# PROPHET

③ EMPIRE

PROPHET, VOL. 3: EMPIRE TP
ISBN#: 978-1-60706-858-7
May 2015. Second printing.

Published by Image Comics, Inc. Office of
publication: 2001 Center Street, Sixth Floor,
Berkeley, California 94704. Copyright © 2015
Rob Liefeld. Originally published in single magazine
form as PROPHET #32 and 34-38. All rights
reserved. PROPHET® (including all prominent
characters featured herein), its logo and all
character likenesses are trademarks of Rob
Liefeld, unless otherwise noted. Image Comics®
is a trademark of Image Comics, Inc. All rights
reserved. No part of this publication may be
reproduced or transmitted in any form or by
any means (except for short excerpts for review
purposes) without the express written permission
of Image Comics, Inc. All names, characters,
events and locales in this publication are entirely
fictional. Any resemblance to actual persons (living
or dead), events or places, without satiric intent,
is coincidental.

PRINTED IN USA.

For information regarding the CPSIA on this
printed material call: 203-595-3636 and
provide reference # RICH – 617795.

For international rights, contact:
foreignlicensing@imagecomics.com

STORY Brandon Graham
with Simon Roy (chapter 1-4 & 6)
and Giannis Milonogiannis (chapter 5)


ART Simon Roy (chapters 1-4 & 6)
with Giannis Milonogiannis (chapter 3-6)
Malachi Ward & Matt Sheean (chapter 2 title page & chapter 3)
Zachary Baldus (chapter 3 title page)
Aaron Conley (chapter 4 title page)
Fil Barlow (chapter 5 title page)
Jim Rugg (chapter 6 title page)
Bayard Baudoin (Venerable the Wake Bio Page)

COLORS Joseph Bergin III
with Simon Roy (chapter 1, 4 & 6)
and Giannis Milonogiannis (chapter 5)
COLOR FLATS Jessica Pollard (chapter 6)


LETTERS Ed Brisson


EDITS Eric Stephenson


COVER Farel Dalrymple



PROPHET created by Rob Liefeld

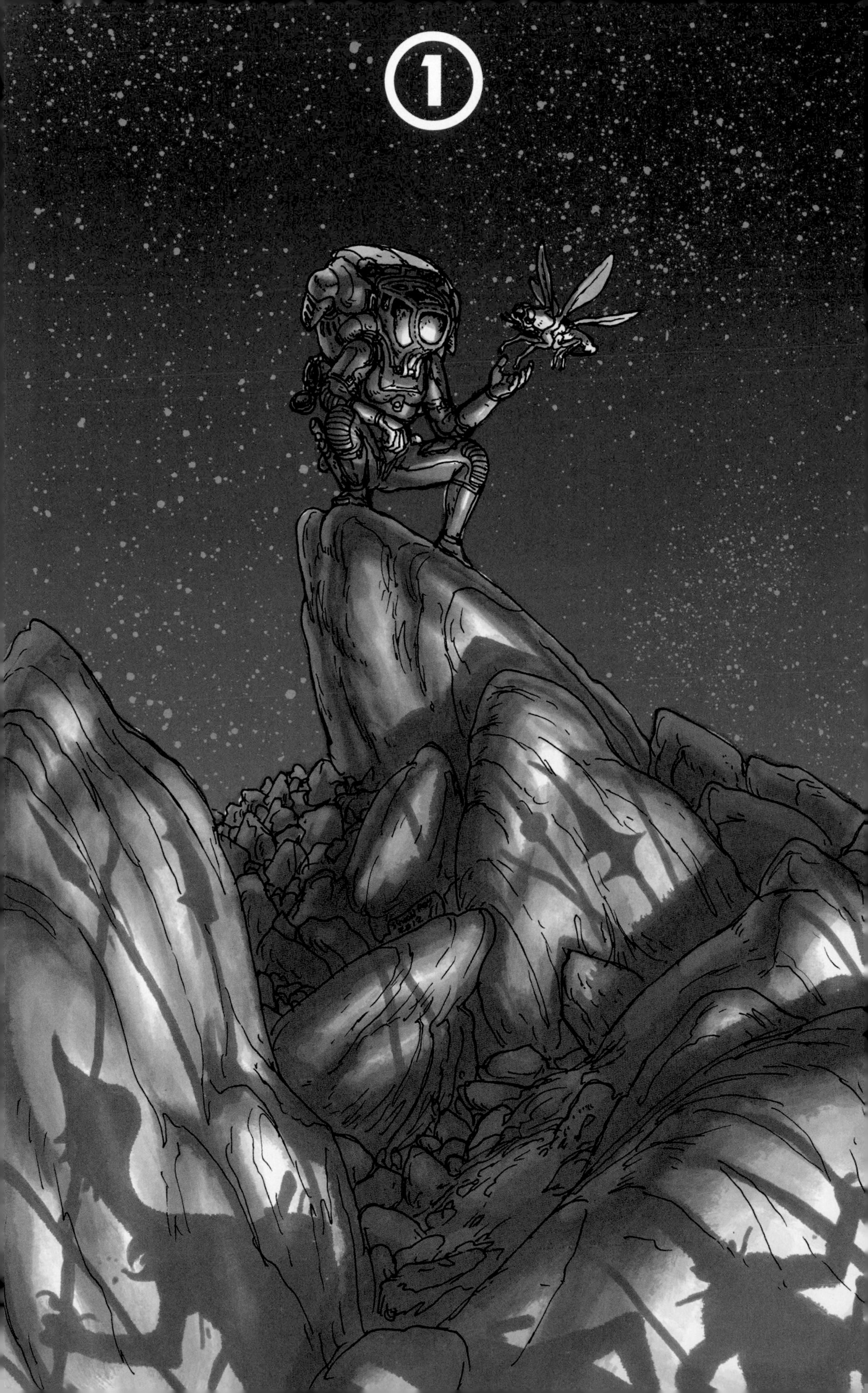
1

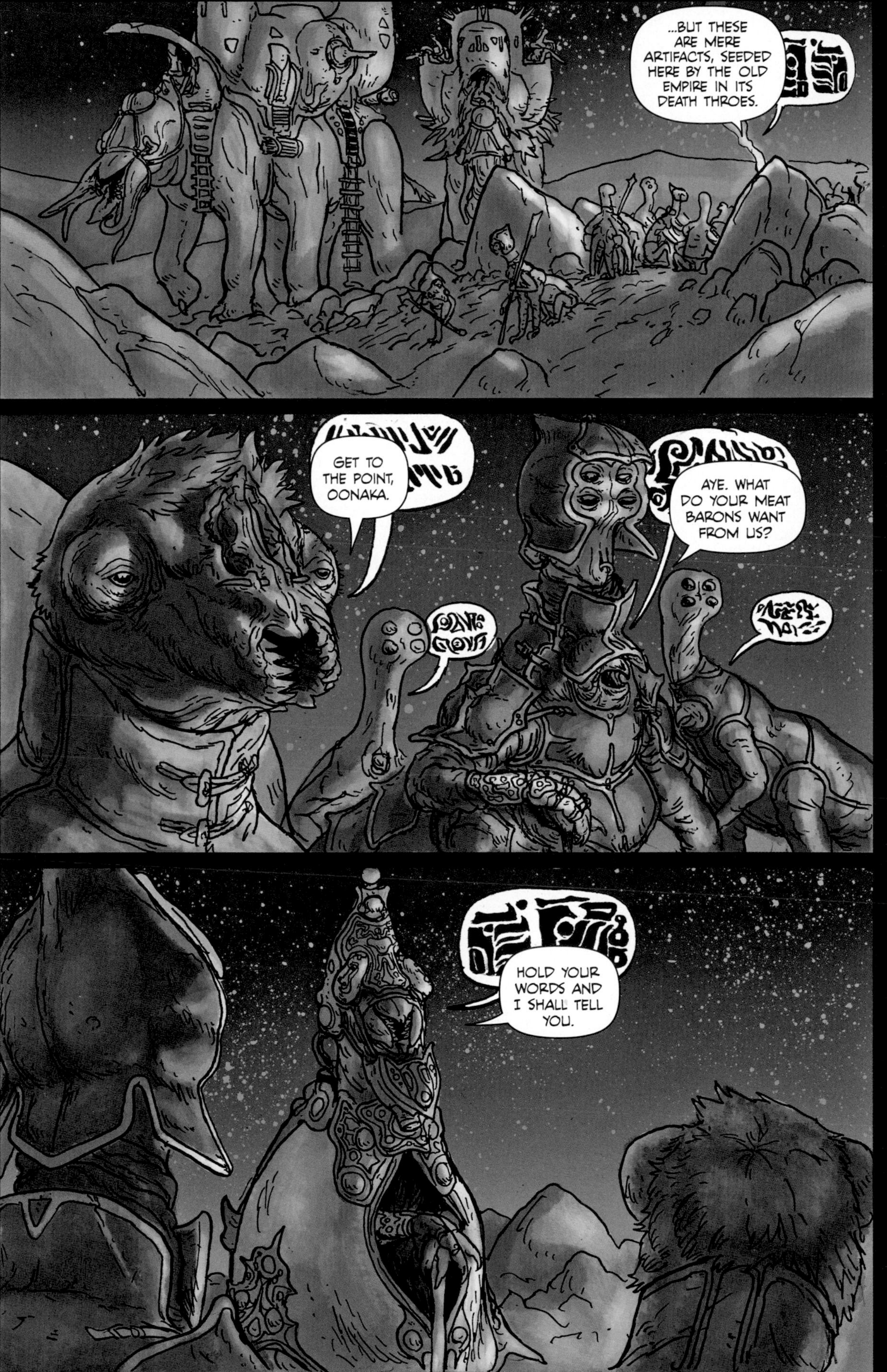
...BUT THESE ARE MERE ARTIFACTS, SEEDED HERE BY THE OLD EMPIRE IN ITS DEATH THROES.
GET TO THE POINT, OONAKA.
AYE. WHAT DO YOUR MEAT BARONS WANT FROM US?
HOLD YOUR WORDS AND I SHALL TELL YOU.

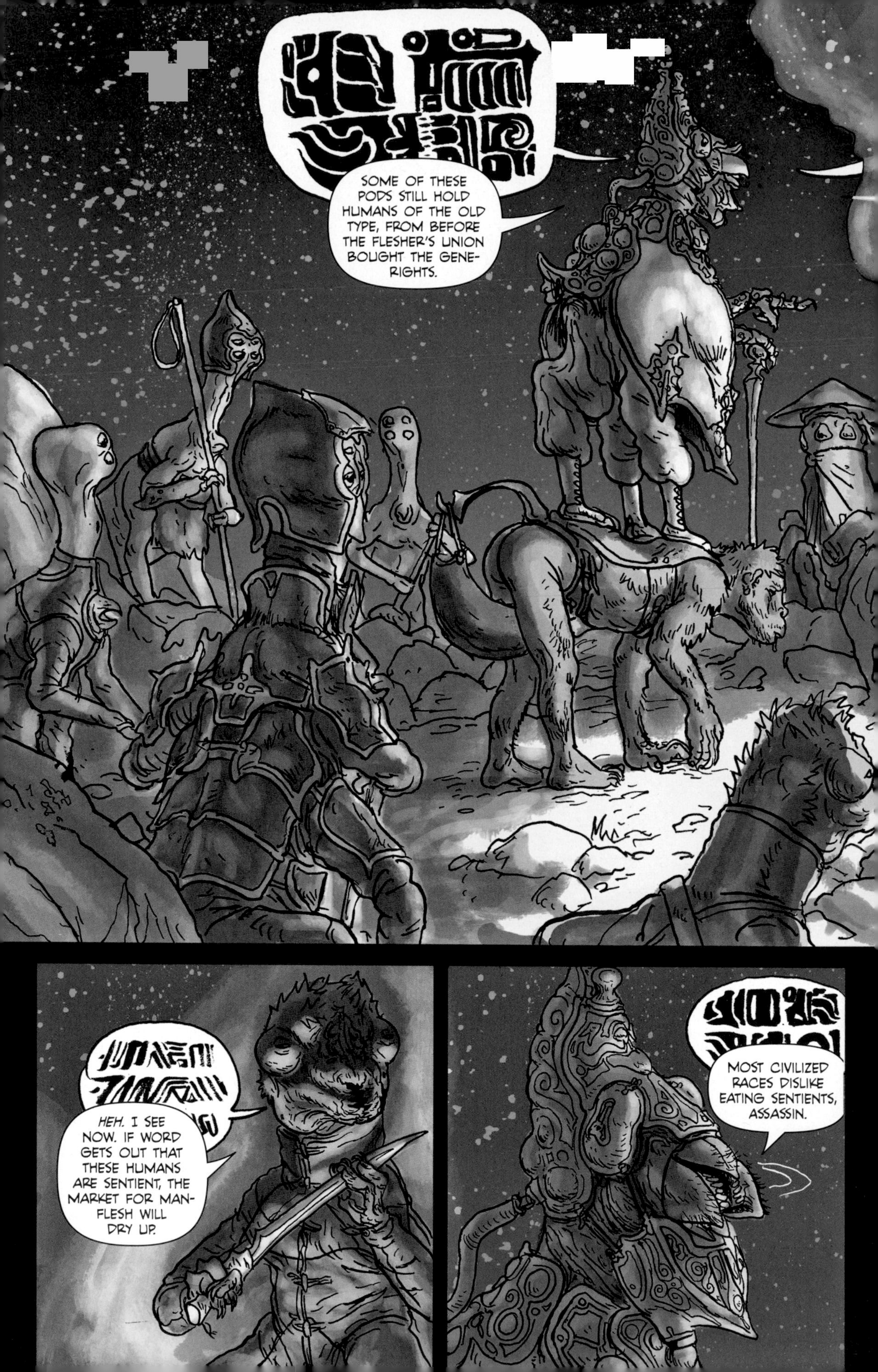
SOME OF THESE PODS STILL HOLD HUMANS OF THE OLD TYPE, FROM BEFORE THE FLESHER'S UNION BOUGHT THE GENE-RIGHTS.
HEH. I SEE NOW. IF WORD GETS OUT THAT THESE HUMANS ARE SENTIENT, THE MARKET FOR MAN-FLESH WILL DRY UP.
MOST CIVILIZED RACES DISLIKE EATING SENTIENTS, ASSASSIN.

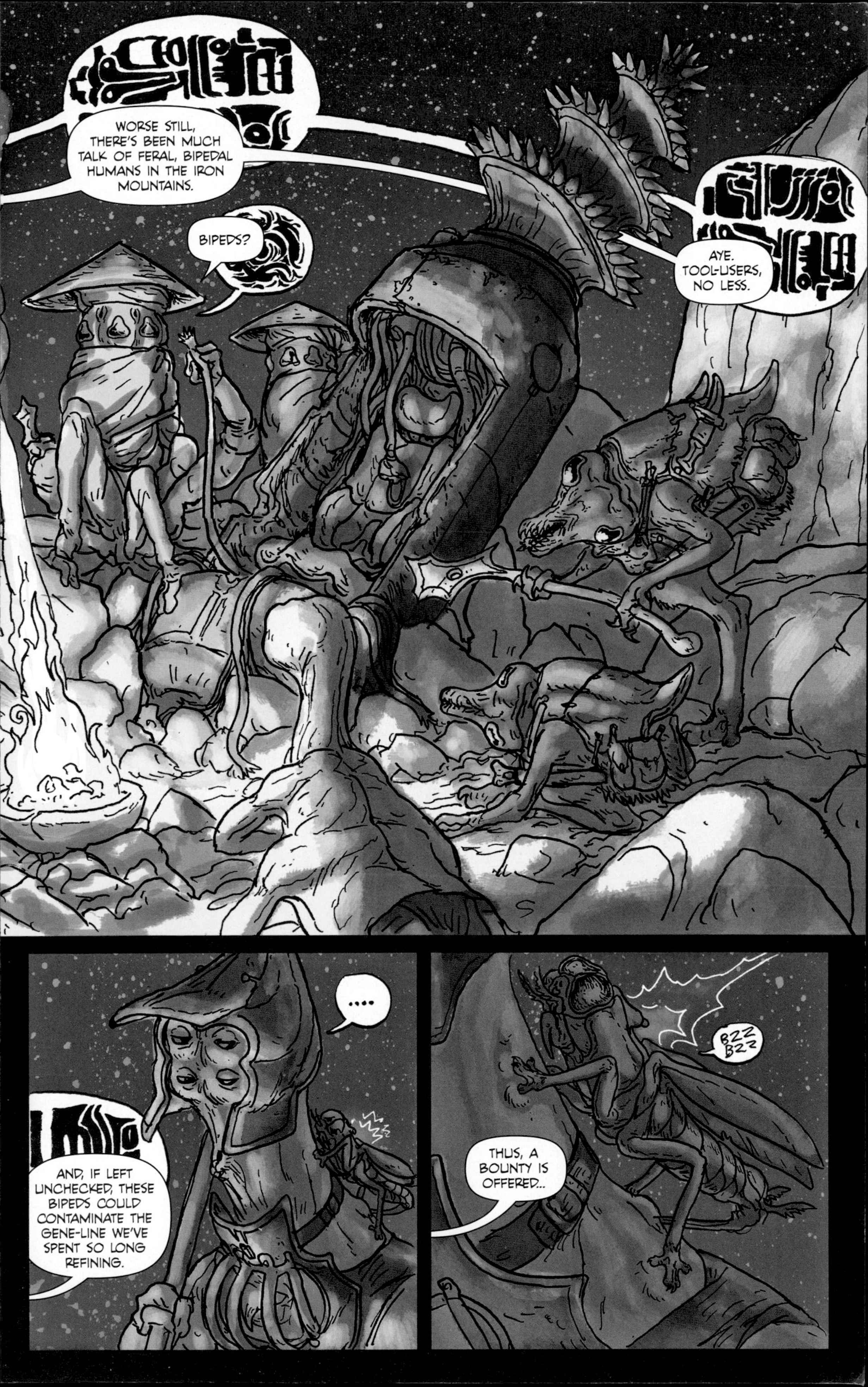
WORSE STILL, THERE'S BEEN MUCH TALK OF FERAL, BIPEDAL HUMANS IN THE IRON MOUNTAINS.
BIPEDS?
AYE. TOOL-USERS, NO LESS.
....
AND, IF LEFT UNCHECKED, THESE BIPEDS COULD CONTAMINATE THE GENE-LINE WE'VE SPENT SO LONG REFINING.
BZZ BZZ
THUS, A BOUNTY IS OFFERED...

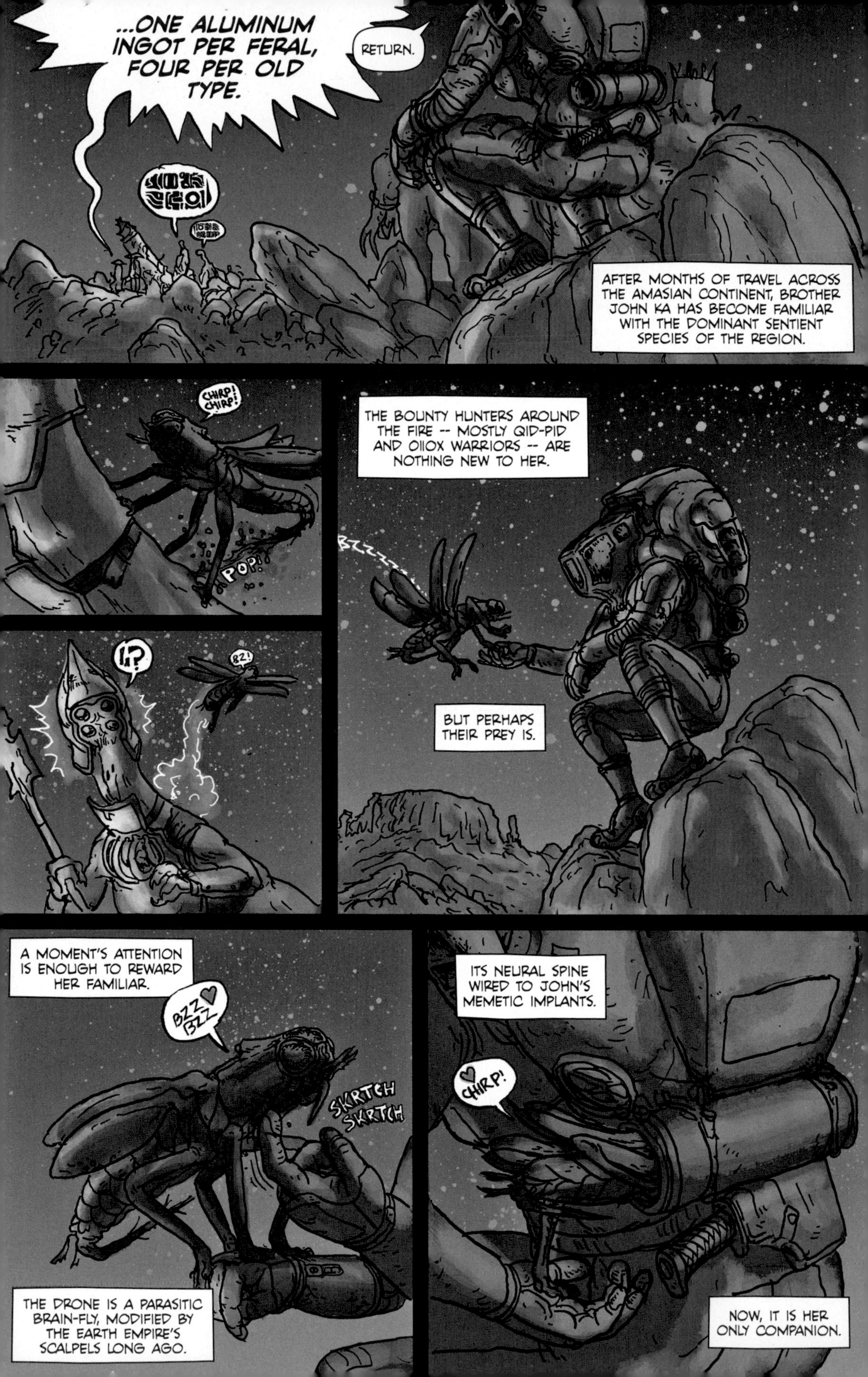
...ONE ALUMINUM INGOT PER FERAL, FOUR PER OLD TYPE.
RETURN.
AFTER MONTHS OF TRAVEL ACROSS THE AMASIAN CONTINENT, BROTHER JOHN KA HAS BECOME FAMILIAR WITH THE DOMINANT SENTIENT SPECIES OF THE REGION.
CHIRP! CHIRP!
POP!
!?
BZ!
THE BOUNTY HUNTERS AROUND THE FIRE -- MOSTLY QID-PID AND OIIOX WARRIORS -- ARE NOTHING NEW TO HER.
BUT PERHAPS THEIR PREY IS.
A MOMENT'S ATTENTION IS ENOUGH TO REWARD HER FAMILIAR.
BZZ BZZ
SKRTCH SKRTCH
THE DRONE IS A PARASITIC BRAIN-FLY, MODIFIED BY THE EARTH EMPIRE'S SCALPELS LONG AGO.
ITS NEURAL SPINE WIRED TO JOHN'S MEMETIC IMPLANTS.
CHIRP!
NOW, IT IS HER ONLY COMPANION.

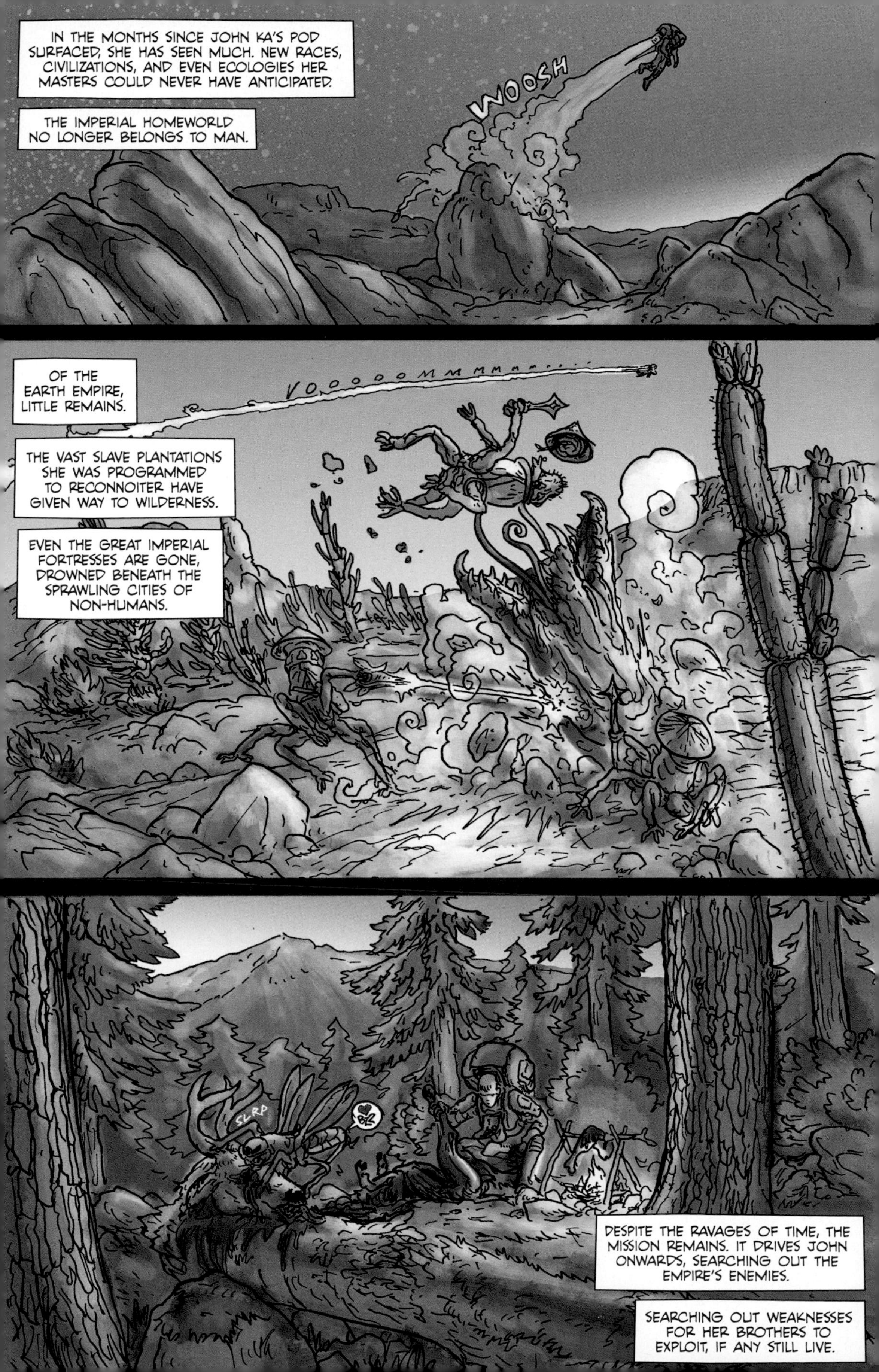
IN THE MONTHS SINCE JOHN KA'S POD SURFACED, SHE HAS SEEN MUCH. NEW RACES, CIVILIZATIONS, AND EVEN ECOLOGIES HER MASTERS COULD NEVER HAVE ANTICIPATED.
THE IMPERIAL HOMEWORLD NO LONGER BELONGS TO MAN.
WOOSH
OF THE EARTH EMPIRE, LITTLE REMAINS.
VOOOOOOMMMMMM
THE VAST SLAVE PLANTATIONS SHE WAS PROGRAMMED TO RECONNOITER HAVE GIVEN WAY TO WILDERNESS.
EVEN THE GREAT IMPERIAL FORTRESSES ARE GONE, DROWNED BENEATH THE SPRAWLING CITIES OF NON-HUMANS.
SLRP
DESPITE THE RAVAGES OF TIME, THE MISSION REMAINS. IT DRIVES JOHN ONWARDS, SEARCHING OUT THE EMPIRE'S ENEMIES.
SEARCHING OUT WEAKNESSES FOR HER BROTHERS TO EXPLOIT, IF ANY STILL LIVE.

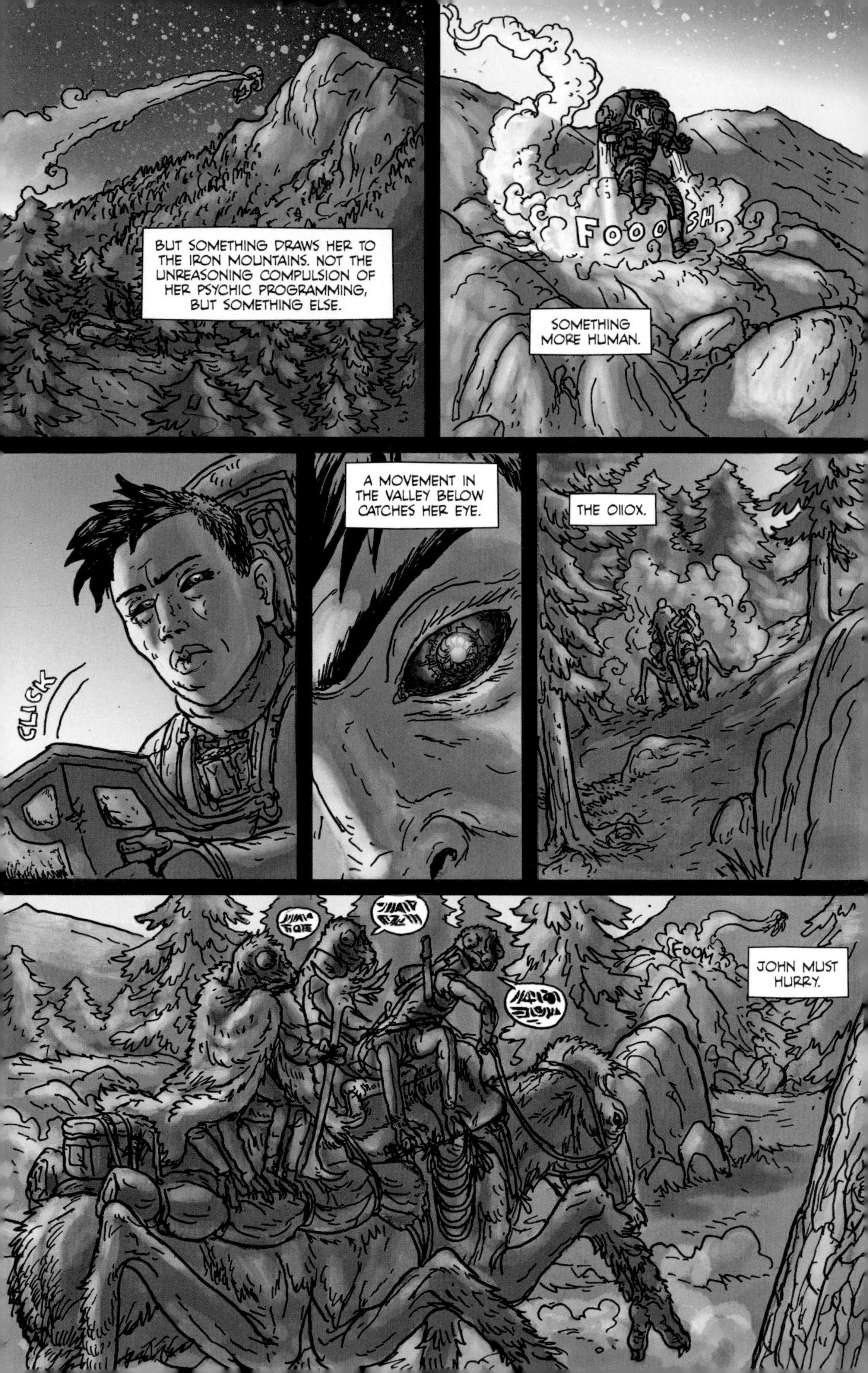
BUT SOMETHING DRAWS HER TO THE IRON MOUNTAINS. NOT THE UNREASONING COMPULSION OF HER PSYCHIC PROGRAMMING, BUT SOMETHING ELSE.
FOOOSH
SOMETHING MORE HUMAN.
CLICK
A MOVEMENT IN THE VALLEY BELOW CATCHES HER EYE.
THE OIIOX.
FOOM
JOHN MUST HURRY.

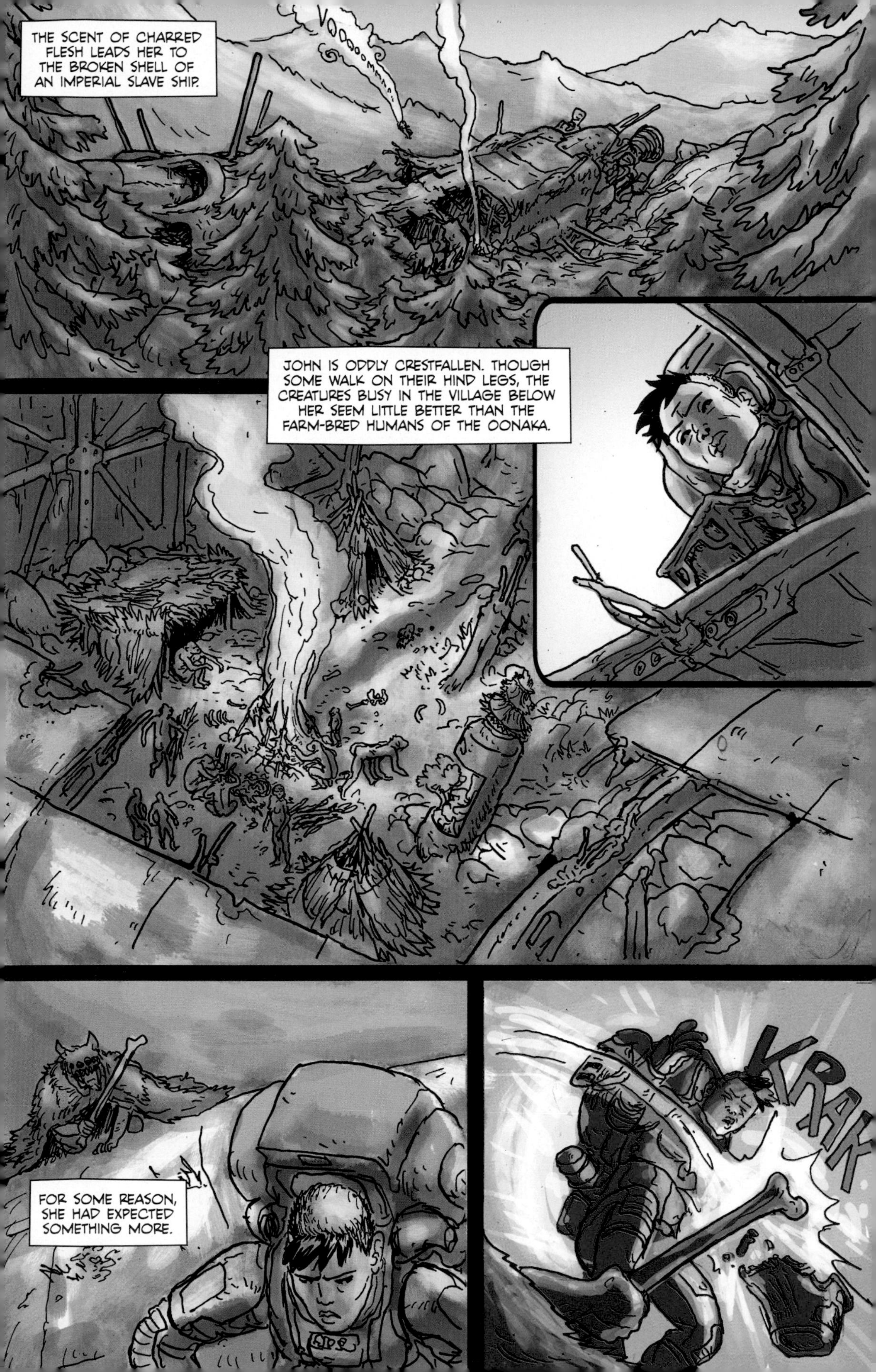
THE SCENT OF CHARRED FLESH LEADS HER TO THE BROKEN SHELL OF AN IMPERIAL SLAVE SHIP.
VOOOOooOMMMN..
JOHN IS ODDLY CRESTFALLEN. THOUGH SOME WALK ON THEIR HIND LEGS, THE CREATURES BUSY IN THE VILLAGE BELOW HER SEEM LITTLE BETTER THAN THE FARM-BRED HUMANS OF THE OONAKA.
FOR SOME REASON, SHE HAD EXPECTED SOMETHING MORE.
KRAK

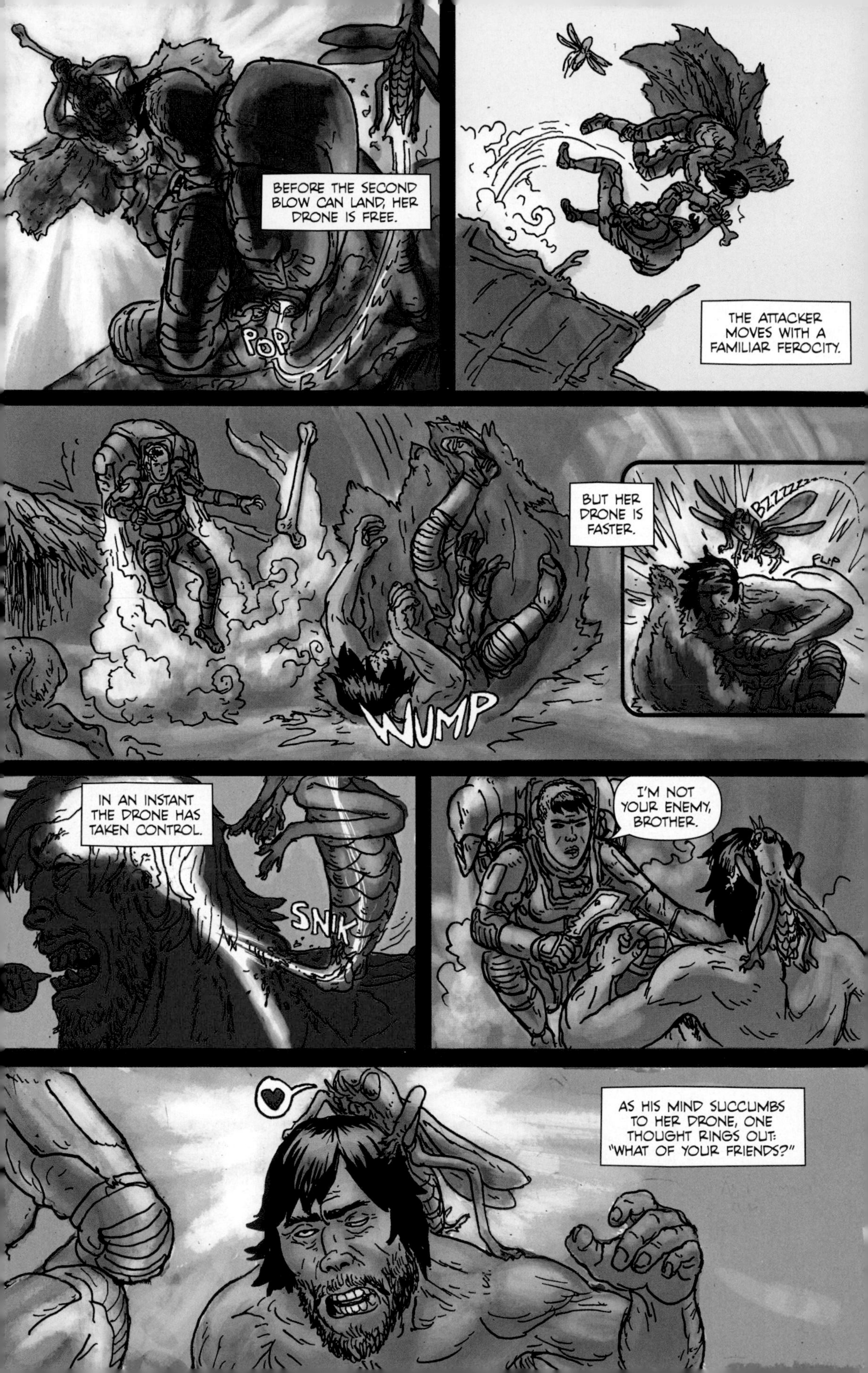
BEFORE THE SECOND BLOW CAN LAND, HER DRONE IS FREE.
POP
THE ATTACKER MOVES WITH A FAMILIAR FEROCITY.
BUT HER DRONE IS FASTER.
BZZZZ
FLIP
WUMP
IN AN INSTANT THE DRONE HAS TAKEN CONTROL.
SNIK
I'M NOT YOUR ENEMY, BROTHER.
AS HIS MIND SUCCUMBS TO HER DRONE, ONE THOUGHT RINGS OUT: "WHAT OF YOUR FRIENDS?"

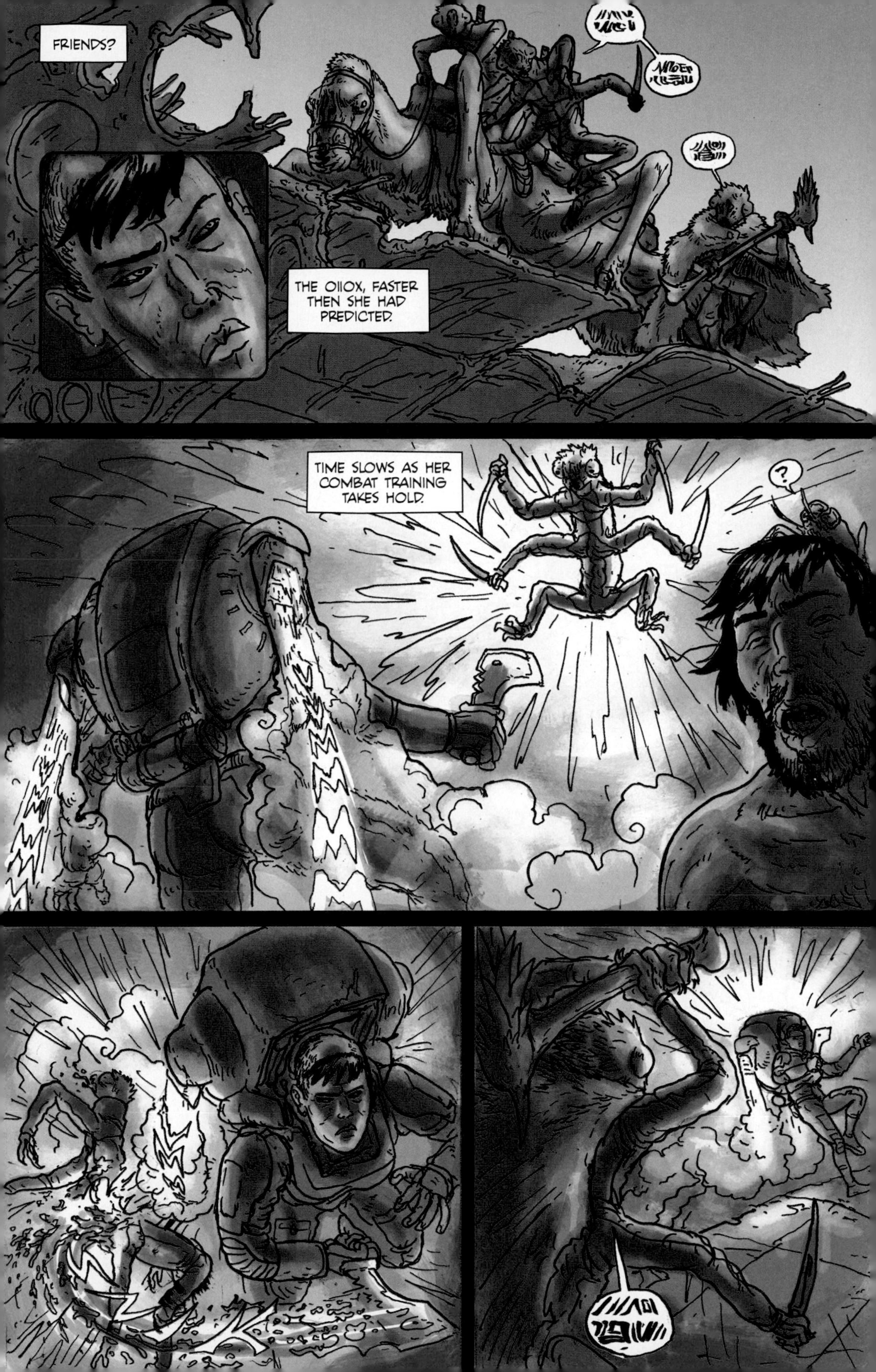
FRIENDS?
THE OIIOX, FASTER THEN SHE HAD PREDICTED.
TIME SLOWS AS HER COMBAT TRAINING TAKES HOLD.
?

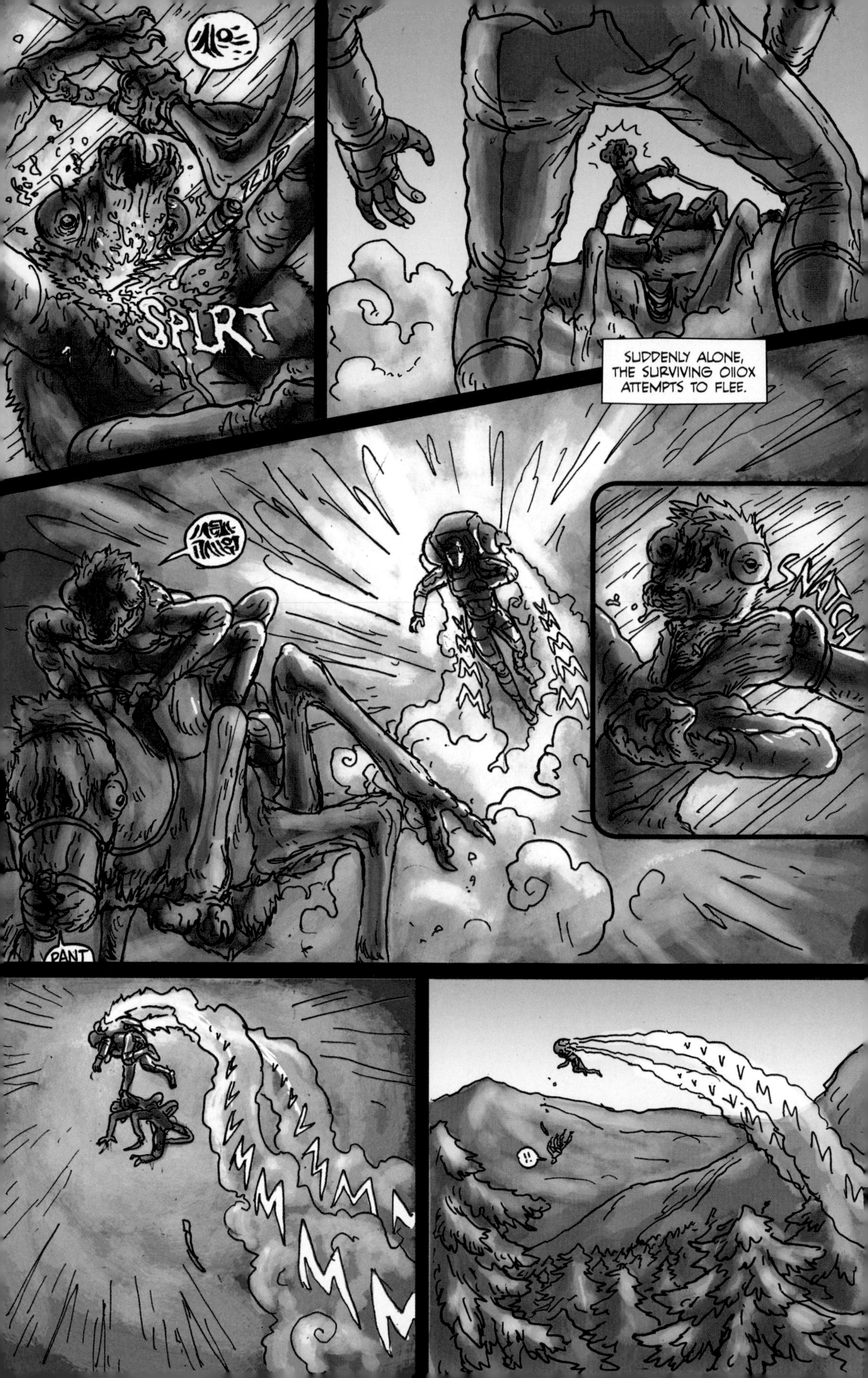
ZIP
SPLRT
SUDDENLY ALONE, THE SURVIVING OIIOX ATTEMPTS TO FLEE.
SNATCH
PANT
!!

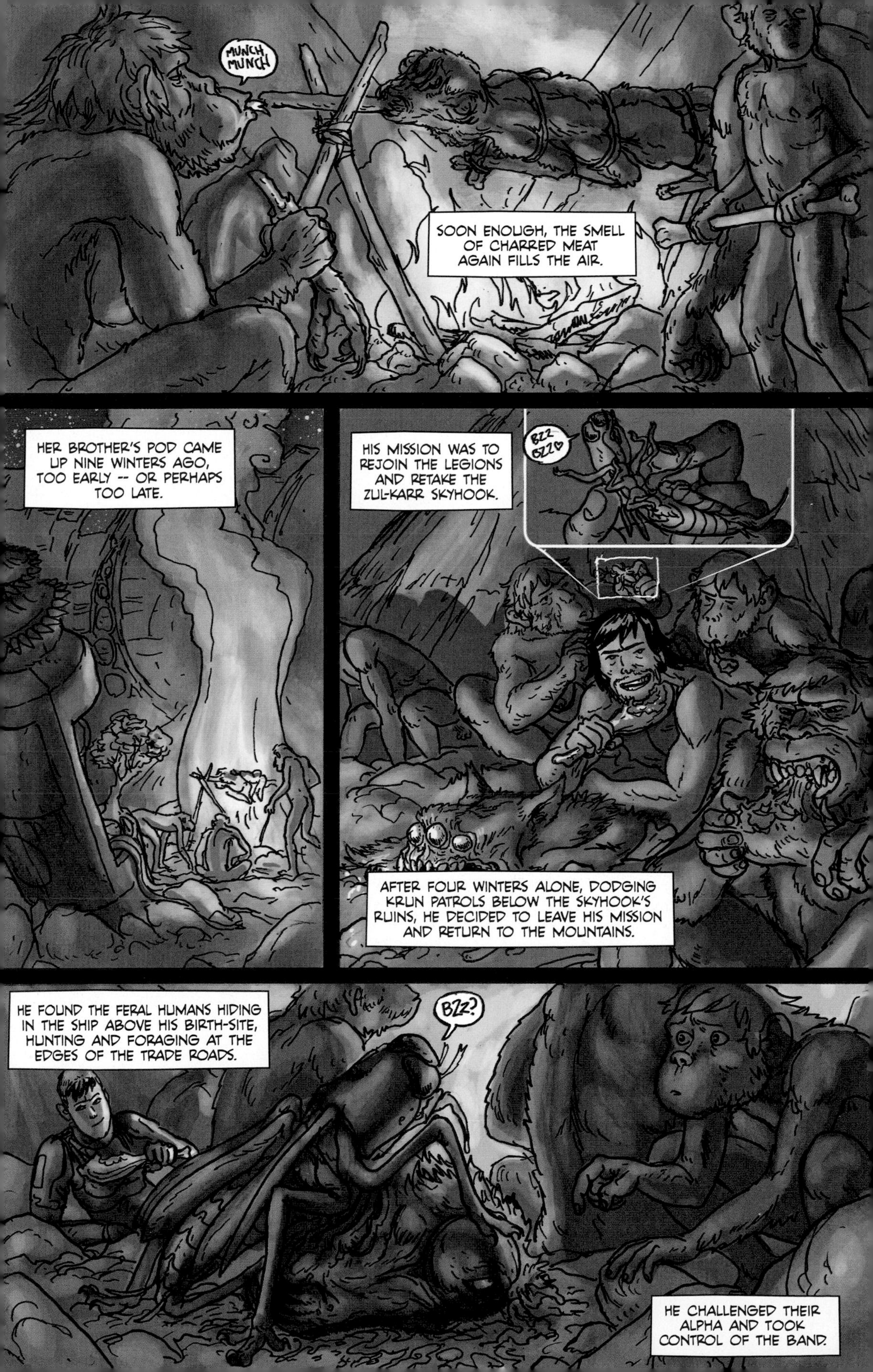
MUNCH MUNCH
SOON ENOUGH, THE SMELL OF CHARRED MEAT AGAIN FILLS THE AIR.
HER BROTHER'S POD CAME UP NINE WINTERS AGO, TOO EARLY -- OR PERHAPS TOO LATE.
HIS MISSION WAS TO REJOIN THE LEGIONS AND RETAKE THE ZUL-KARR SKYHOOK.
BZZ BZZ♡
AFTER FOUR WINTERS ALONE, DODGING KRUN PATROLS BELOW THE SKYHOOK'S RUINS, HE DECIDED TO LEAVE HIS MISSION AND RETURN TO THE MOUNTAINS.
HE FOUND THE FERAL HUMANS HIDING IN THE SHIP ABOVE HIS BIRTH-SITE, HUNTING AND FORAGING AT THE EDGES OF THE TRADE ROADS.
BZZ?
HE CHALLENGED THEIR ALPHA AND TOOK CONTROL OF THE BAND.

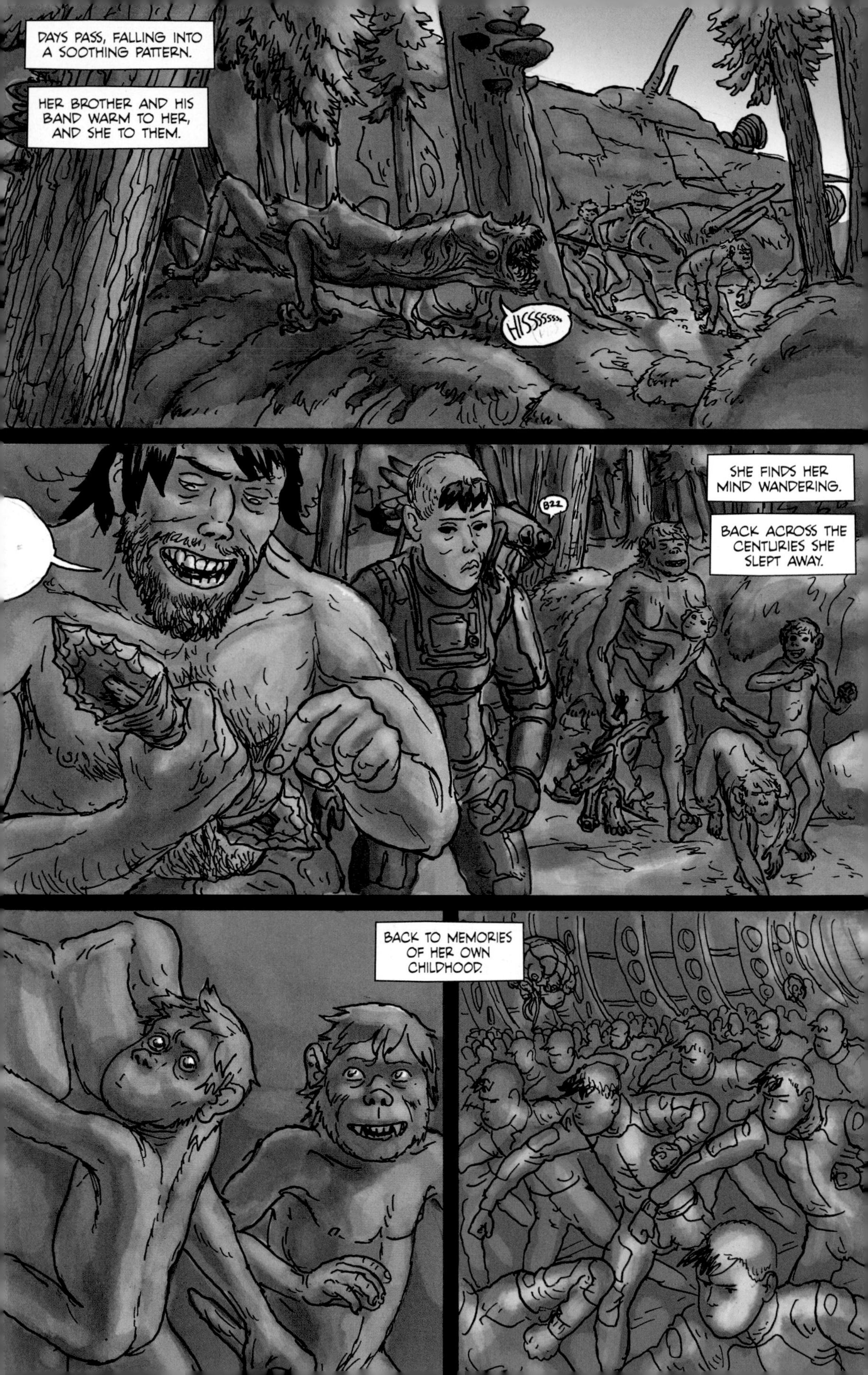
DAYS PASS, FALLING INTO A SOOTHING PATTERN.
HER BROTHER AND HIS BAND WARM TO HER, AND SHE TO THEM.
HISSSSSS.
SHE FINDS HER MIND WANDERING.
BZZ
BACK ACROSS THE CENTURIES SHE SLEPT AWAY.
BACK TO MEMORIES OF HER OWN CHILDHOOD.

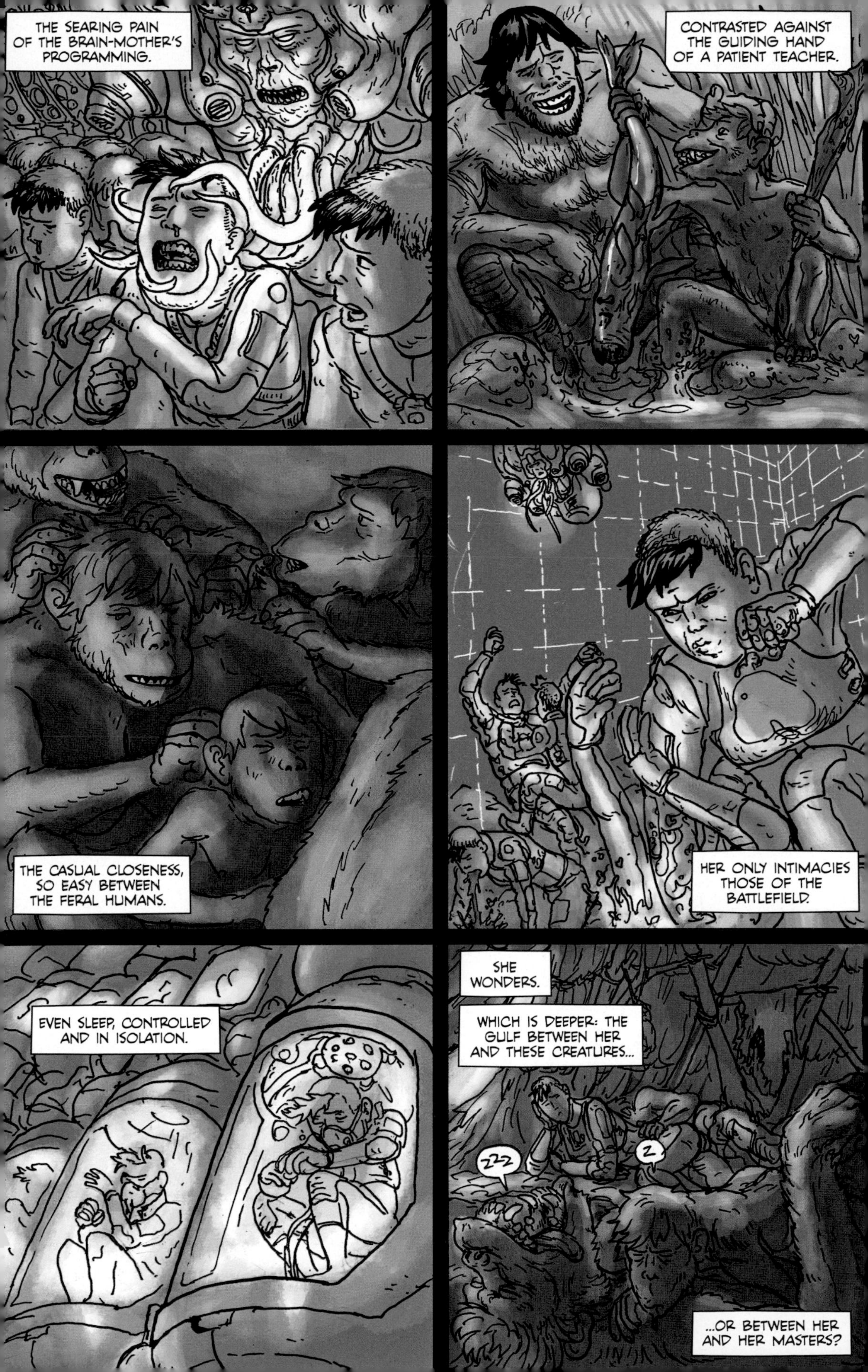
THE SEARING PAIN OF THE BRAIN-MOTHER'S PROGRAMMING.
CONTRASTED AGAINST THE GUIDING HAND OF A PATIENT TEACHER.
THE CASUAL CLOSENESS, SO EASY BETWEEN THE FERAL HUMANS.
HER ONLY INTIMACIES THOSE OF THE BATTLEFIELD.
EVEN SLEEP, CONTROLLED AND IN ISOLATION.
SHE WONDERS.
WHICH IS DEEPER: THE GULF BETWEEN HER AND THESE CREATURES...
ZZZ
Z
...OR BETWEEN HER AND HER MASTERS?

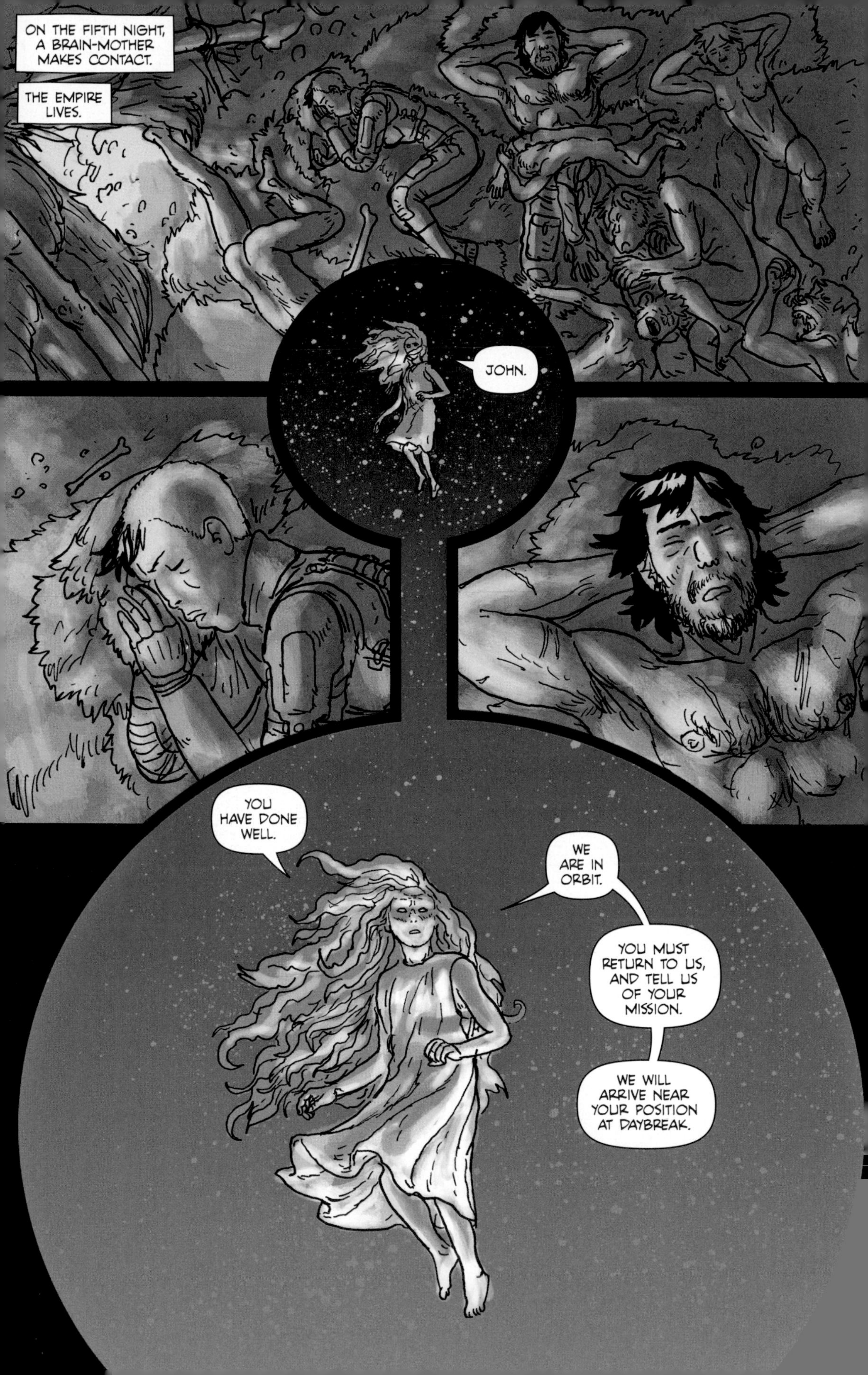

ON THE FIFTH NIGHT, A BRAIN-MOTHER MAKES CONTACT.
THE EMPIRE LIVES.
JOHN.
YOU HAVE DONE WELL.
WE ARE IN ORBIT.
YOU MUST RETURN TO US, AND TELL US OF YOUR MISSION.
WE WILL ARRIVE NEAR YOUR POSITION AT DAYBREAK.

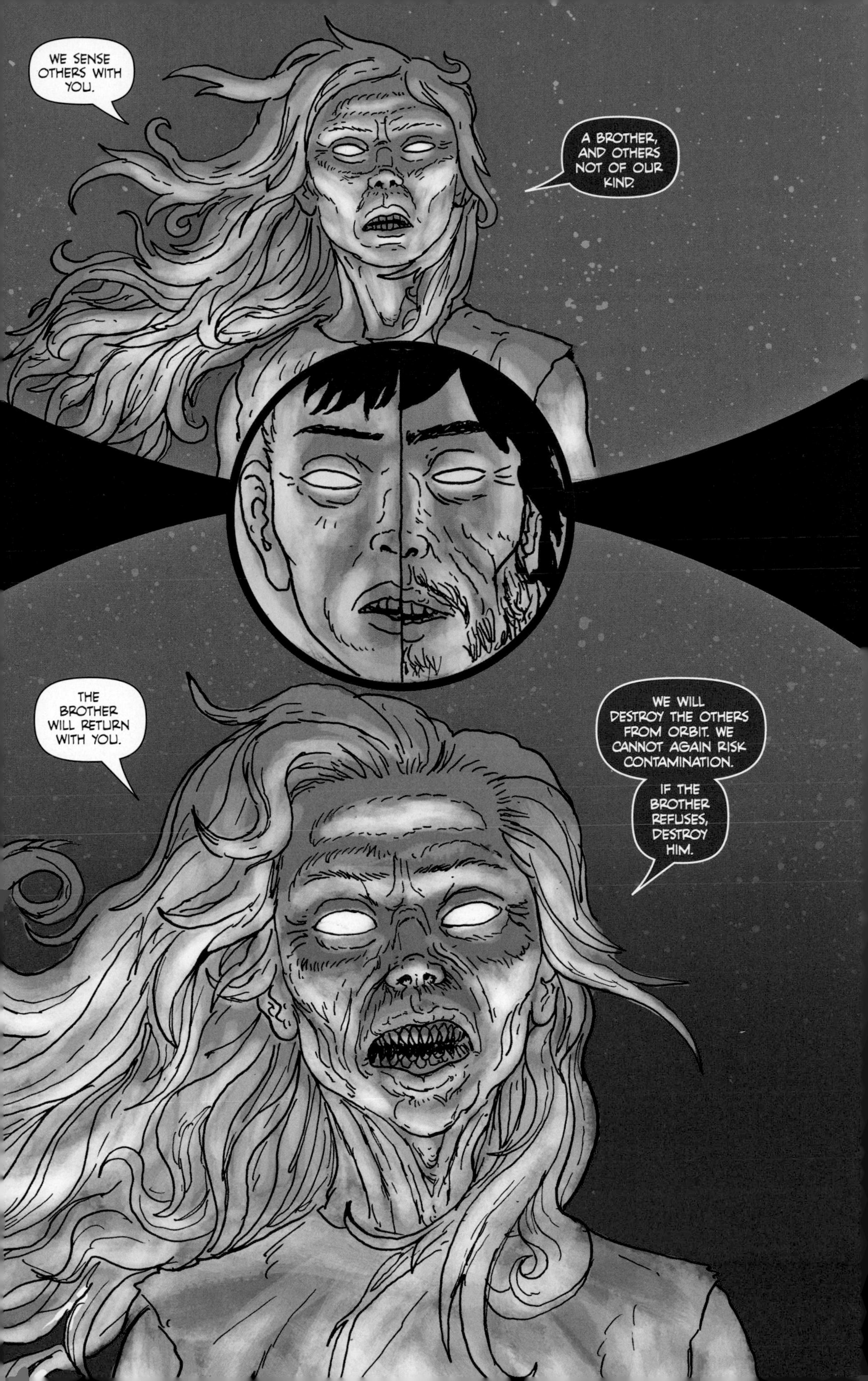
WE SENSE OTHERS WITH YOU.
A BROTHER, AND OTHERS NOT OF OUR KIND.
THE BROTHER WILL RETURN WITH YOU.
WE WILL DESTROY THE OTHERS FROM ORBIT. WE CANNOT AGAIN RISK CONTAMINATION.
IF THE BROTHER REFUSES, DESTROY HIM.

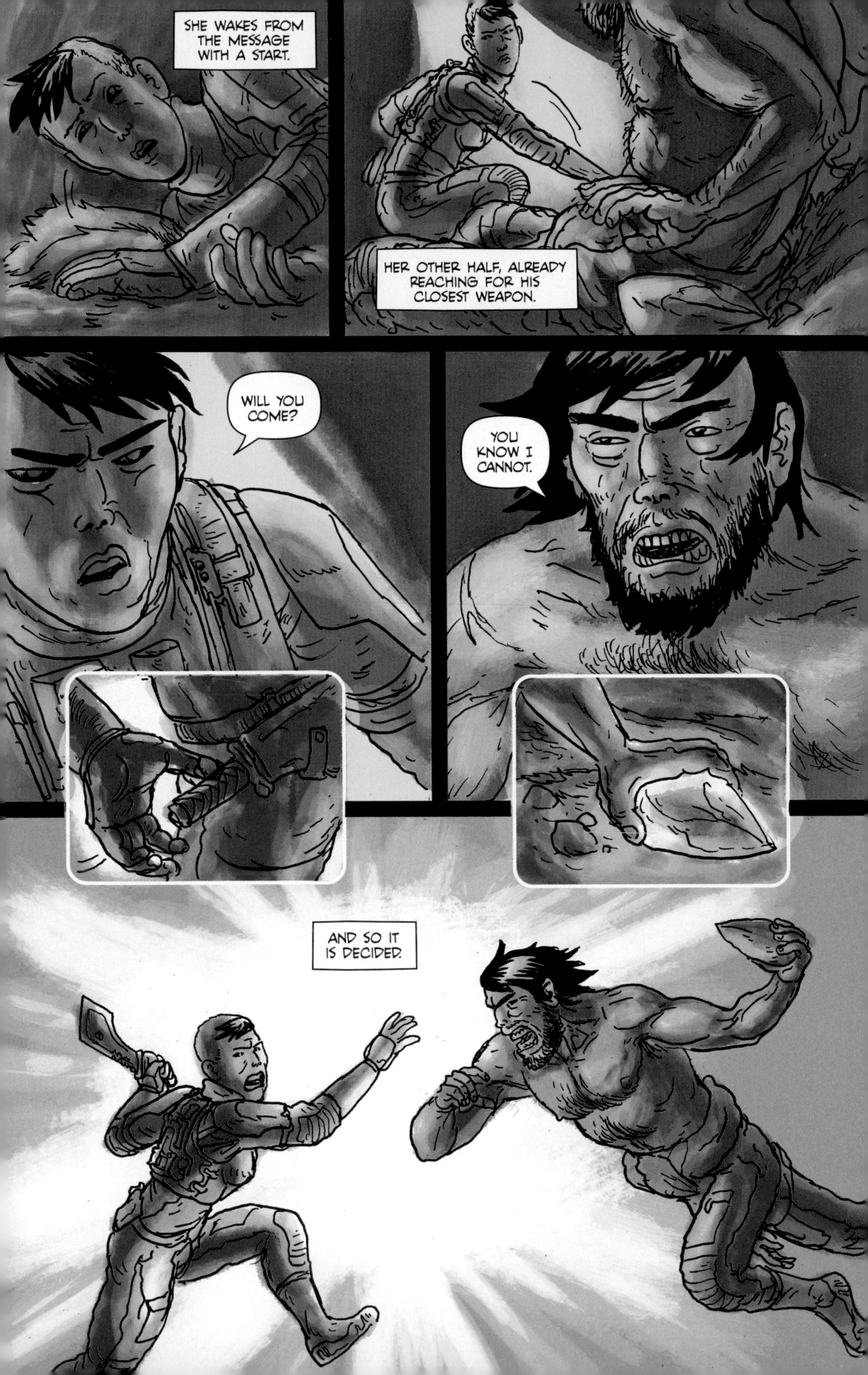
SHE WAKES FROM THE MESSAGE WITH A START.
HER OTHER HALF, ALREADY REACHING FOR HIS CLOSEST WEAPON.
WILL YOU COME?
YOU KNOW I CANNOT.
AND SO IT IS DECIDED.

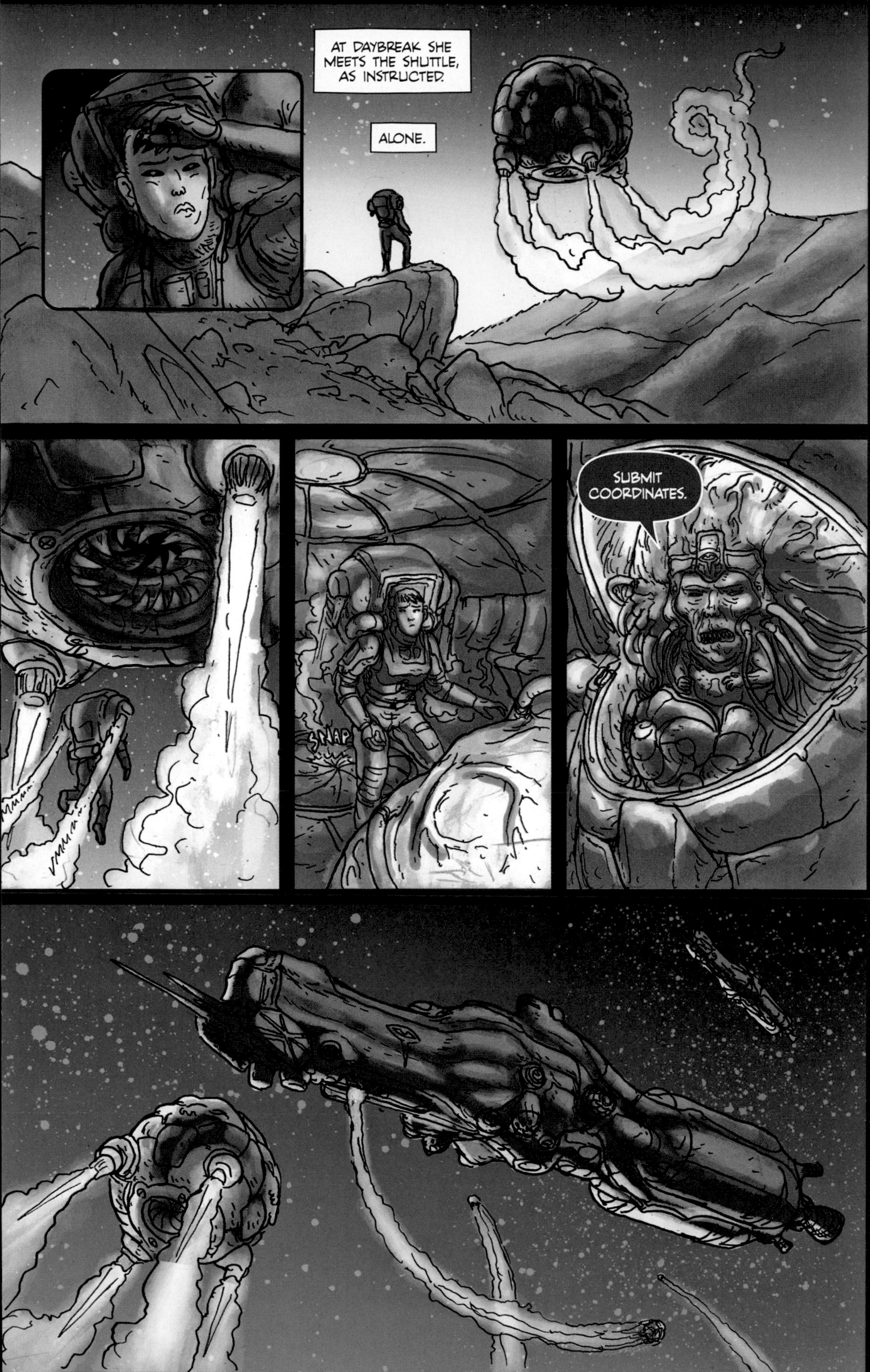
AT DAYBREAK SHE MEETS THE SHUTTLE, AS INSTRUCTED.
ALONE.
SNAP!
SUBMIT COORDINATES.

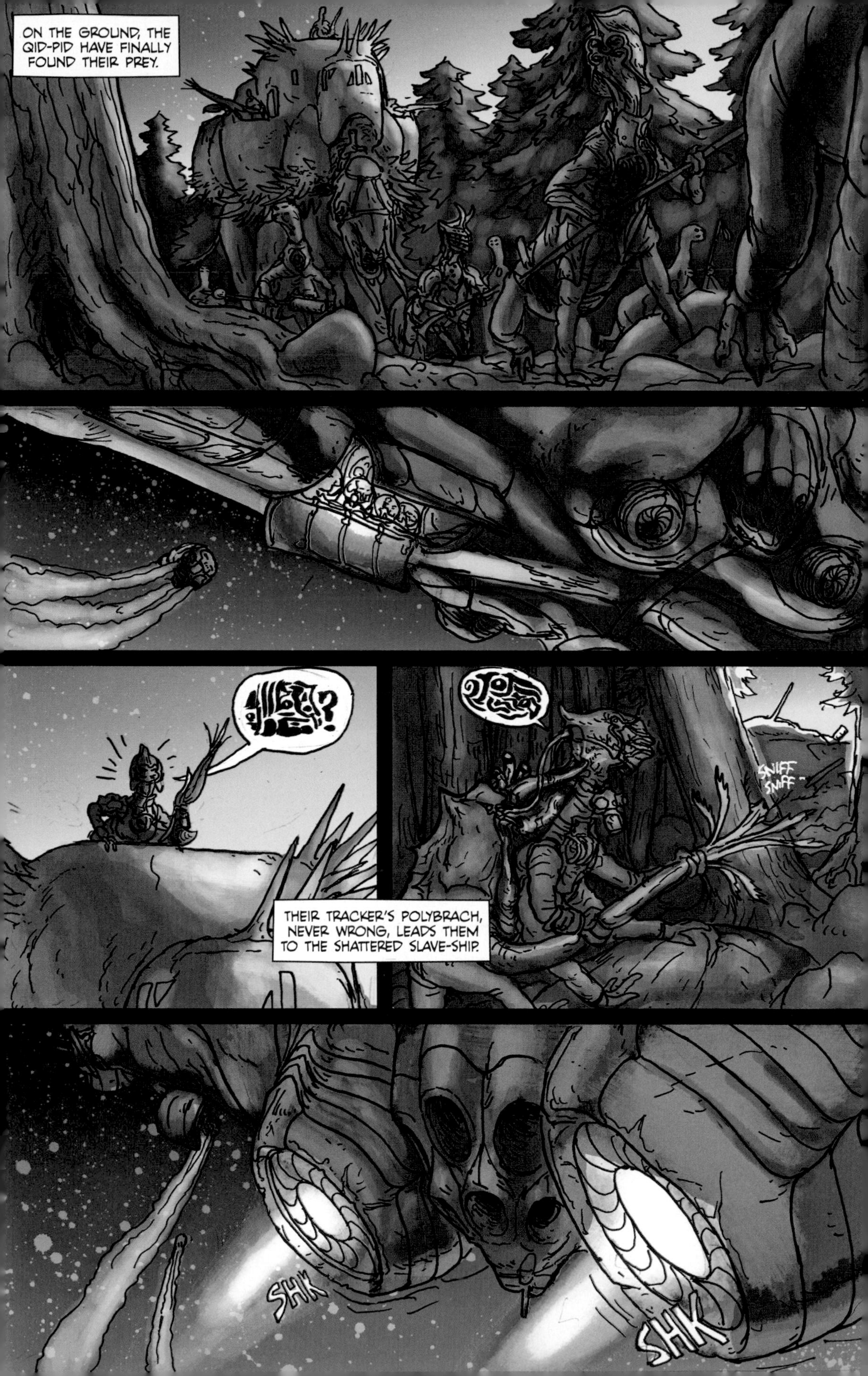
ON THE GROUND, THE QID-PID HAVE FINALLY FOUND THEIR PREY.
SNIFF SNIFF -
THEIR TRACKER'S POLYBRACH, NEVER WRONG, LEADS THEM TO THE SHATTERED SLAVE-SHIP.
SHK
SHK

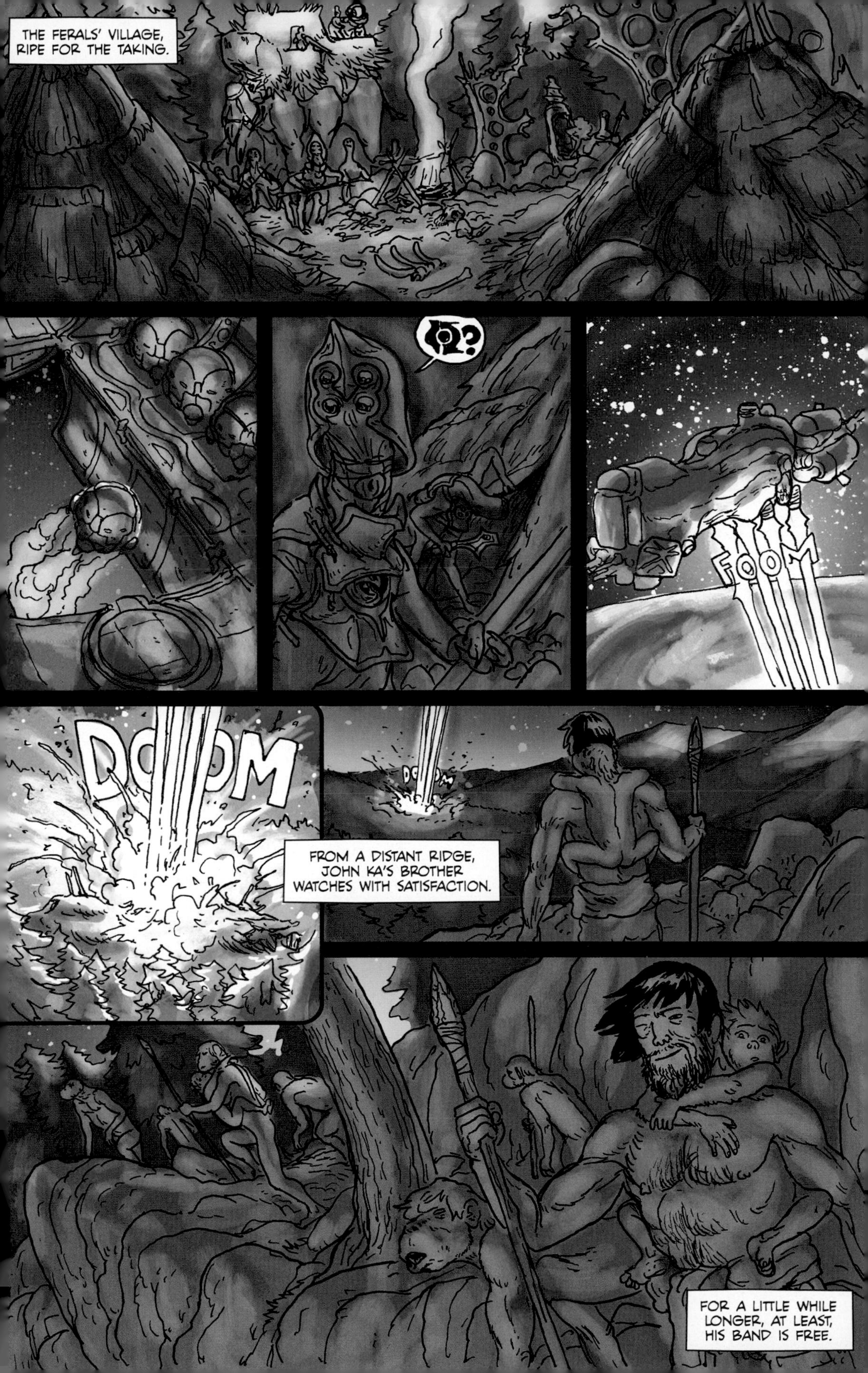
THE FERALS' VILLAGE, RIPE FOR THE TAKING.
?
FOOM
DOOM
DOOM
FROM A DISTANT RIDGE, JOHN KA'S BROTHER WATCHES WITH SATISFACTION.
FOR A LITTLE WHILE LONGER, AT LEAST, HIS BAND IS FREE.

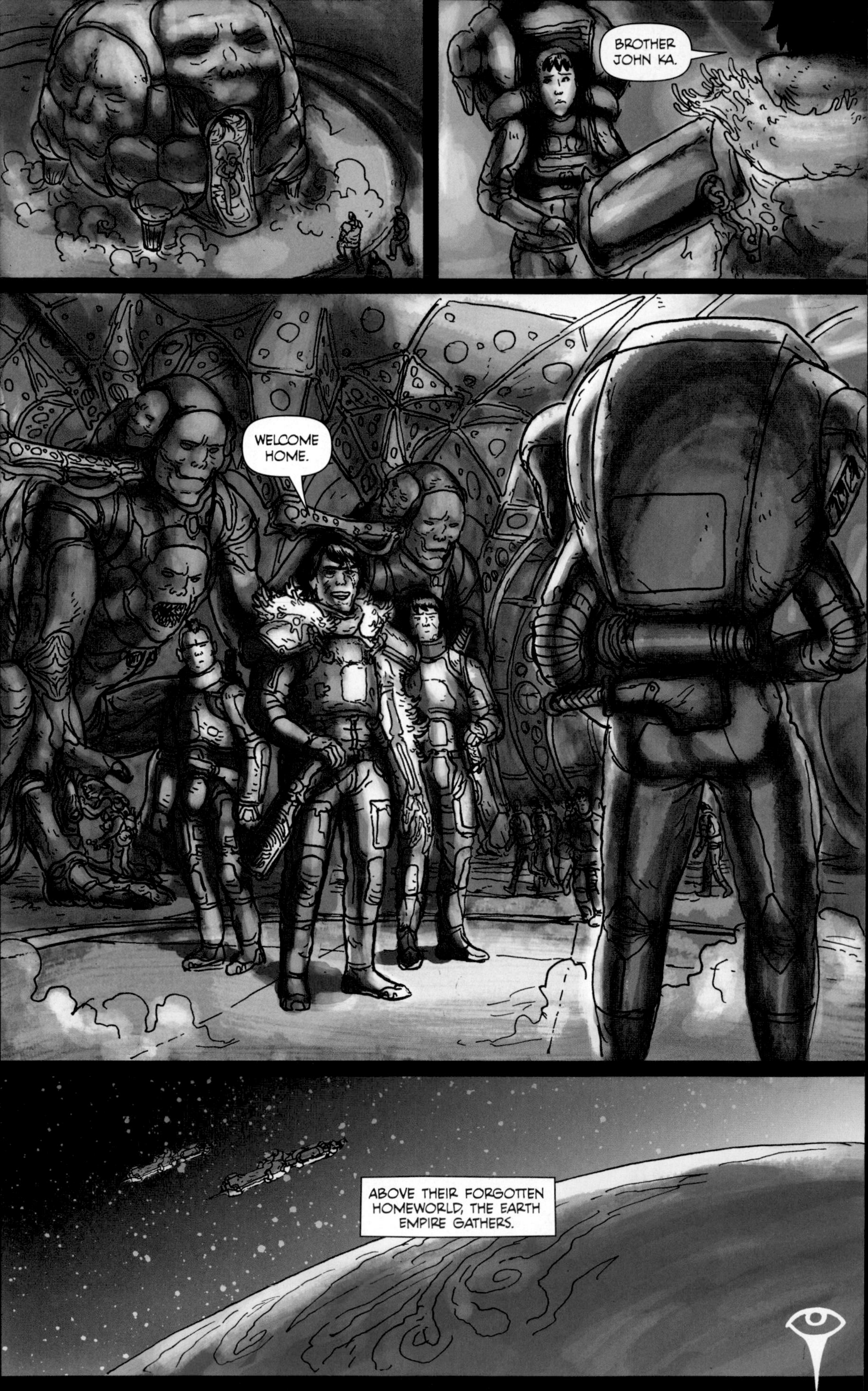
BROTHER JOHN KA.
WELCOME HOME.
ABOVE THEIR FORGOTTEN HOMEWORLD, THE EARTH EMPIRE GATHERS.

# 2

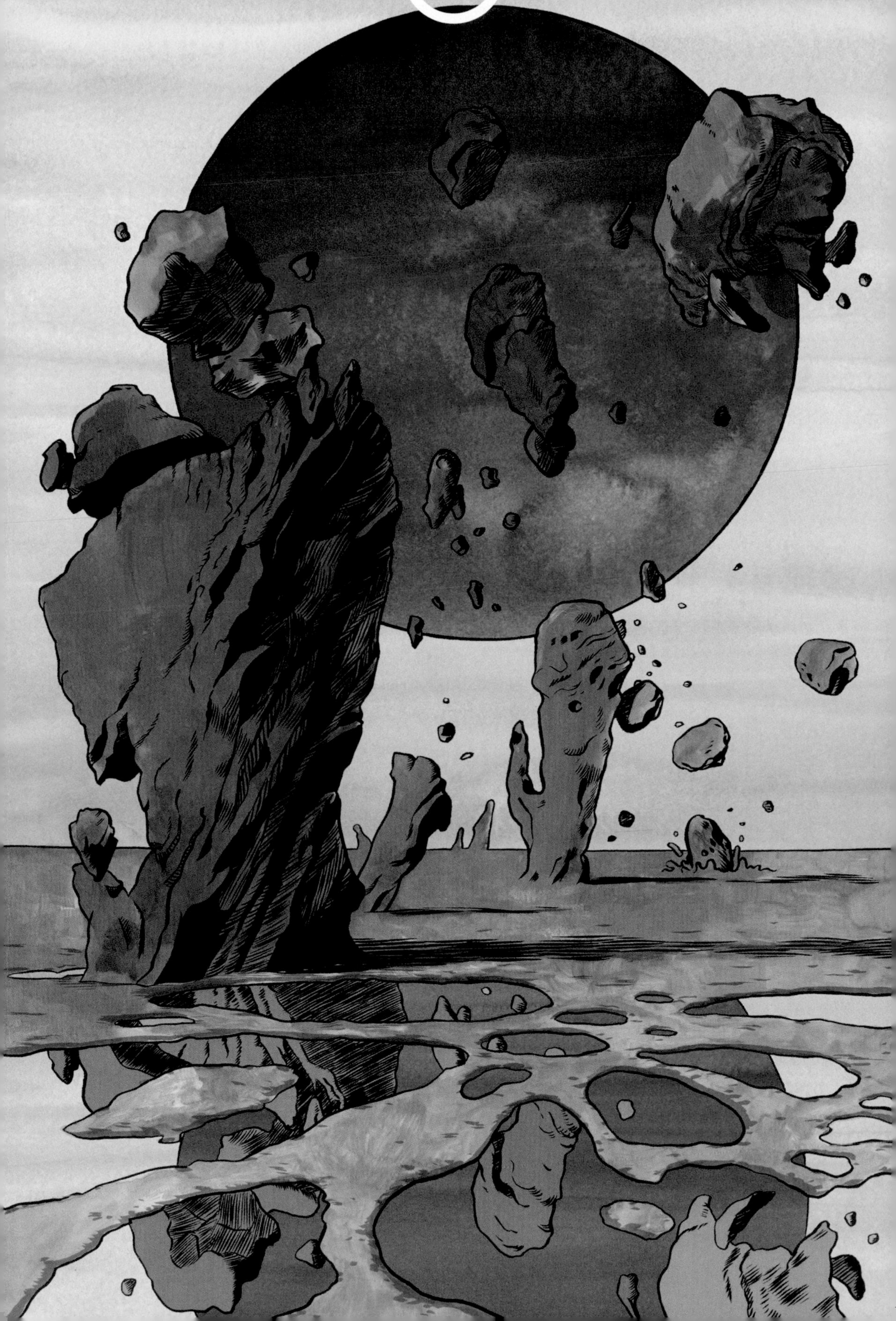

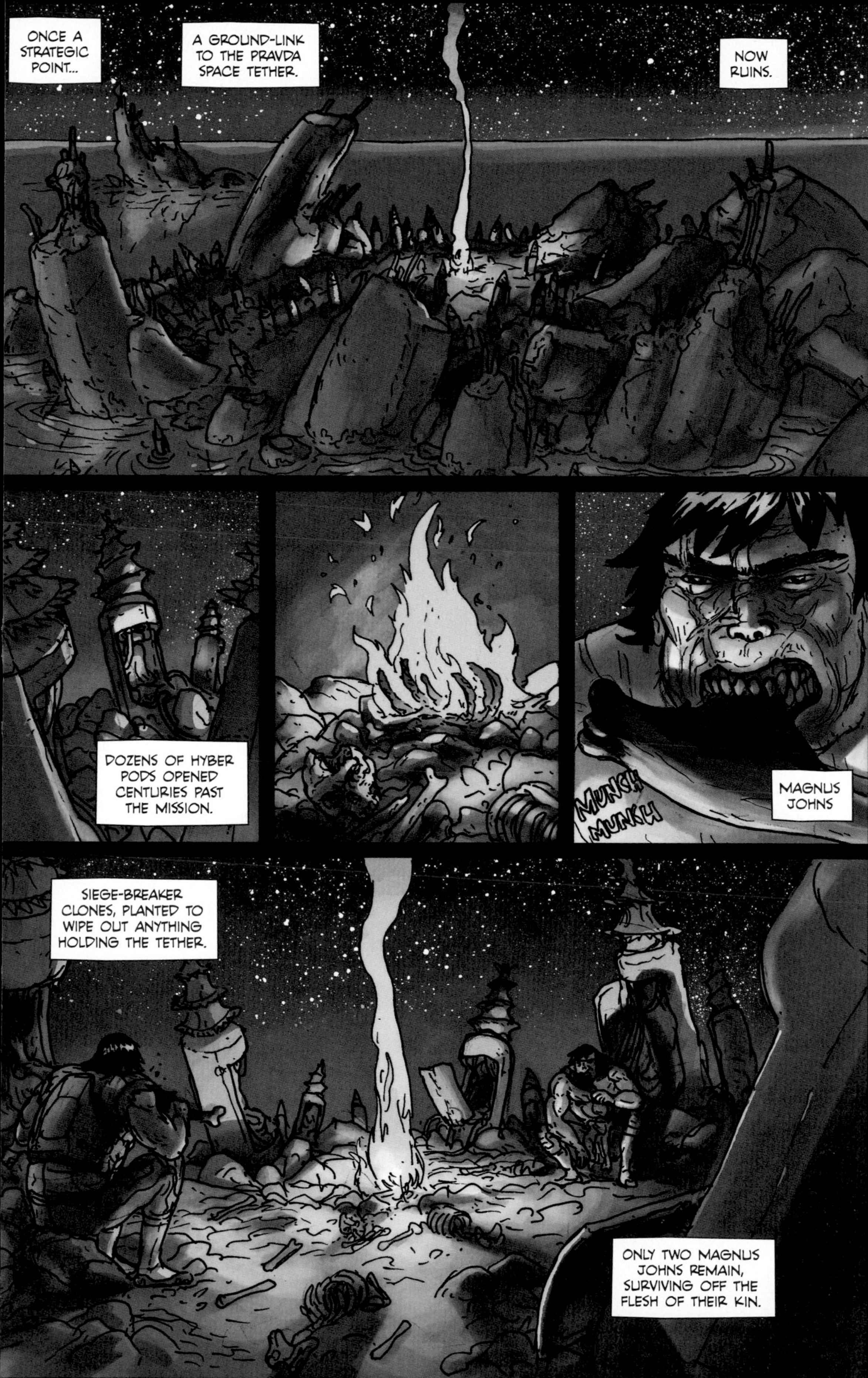
ONCE A STRATEGIC POINT...
A GROUND-LINK TO THE PRAVDA SPACE TETHER.
NOW RUINS.
DOZENS OF HYBER PODS OPENED CENTURIES PAST THE MISSION.
MUNCH MUNCH
MAGNUS JOHNS
SIEGE-BREAKER CLONES, PLANTED TO WIPE OUT ANYTHING HOLDING THE TETHER.
ONLY TWO MAGNUS JOHNS REMAIN, SURVIVING OFF THE FLESH OF THEIR KIN.

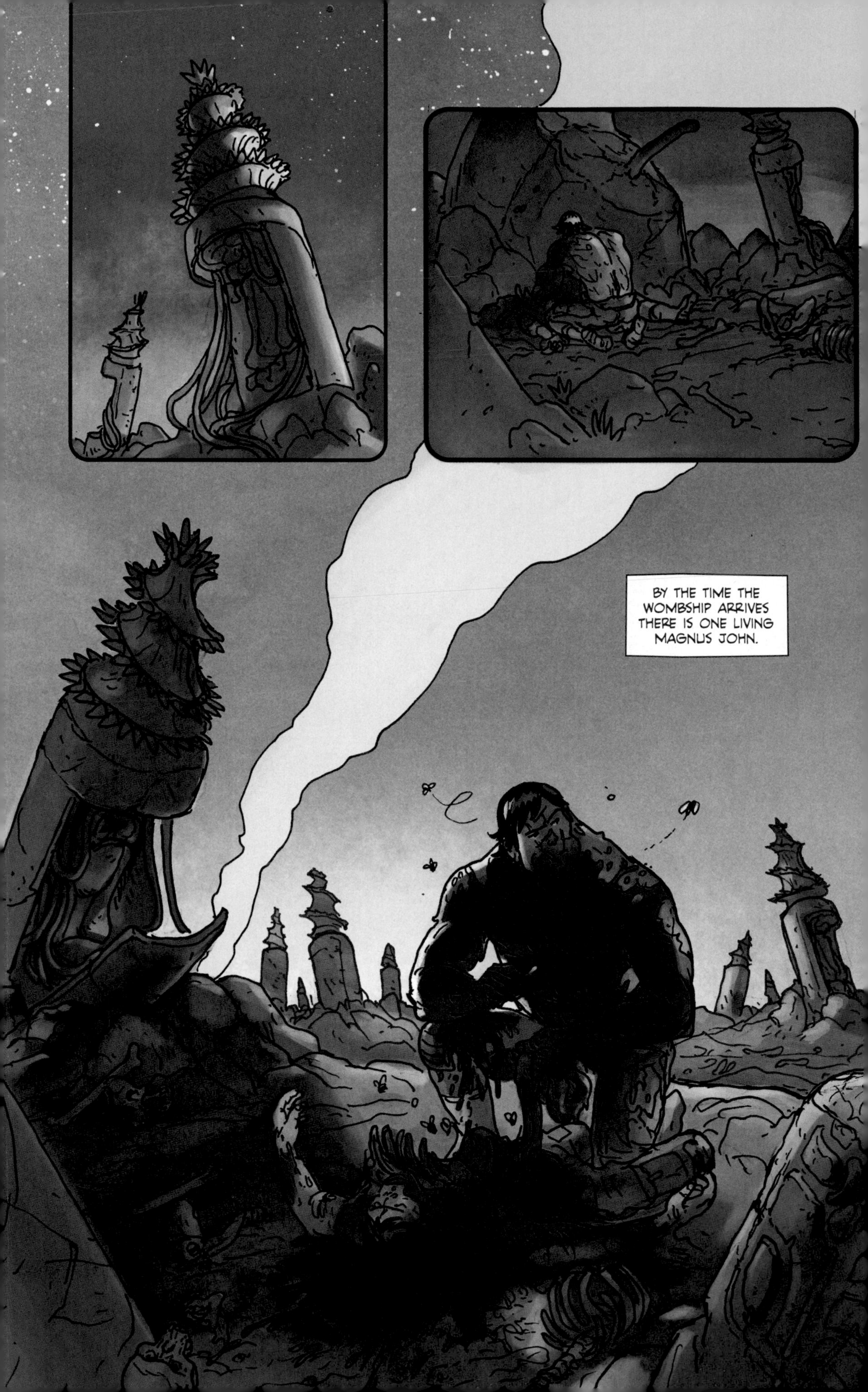
BY THE TIME THE WOMBSHIP ARRIVES THERE IS ONE LIVING MAGNUS JOHN.

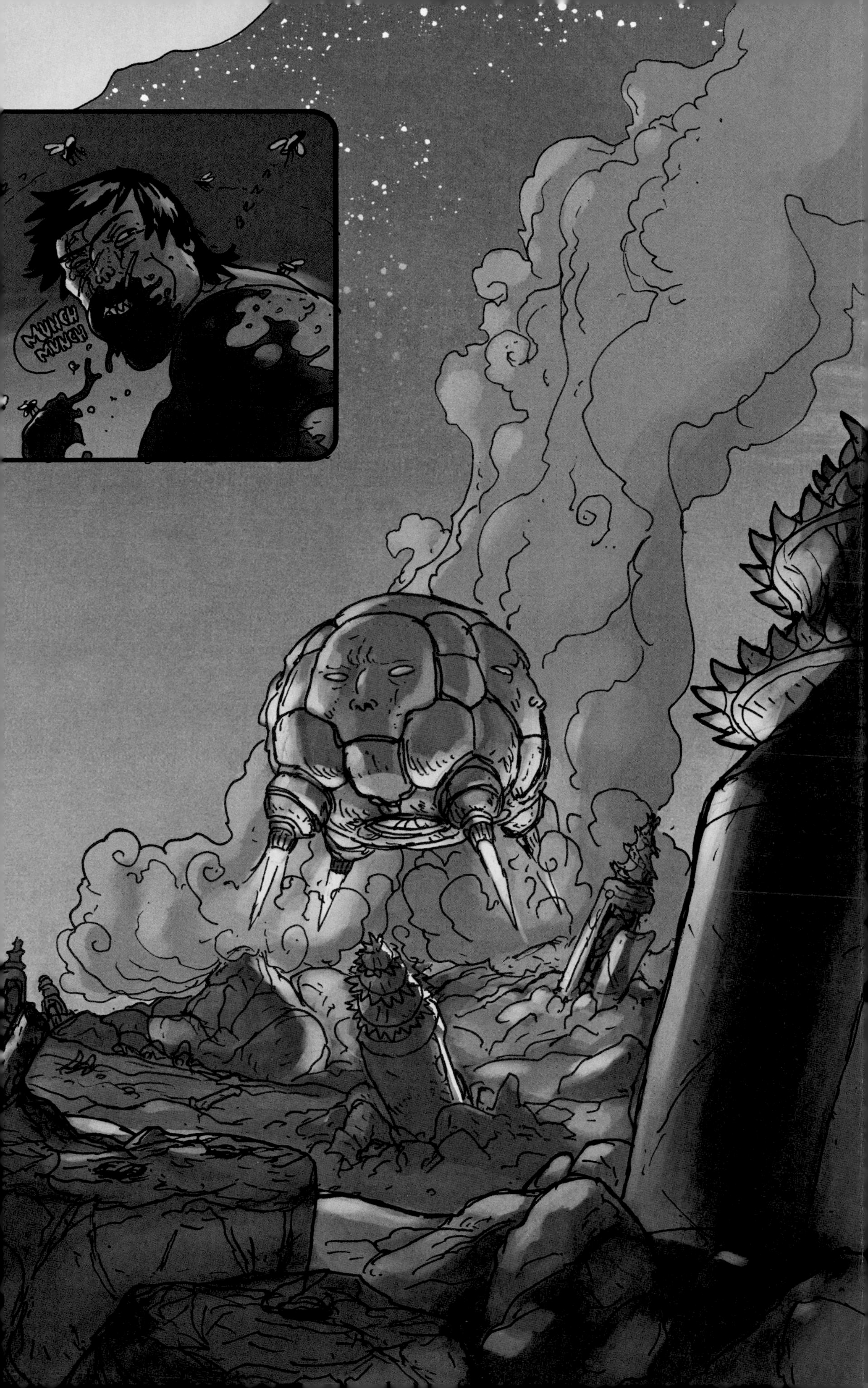
MUNCH MUNCH

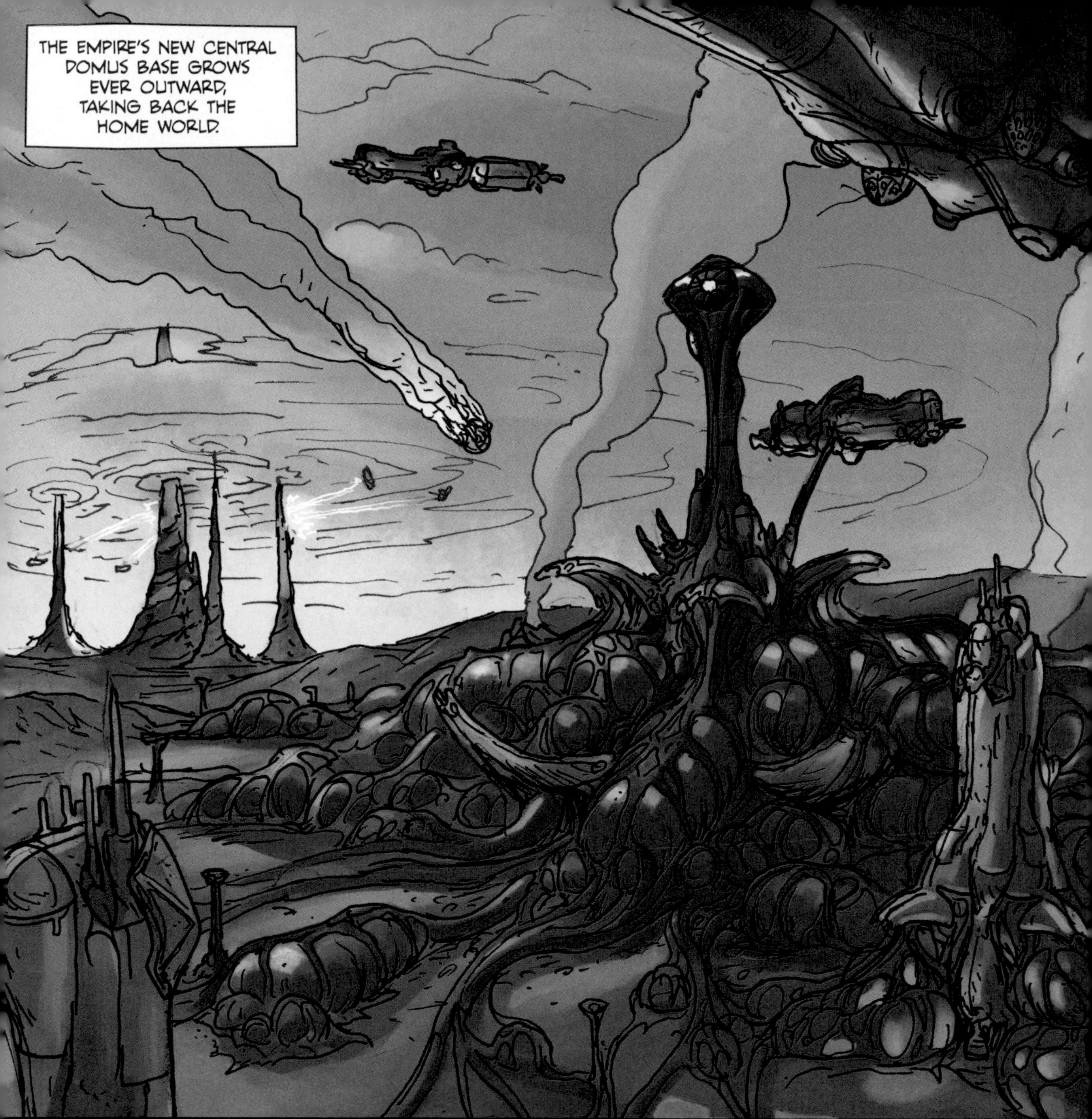
THE EMPIRE'S NEW CENTRAL DOMUS BASE GROWS EVER OUTWARD, TAKING BACK THE HOME WORLD.
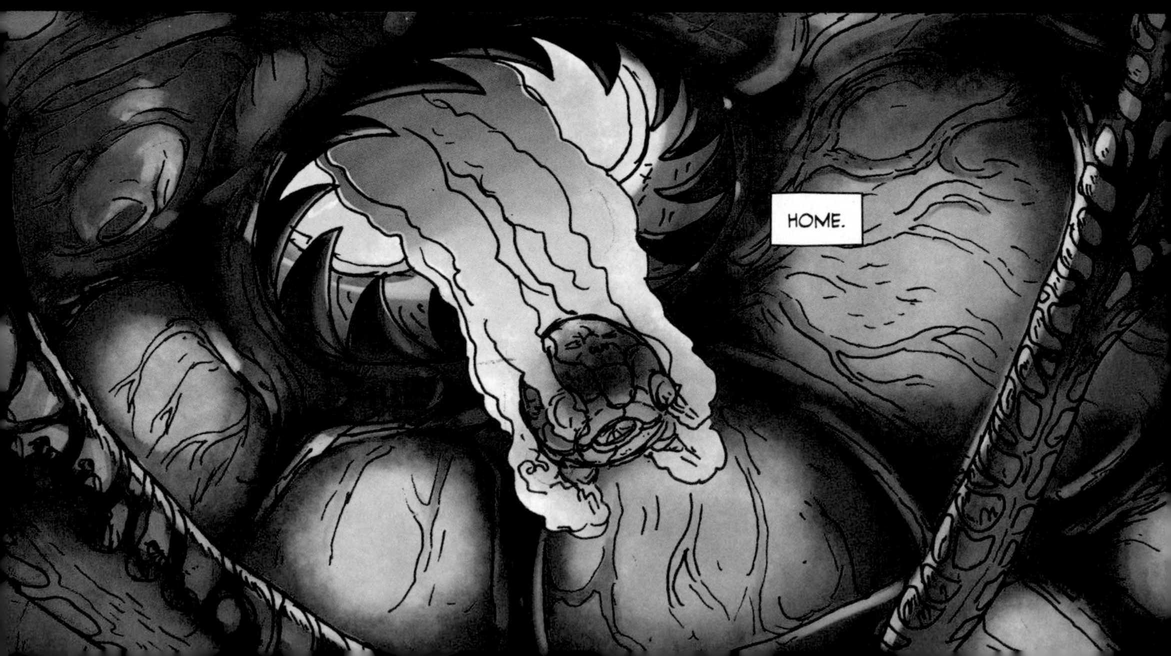
HOME.

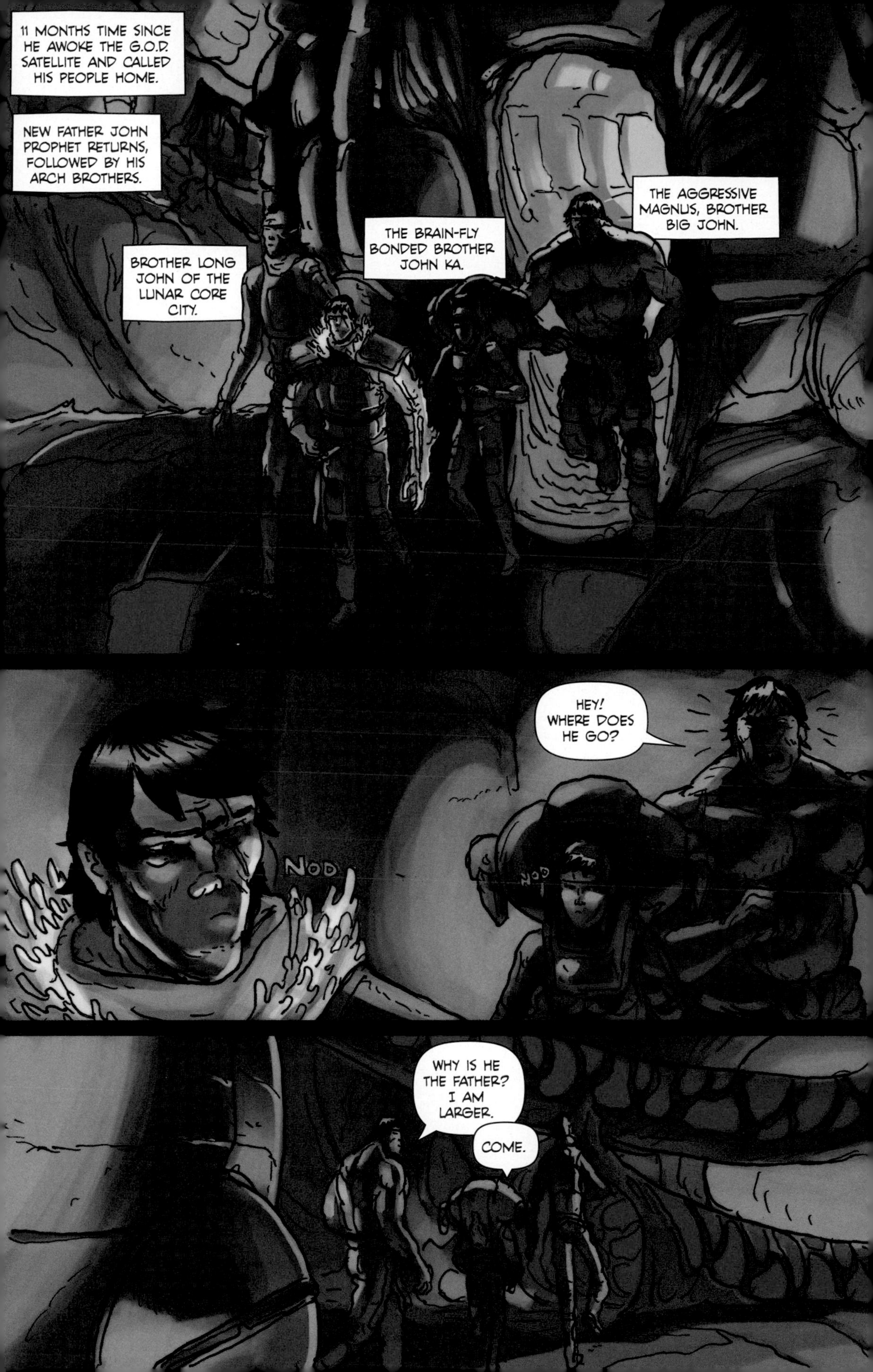
11 MONTHS TIME SINCE HE AWOKE THE G.O.D. SATELLITE AND CALLED HIS PEOPLE HOME.
NEW FATHER JOHN PROPHET RETURNS, FOLLOWED BY HIS ARCH BROTHERS.
BROTHER LONG JOHN OF THE LUNAR CORE CITY.
THE BRAIN-FLY BONDED BROTHER JOHN KA.
THE AGGRESSIVE MAGNUS, BROTHER BIG JOHN.
HEY! WHERE DOES HE GO?
NOD
NOD
WHY IS HE THE FATHER? I AM LARGER.
COME.

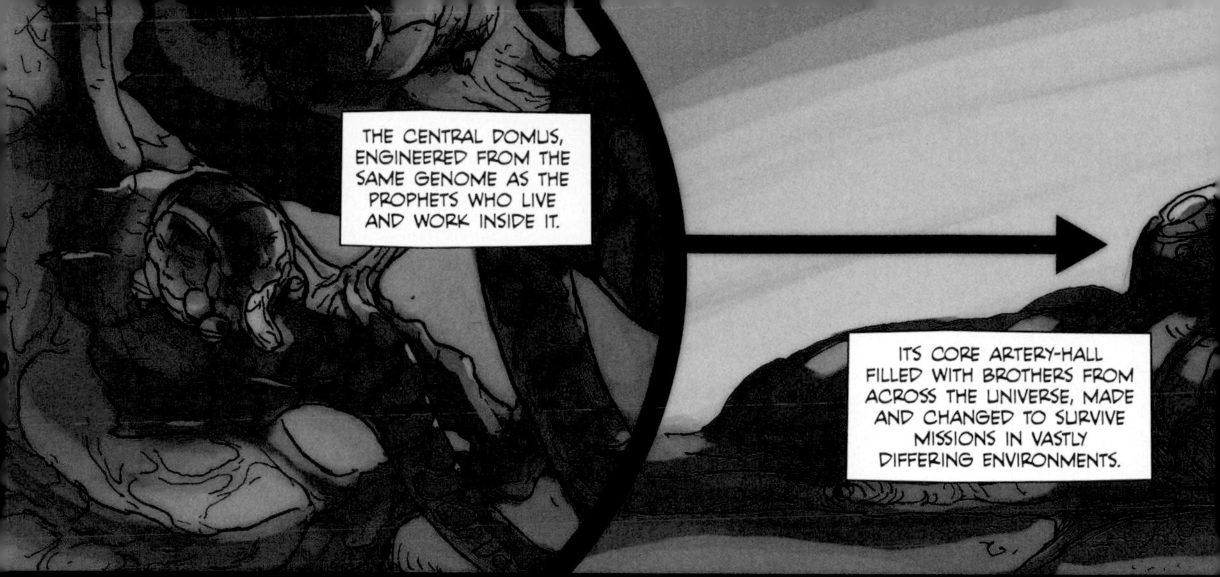
THE CENTRAL DOMUS, ENGINEERED FROM THE SAME GENOME AS THE PROPHETS WHO LIVE AND WORK INSIDE IT.
ITS CORE ARTERY-HALL FILLED WITH BROTHERS FROM ACROSS THE UNIVERSE, MADE AND CHANGED TO SURVIVE MISSIONS IN VASTLY DIFFERING ENVIRONMENTS.

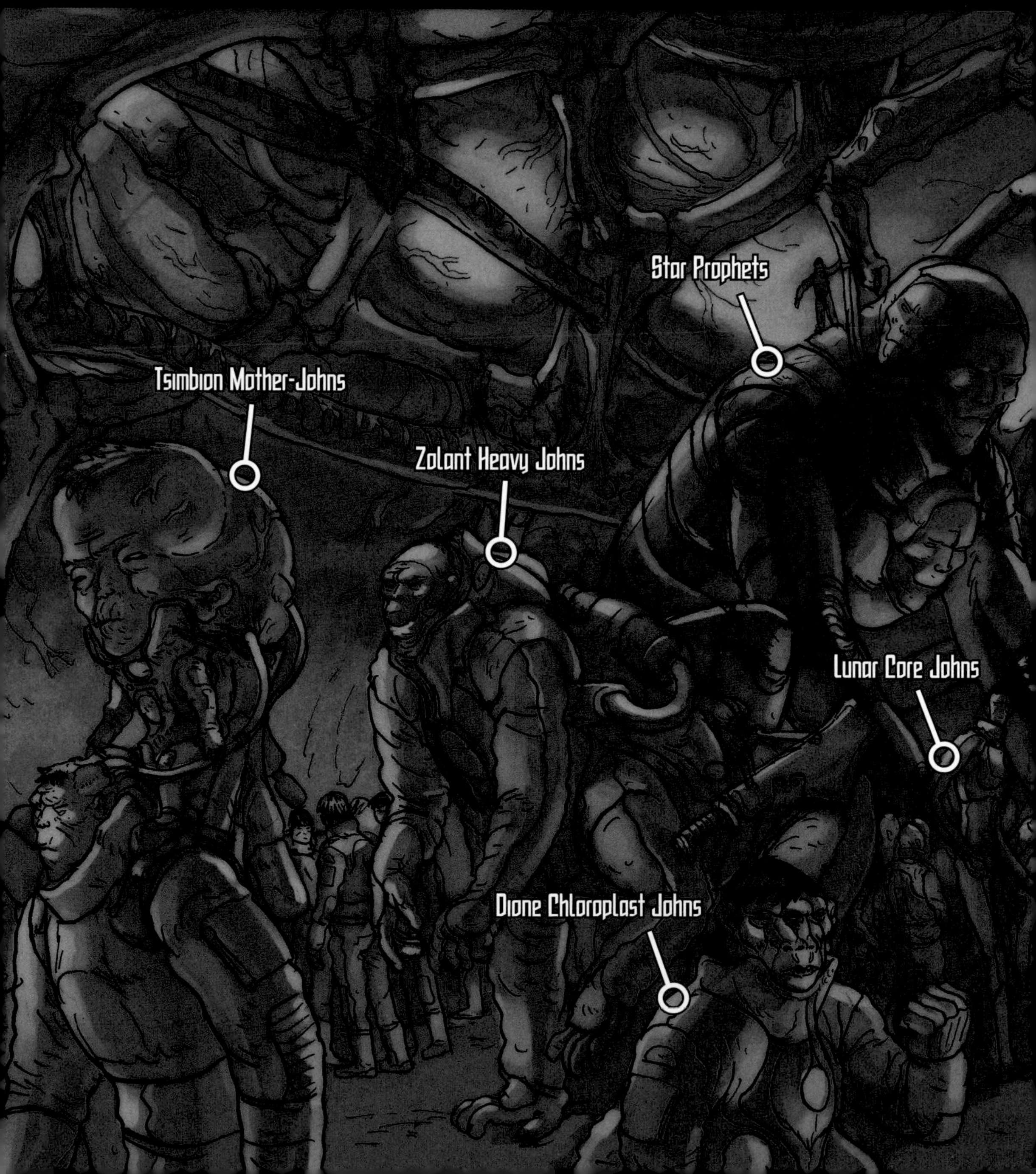
Star Prophets
Tsimbion Mother-Johns
Zolant Heavy Johns
Lunar Core Johns
Dione Chloroplast Johns

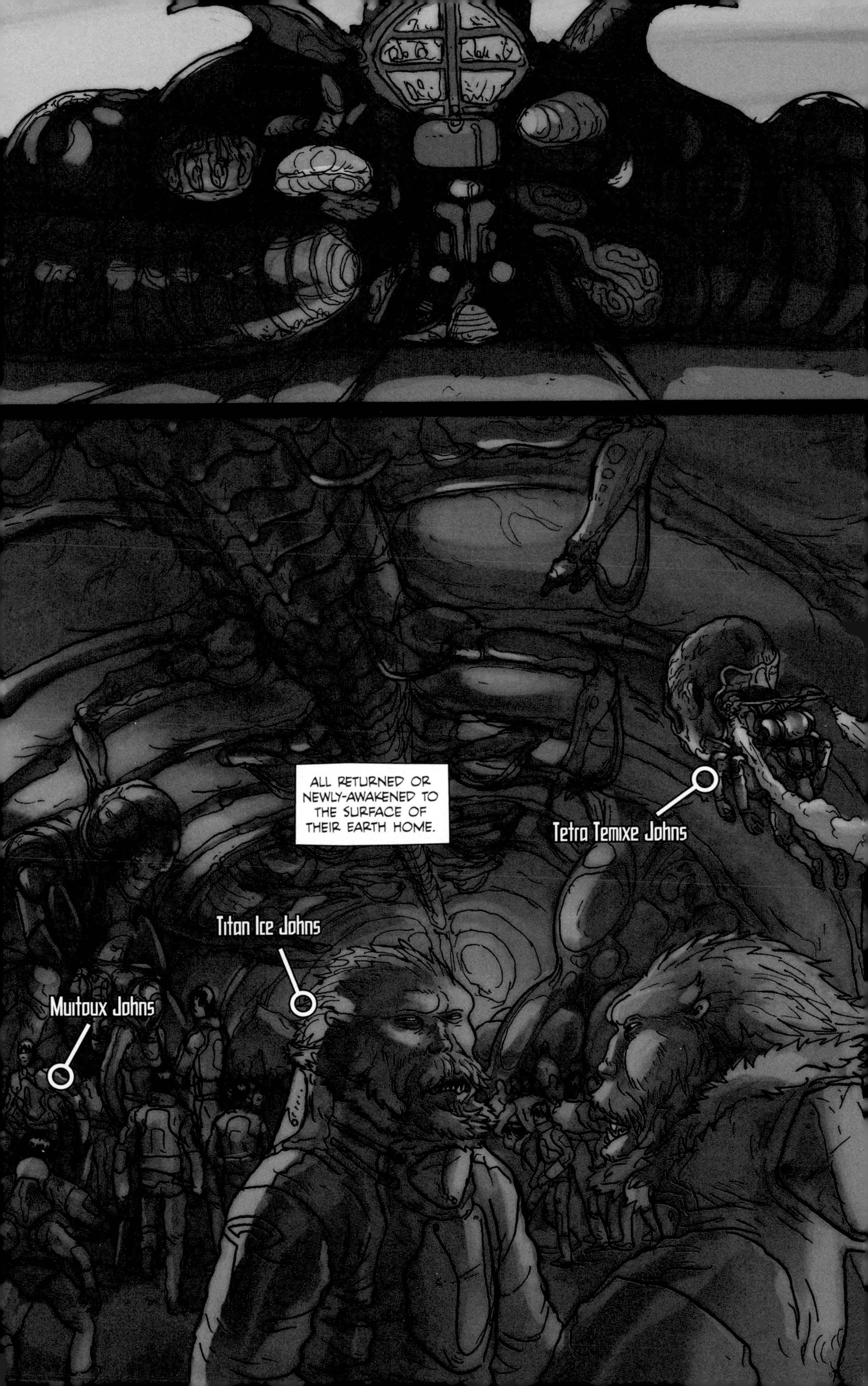
ALL RETURNED OR NEWLY-AWAKENED TO THE SURFACE OF THEIR EARTH HOME.
Tetra Temixe Johns
Titan Ice Johns
Muitoux Johns

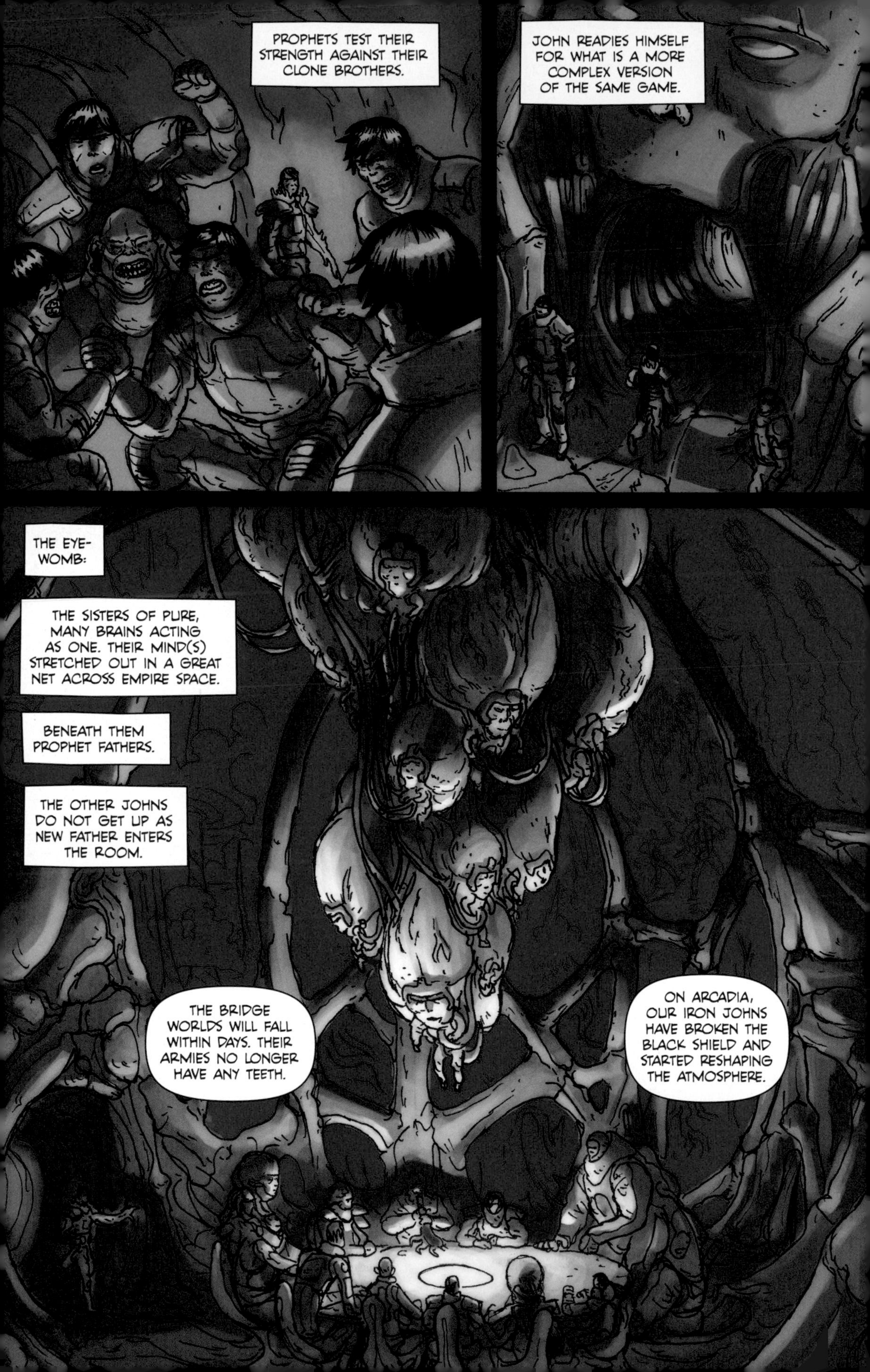
PROPHETS TEST THEIR STRENGTH AGAINST THEIR CLONE BROTHERS.
JOHN READIES HIMSELF FOR WHAT IS A MORE COMPLEX VERSION OF THE SAME GAME.
THE EYE-WOMB:
THE SISTERS OF PURE, MANY BRAINS ACTING AS ONE. THEIR MIND(S) STRETCHED OUT IN A GREAT NET ACROSS EMPIRE SPACE.
BENEATH THEM PROPHET FATHERS.
THE OTHER JOHNS DO NOT GET UP AS NEW FATHER ENTERS THE ROOM.
THE BRIDGE WORLDS WILL FALL WITHIN DAYS. THEIR ARMIES NO LONGER HAVE ANY TEETH.
ON ARCADIA, OUR IRON JOHNS HAVE BROKEN THE BLACK SHIELD AND STARTED RESHAPING THE ATMOSPHERE.

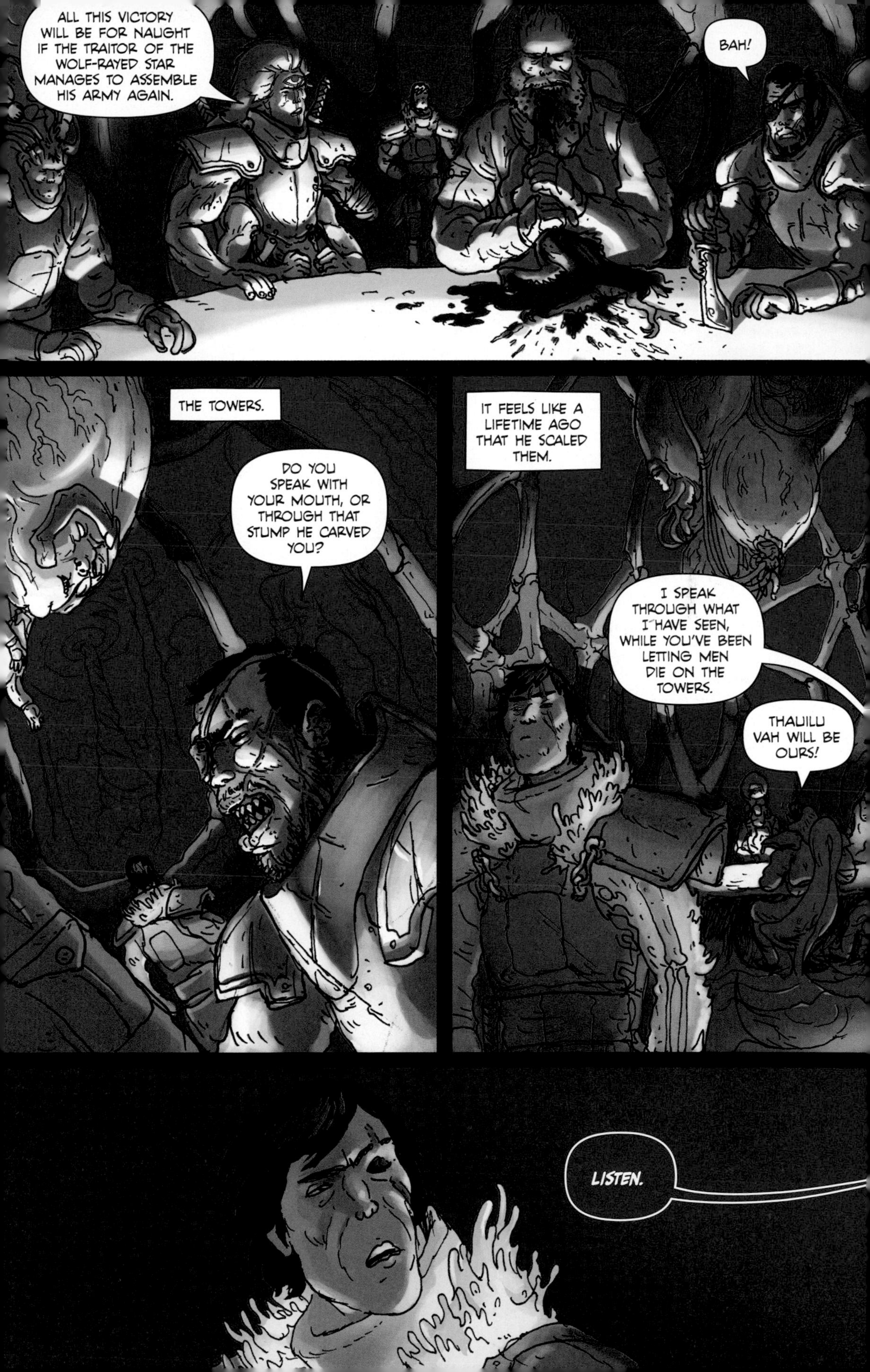
ALL THIS VICTORY WILL BE FOR NAUGHT IF THE TRAITOR OF THE WOLF-RAYED STAR MANAGES TO ASSEMBLE HIS ARMY AGAIN.
BAH!
THE TOWERS.
DO YOU SPEAK WITH YOUR MOUTH, OR THROUGH THAT STUMP HE CARVED YOU?
IT FEELS LIKE A LIFETIME AGO THAT HE SCALED THEM.
I SPEAK THROUGH WHAT I HAVE SEEN, WHILE YOU'VE BEEN LETTING MEN DIE ON THE TOWERS.
THAUILU VAH WILL BE OURS!
LISTEN.

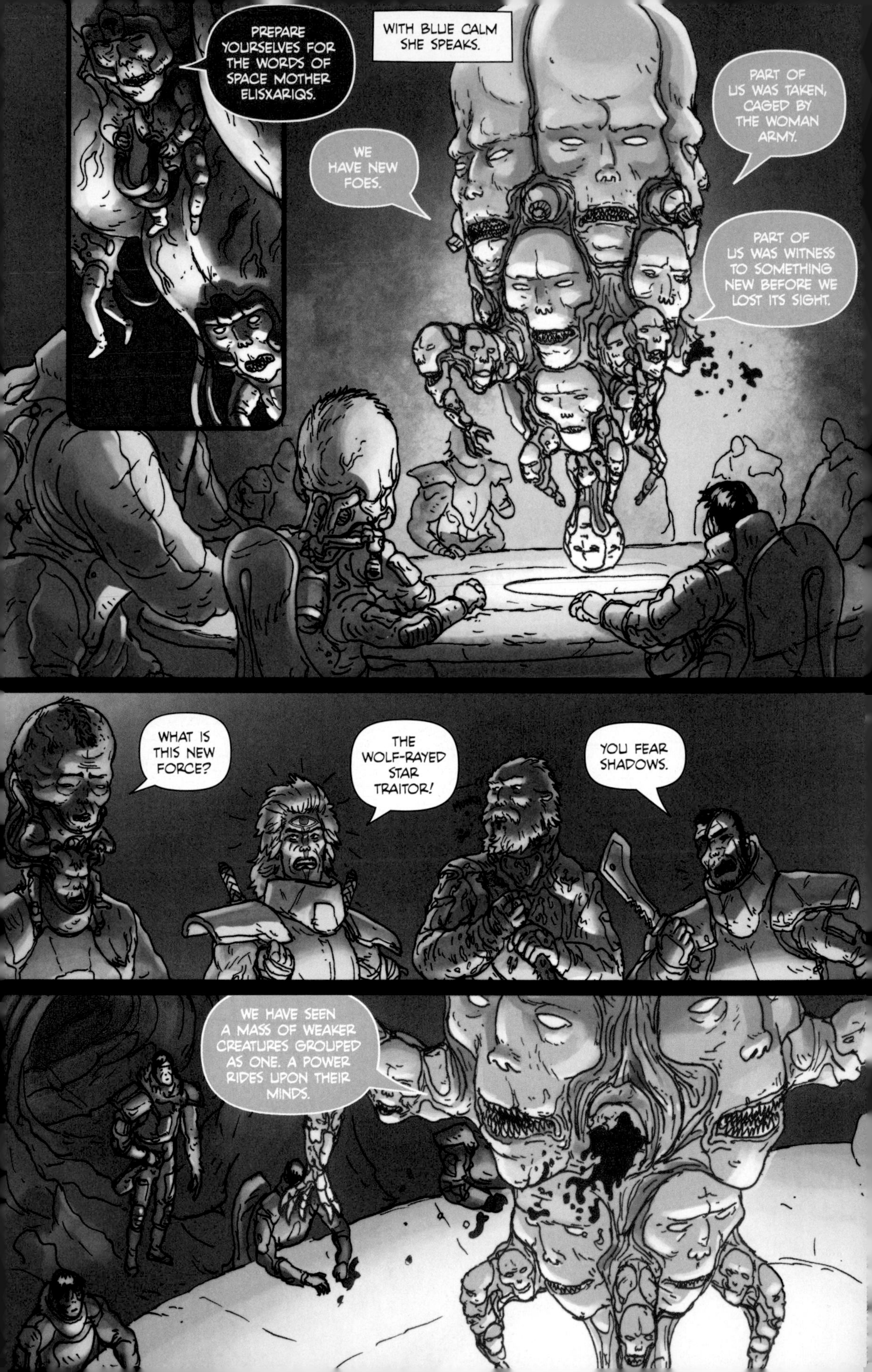
PREPARE YOURSELVES FOR THE WORDS OF SPACE MOTHER ELISXARIQS.
WITH BLUE CALM SHE SPEAKS.
WE HAVE NEW FOES.
PART OF US WAS TAKEN, CAGED BY THE WOMAN ARMY.
PART OF US WAS WITNESS TO SOMETHING NEW BEFORE WE LOST ITS SIGHT.
WHAT IS THIS NEW FORCE?
THE WOLF-RAYED STAR TRAITOR!
YOU FEAR SHADOWS.
WE HAVE SEEN A MASS OF WEAKER CREATURES GROUPED AS ONE. A POWER RIDES UPON THEIR MINDS.

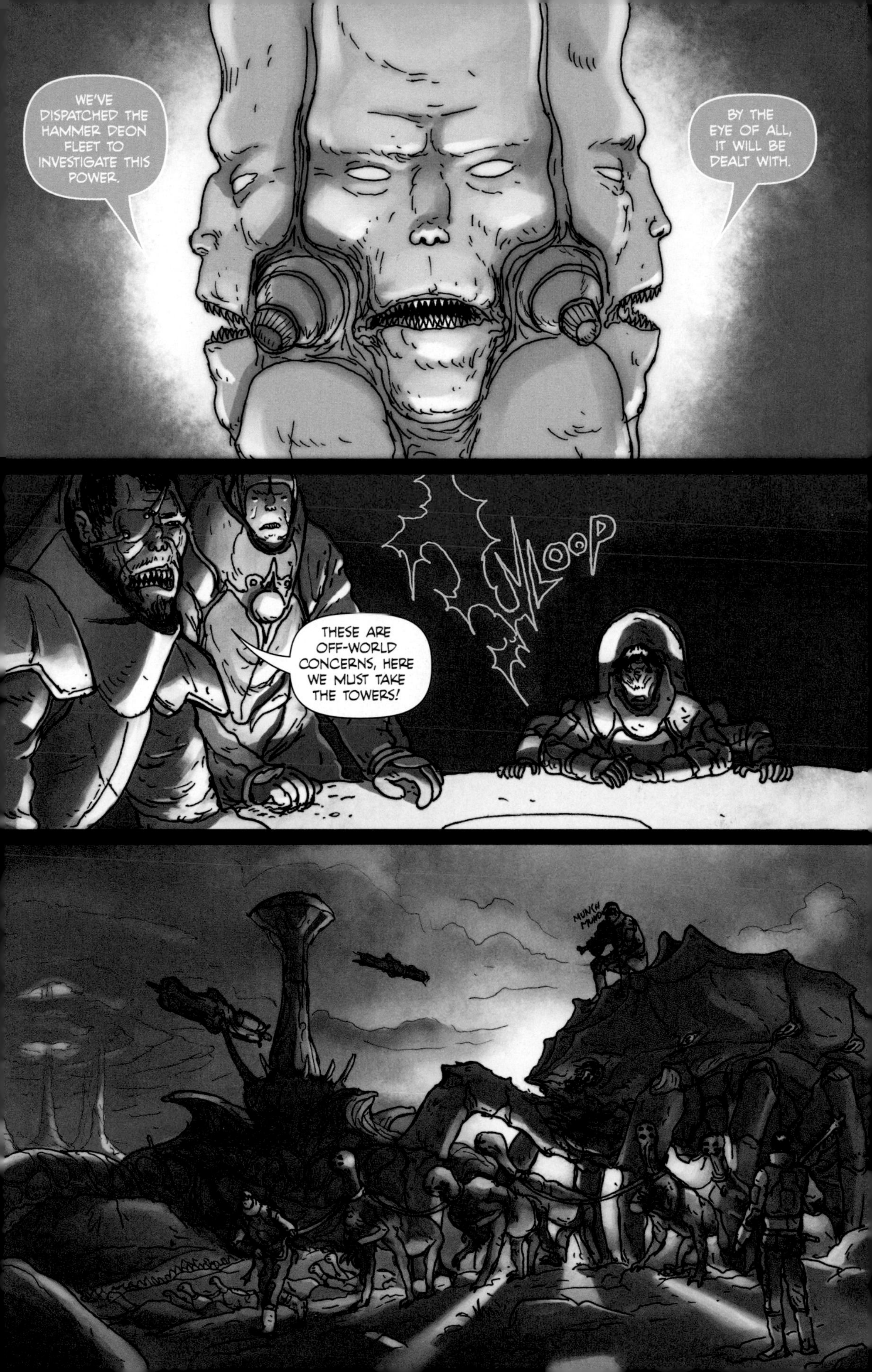
WE'VE DISPATCHED THE HAMMER DEON FLEET TO INVESTIGATE THIS POWER.
BY THE EYE OF ALL, IT WILL BE DEALT WITH.
VVLOOP
THESE ARE OFF-WORLD CONCERNS, HERE WE MUST TAKE THE TOWERS!
MUNCH

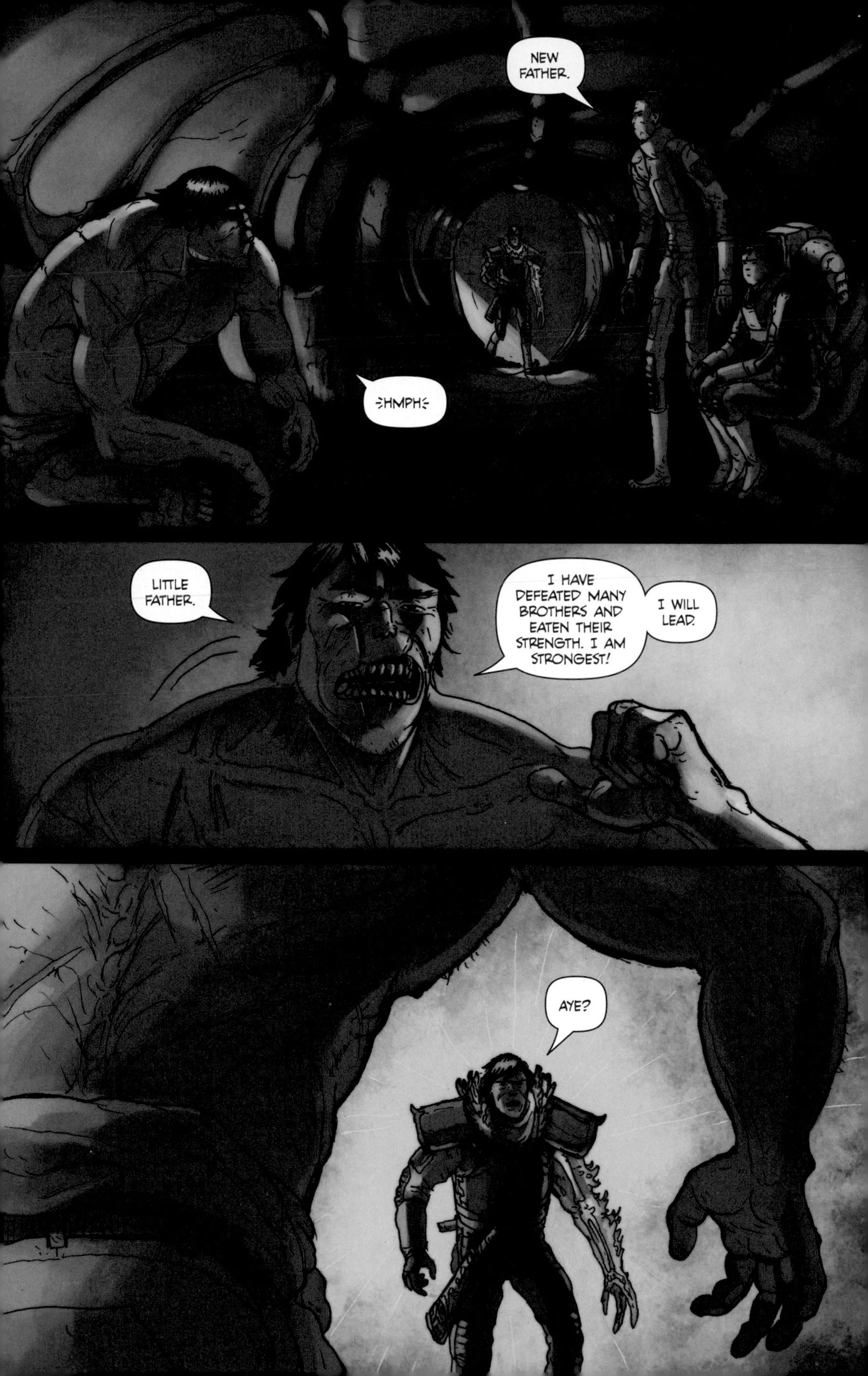
NEW FATHER.
HMPH
LITTLE FATHER.
I HAVE DEFEATED MANY BROTHERS AND EATEN THEIR STRENGTH. I AM STRONGEST!
I WILL LEAD.
AYE?

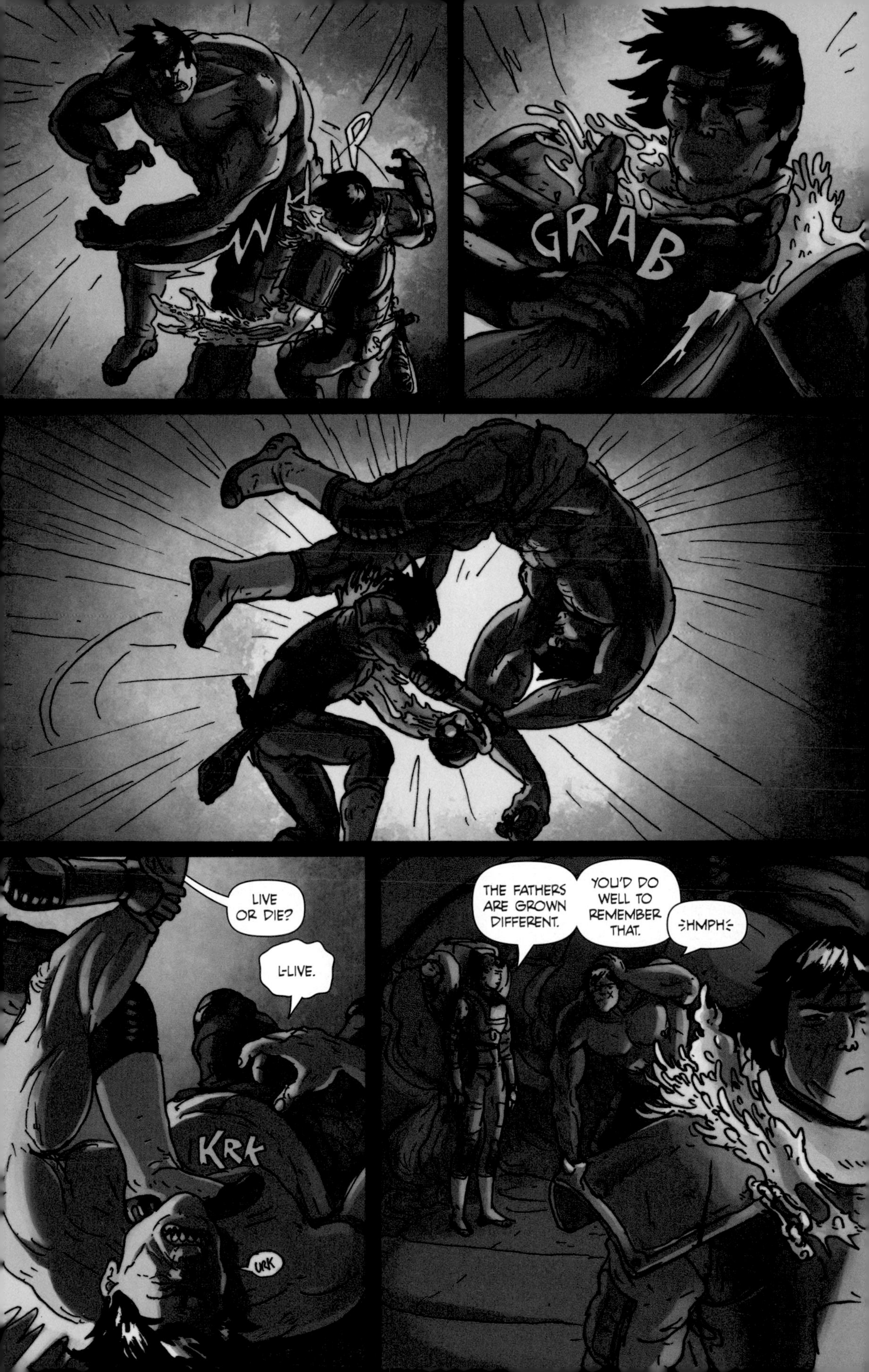
WHAP
GRAB
LIVE OR DIE?
L-LIVE.
KRK
URK
THE FATHERS ARE GROWN DIFFERENT.
YOU'D DO WELL TO REMEMBER THAT.
HMPH

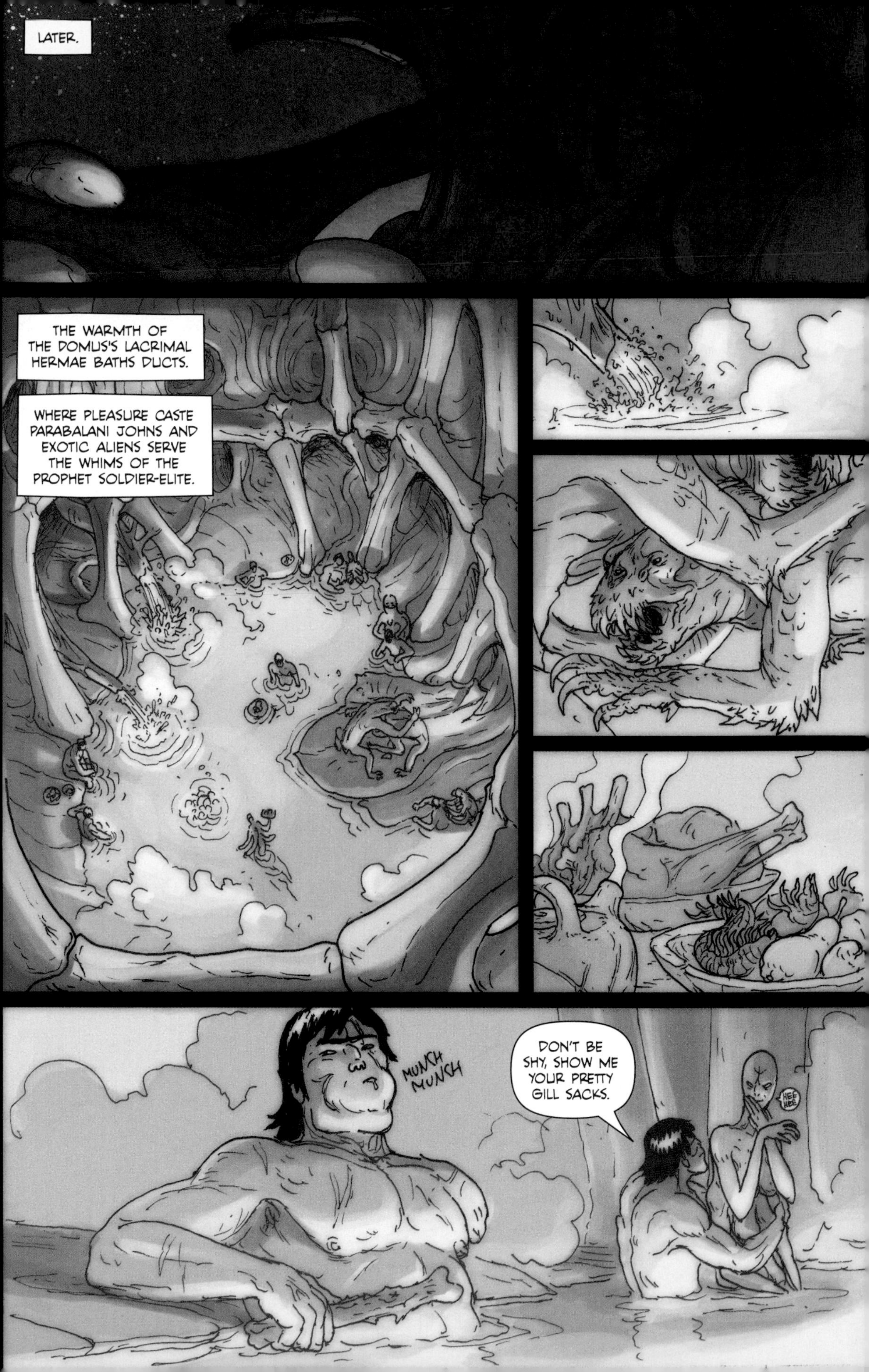
LATER.
THE WARMTH OF THE DOMUS'S LACRIMAL HERMAE BATHS DUCTS.
WHERE PLEASURE CASTE PARABALANI JOHNS AND EXOTIC ALIENS SERVE THE WHIMS OF THE PROPHET SOLDIER-ELITE.
MUNCH MUNCH
DON'T BE SHY, SHOW ME YOUR PRETTY GILL SACKS.
HEE HEE

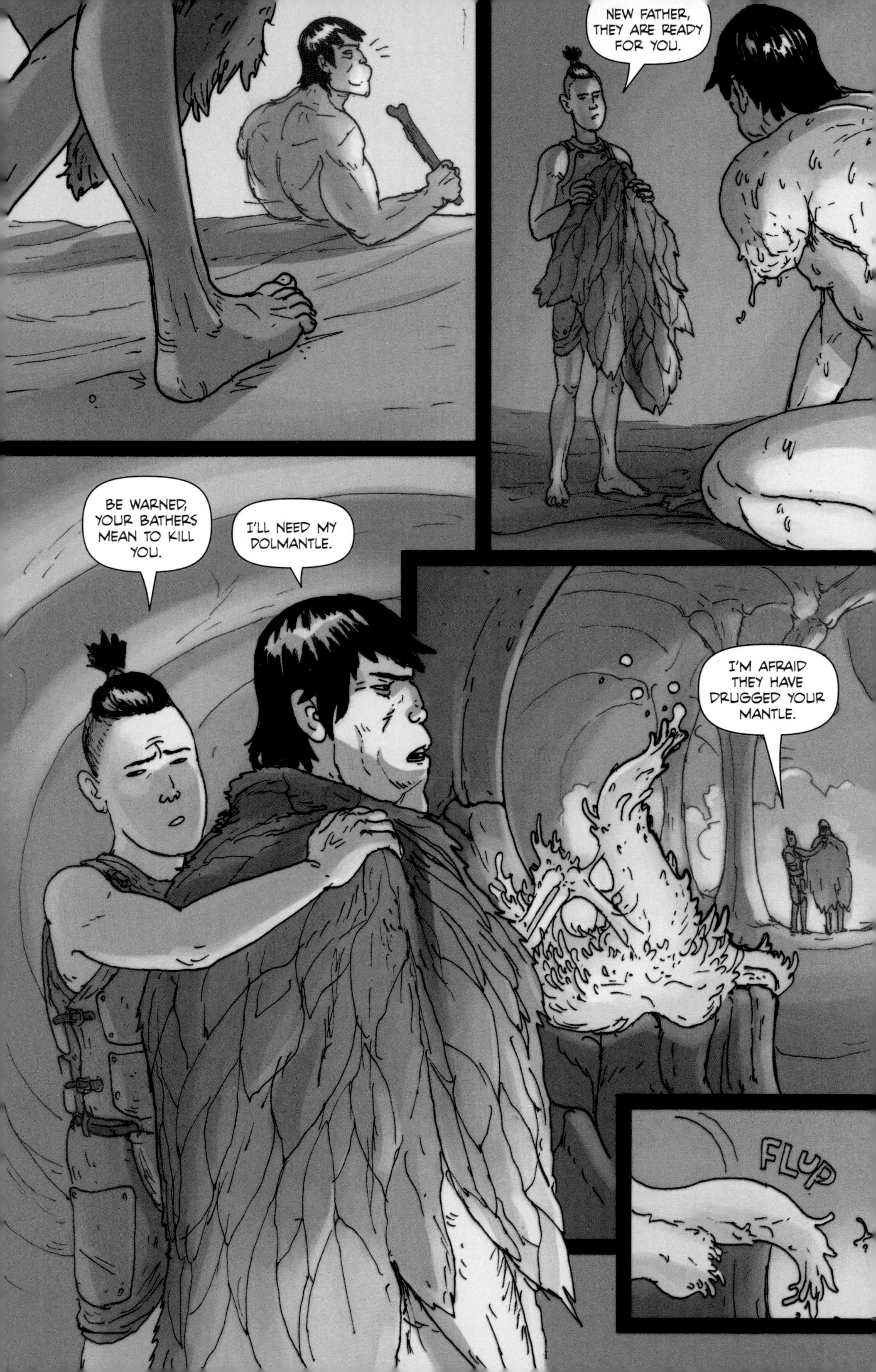
NEW FATHER, THEY ARE READY FOR YOU.
BE WARNED, YOUR BATHERS MEAN TO KILL YOU.
I'LL NEED MY DOLMANTLE.
I'M AFRAID THEY HAVE DRUGGED YOUR MANTLE.
FLUP

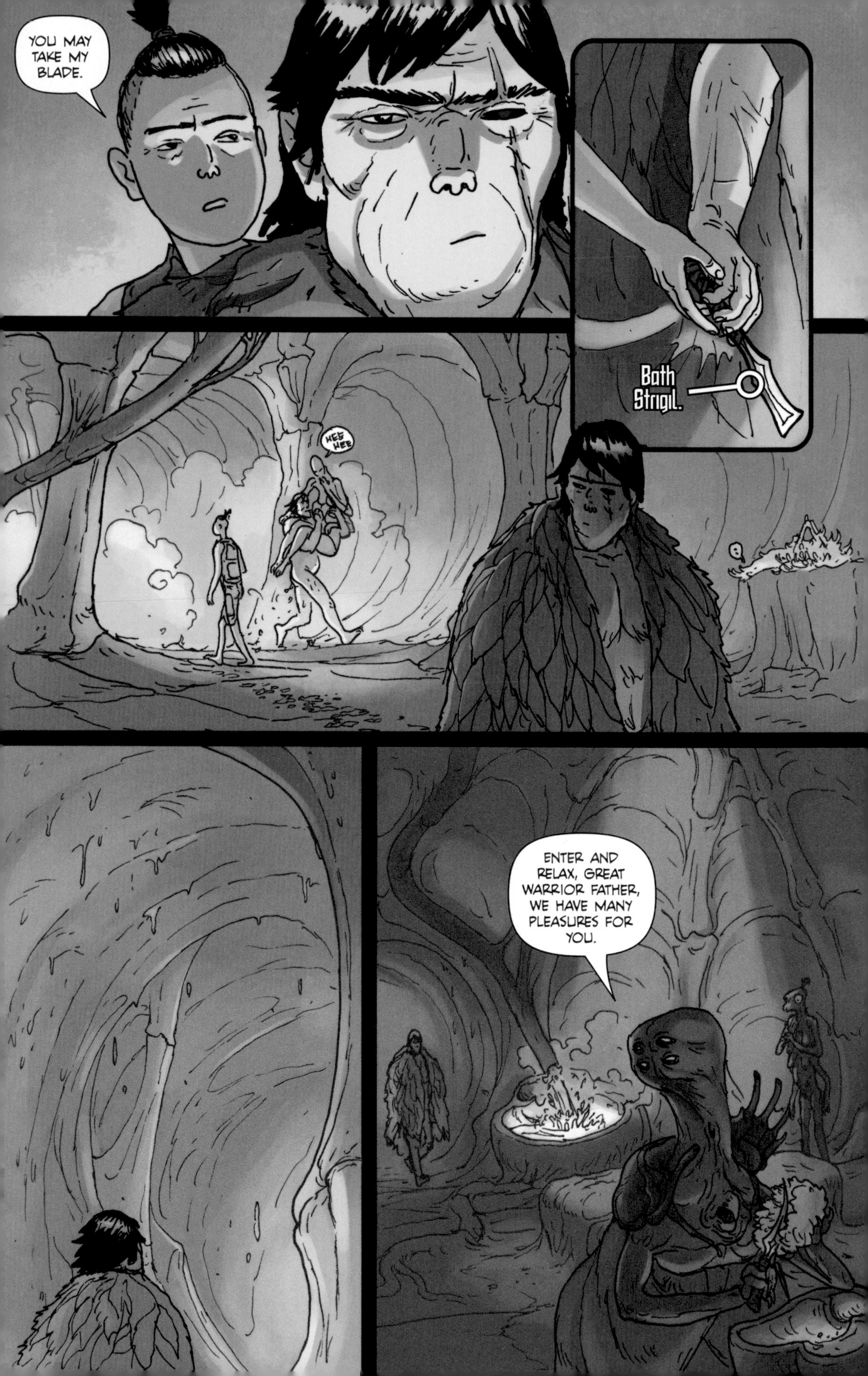
YOU MAY TAKE MY BLADE.
Bath Strigil.
HEE HEE
ENTER AND RELAX, GREAT WARRIOR FATHER, WE HAVE MANY PLEASURES FOR YOU.

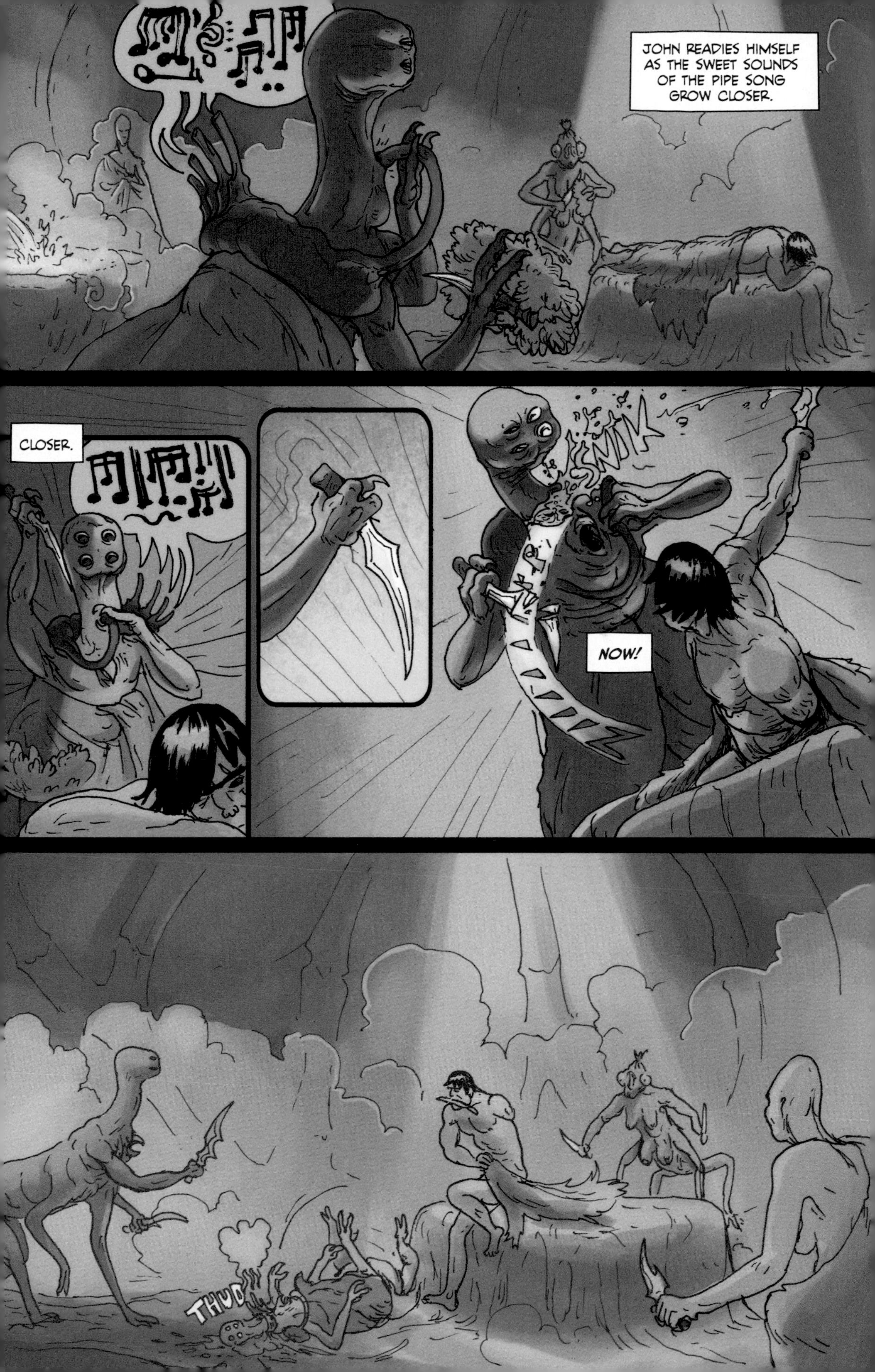
JOHN READIES HIMSELF AS THE SWEET SOUNDS OF THE PIPE SONG GROW CLOSER.
CLOSER.
SNIK
NOW!
THUD

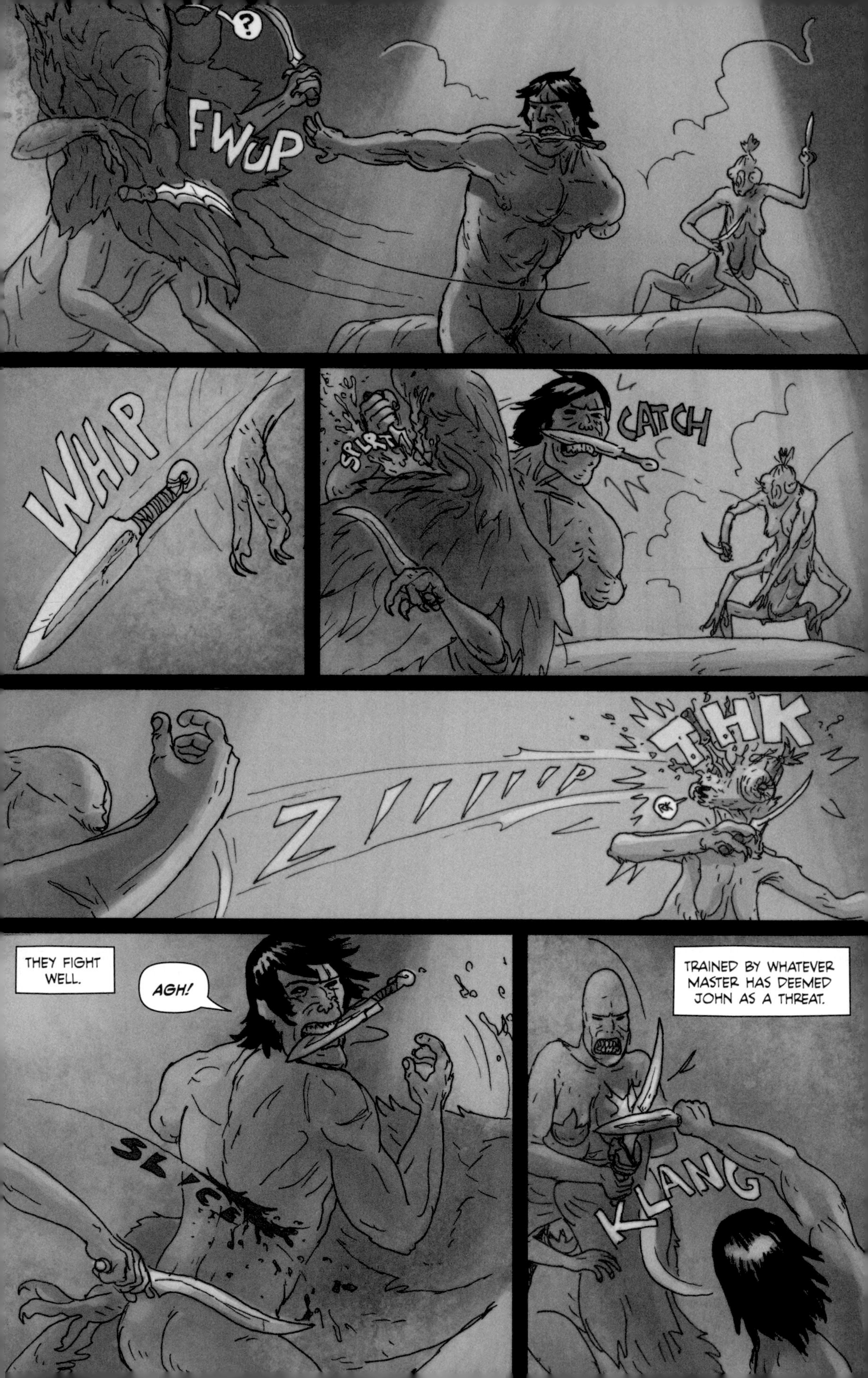
?
FWUP
WHIP
SPLRT
CATCH
ZIIIIIP
THK
THEY FIGHT WELL.
AGH!
SLICE
TRAINED BY WHATEVER MASTER HAS DEEMED JOHN AS A THREAT.
KLANG

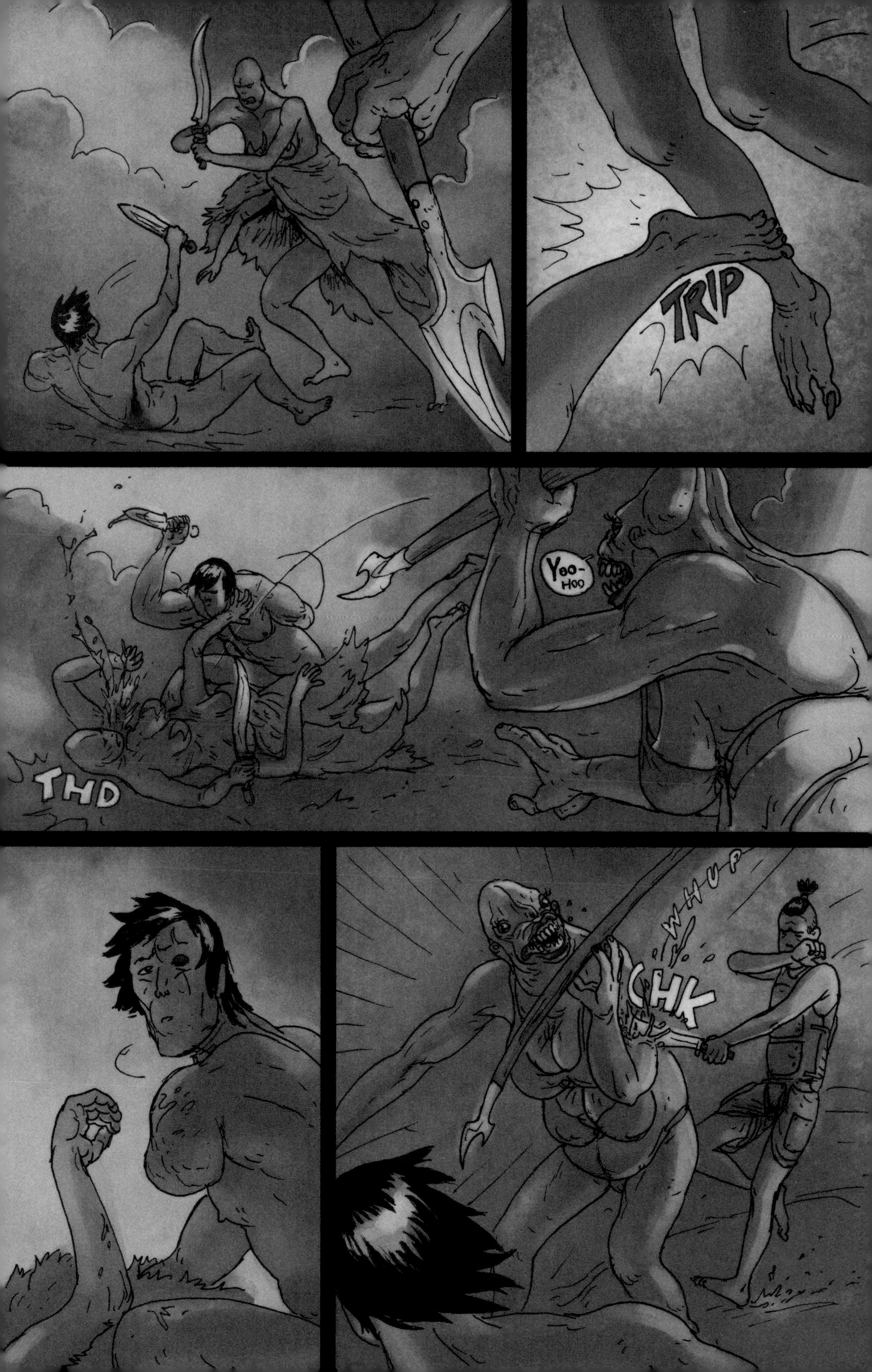
TRIP
YOO-HOO
THD
WHUP
CHK

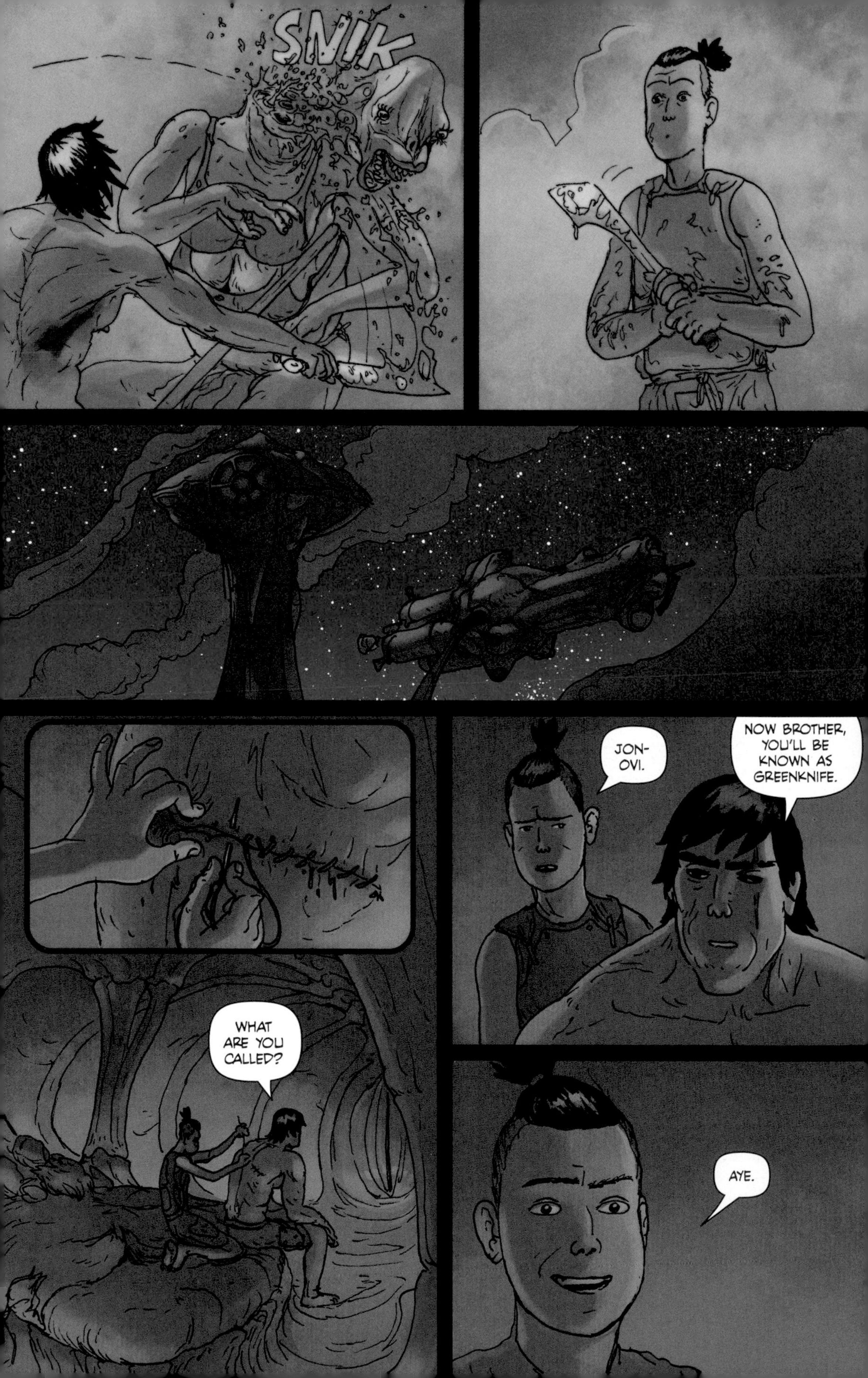
SNIK
JON-OVI.
NOW BROTHER, YOU'LL BE KNOWN AS GREENKNIFE.
WHAT ARE YOU CALLED?
AYE.

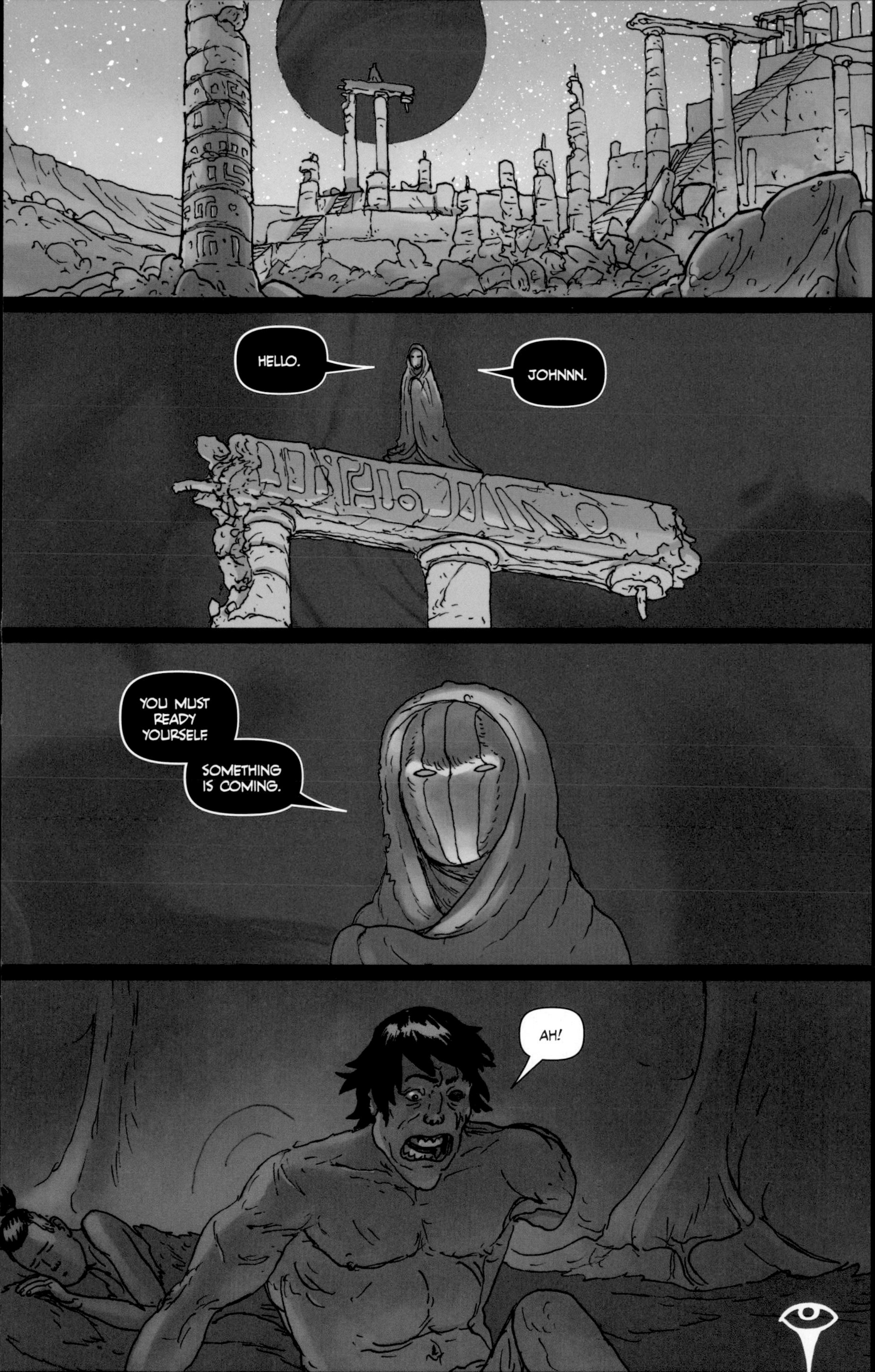
HELLO.
JOHNNN.
YOU MUST READY YOURSELF.
SOMETHING IS COMING.
AH!

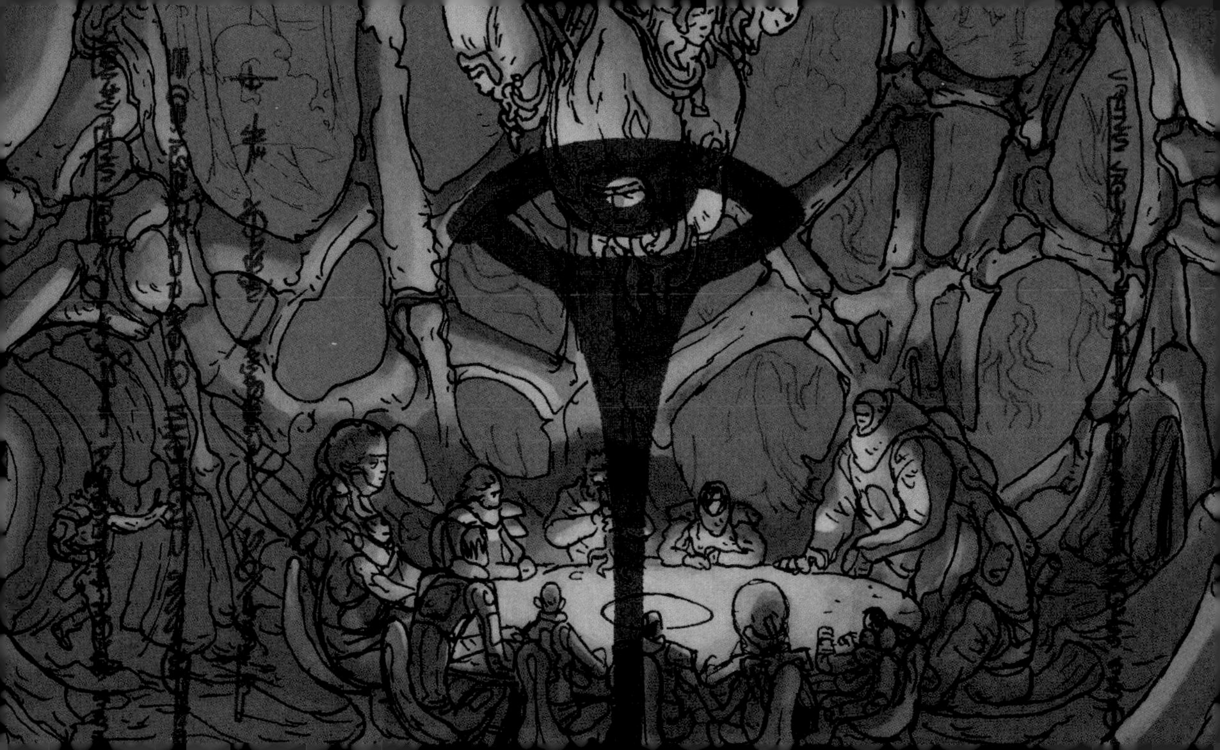

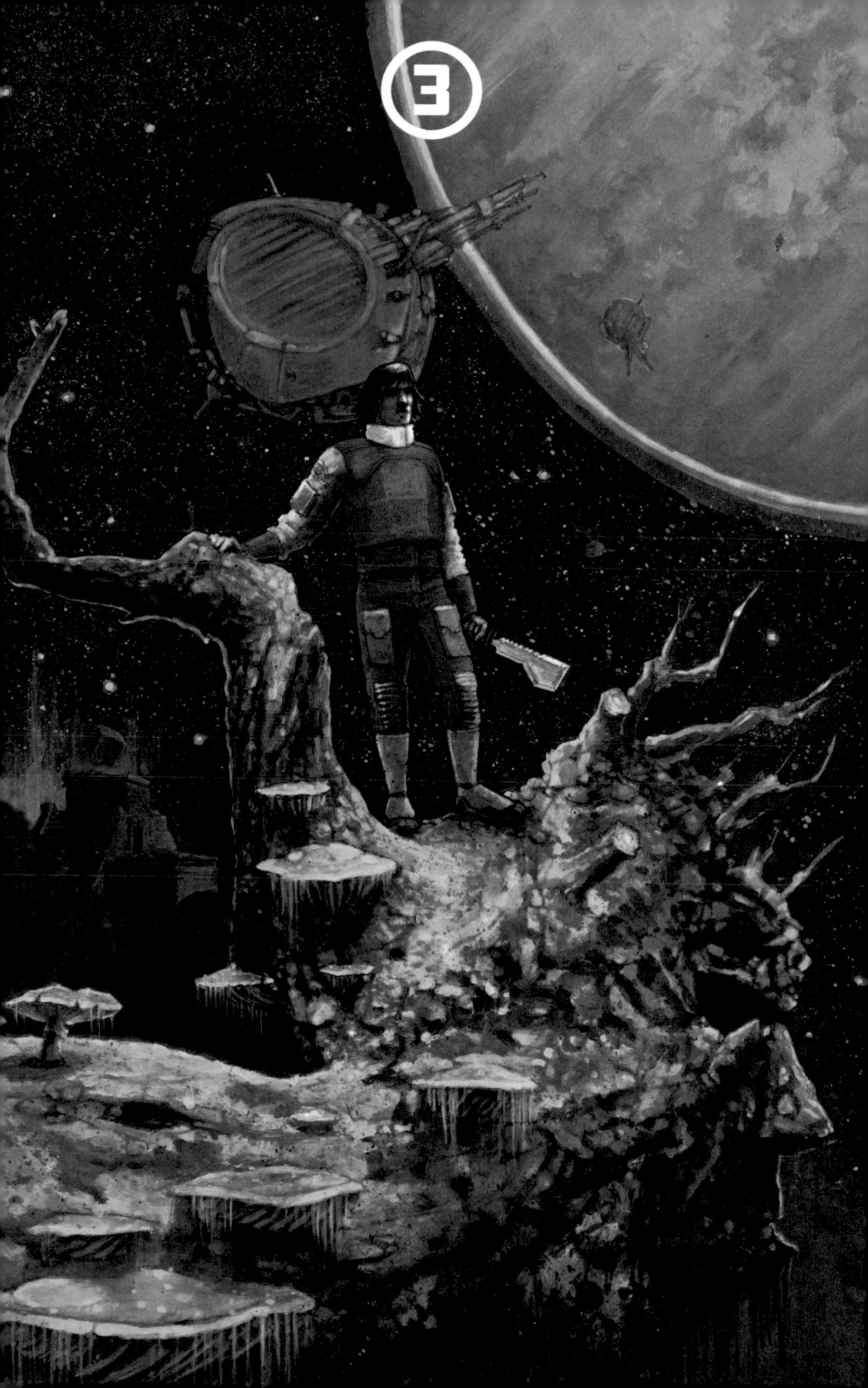
3

PRO

HET

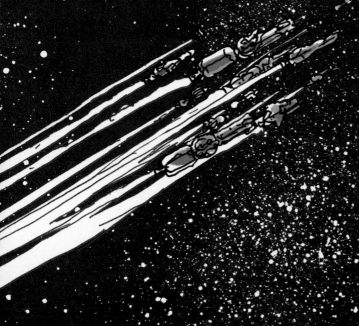

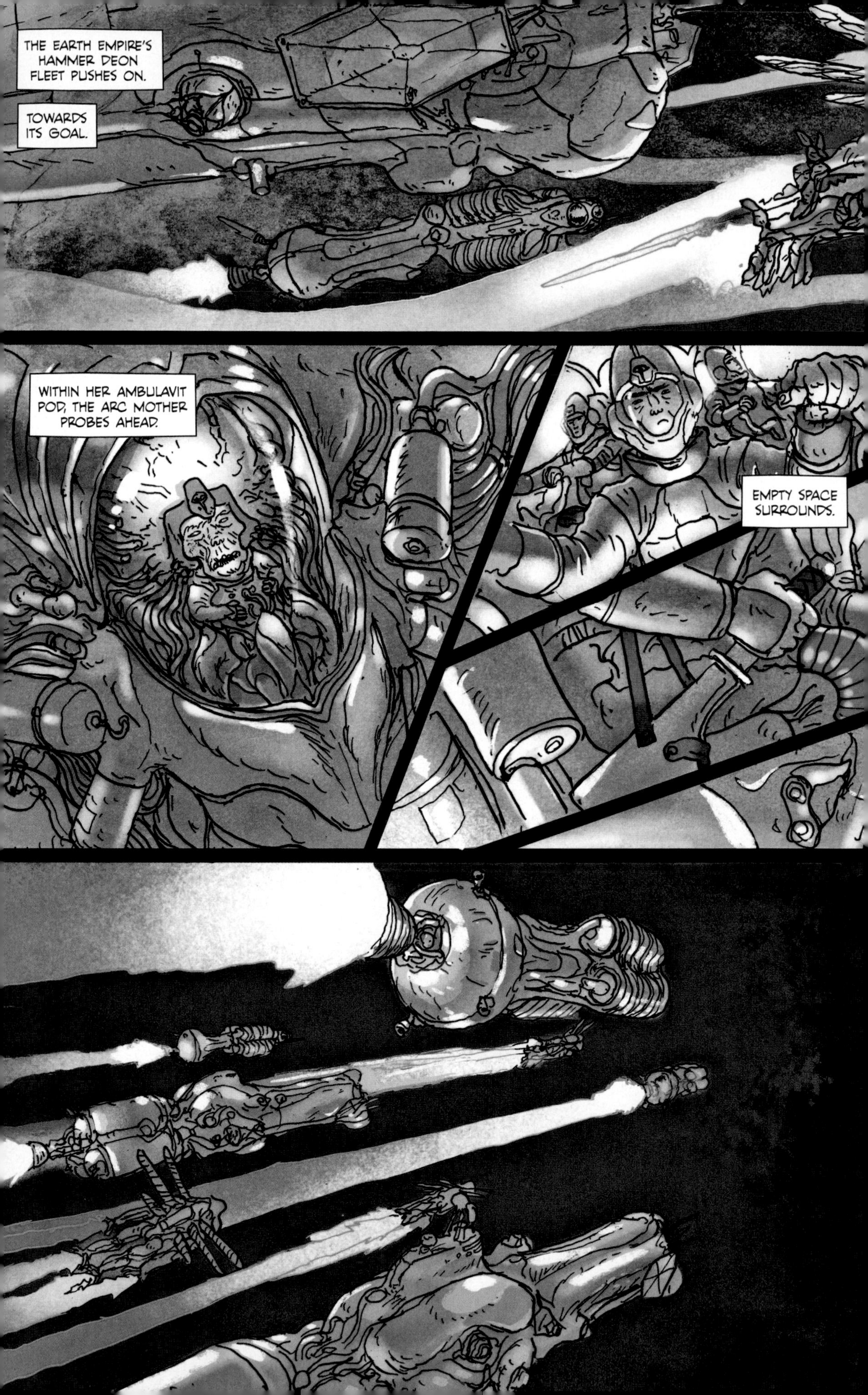
THE EARTH EMPIRE'S HAMMER DEON FLEET PUSHES ON.
TOWARDS ITS GOAL.
WITHIN HER AMBULAVIT POD, THE ARC MOTHER PROBES AHEAD.
EMPTY SPACE SURROUNDS.

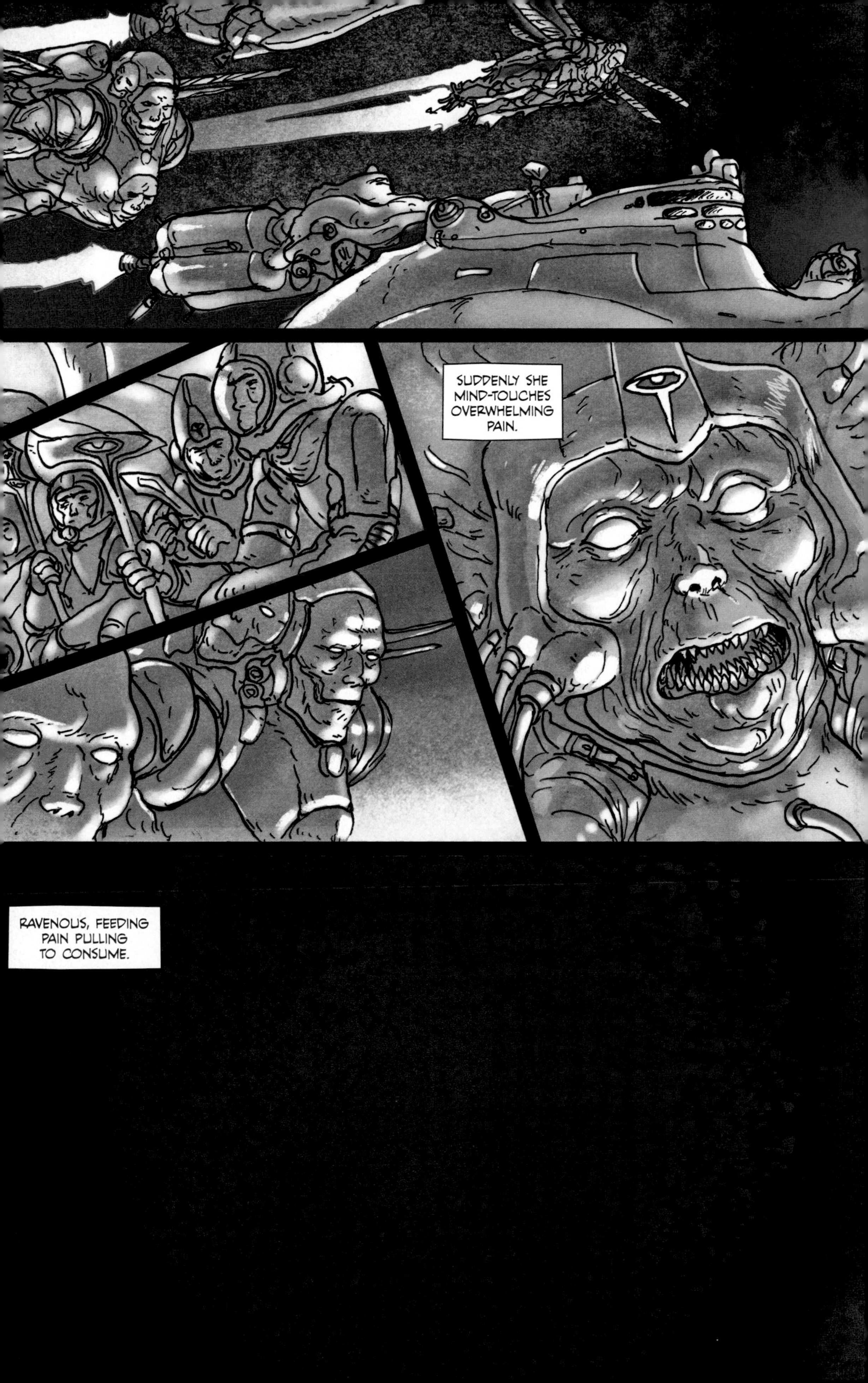
SUDDENLY SHE MIND-TOUCHES OVERWHELMING PAIN.
RAVENOUS, FEEDING PAIN PULLING TO CONSUME.

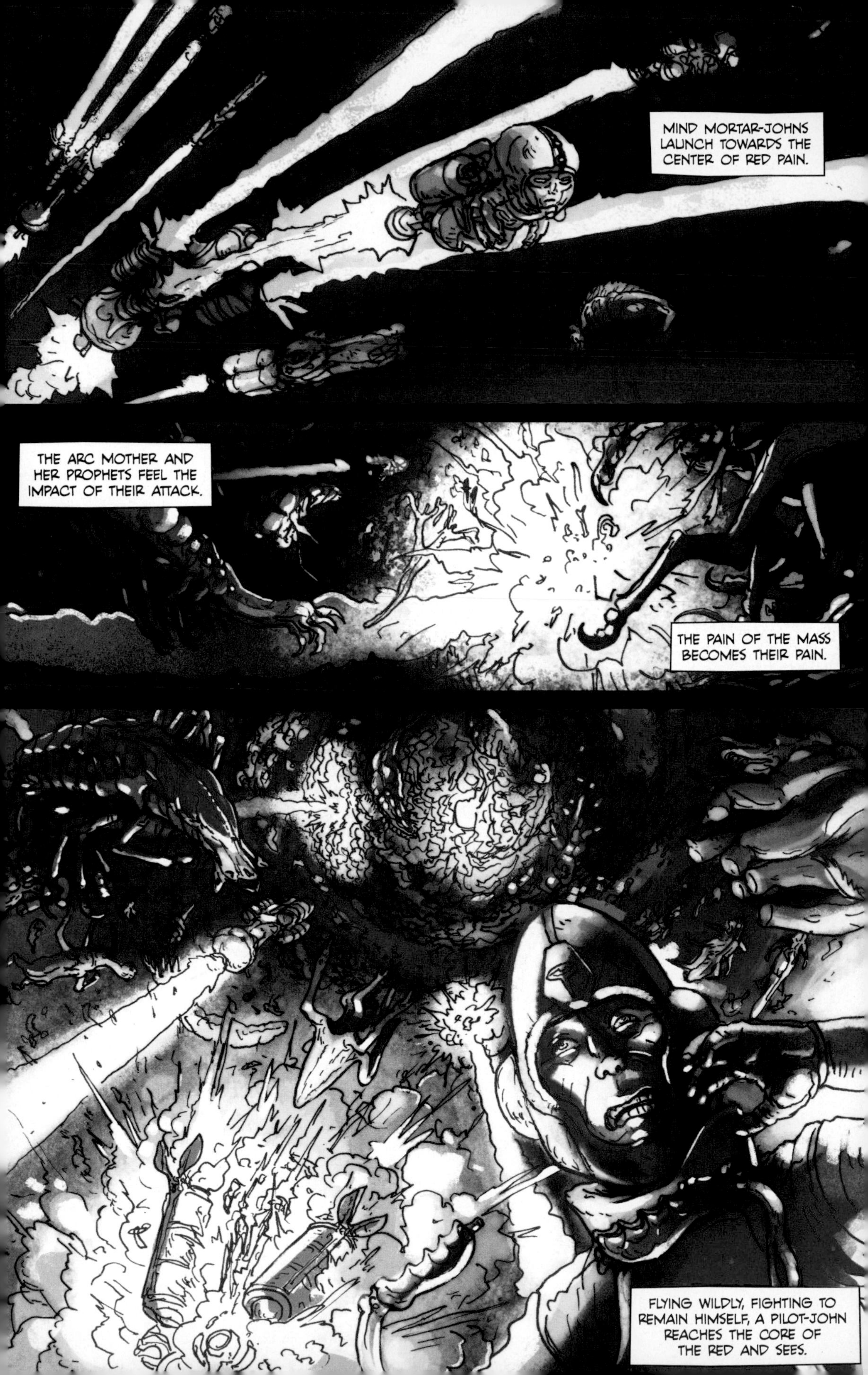
MIND MORTAR-JOHNS LAUNCH TOWARDS THE CENTER OF RED PAIN.
THE ARC MOTHER AND HER PROPHETS FEEL THE IMPACT OF THEIR ATTACK.
THE PAIN OF THE MASS BECOMES THEIR PAIN.
FLYING WILDLY, FIGHTING TO REMAIN HIMSELF, A PILOT-JOHN REACHES THE CORE OF THE RED AND SEES.

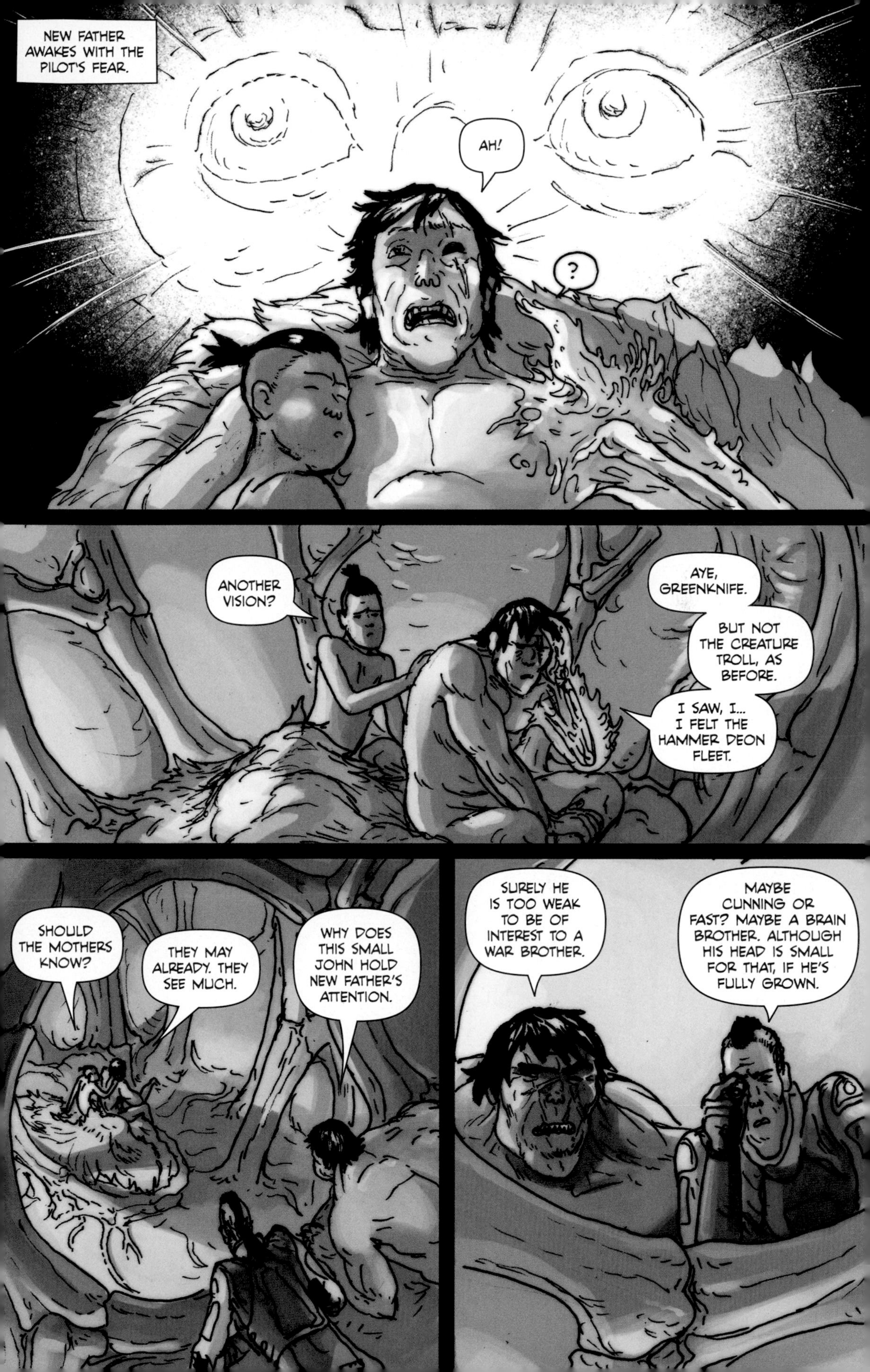
NEW FATHER AWAKES WITH THE PILOT'S FEAR.
AH!
?
ANOTHER VISION?
AYE, GREENKNIFE.
BUT NOT THE CREATURE TROLL, AS BEFORE.
I SAW, I... I FELT THE HAMMER DEON FLEET.
SHOULD THE MOTHERS KNOW?
THEY MAY ALREADY. THEY SEE MUCH.
WHY DOES THIS SMALL JOHN HOLD NEW FATHER'S ATTENTION.
SURELY HE IS TOO WEAK TO BE OF INTEREST TO A WAR BROTHER.
MAYBE CUNNING OR FAST? MAYBE A BRAIN BROTHER. ALTHOUGH HIS HEAD IS SMALL FOR THAT, IF HE'S FULLY GROWN.

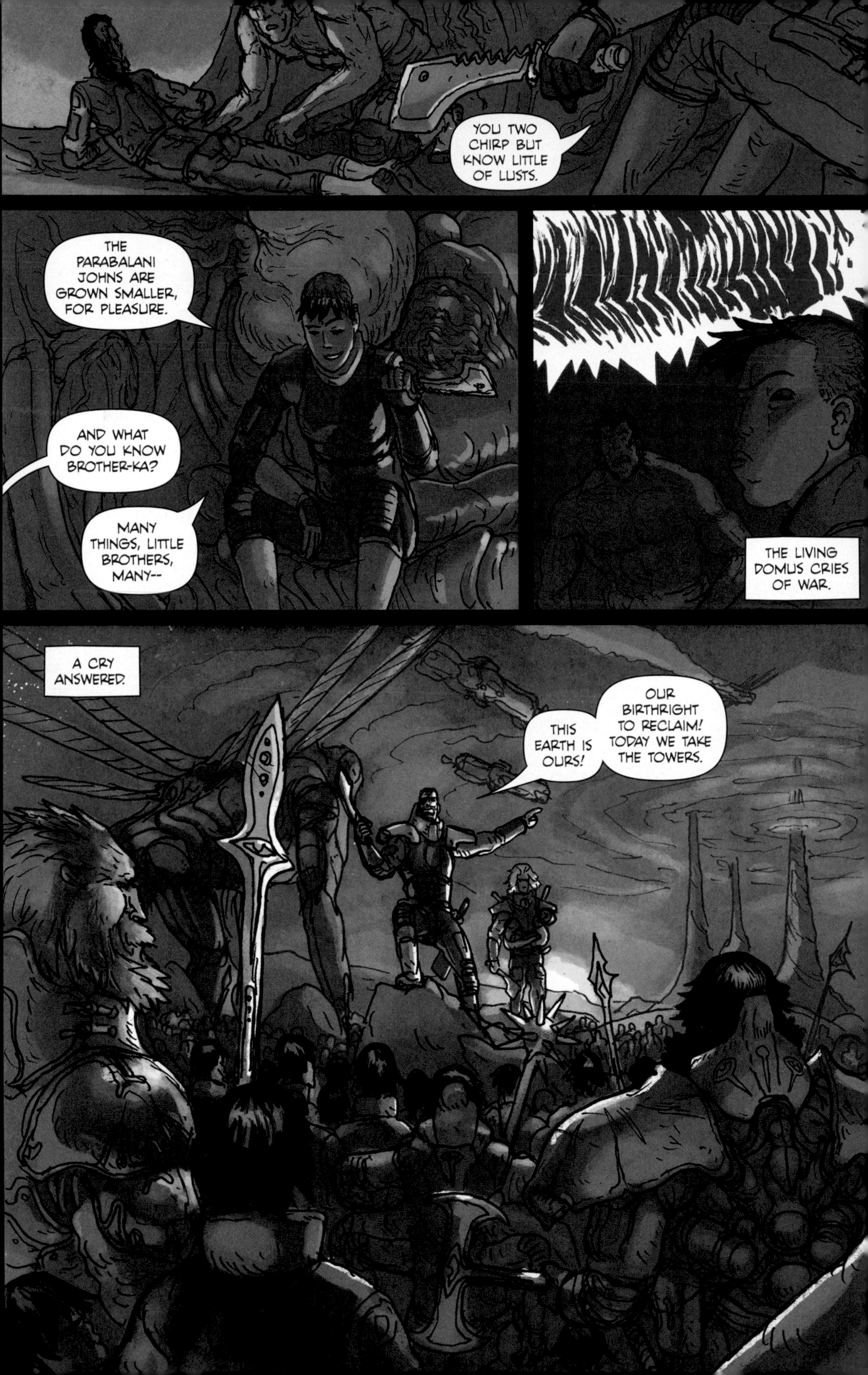
YOU TWO CHIRP BUT KNOW LITTLE OF LUSTS.
THE PARABALANI JOHNS ARE GROWN SMALLER, FOR PLEASURE.
AND WHAT DO YOU KNOW BROTHER-KA?
MANY THINGS, LITTLE BROTHERS, MANY--
THE LIVING DOMUS CRIES OF WAR.
A CRY ANSWERED.
THIS EARTH IS OURS!
OUR BIRTHRIGHT TO RECLAIM! TODAY WE TAKE THE TOWERS.

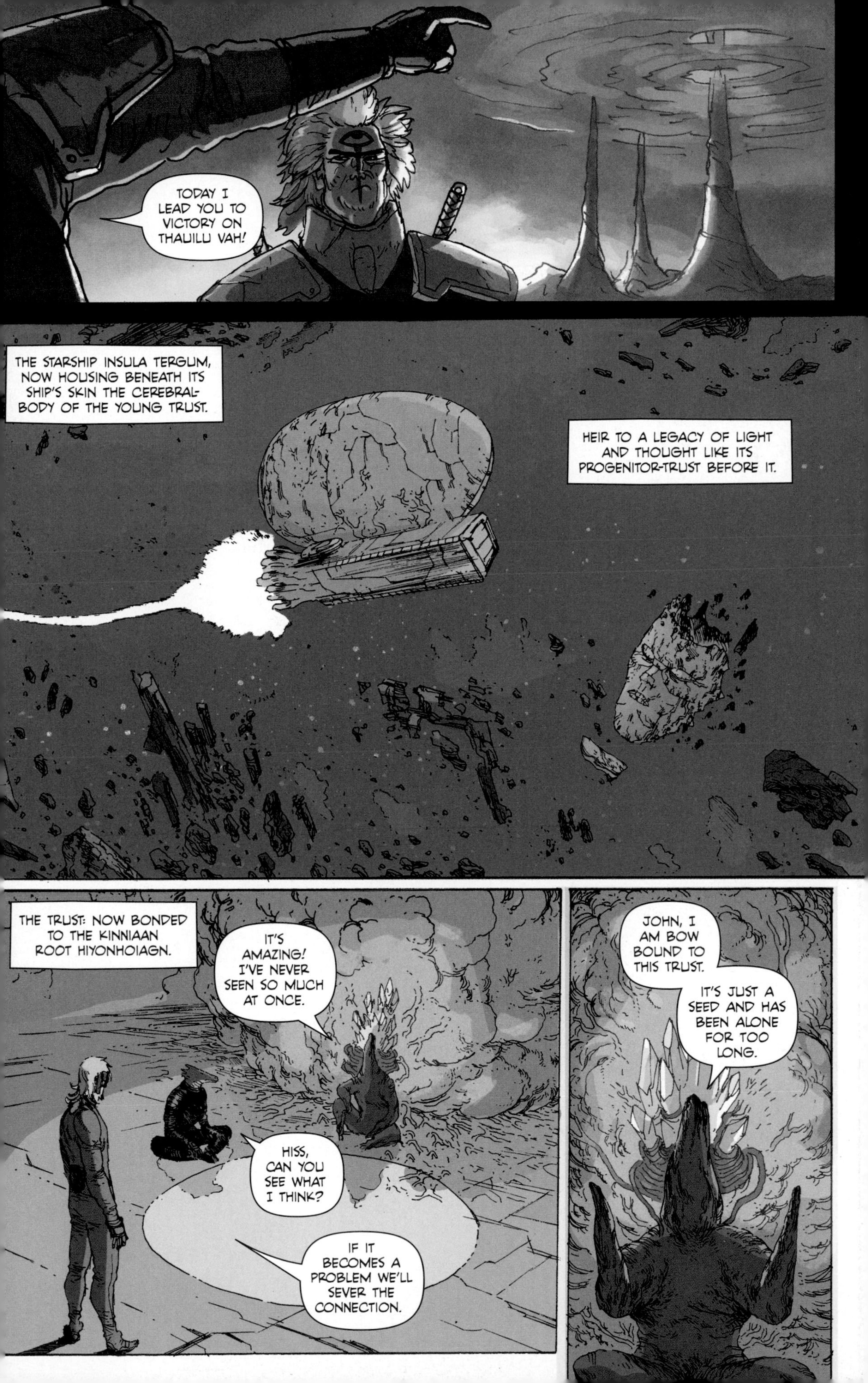
TODAY I LEAD YOU TO VICTORY ON THAUILU VAH!
THE STARSHIP INSULA TERGUM, NOW HOUSING BENEATH ITS SHIP'S SKIN THE CEREBRAL-BODY OF THE YOUNG TRUST.
HEIR TO A LEGACY OF LIGHT AND THOUGHT LIKE ITS PROGENITOR-TRUST BEFORE IT.
THE TRUST: NOW BONDED TO THE KINNIAAN ROOT HIYONHOIAGN.
IT'S AMAZING! I'VE NEVER SEEN SO MUCH AT ONCE.
HISS, CAN YOU SEE WHAT I THINK?
IF IT BECOMES A PROBLEM WE'LL SEVER THE CONNECTION.
JOHN, I AM BOW BOUND TO THIS TRUST.
IT'S JUST A SEED AND HAS BEEN ALONE FOR TOO LONG.

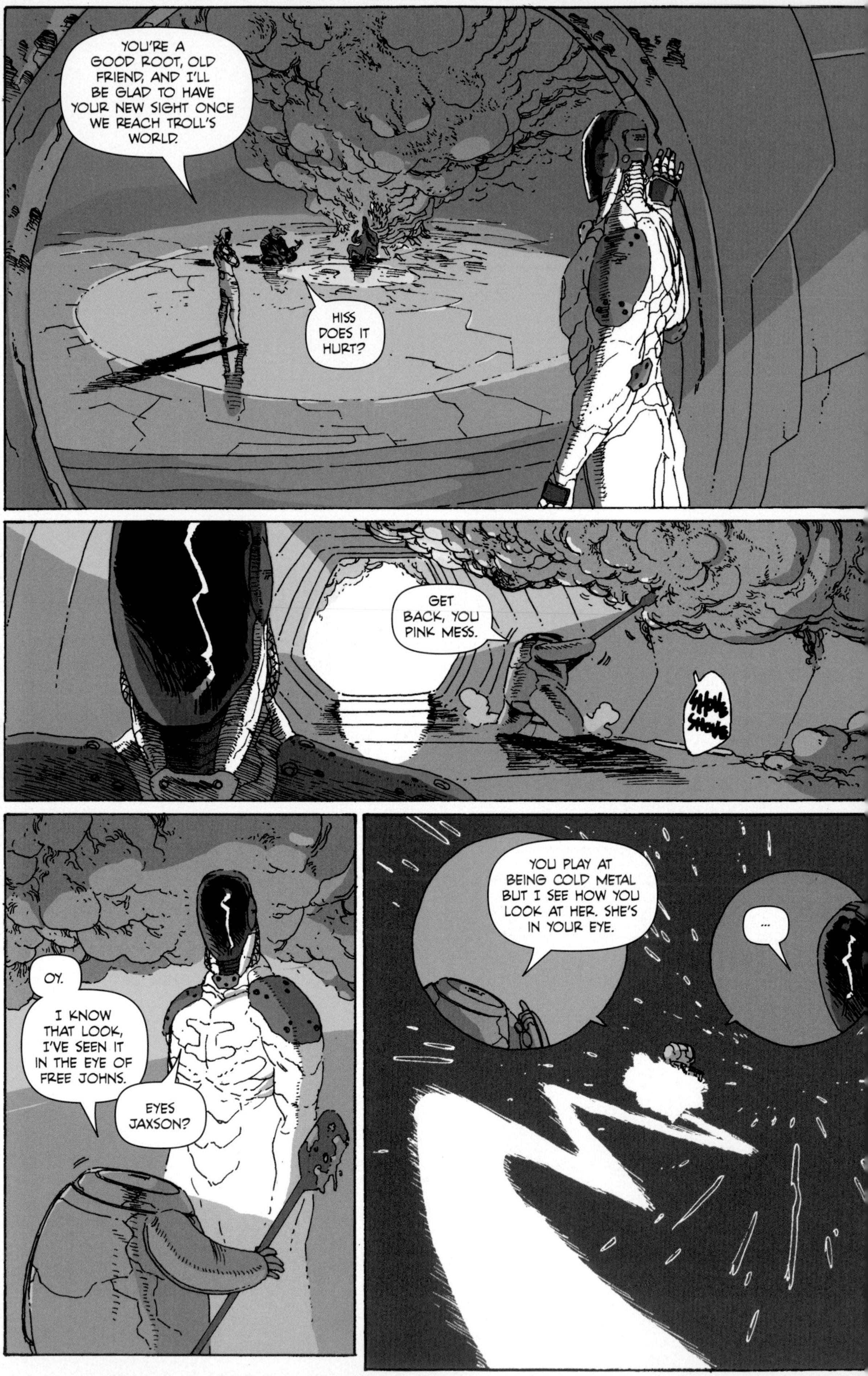
YOU'RE A GOOD ROOT, OLD FRIEND, AND I'LL BE GLAD TO HAVE YOUR NEW SIGHT ONCE WE REACH TROLL'S WORLD.
HISS DOES IT HURT?
GET BACK, YOU PINK MESS.
OY.
I KNOW THAT LOOK, I'VE SEEN IT IN THE EYE OF FREE JOHNS.
EYES JAXSON?
YOU PLAY AT BEING COLD METAL BUT I SEE HOW YOU LOOK AT HER. SHE'S IN YOUR EYE.
...

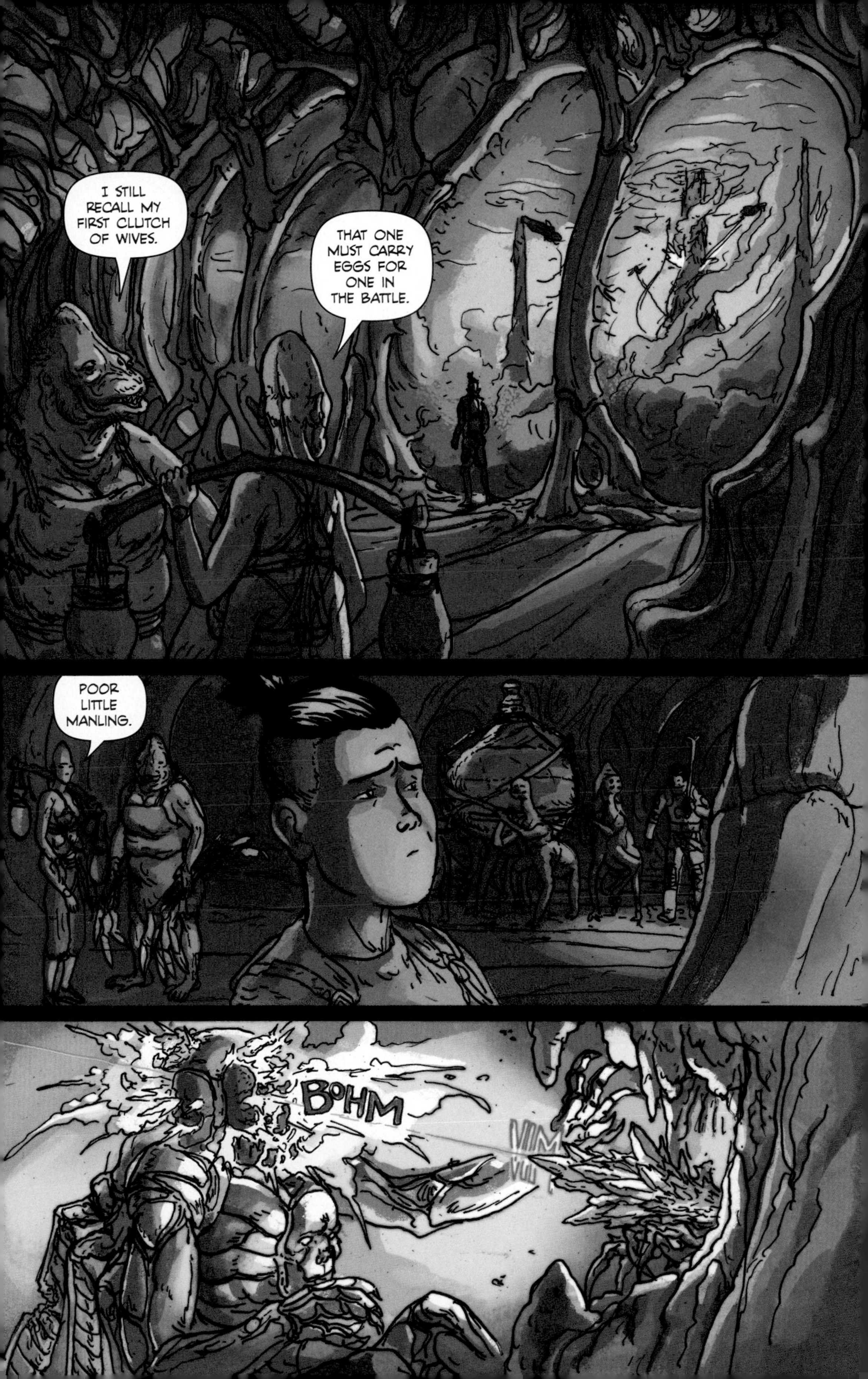
I STILL RECALL MY FIRST CLUTCH OF WIVES.
THAT ONE MUST CARRY EGGS FOR ONE IN THE BATTLE.
POOR LITTLE MANLING.
BoHM

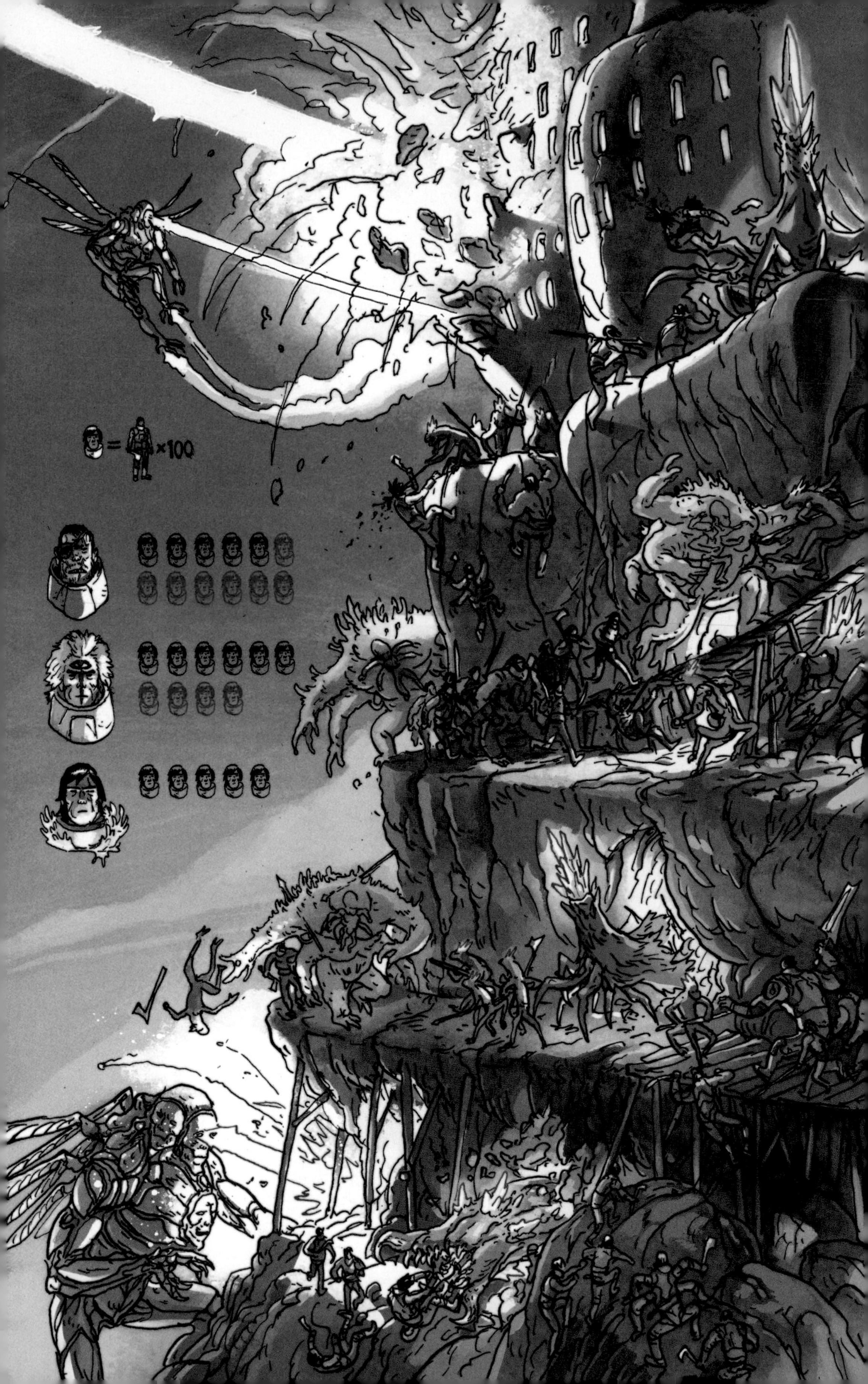

= ×100

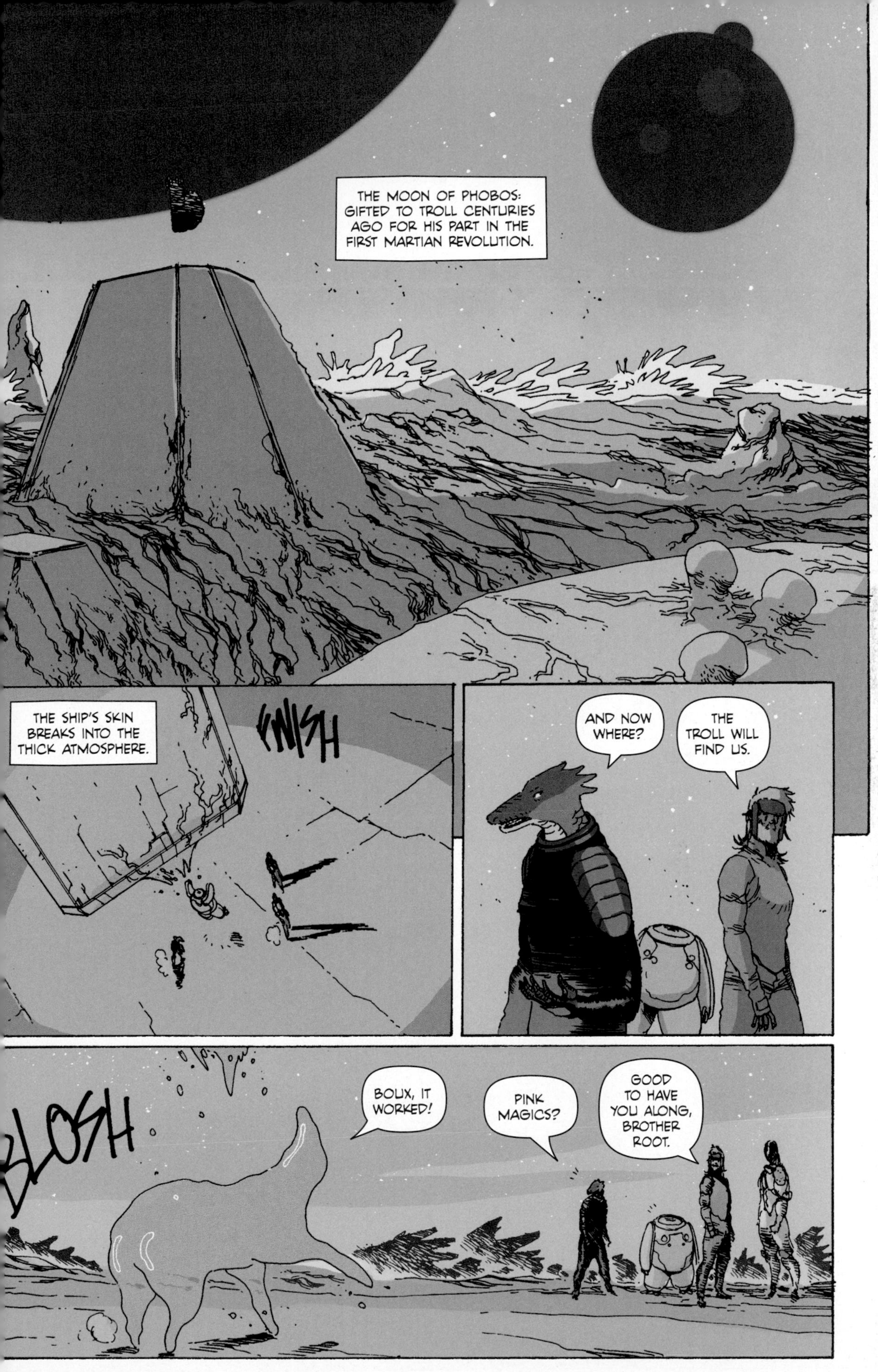
THE MOON OF PHOBOS: GIFTED TO TROLL CENTURIES AGO FOR HIS PART IN THE FIRST MARTIAN REVOLUTION.
THE SHIP'S SKIN BREAKS INTO THE THICK ATMOSPHERE.
FNISH
AND NOW WHERE?
THE TROLL WILL FIND US.
BLOSH
BOUX, IT WORKED!
PINK MAGICS?
GOOD TO HAVE YOU ALONG, BROTHER ROOT.

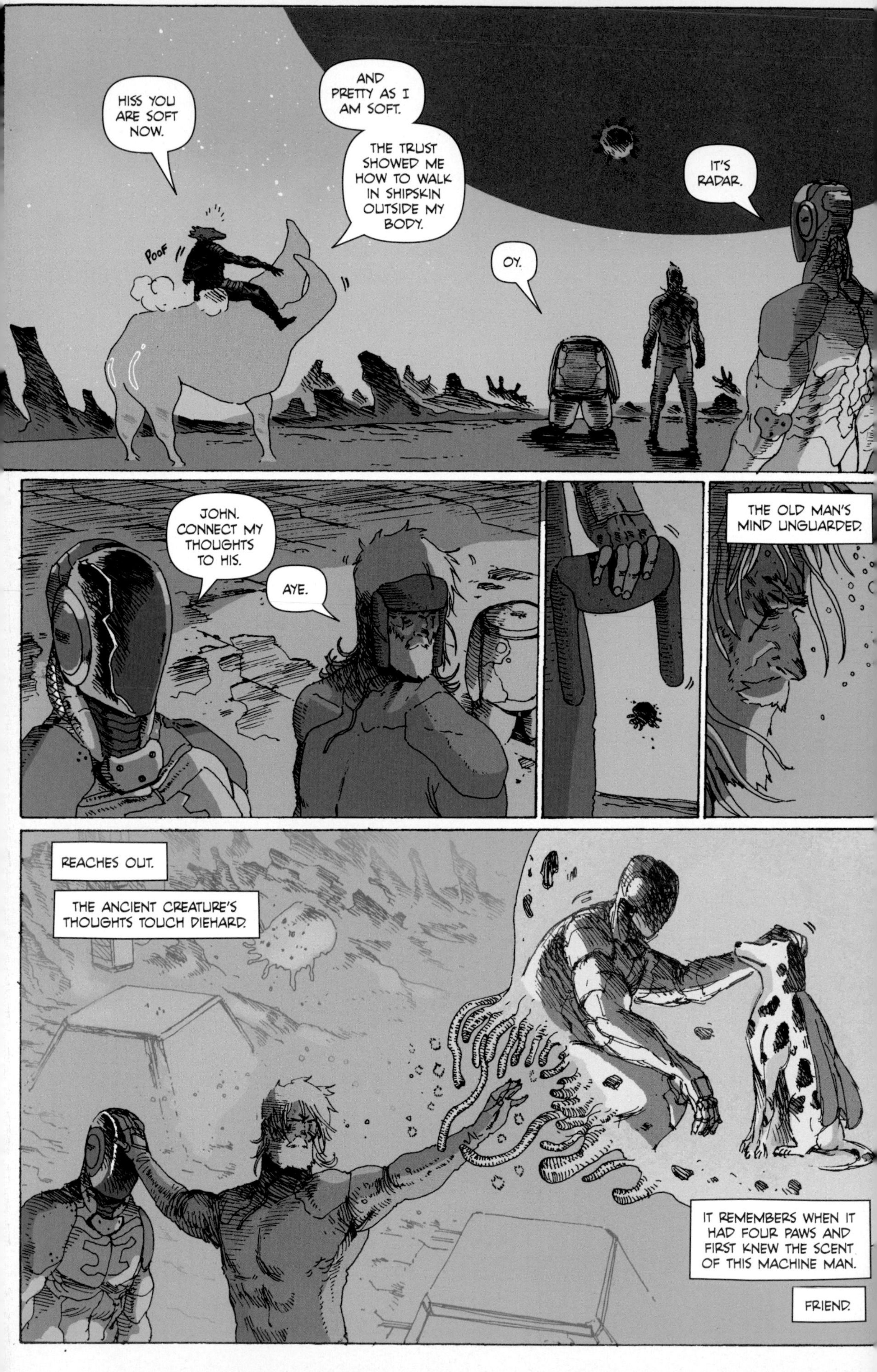
HISS YOU ARE SOFT NOW.
POOF
AND PRETTY AS I AM SOFT.
THE TRUST SHOWED ME HOW TO WALK IN SHIPSKIN OUTSIDE MY BODY.
OY.
IT'S RADAR.
JOHN. CONNECT MY THOUGHTS TO HIS.
AYE.
THE OLD MAN'S MIND UNGUARDED.
REACHES OUT.
THE ANCIENT CREATURE'S THOUGHTS TOUCH DIEHARD.
IT REMEMBERS WHEN IT HAD FOUR PAWS AND FIRST KNEW THE SCENT OF THIS MACHINE MAN.
FRIEND.

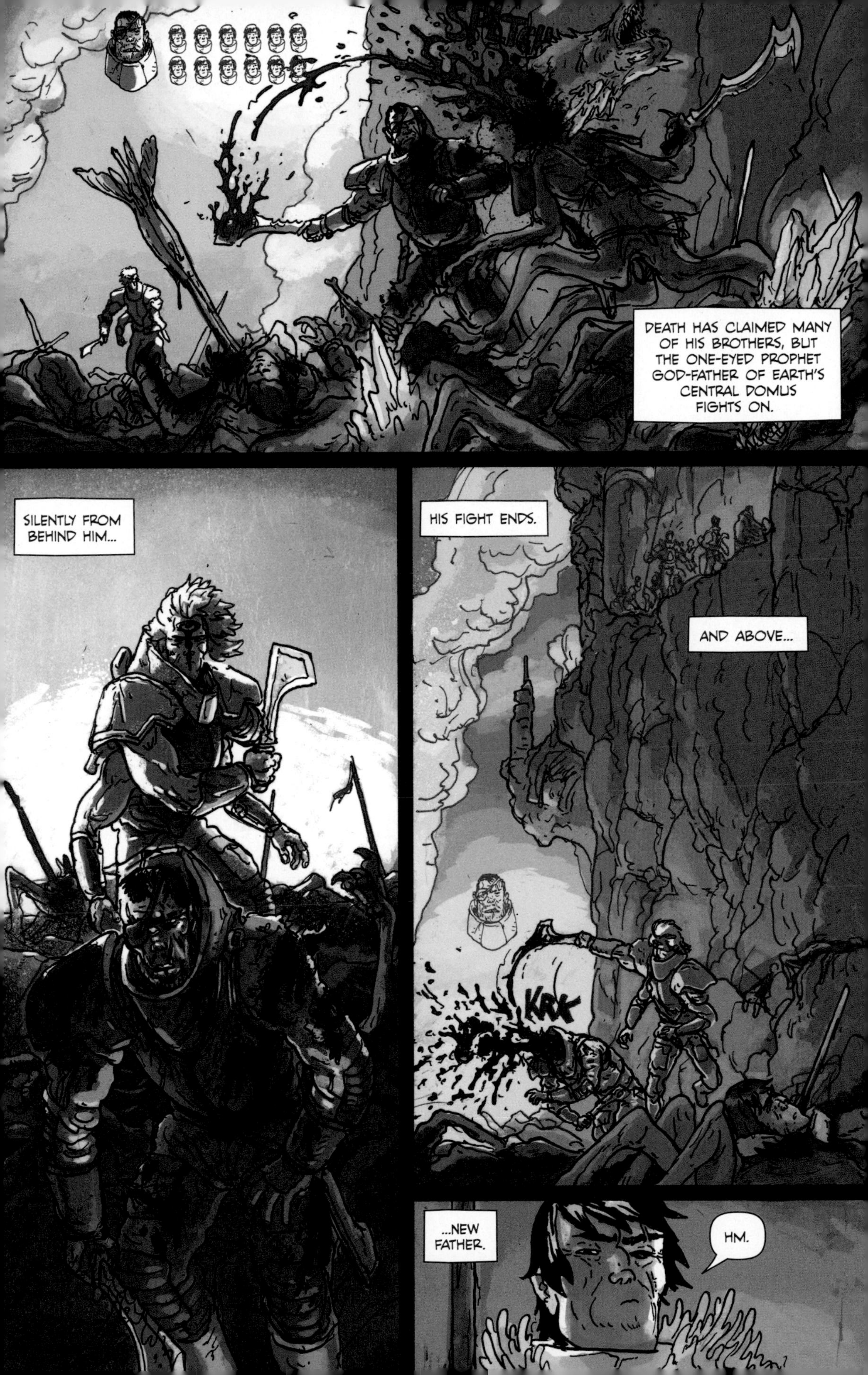
SPLTCH
DEATH HAS CLAIMED MANY OF HIS BROTHERS, BUT THE ONE-EYED PROPHET GOD-FATHER OF EARTH'S CENTRAL DOMUS FIGHTS ON.
SILENTLY FROM BEHIND HIM...
HIS FIGHT ENDS.
AND ABOVE...
KRK
...NEW FATHER.
HM.

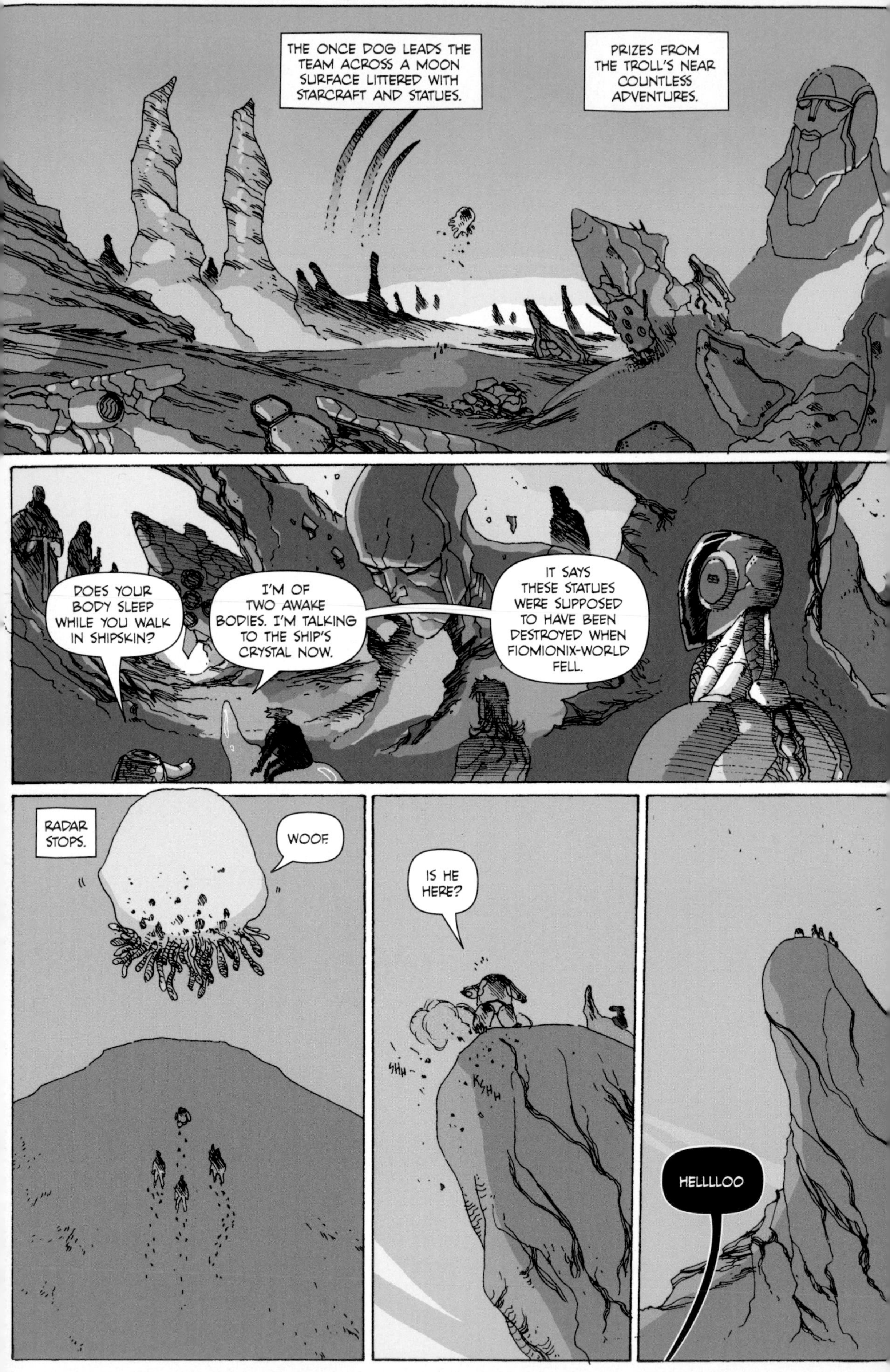
THE ONCE DOG LEADS THE TEAM ACROSS A MOON SURFACE LITTERED WITH STARCRAFT AND STATUES.
PRIZES FROM THE TROLL'S NEAR COUNTLESS ADVENTURES.
DOES YOUR BODY SLEEP WHILE YOU WALK IN SHIPSKIN?
I'M OF TWO AWAKE BODIES. I'M TALKING TO THE SHIP'S CRYSTAL NOW.
IT SAYS THESE STATUES WERE SUPPOSED TO HAVE BEEN DESTROYED WHEN FIOMIONIX-WORLD FELL.
RADAR STOPS.
WOOF.
IS HE HERE?
SHH
KSHH
HELLLLOO

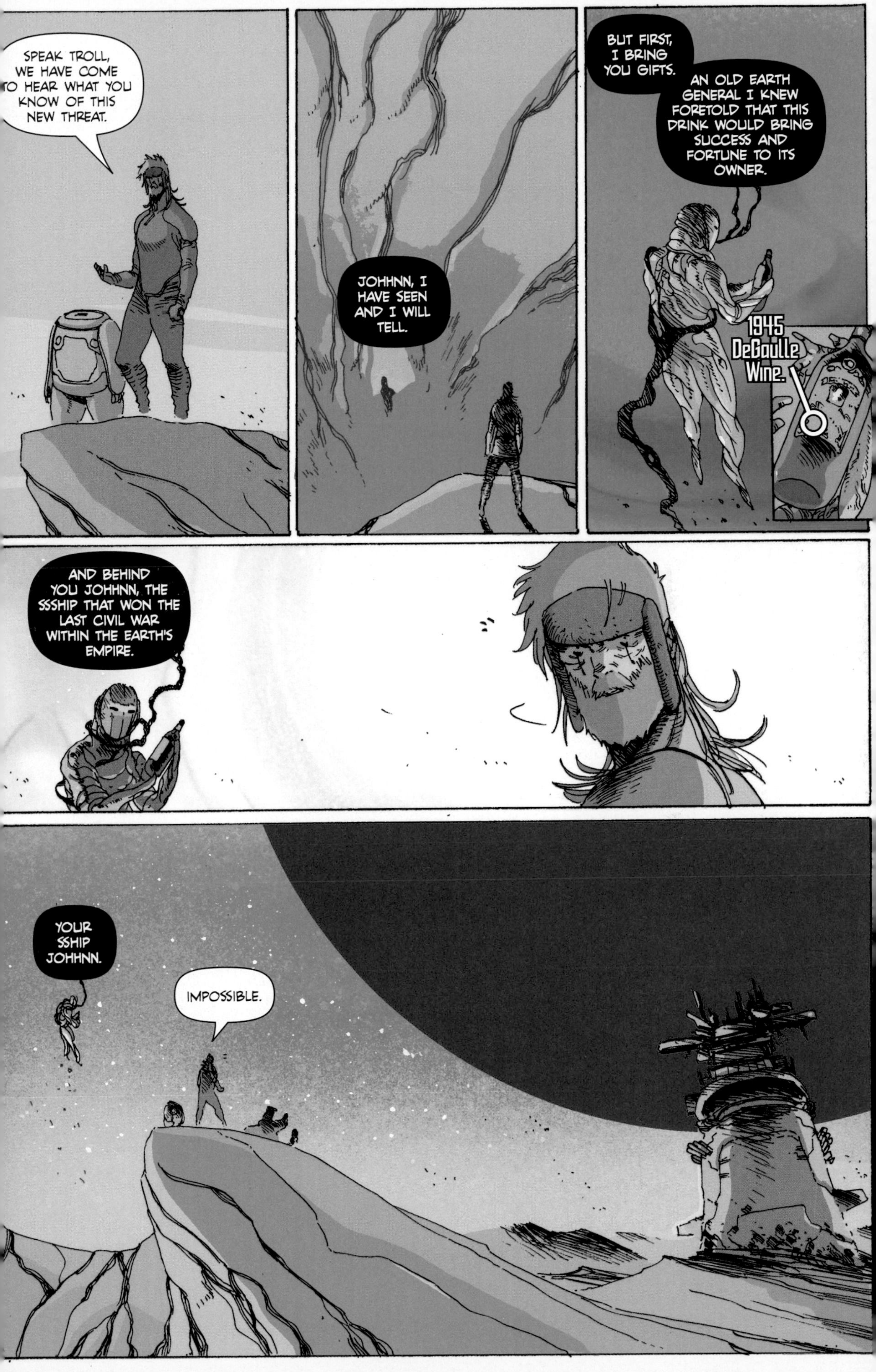
SPEAK TROLL, WE HAVE COME TO HEAR WHAT YOU KNOW OF THIS NEW THREAT.
JOHHNN, I HAVE SEEN AND I WILL TELL.
BUT FIRST, I BRING YOU GIFTS.
AN OLD EARTH GENERAL I KNEW FORETOLD THAT THIS DRINK WOULD BRING SUCCESS AND FORTUNE TO ITS OWNER.
1945 DeGaulle Wine.
AND BEHIND YOU JOHHNN, THE SSSHIP THAT WON THE LAST CIVIL WAR WITHIN THE EARTH'S EMPIRE.
YOUR SSHIP JOHHNN.
IMPOSSIBLE.

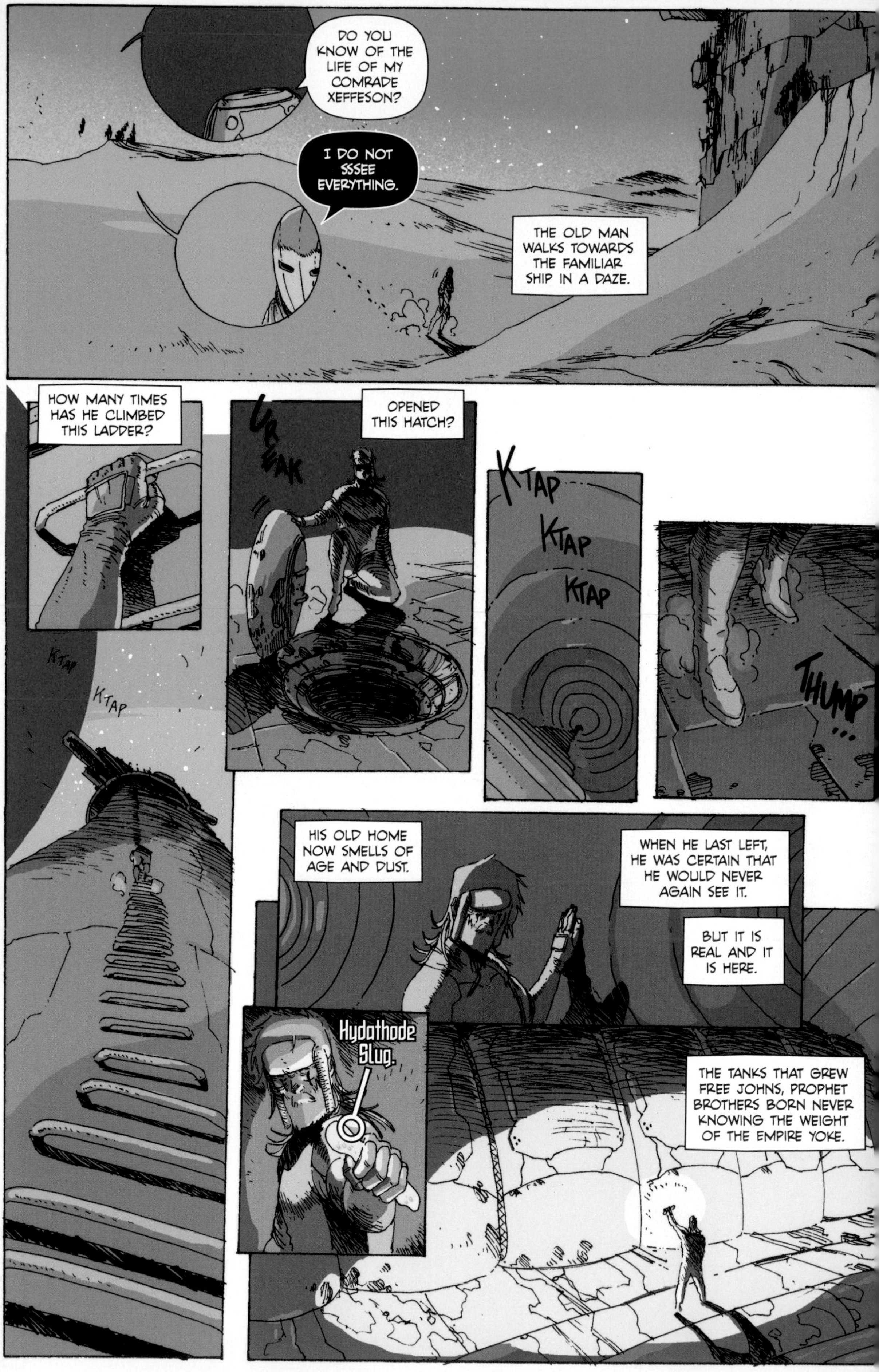
DO YOU KNOW OF THE LIFE OF MY COMRADE XEFFESON?
I DO NOT SSSEE EVERYTHING.
THE OLD MAN WALKS TOWARDS THE FAMILIAR SHIP IN A DAZE.
HOW MANY TIMES HAS HE CLIMBED THIS LADDER?
KTAP
KTAP
UREAK
OPENED THIS HATCH?
KTAP
KTAP
KTAP
THUMP...
HIS OLD HOME NOW SMELLS OF AGE AND DUST.
WHEN HE LAST LEFT, HE WAS CERTAIN THAT HE WOULD NEVER AGAIN SEE IT.
BUT IT IS REAL AND IT IS HERE.
Hydathode Slug.
THE TANKS THAT GREW FREE JOHNS, PROPHET BROTHERS BORN NEVER KNOWING THE WEIGHT OF THE EMPIRE YOKE.

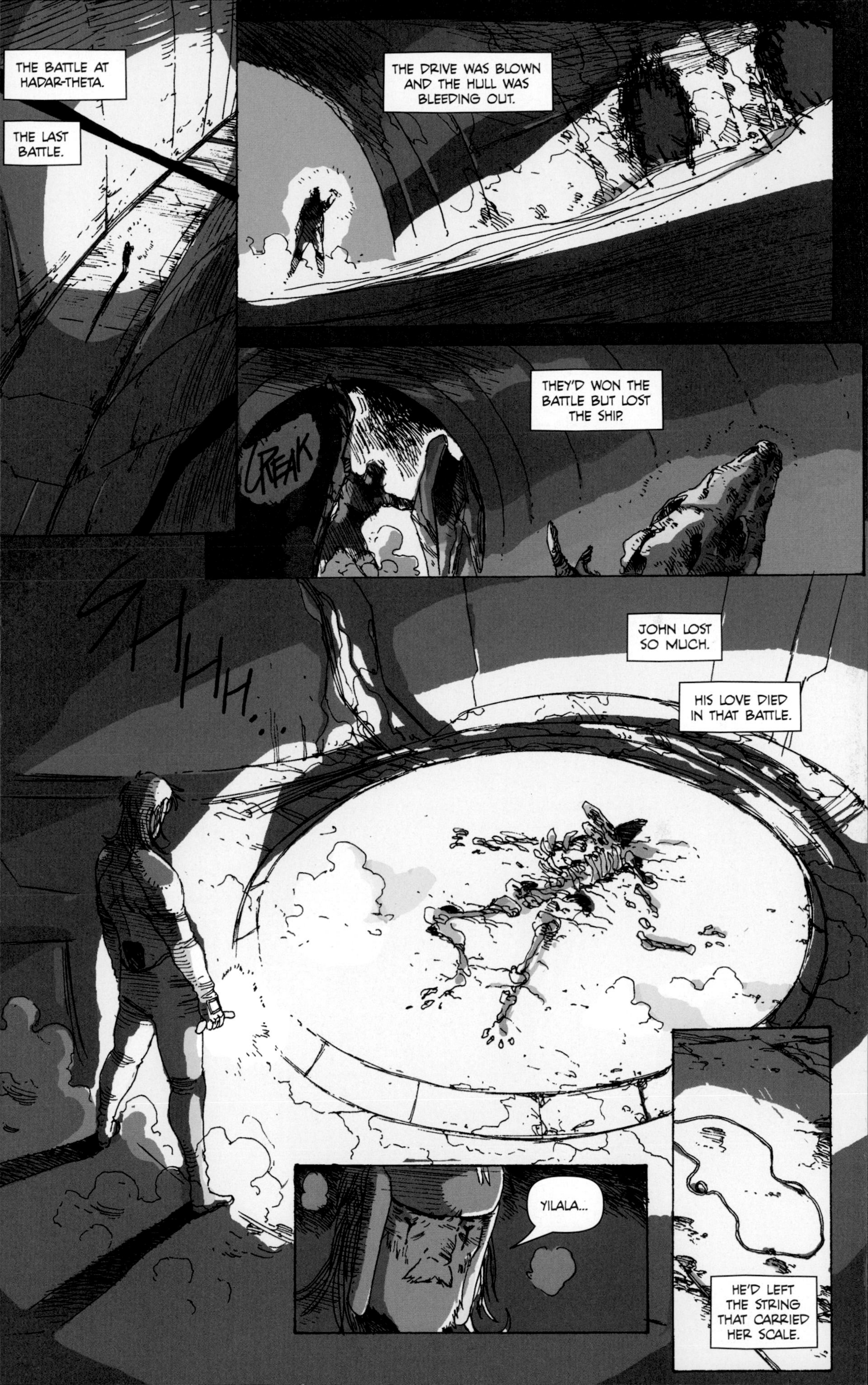
THE BATTLE AT HADAR-THETA.
THE LAST BATTLE.
THE DRIVE WAS BLOWN AND THE HULL WAS BLEEDING OUT.
CREAK
THEY'D WON THE BATTLE BUT LOST THE SHIP.
SHHH...
JOHN LOST SO MUCH.
HIS LOVE DIED IN THAT BATTLE.
YILALA...
HE'D LEFT THE STRING THAT CARRIED HER SCALE.

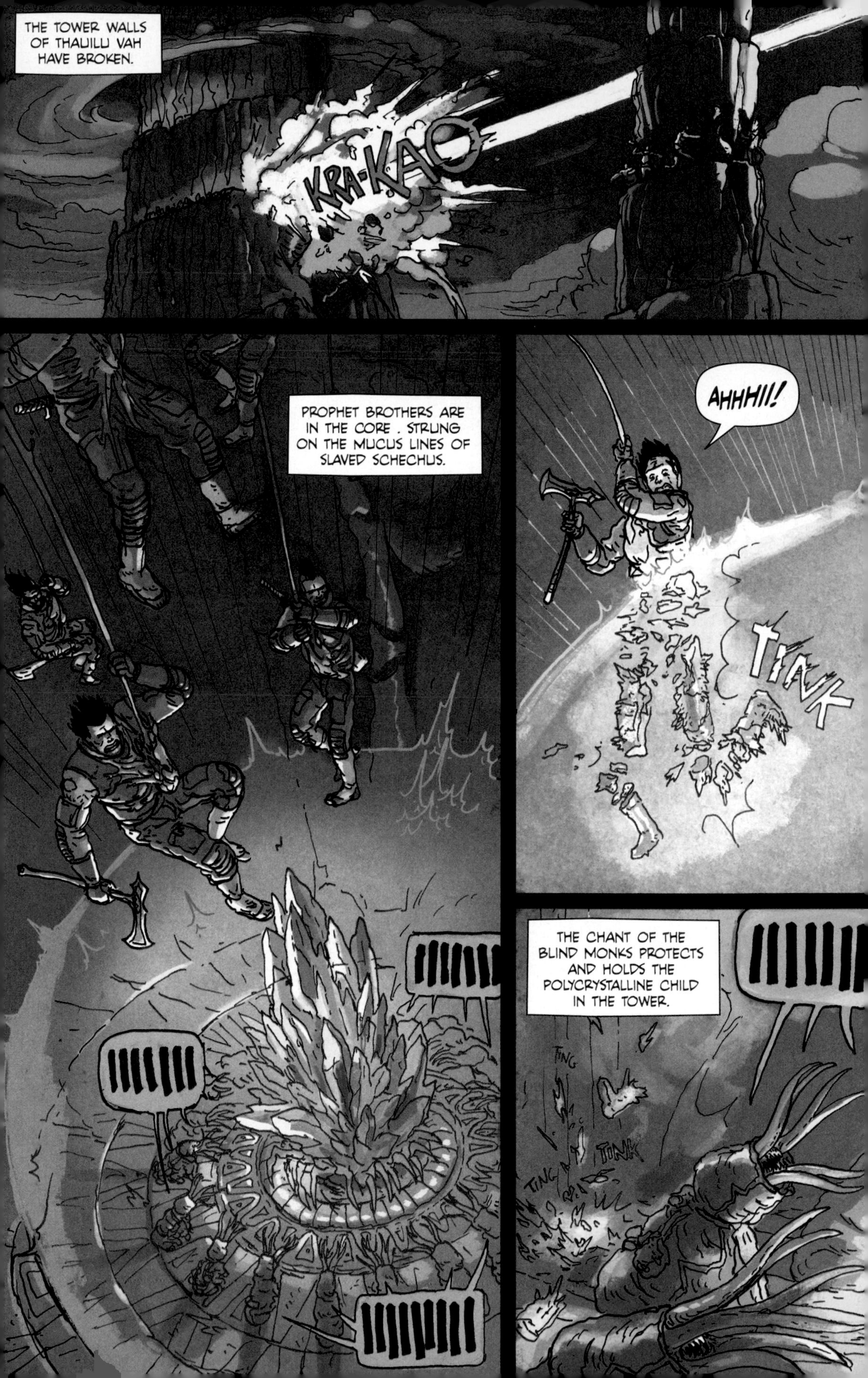
THE TOWER WALLS OF THAUILU VAH HAVE BROKEN.
KRA-KAO
PROPHET BROTHERS ARE IN THE CORE . STRUNG ON THE MUCUS LINES OF SLAVED SCHECHUS.
AHHHII!
TINK
THE CHANT OF THE BLIND MONKS PROTECTS AND HOLDS THE POLYCRYSTALLINE CHILD IN THE TOWER.
TING
TINK
TING

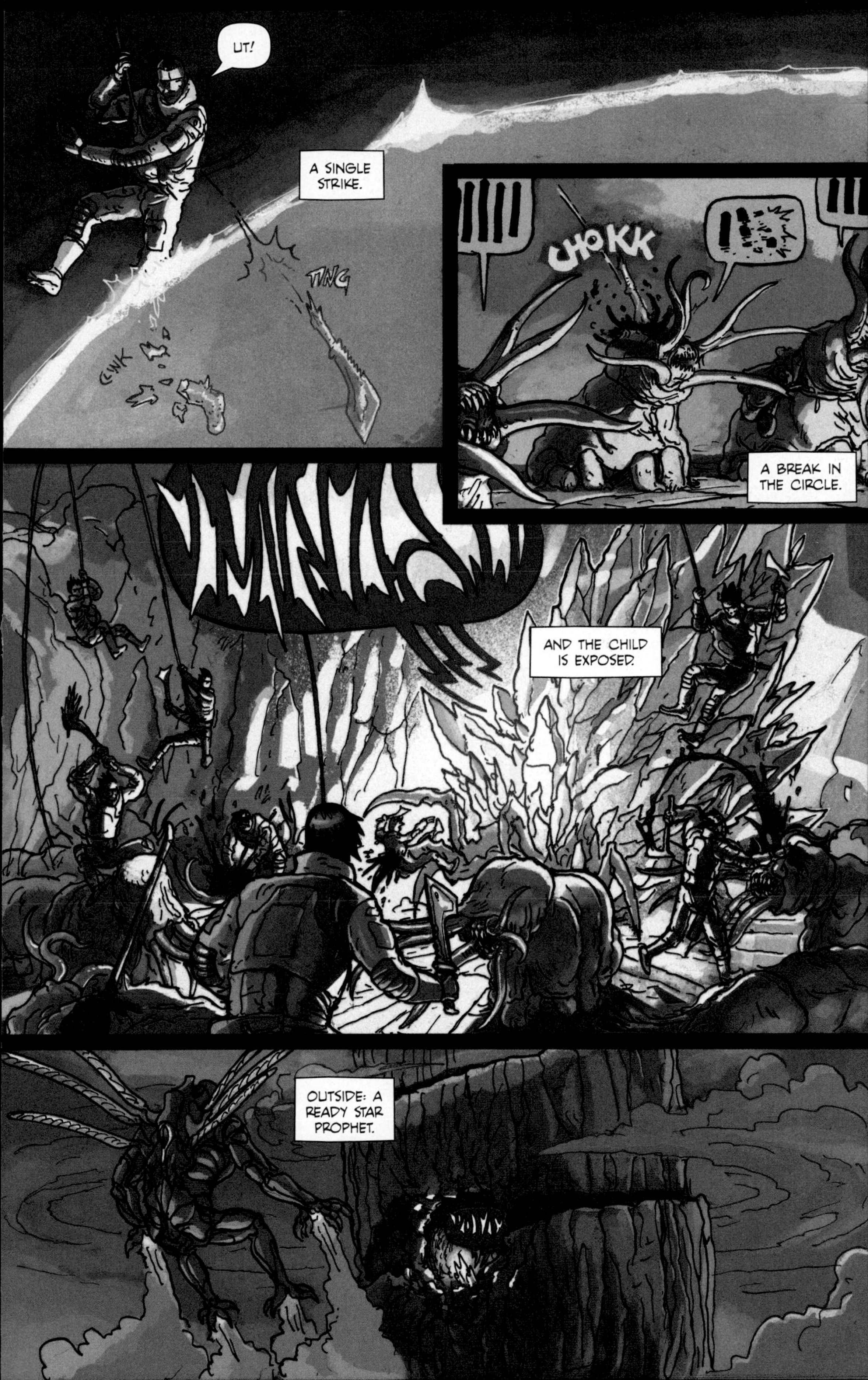

UT!
A SINGLE STRIKE.
TING
CLINK
CHOKK
A BREAK IN THE CIRCLE.
AND THE CHILD IS EXPOSED.
OUTSIDE: A READY STAR PROPHET.

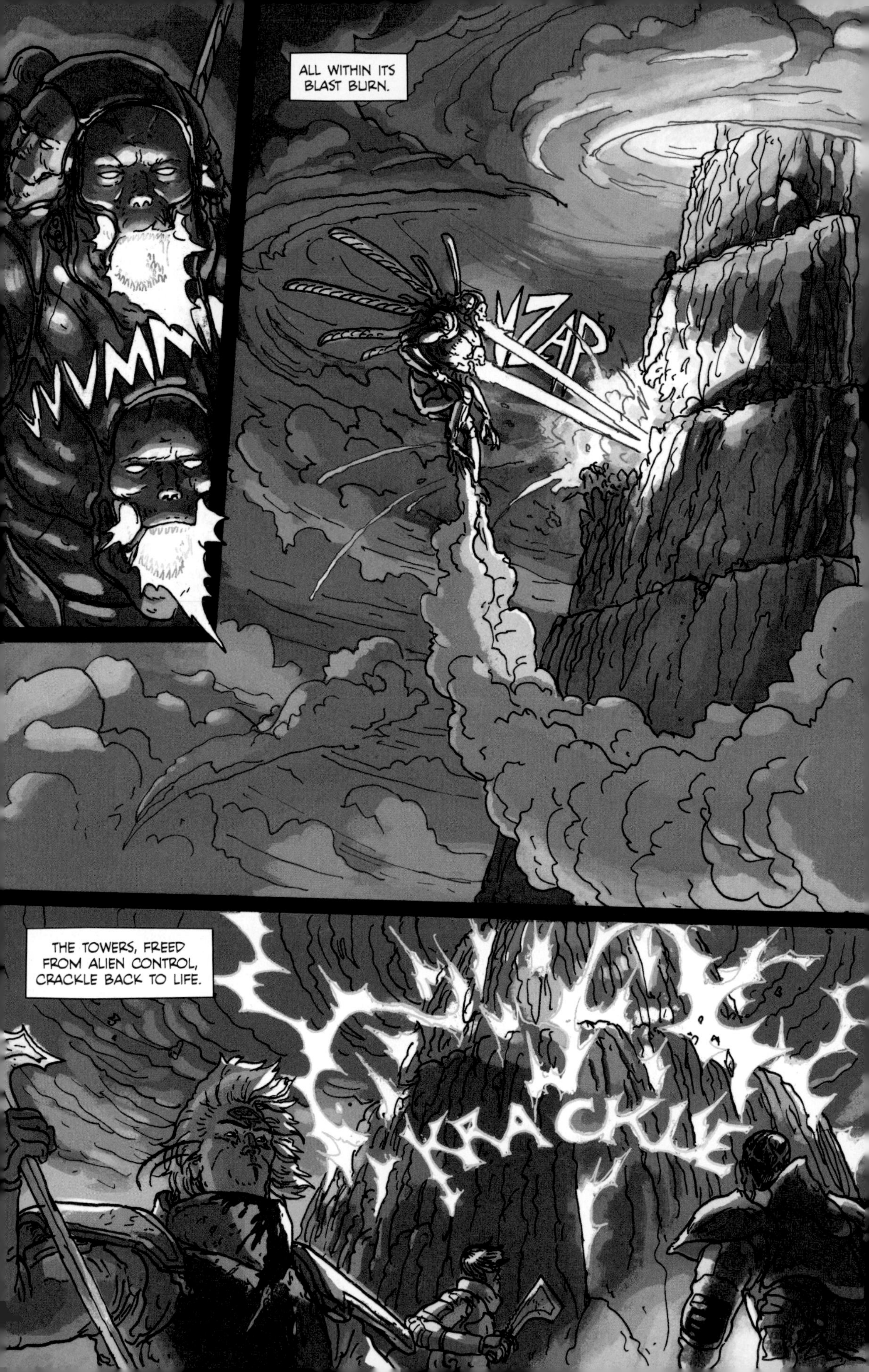
WVMM
ALL WITHIN ITS BLAST BURN.
VZAP
THE TOWERS, FREED FROM ALIEN CONTROL, CRACKLE BACK TO LIFE.
KRACKLE

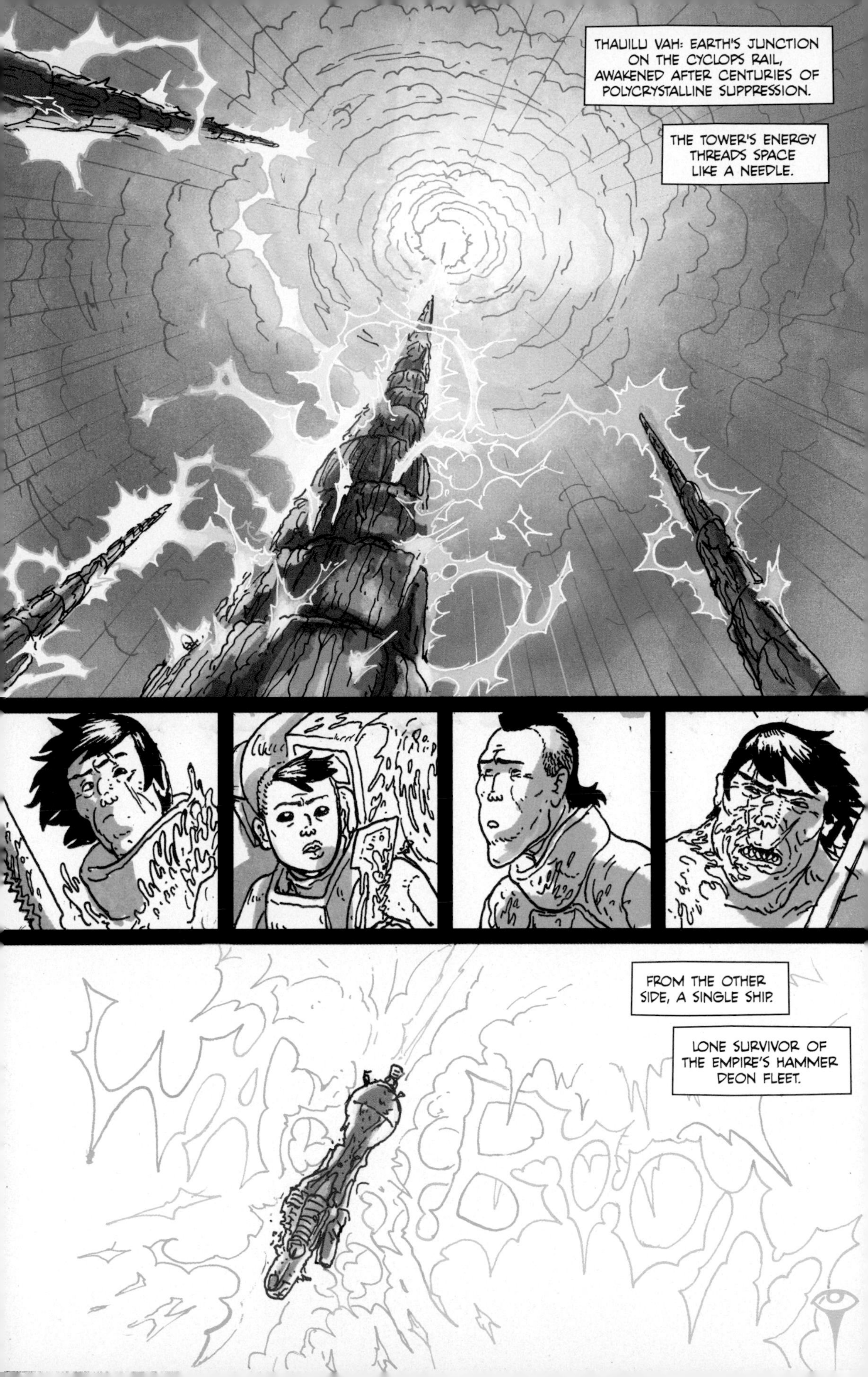
THAVILU VAH: EARTH'S JUNCTION ON THE CYCLOPS RAIL, AWAKENED AFTER CENTURIES OF POLYCRYSTALLINE SUPPRESSION.
THE TOWER'S ENERGY THREADS SPACE LIKE A NEEDLE.
FROM THE OTHER SIDE, A SINGLE SHIP.
LONE SURVIVOR OF THE EMPIRE'S HAMMER DEON FLEET.

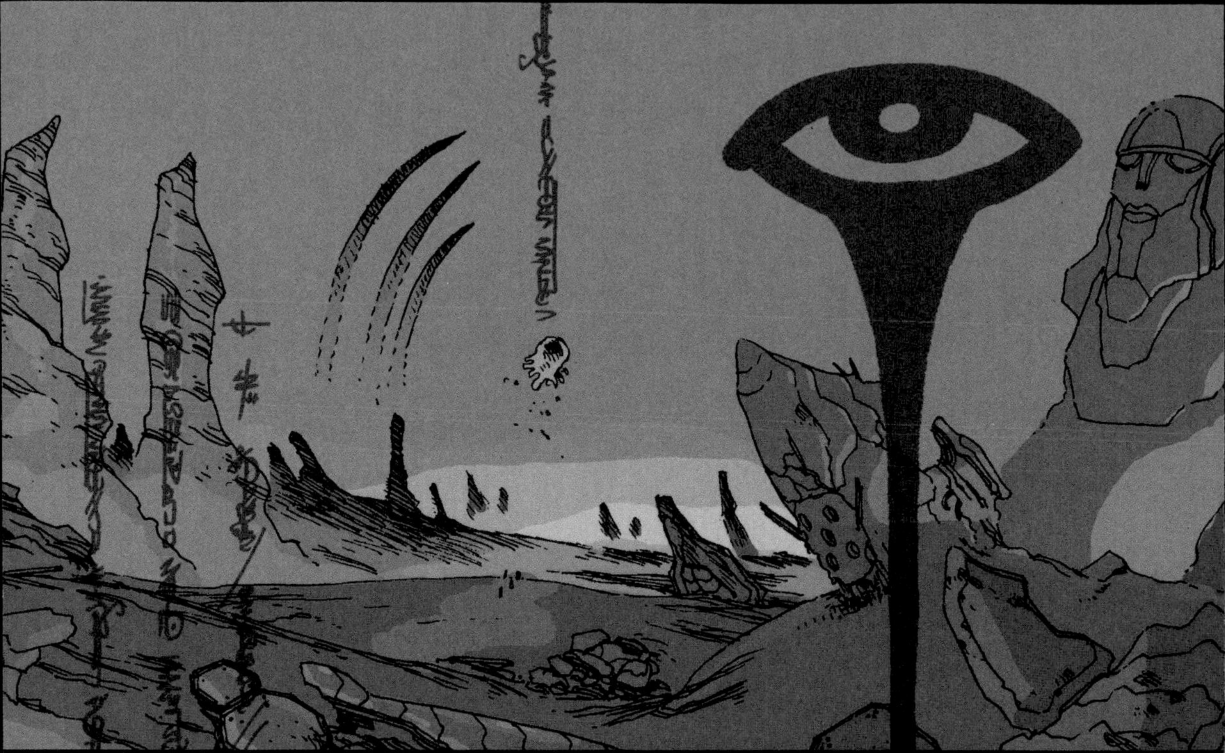

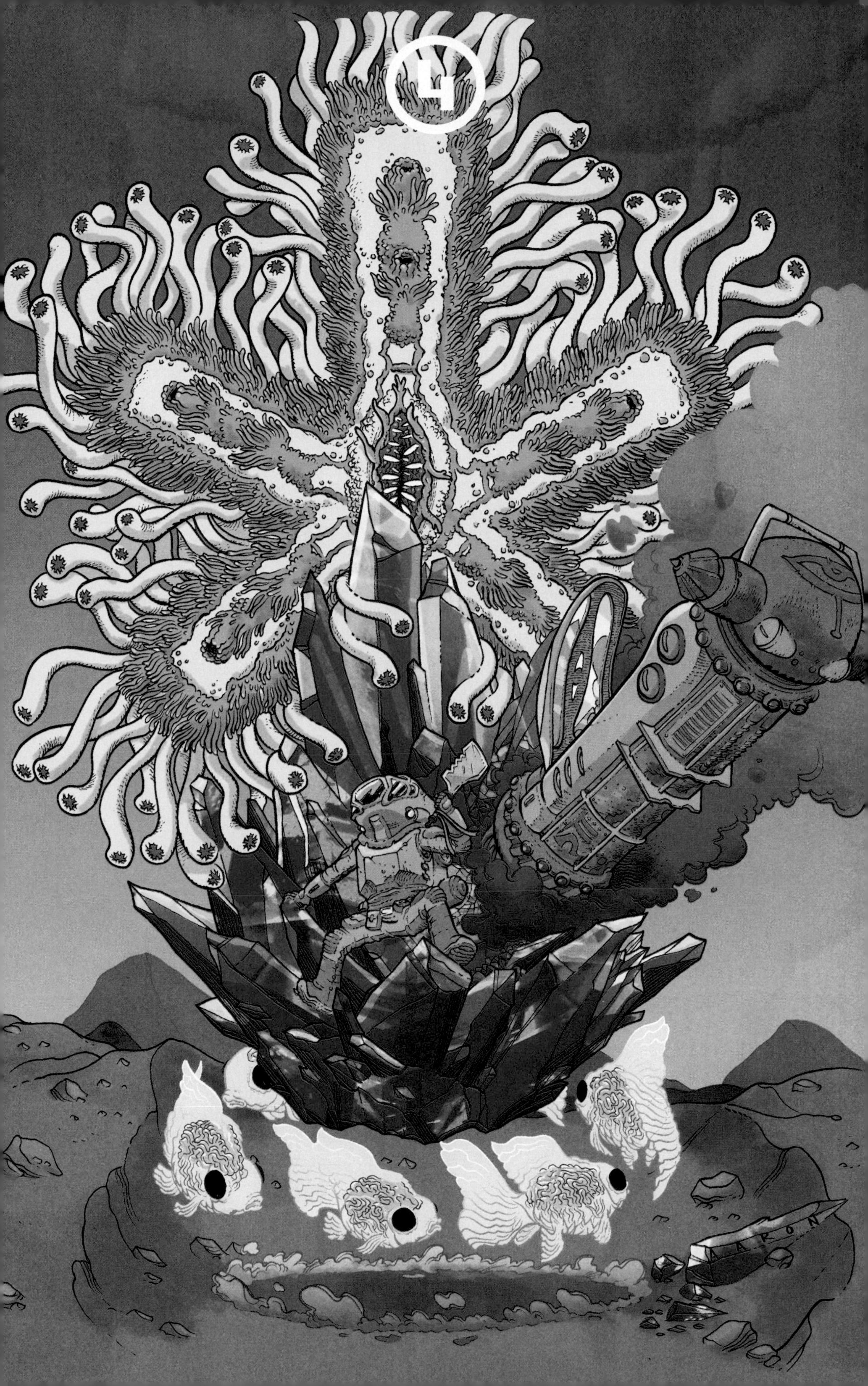
4
AARON

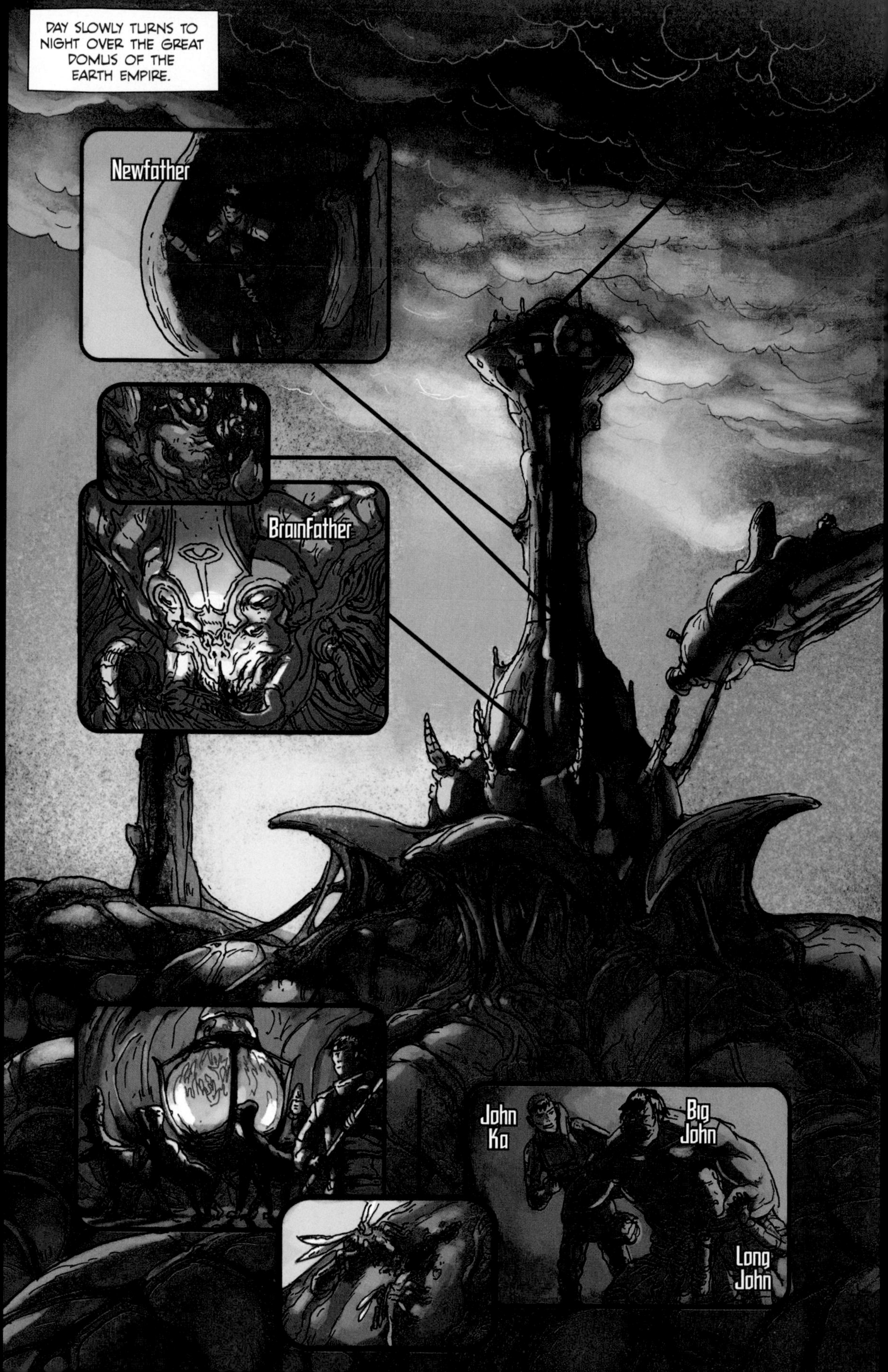
DAY SLOWLY TURNS TO NIGHT OVER THE GREAT DOMUS OF THE EARTH EMPIRE.
Newfather
BrainFather
John Ka
Big John
Long John

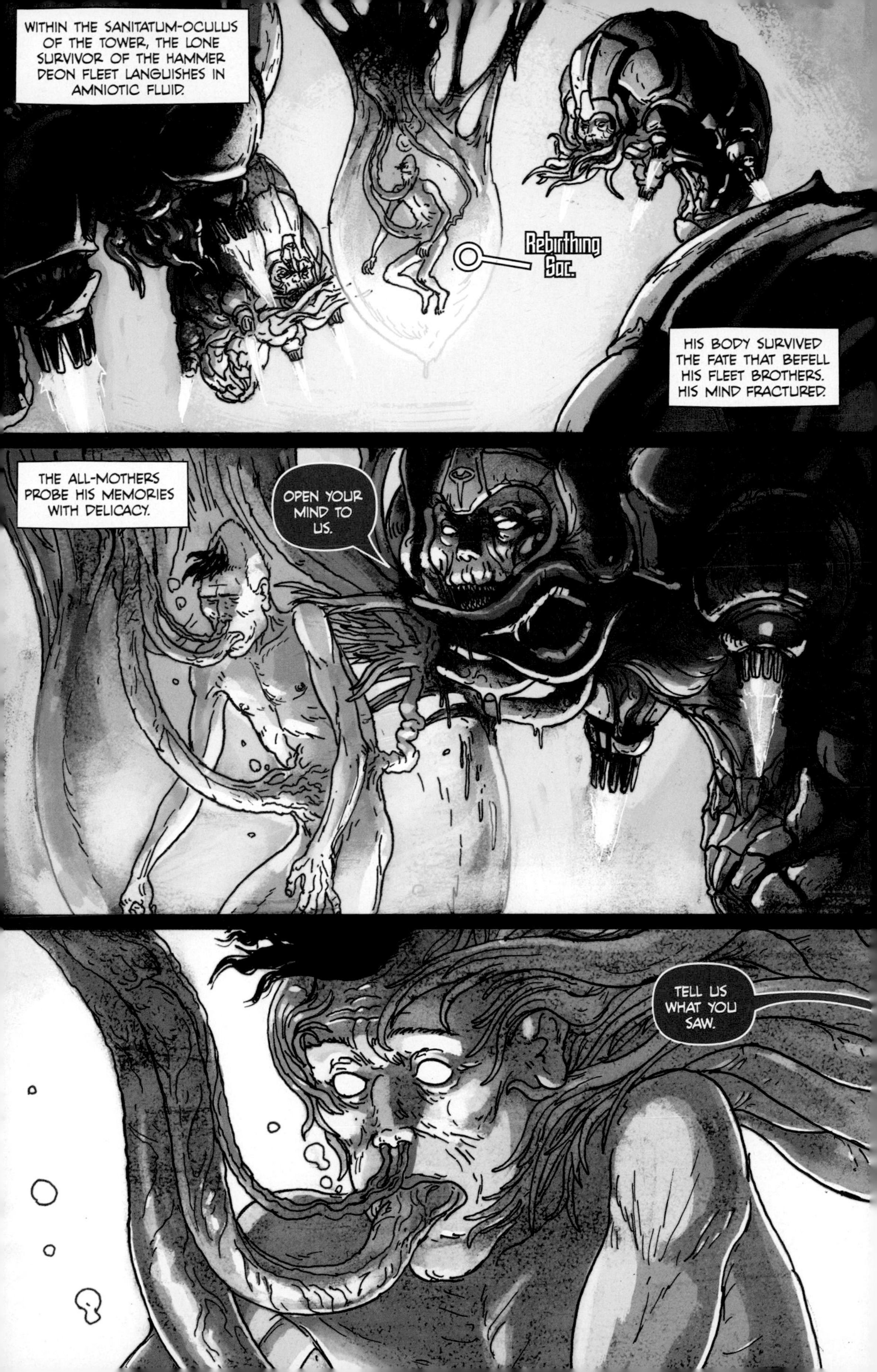
WITHIN THE SANITATUM-OCULUS OF THE TOWER, THE LONE SURVIVOR OF THE HAMMER DEON FLEET LANGUISHES IN AMNIOTIC FLUID.
Rebirthing Sac.
HIS BODY SURVIVED THE FATE THAT BEFELL HIS FLEET BROTHERS. HIS MIND FRACTURED.
THE ALL-MOTHERS PROBE HIS MEMORIES WITH DELICACY.
OPEN YOUR MIND TO US.
TELL US WHAT YOU SAW.

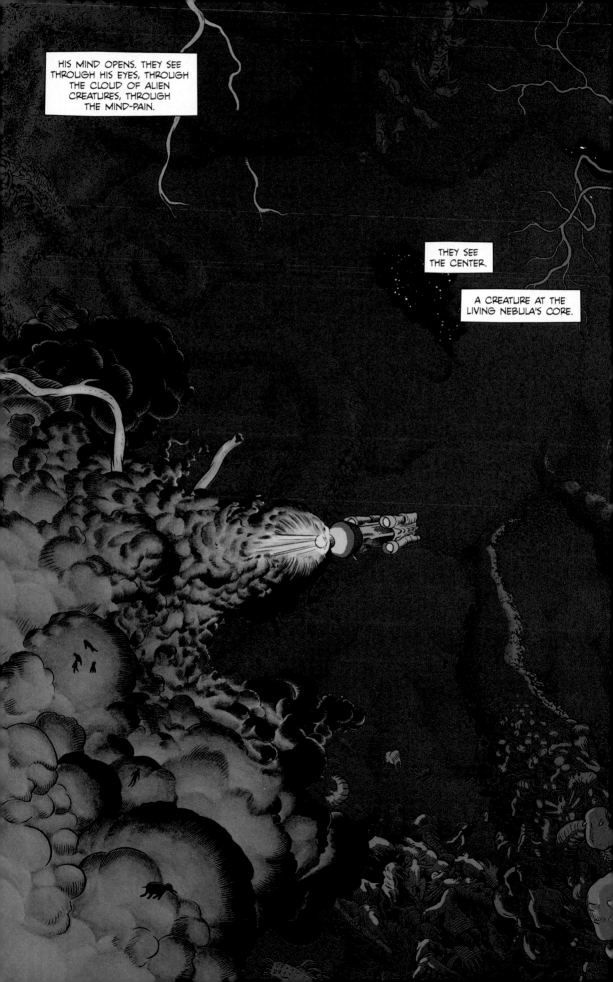

HIS MIND OPENS. THEY SEE THROUGH HIS EYES, THROUGH THE CLOUD OF ALIEN CREATURES, THROUGH THE MIND-PAIN.

THEY SEE THE CENTER.

A CREATURE AT THE LIVING NEBULA'S CORE.

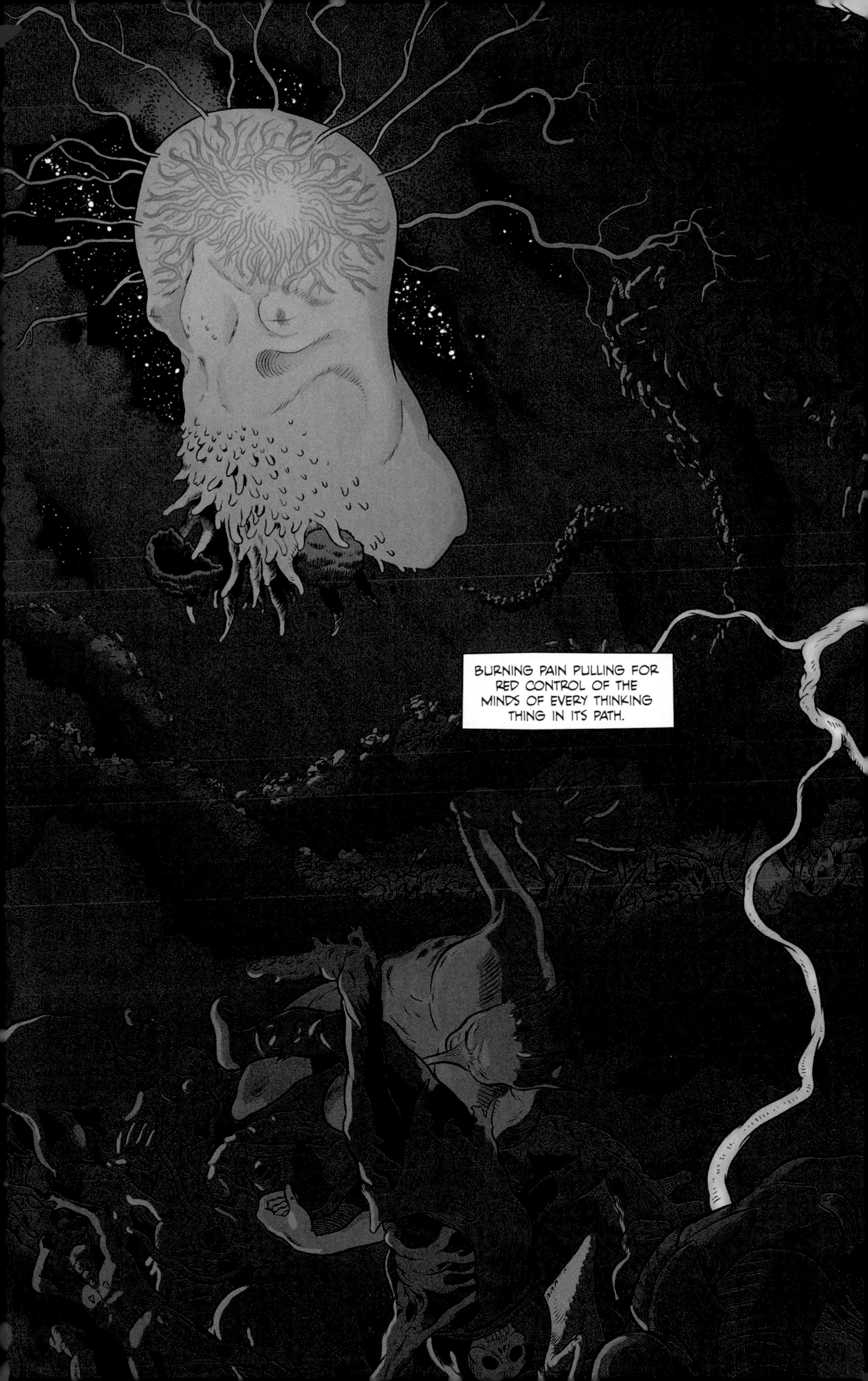
BURNING PAIN PULLING FOR RED CONTROL OF THE MINDS OF EVERY THINKING THING IN ITS PATH.

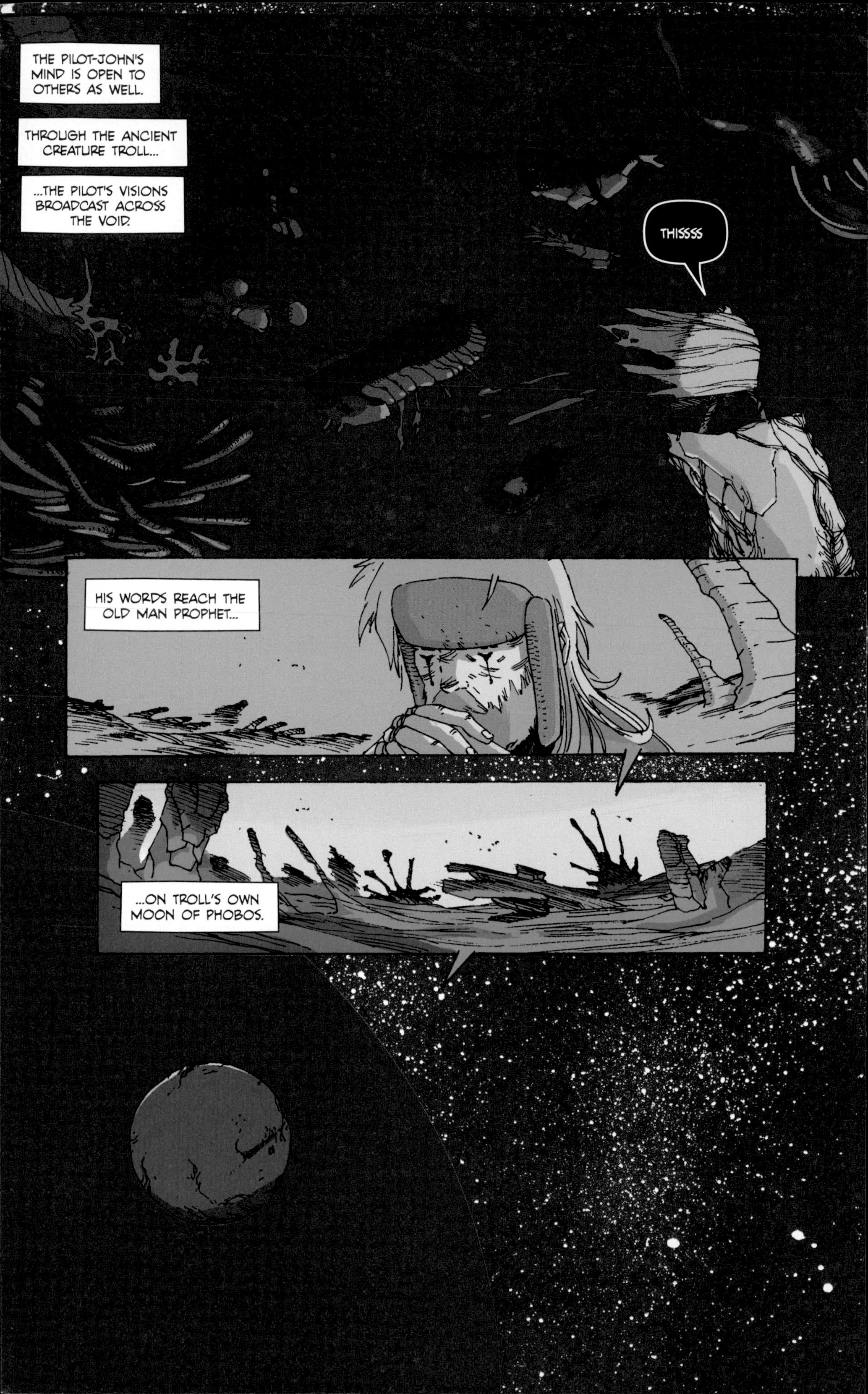
THE PILOT-JOHN'S MIND IS OPEN TO OTHERS AS WELL.
THROUGH THE ANCIENT CREATURE TROLL...
...THE PILOT'S VISIONS BROADCAST ACROSS THE VOID.
THISSSS
HIS WORDS REACH THE OLD MAN PROPHET...
...ON TROLL'S OWN MOON OF PHOBOS.

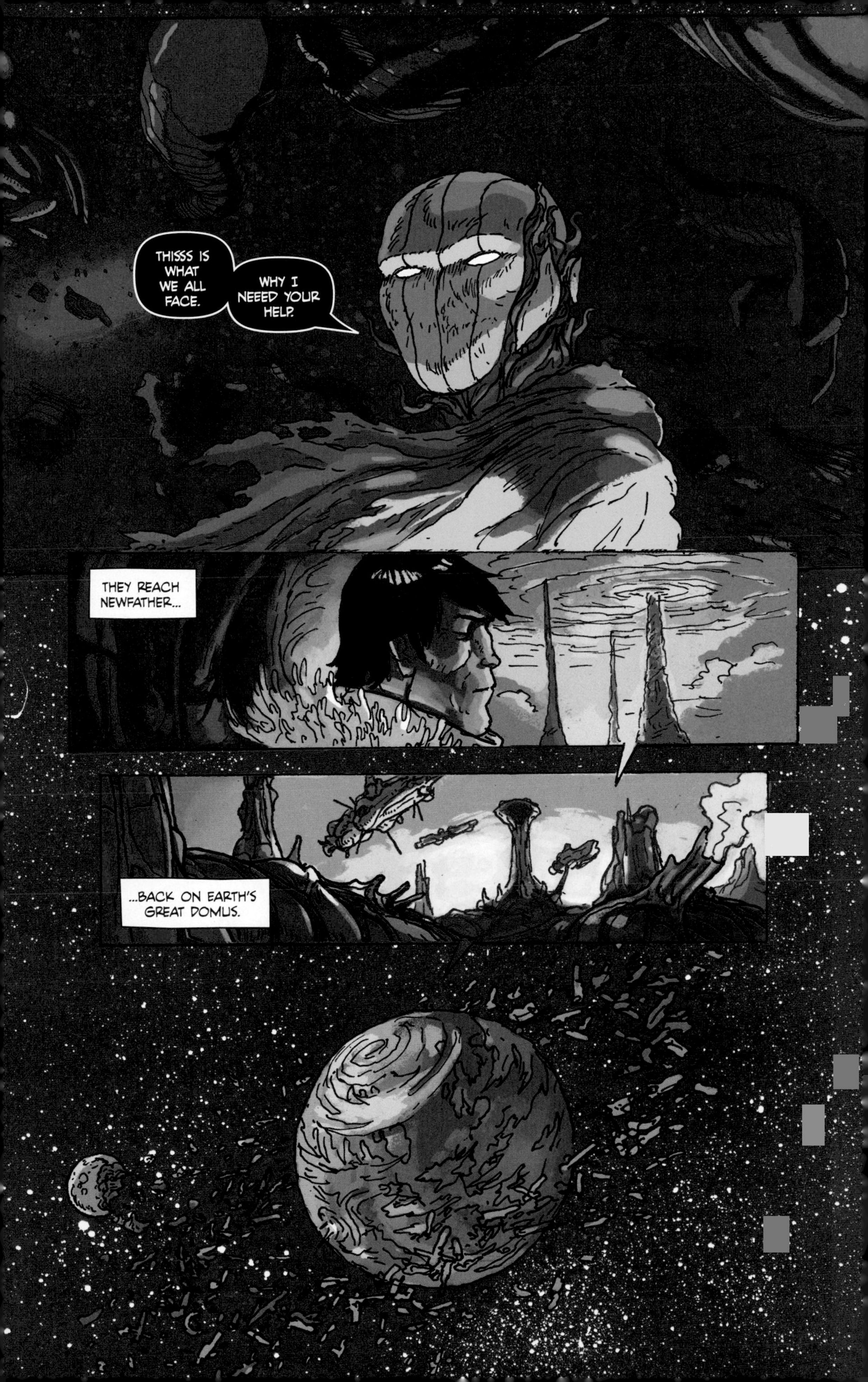
THISSS IS WHAT WE ALL FACE.
WHY I NEEED YOUR HELP.
THEY REACH NEWFATHER...
...BACK ON EARTH'S GREAT DOMUS.

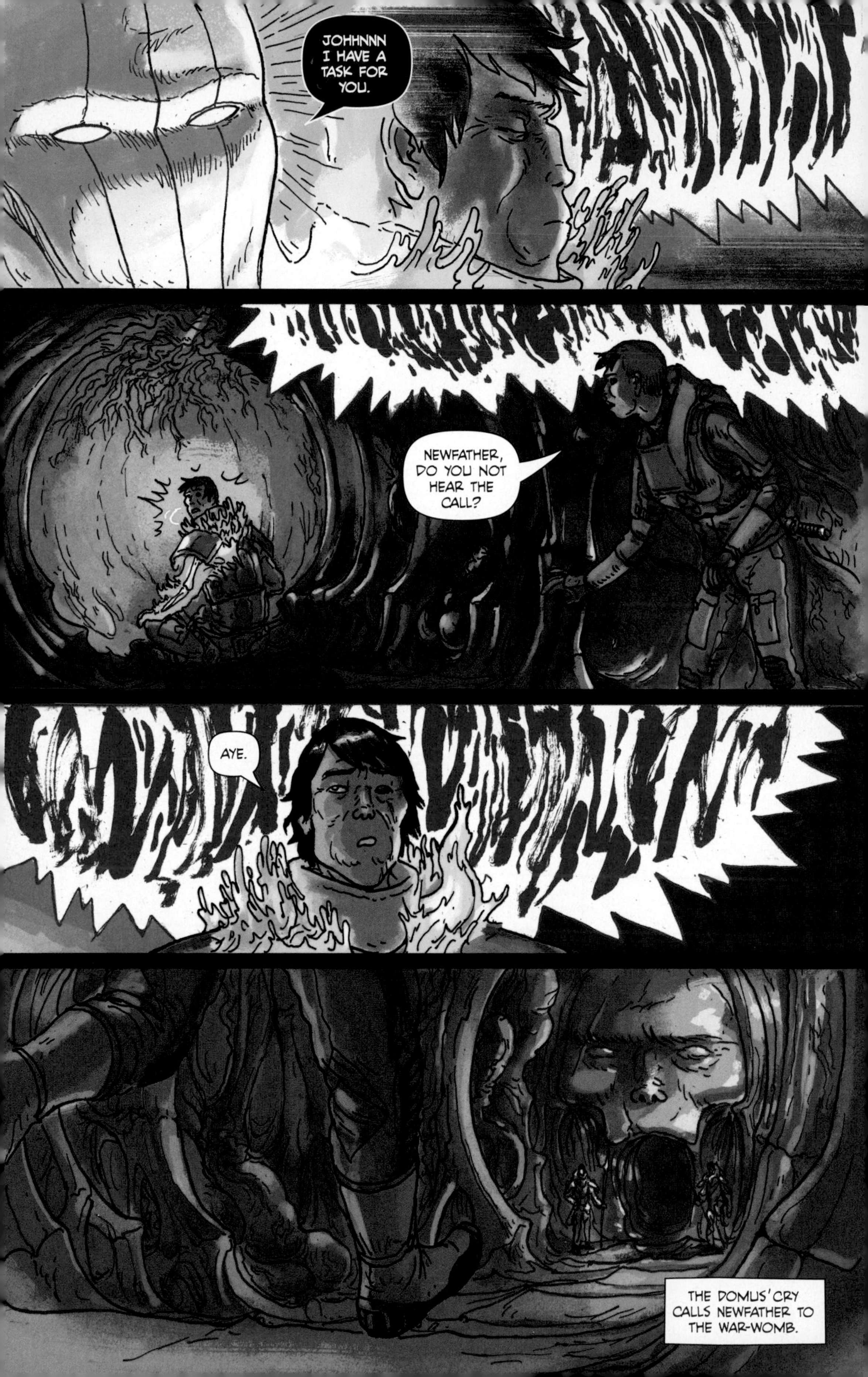
JOHHNNN I HAVE A TASK FOR YOU.
NEWFATHER, DO YOU NOT HEAR THE CALL?
AYE.
THE DOMUS' CRY CALLS NEWFATHER TO THE WAR-WOMB.

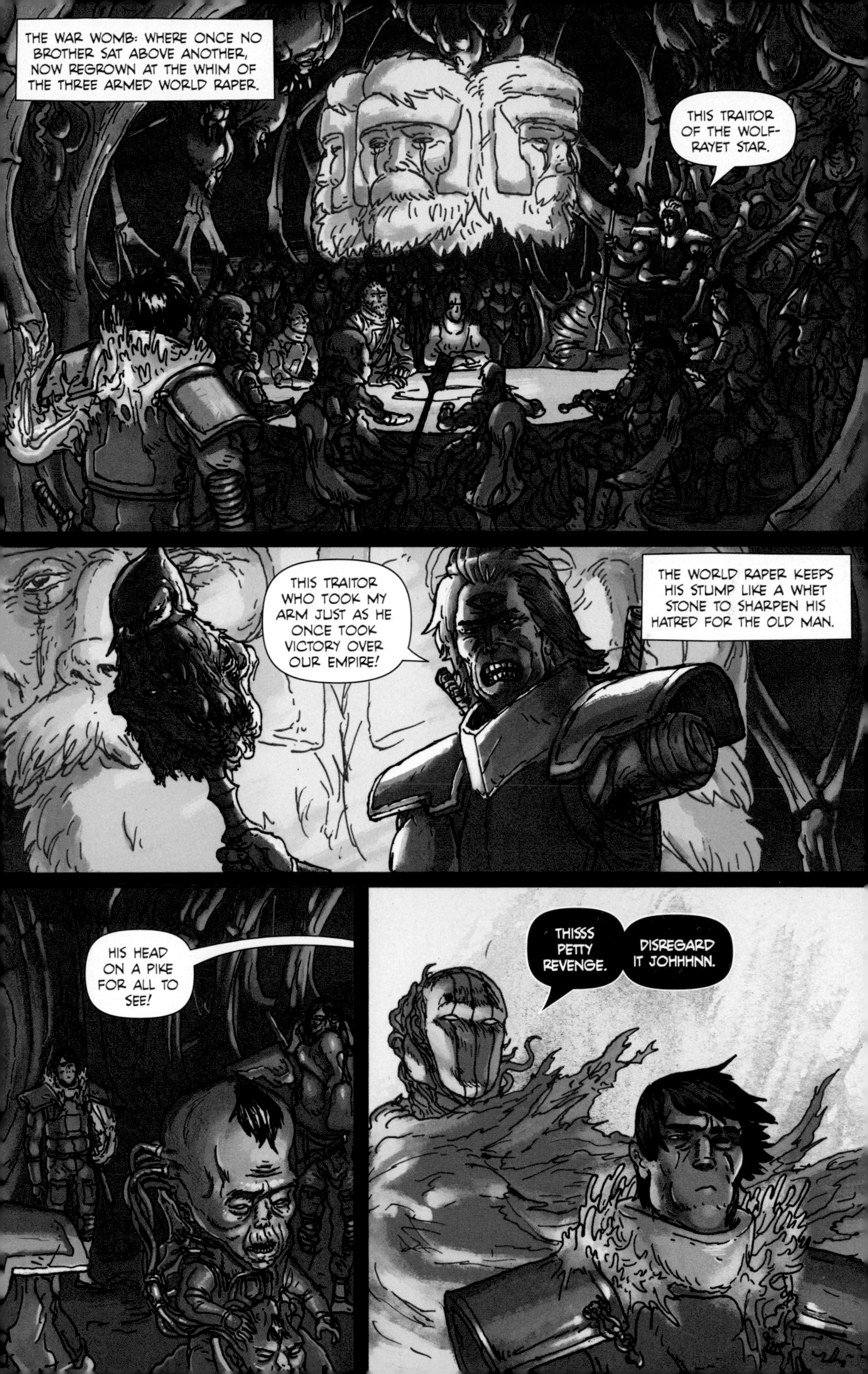
THE WAR WOMB: WHERE ONCE NO BROTHER SAT ABOVE ANOTHER, NOW REGROWN AT THE WHIM OF THE THREE ARMED WORLD RAPER.
THIS TRAITOR OF THE WOLF-RAYET STAR.
THIS TRAITOR WHO TOOK MY ARM JUST AS HE ONCE TOOK VICTORY OVER OUR EMPIRE!
THE WORLD RAPER KEEPS HIS STUMP LIKE A WHET STONE TO SHARPEN HIS HATRED FOR THE OLD MAN.
HIS HEAD ON A PIKE FOR ALL TO SEE!
THISSS PETTY REVENGE.
DISREGARD IT JOHHHNN.

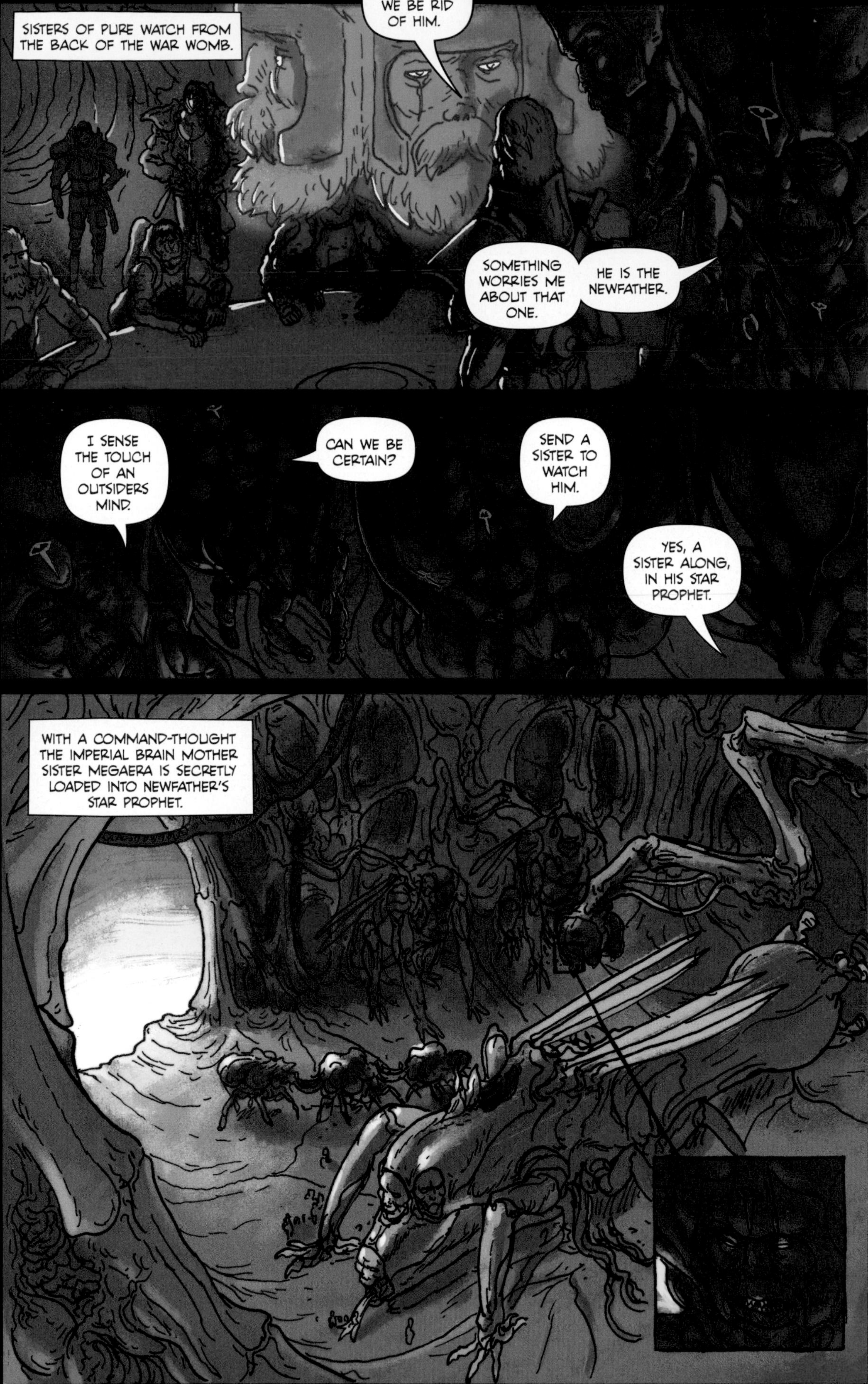
SISTERS OF PURE WATCH FROM THE BACK OF THE WAR WOMB.
ONLY THEN WE BE RID OF HIM.
SOMETHING WORRIES ME ABOUT THAT ONE.
HE IS THE NEWFATHER.
I SENSE THE TOUCH OF AN OUTSIDERS MIND.
CAN WE BE CERTAIN?
SEND A SISTER TO WATCH HIM.
YES, A SISTER ALONG, IN HIS STAR PROPHET.
WITH A COMMAND-THOUGHT THE IMPERIAL BRAIN MOTHER SISTER MEGAERA IS SECRETLY LOADED INTO NEWFATHER'S STAR PROPHET.

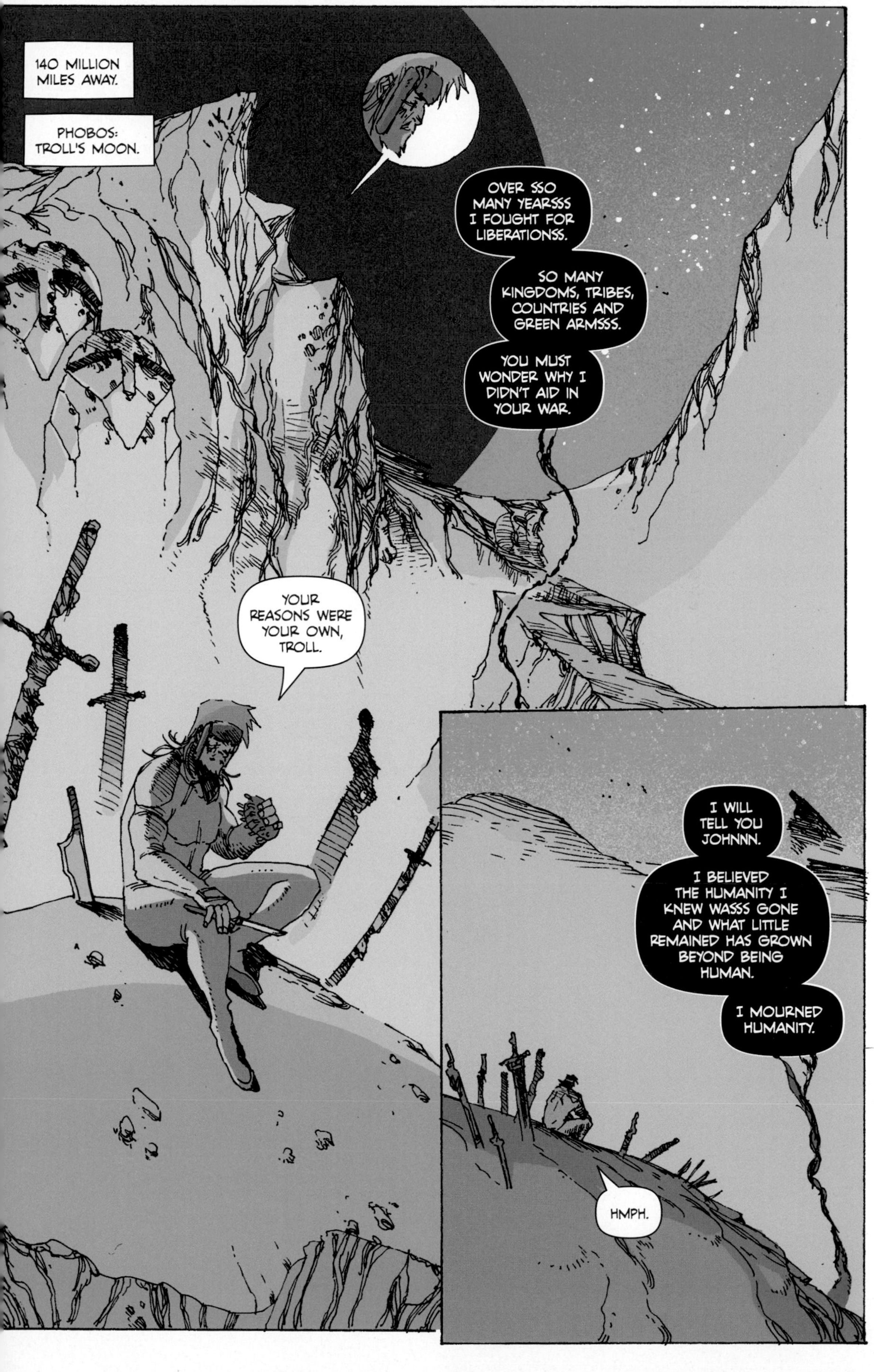
140 MILLION MILES AWAY.
PHOBOS: TROLL'S MOON.
OVER SSO MANY YEARSSS I FOUGHT FOR LIBERATIONSS.
SO MANY KINGDOMS, TRIBES, COUNTRIES AND GREEN ARMSSS.
YOU MUST WONDER WHY I DIDN'T AID IN YOUR WAR.
YOUR REASONS WERE YOUR OWN, TROLL.
I WILL TELL YOU JOHNNN.
I BELIEVED THE HUMANITY I KNEW WASSS GONE AND WHAT LITTLE REMAINED HAS GROWN BEYOND BEING HUMAN.
I MOURNED HUMANITY.
HMPH.

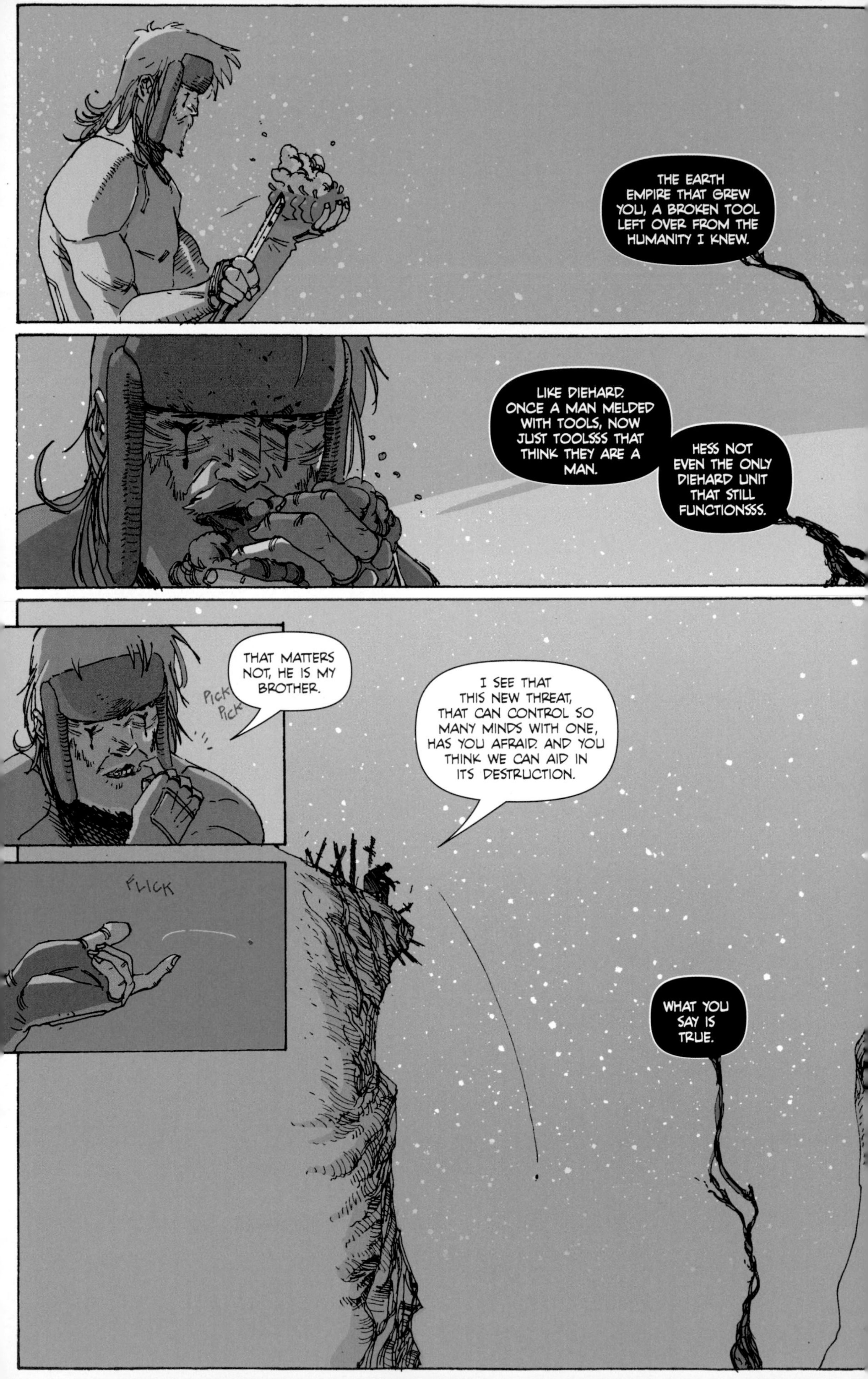
THE EARTH EMPIRE THAT GREW YOU, A BROKEN TOOL LEFT OVER FROM THE HUMANITY I KNEW.
LIKE DIEHARD. ONCE A MAN MELDED WITH TOOLS, NOW JUST TOOLSSS THAT THINK THEY ARE A MAN.
HESS NOT EVEN THE ONLY DIEHARD UNIT THAT STILL FUNCTIONSSS.
PICK PICK
THAT MATTERS NOT, HE IS MY BROTHER.
I SEE THAT THIS NEW THREAT, THAT CAN CONTROL SO MANY MINDS WITH ONE, HAS YOU AFRAID. AND YOU THINK WE CAN AID IN ITS DESTRUCTION.
FLICK
WHAT YOU SAY IS TRUE.

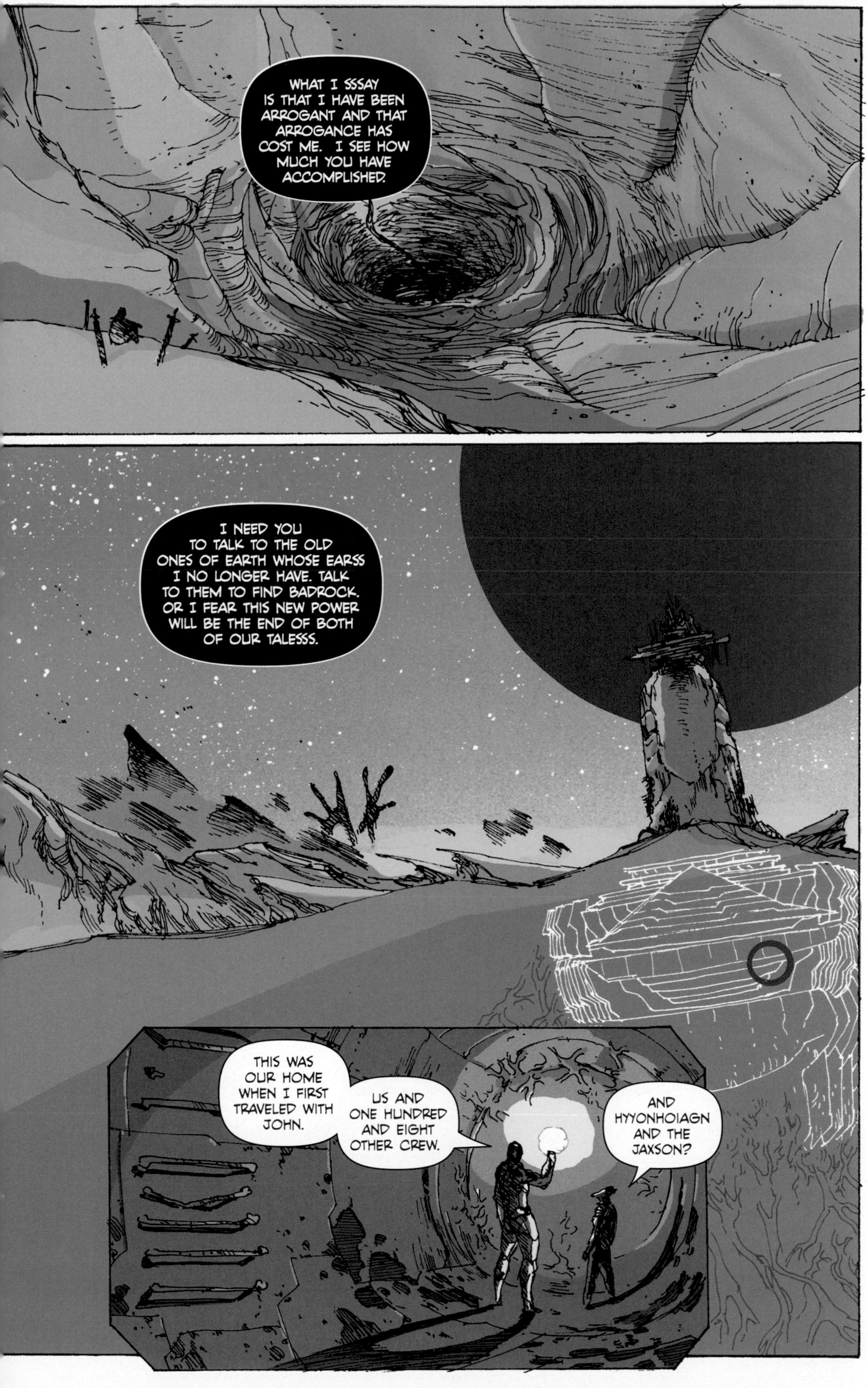
WHAT I SSSAY IS THAT I HAVE BEEN ARROGANT AND THAT ARROGANCE HAS COST ME. I SEE HOW MUCH YOU HAVE ACCOMPLISHED.
I NEED YOU TO TALK TO THE OLD ONES OF EARTH WHOSE EARSS I NO LONGER HAVE. TALK TO THEM TO FIND BADROCK. OR I FEAR THIS NEW POWER WILL BE THE END OF BOTH OF OUR TALESSS.
THIS WAS OUR HOME WHEN I FIRST TRAVELED WITH JOHN.
US AND ONE HUNDRED AND EIGHT OTHER CREW.
AND HYYONHOIAGN AND THE JAXSON?

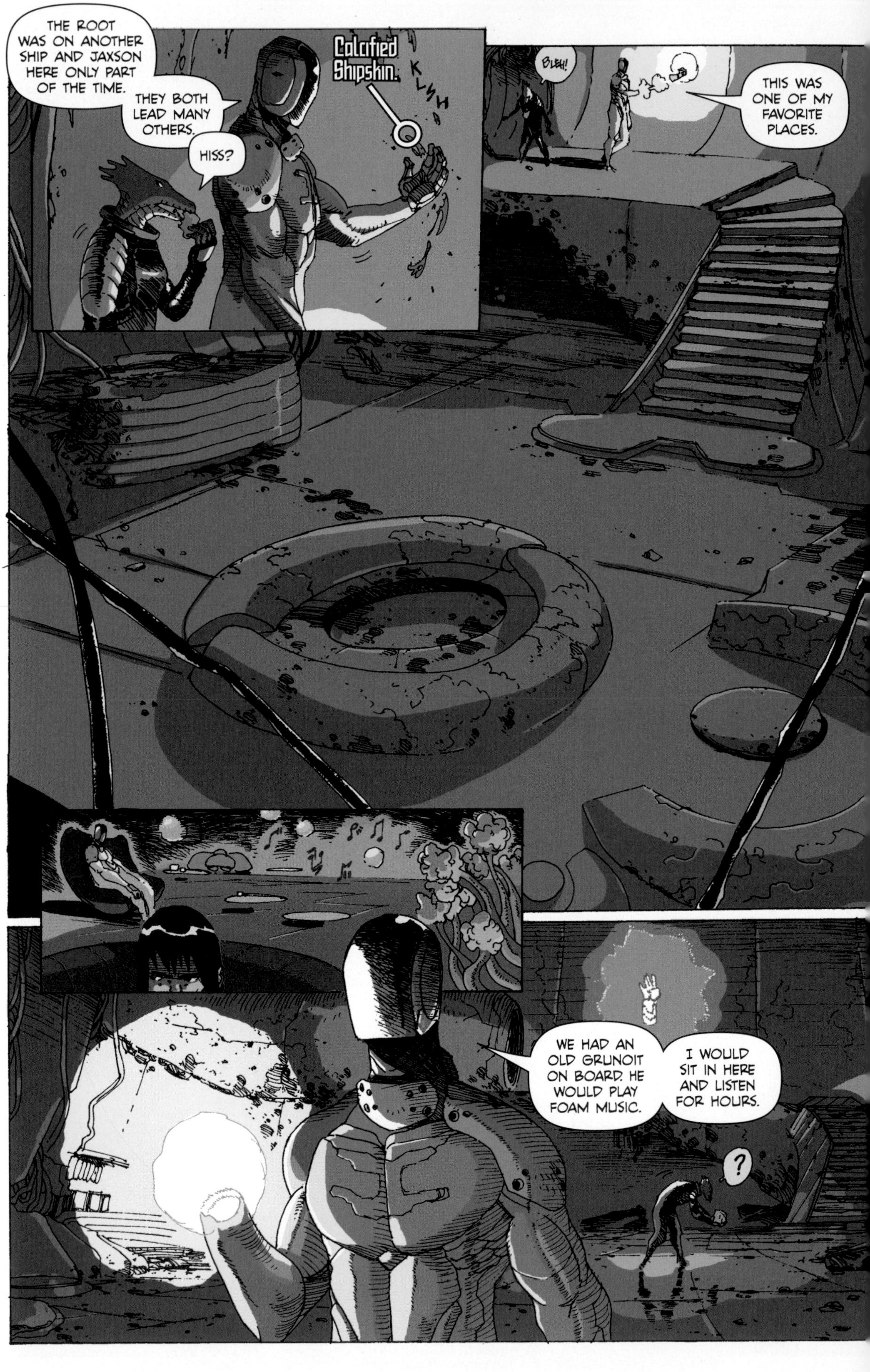
THE ROOT WAS ON ANOTHER SHIP AND JAXSON HERE ONLY PART OF THE TIME.
THEY BOTH LEAD MANY OTHERS.
HISS?
Calcified Shipskin.
KLSH
BLEH!
THIS WAS ONE OF MY FAVORITE PLACES.
WE HAD AN OLD GRUNOIT ON BOARD. HE WOULD PLAY FOAM MUSIC.
I WOULD SIT IN HERE AND LISTEN FOR HOURS.
?

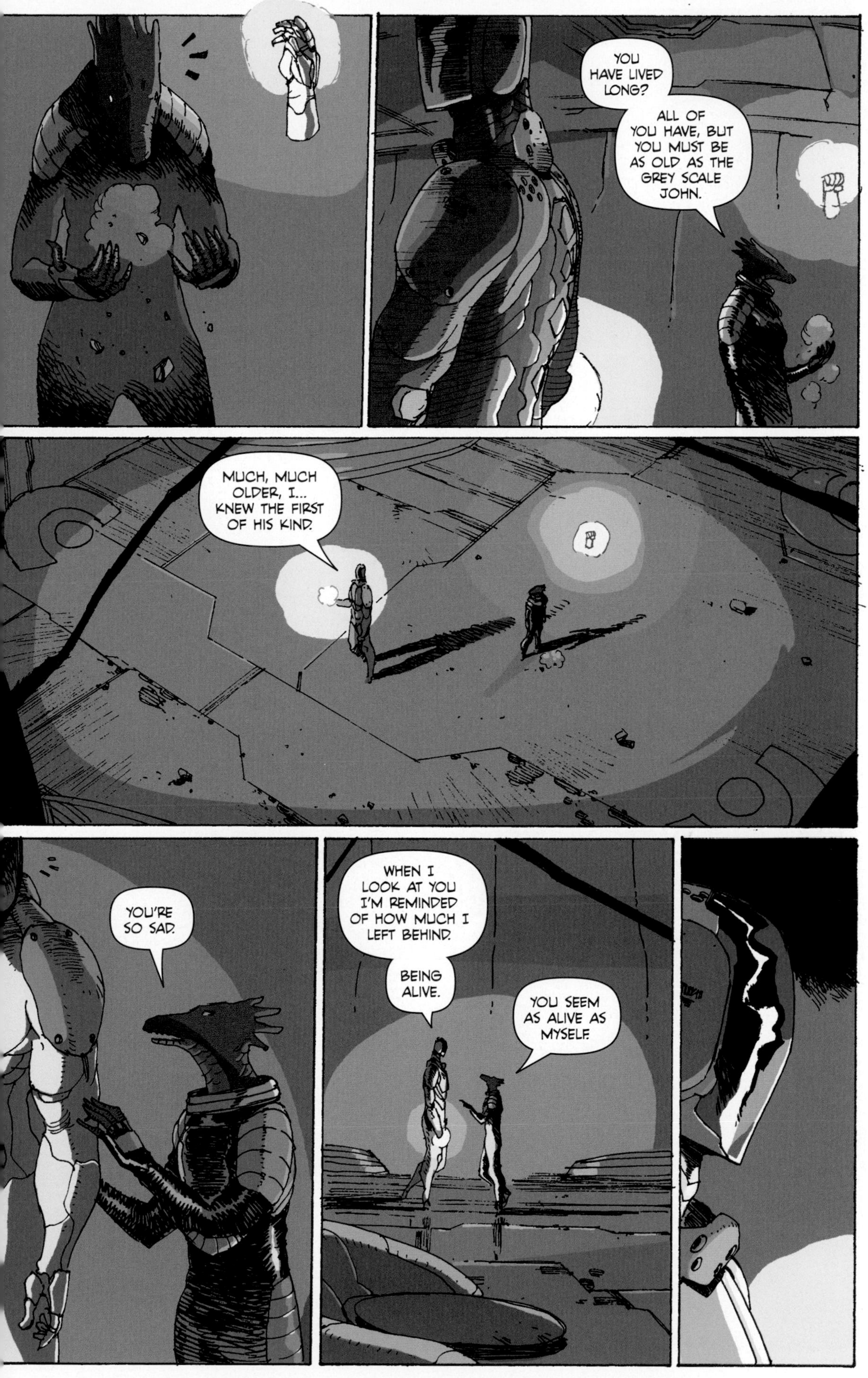
YOU HAVE LIVED LONG?
ALL OF YOU HAVE, BUT YOU MUST BE AS OLD AS THE GREY SCALE JOHN.
MUCH, MUCH OLDER, I... KNEW THE FIRST OF HIS KIND.
YOU'RE SO SAD.
WHEN I LOOK AT YOU I'M REMINDED OF HOW MUCH I LEFT BEHIND.
BEING ALIVE.
YOU SEEM AS ALIVE AS MYSELF.

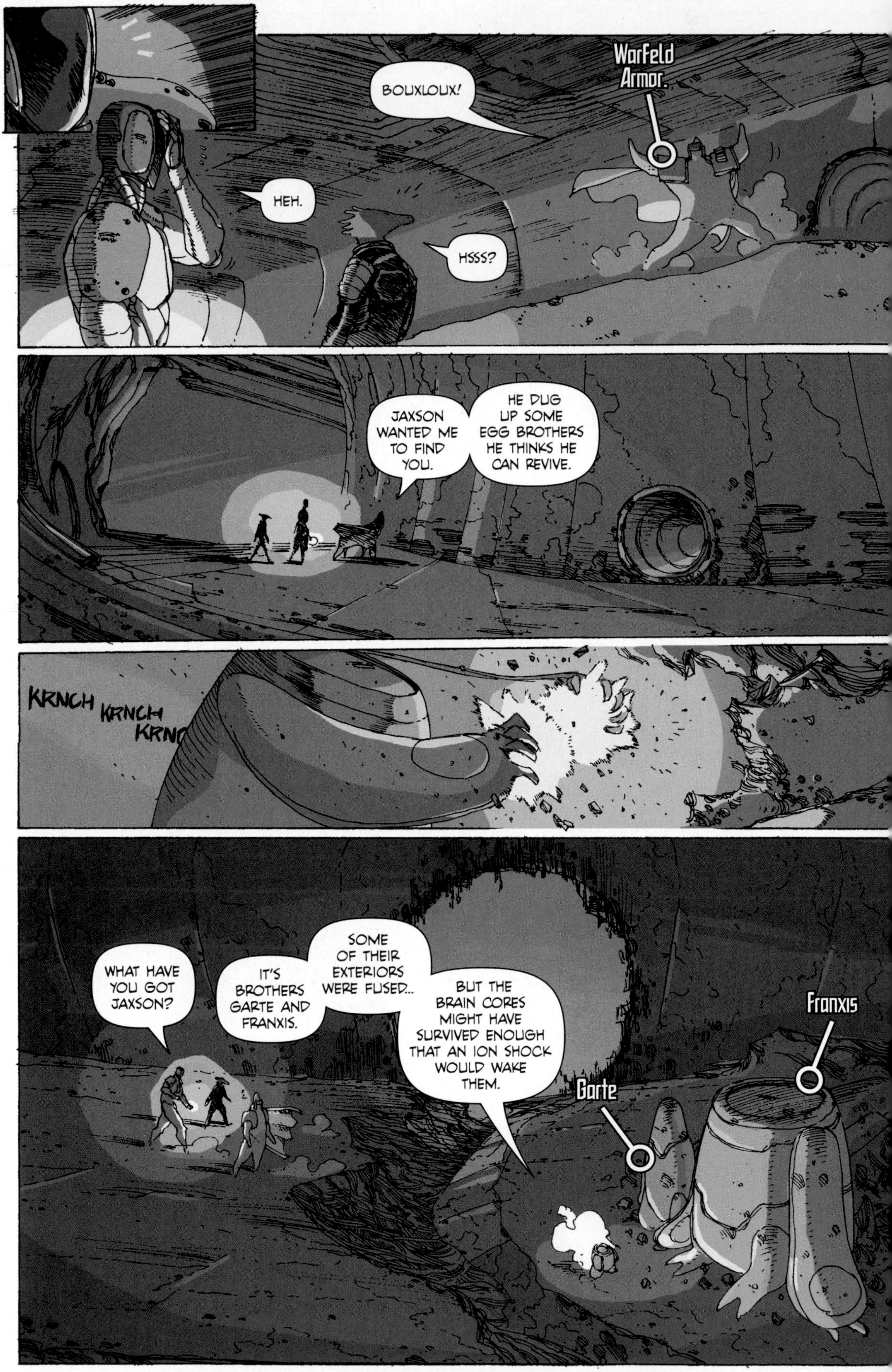

BOUXLOUX!
WarFeld Armor.
HEH.
HSSS?
JAXSON WANTED ME TO FIND YOU.
HE DUG UP SOME EGG BROTHERS HE THINKS HE CAN REVIVE.
KRNCH KRNCH
WHAT HAVE YOU GOT JAXSON?
IT'S BROTHERS GARTE AND FRANXIS.
SOME OF THEIR EXTERIORS WERE FUSED...
BUT THE BRAIN CORES MIGHT HAVE SURVIVED ENOUGH THAT AN ION SHOCK WOULD WAKE THEM.
Garte
Franxis

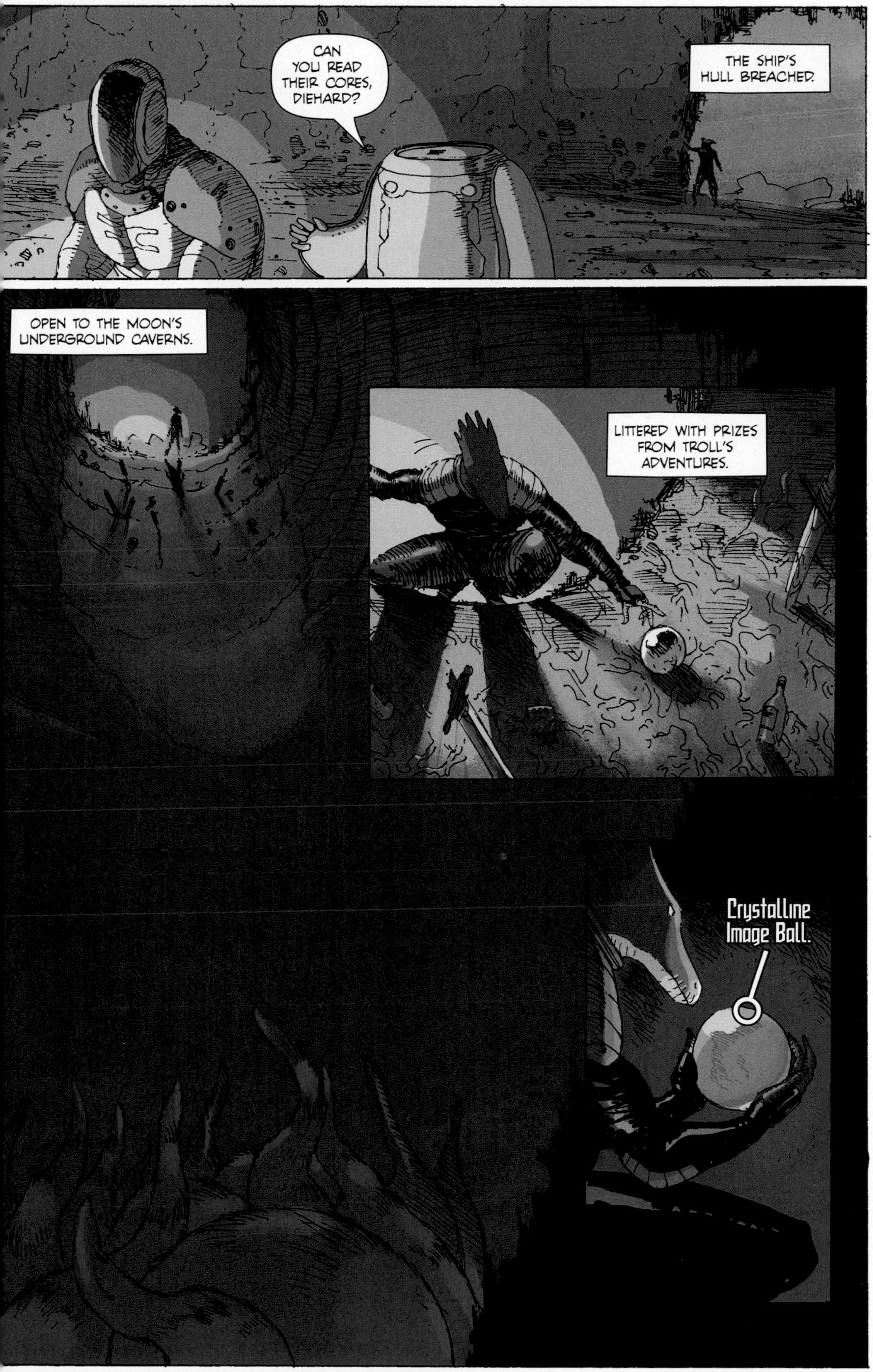

CAN YOU READ THEIR CORES, DIEHARD?
THE SHIP'S HULL BREACHED.
OPEN TO THE MOON'S UNDERGROUND CAVERNS.
LITTERED WITH PRIZES FROM TROLL'S ADVENTURES.
Crystalline Image Ball.

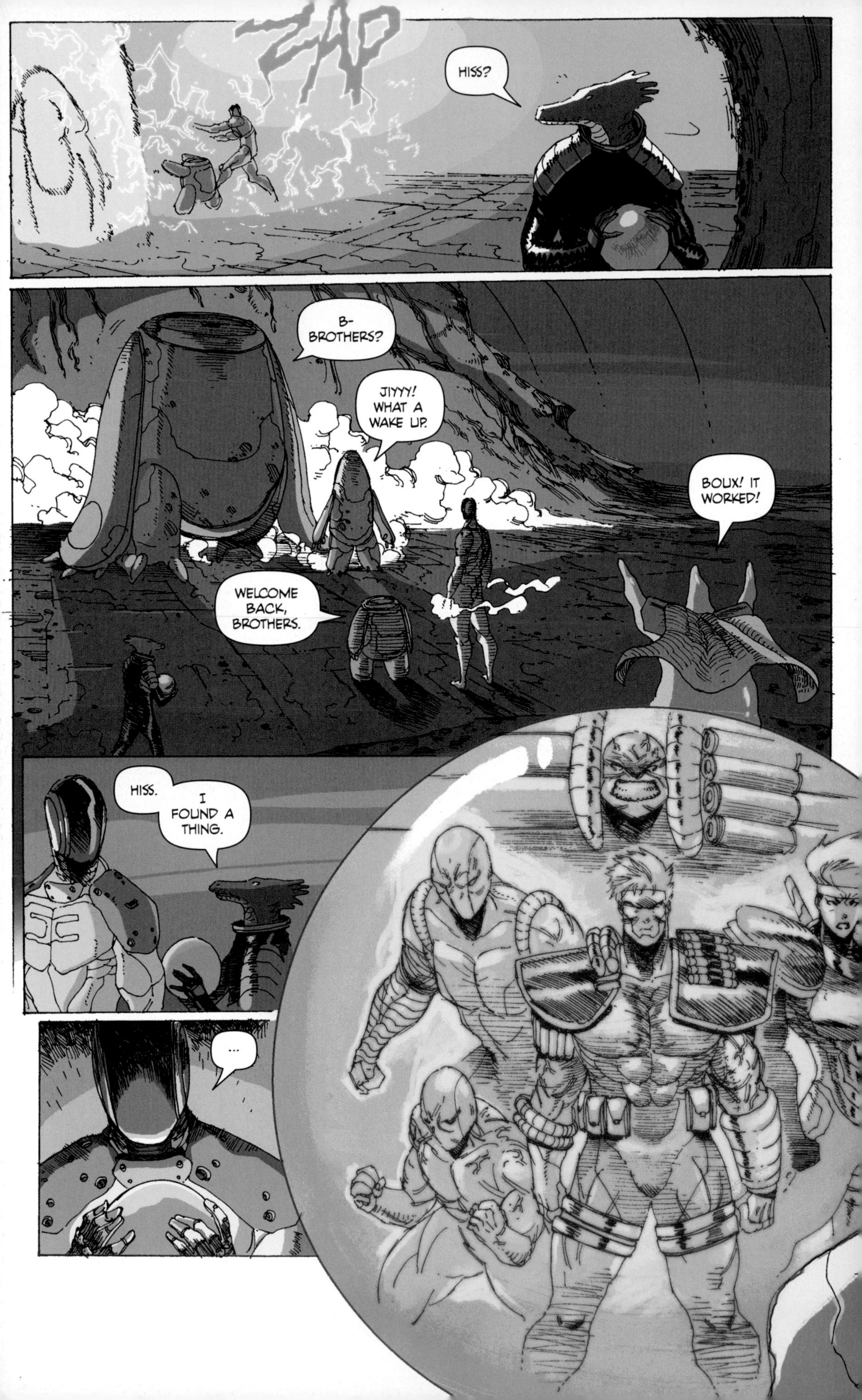
ZAP
HISS?
B- BROTHERS?
JIYYY! WHAT A WAKE UP.
BOUX! IT WORKED!
WELCOME BACK, BROTHERS.
HISS.
I FOUND A THING.
...

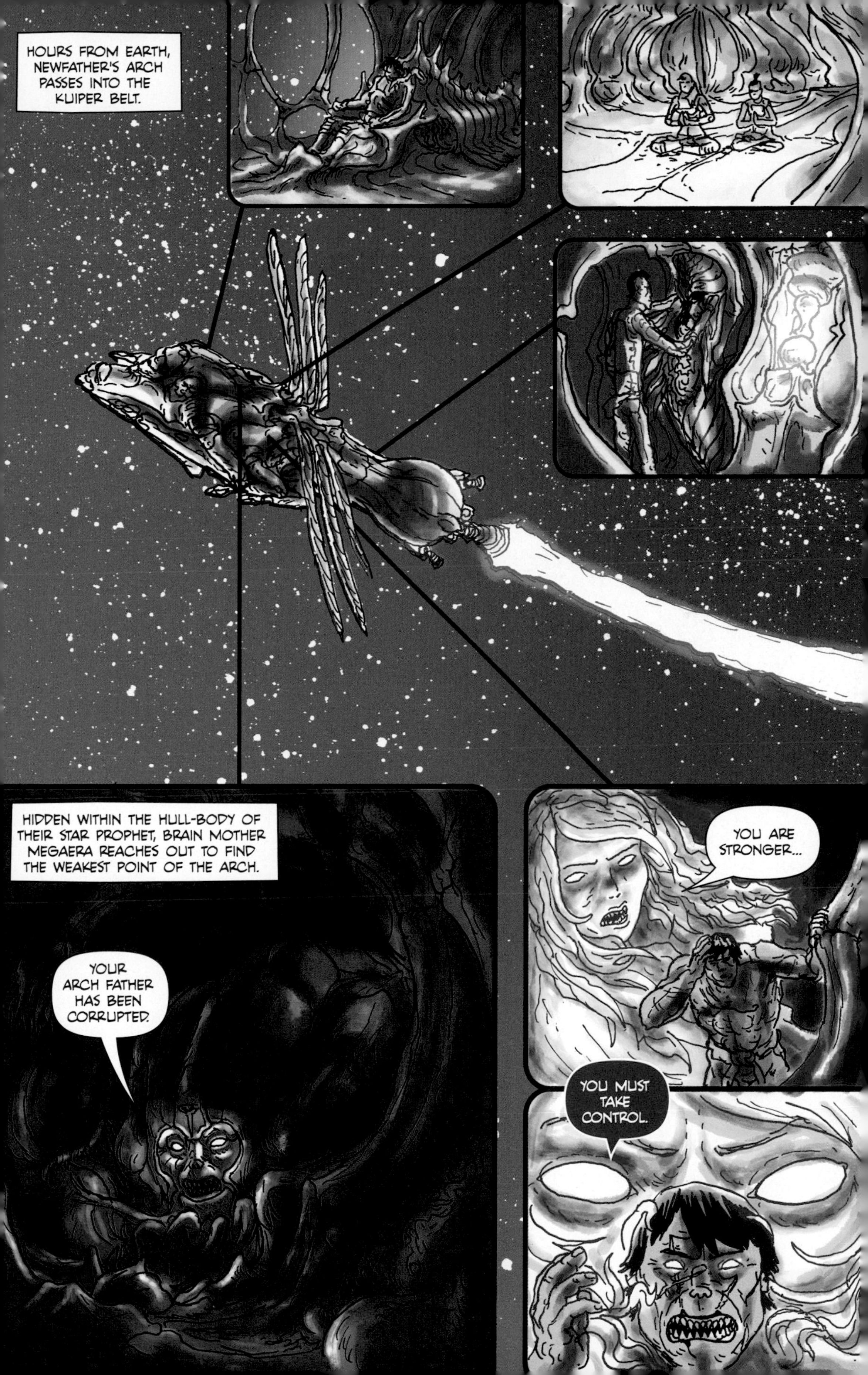
HOURS FROM EARTH, NEWFATHER'S ARCH PASSES INTO THE KUIPER BELT.
HIDDEN WITHIN THE HULL-BODY OF THEIR STAR PROPHET, BRAIN MOTHER MEGAERA REACHES OUT TO FIND THE WEAKEST POINT OF THE ARCH.
YOUR ARCH FATHER HAS BEEN CORRUPTED.
YOU ARE STRONGER...
YOU MUST TAKE CONTROL.

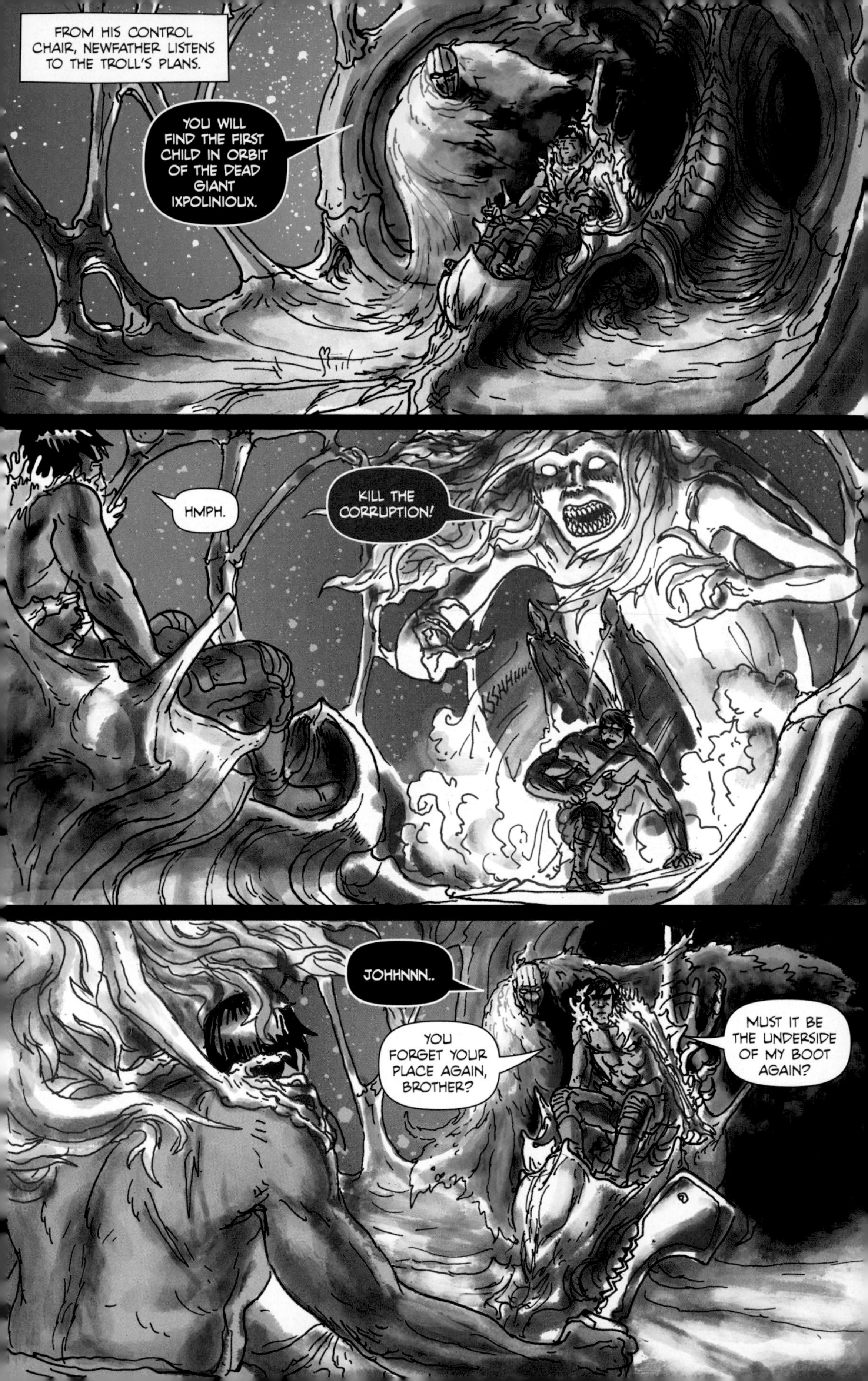
FROM HIS CONTROL CHAIR, NEWFATHER LISTENS TO THE TROLL'S PLANS.
YOU WILL FIND THE FIRST CHILD IN ORBIT OF THE DEAD GIANT IXPOLINIOUX.
HMPH.
KILL THE CORRUPTION!
JOHHNNN..
YOU FORGET YOUR PLACE AGAIN, BROTHER?
MUST IT BE THE UNDERSIDE OF MY BOOT AGAIN?

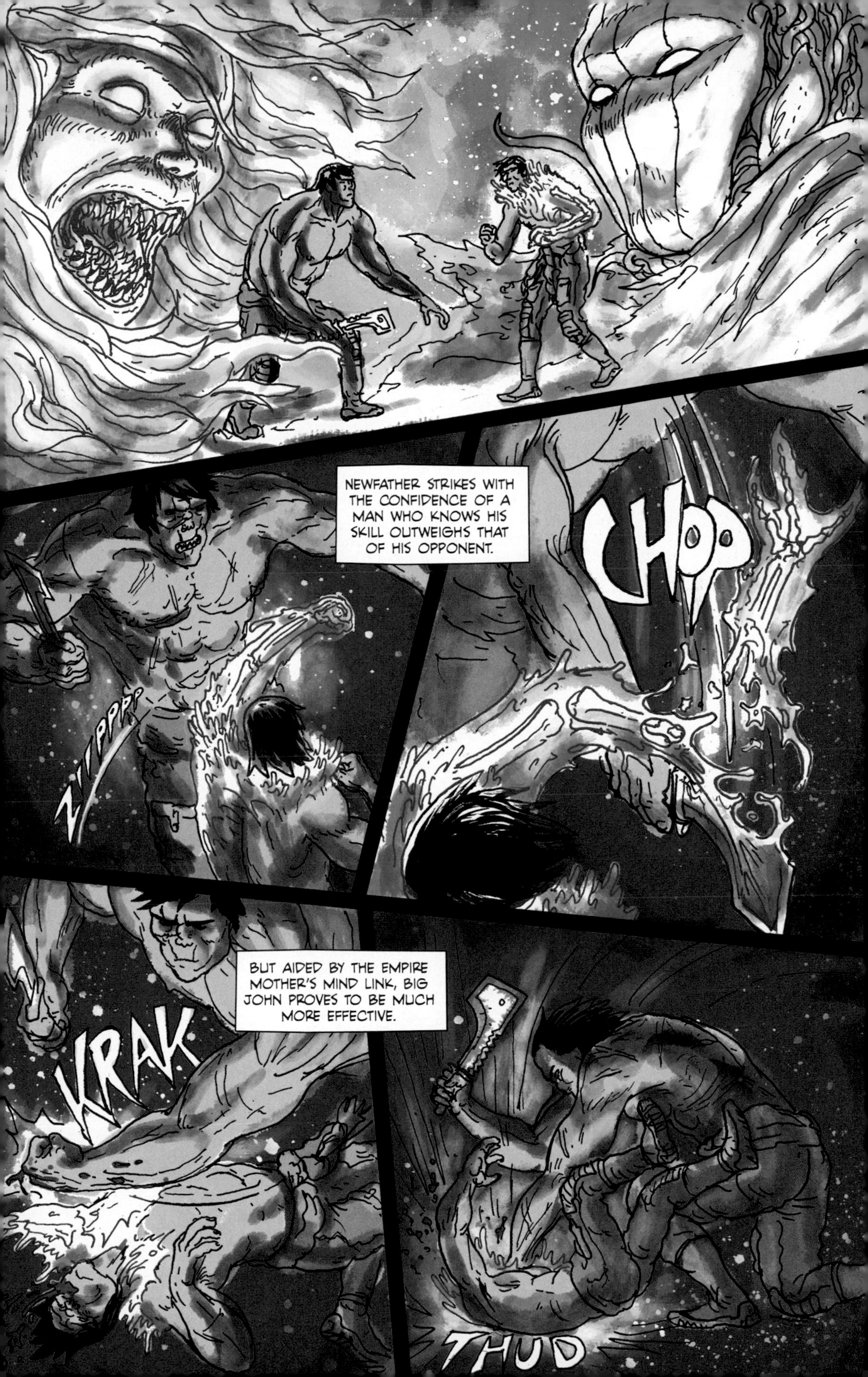
NEWFATHER STRIKES WITH THE CONFIDENCE OF A MAN WHO KNOWS HIS SKILL OUTWEIGHS THAT OF HIS OPPONENT.
ZZIPPPP
CHOP
BUT AIDED BY THE EMPIRE MOTHER'S MIND LINK, BIG JOHN PROVES TO BE MUCH MORE EFFECTIVE.
KRAK
THUD

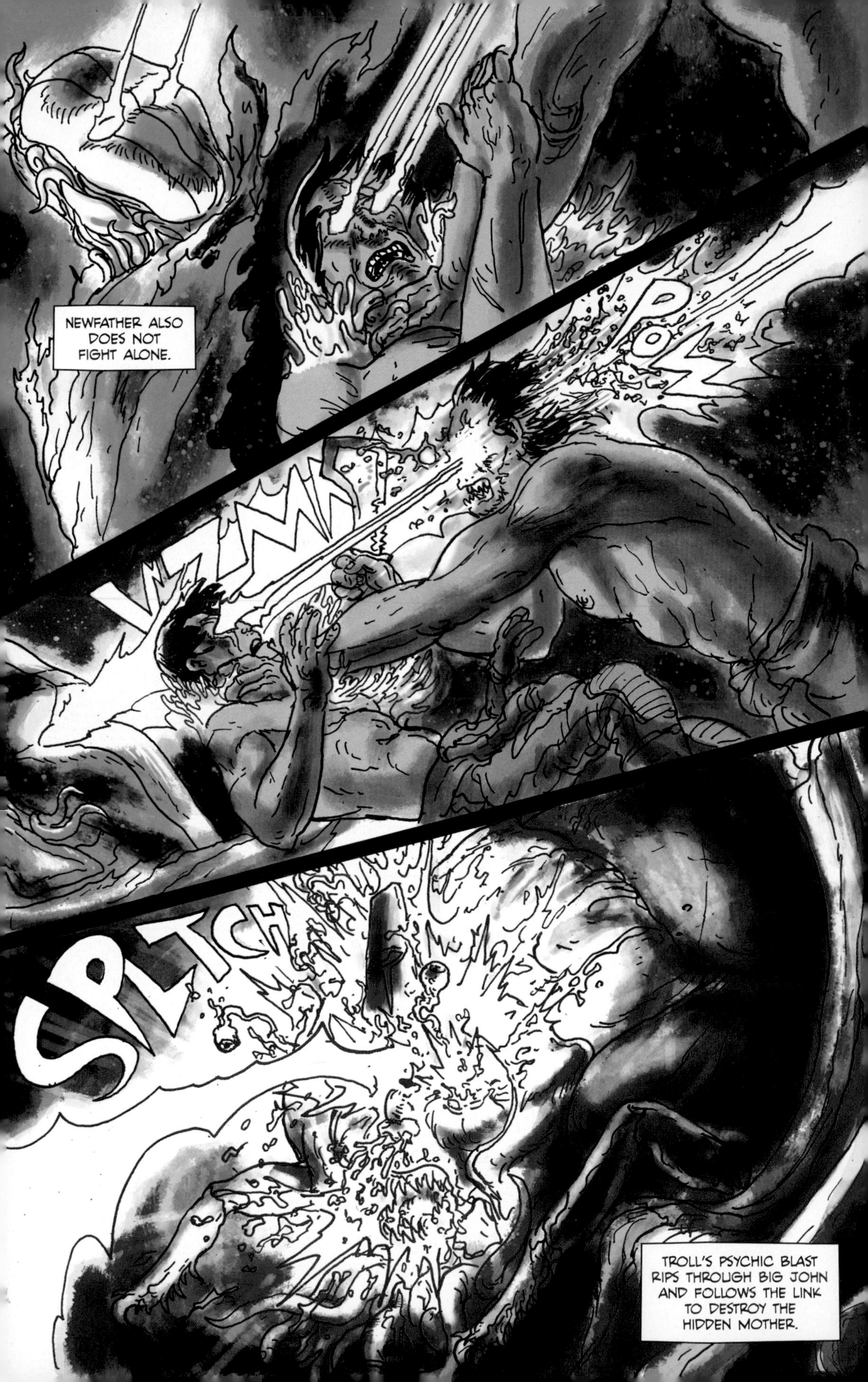
NEWFATHER ALSO DOES NOT FIGHT ALONE.
SPLTCH
TROLL'S PSYCHIC BLAST RIPS THROUGH BIG JOHN AND FOLLOWS THE LINK TO DESTROY THE HIDDEN MOTHER.

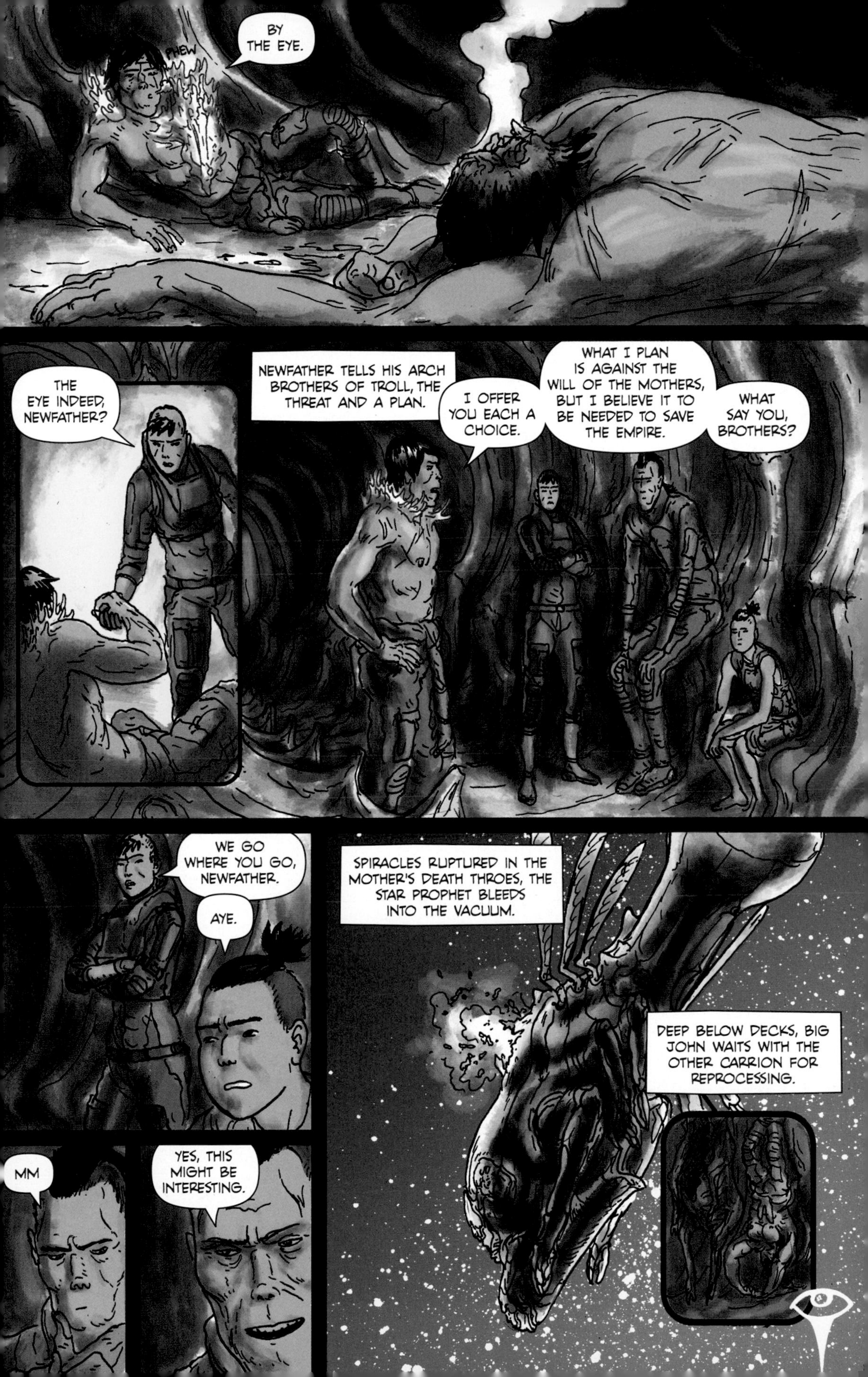
PHEW
BY THE EYE.
THE EYE INDEED, NEWFATHER?
NEWFATHER TELLS HIS ARCH BROTHERS OF TROLL, THE THREAT AND A PLAN.
I OFFER YOU EACH A CHOICE.
WHAT I PLAN IS AGAINST THE WILL OF THE MOTHERS, BUT I BELIEVE IT TO BE NEEDED TO SAVE THE EMPIRE.
WHAT SAY YOU, BROTHERS?
WE GO WHERE YOU GO, NEWFATHER.
AYE.
MM
YES, THIS MIGHT BE INTERESTING.
SPIRACLES RUPTURED IN THE MOTHER'S DEATH THROES, THE STAR PROPHET BLEEDS INTO THE VACUUM.
DEEP BELOW DECKS, BIG JOHN WAITS WITH THE OTHER CARRION FOR REPROCESSING.

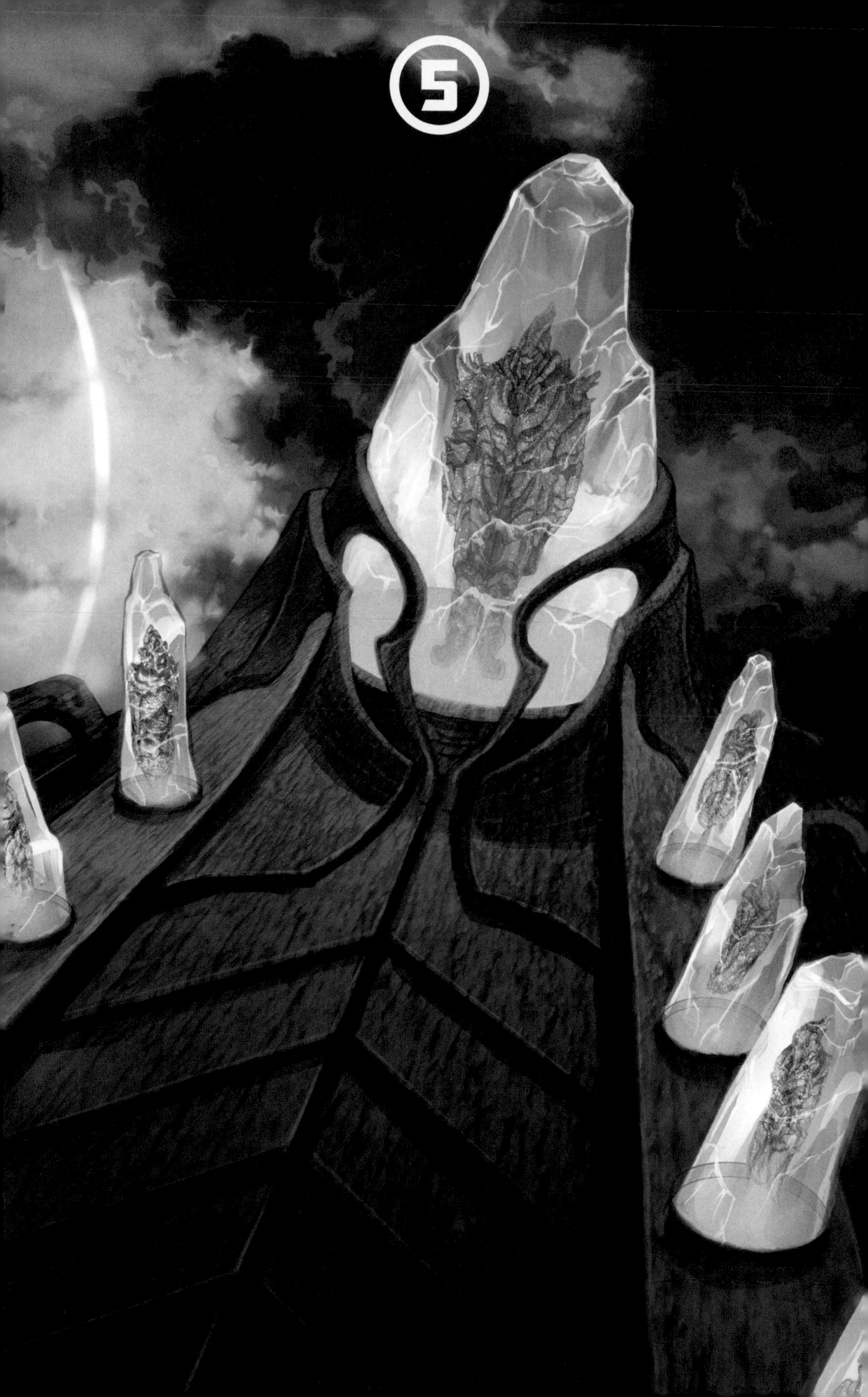
5

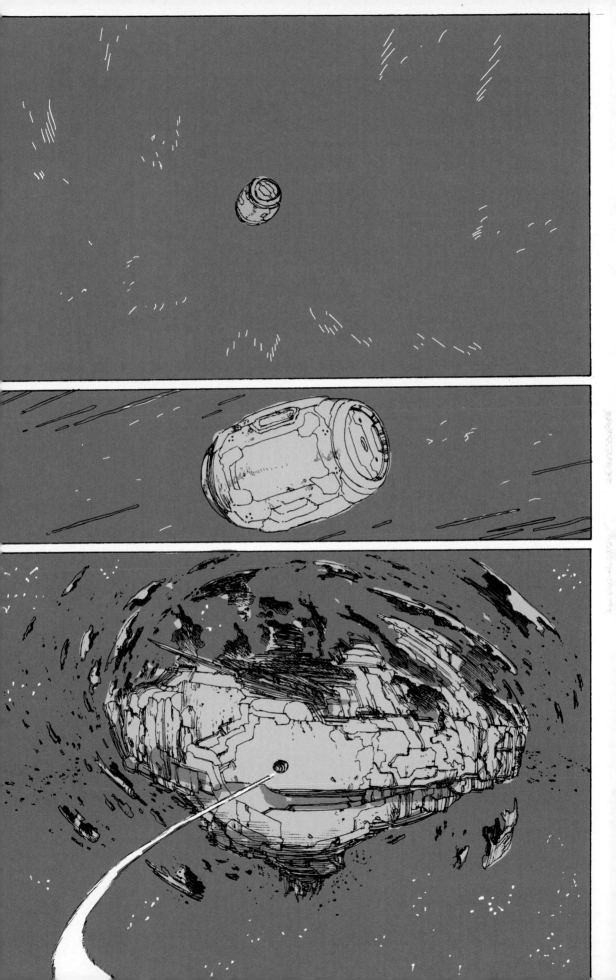

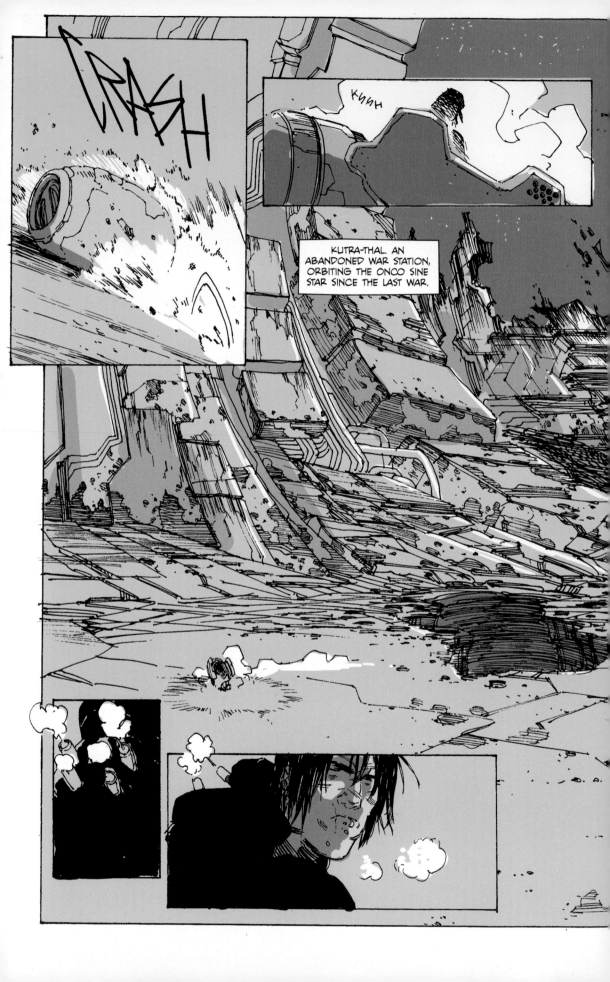

KUTRA-THAL. AN ABANDONED WAR STATION, ORBITING THE ONCO SINE STAR SINCE THE LAST WAR.

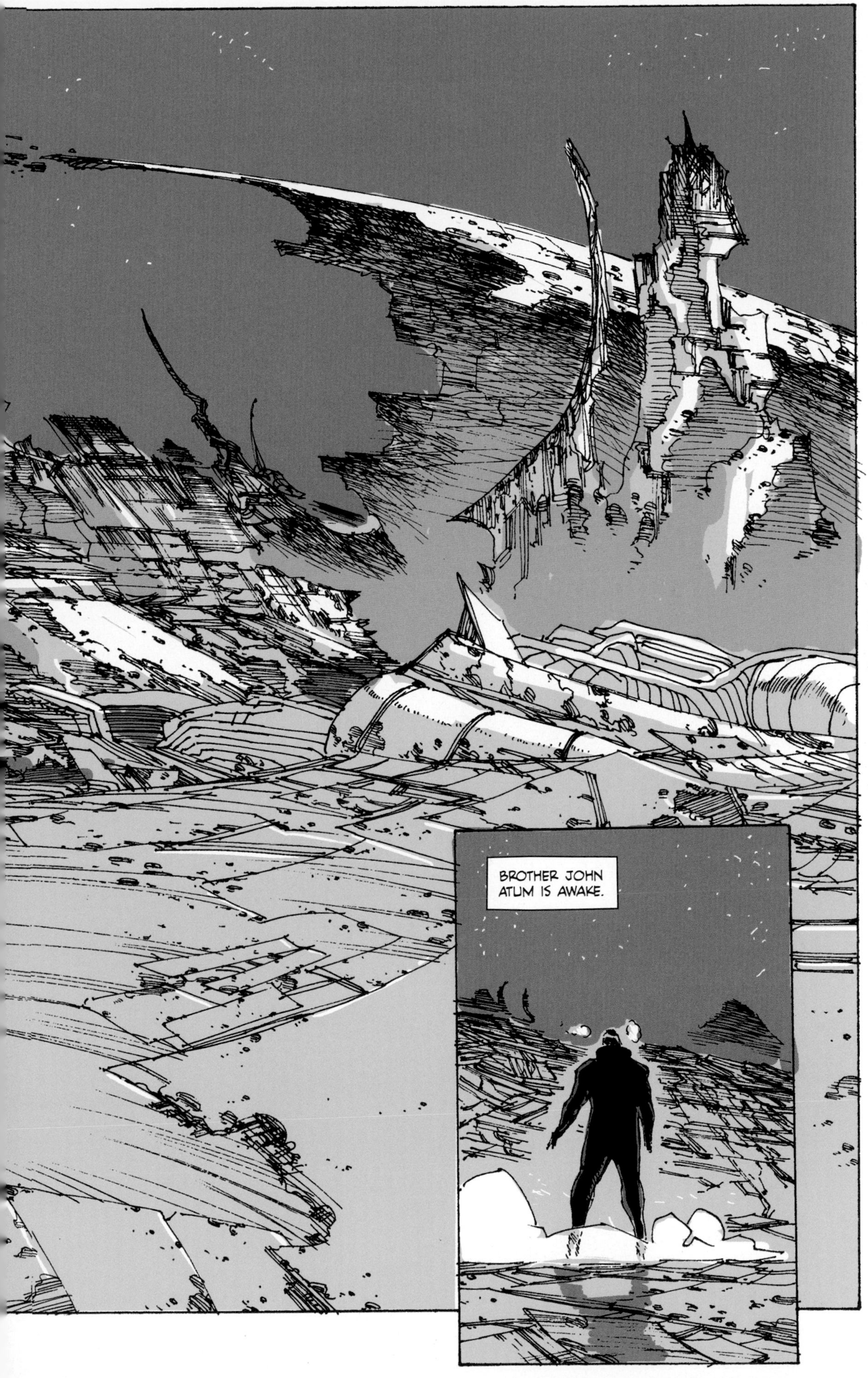
BROTHER JOHN
ATUM IS AWAKE.

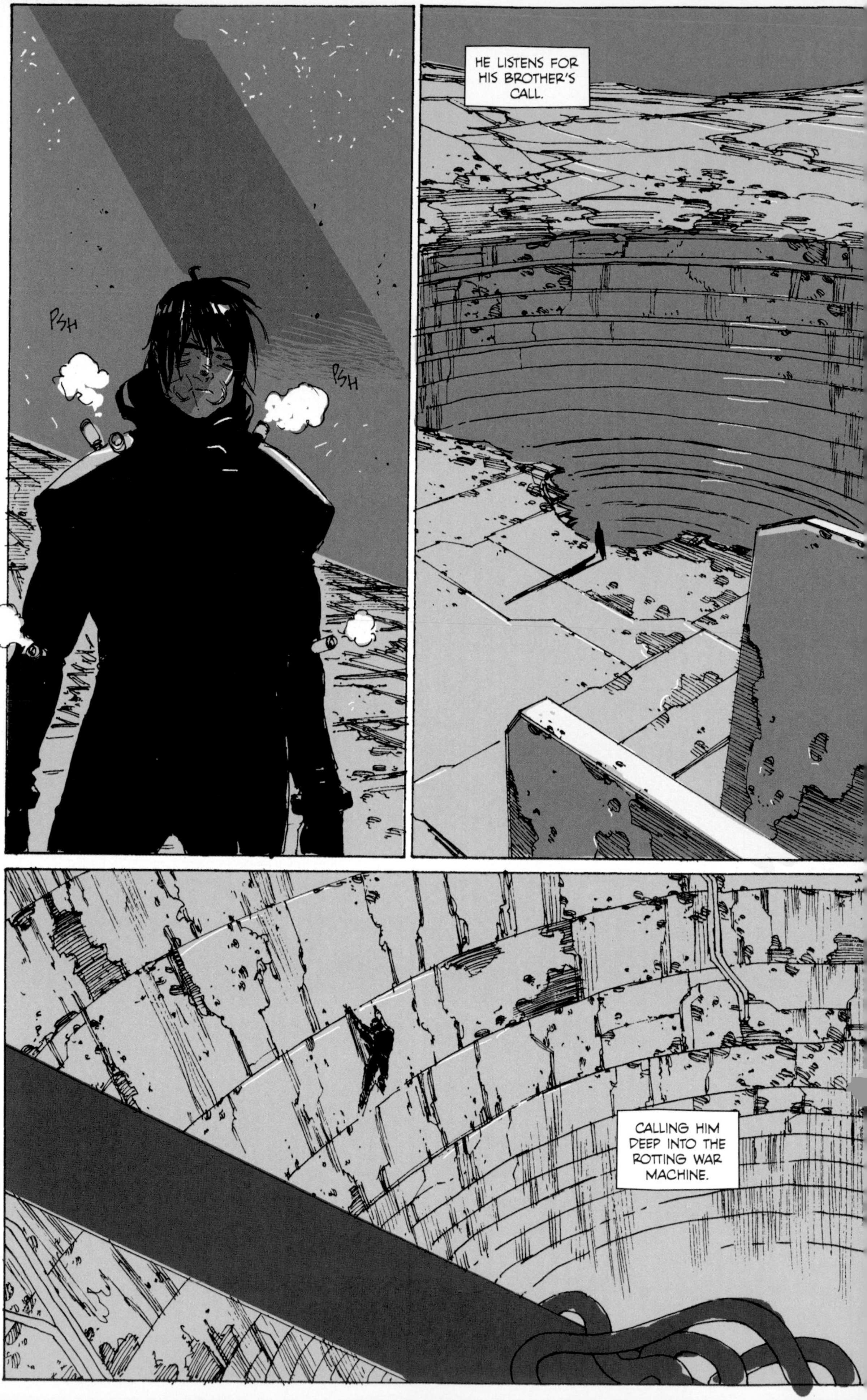
PSH
PSH
HE LISTENS FOR HIS BROTHER'S CALL.
CALLING HIM DEEP INTO THE ROTTING WAR MACHINE.

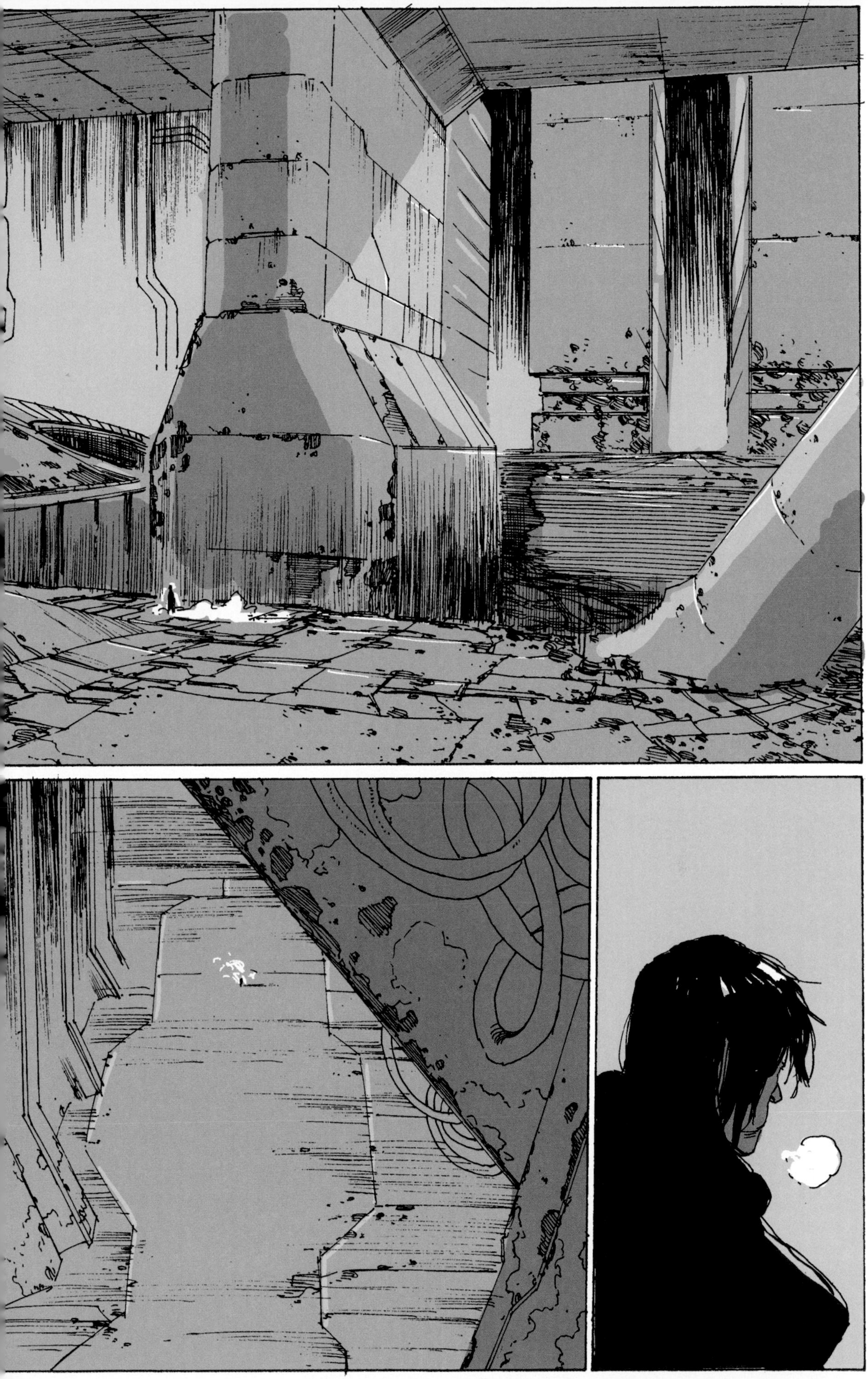

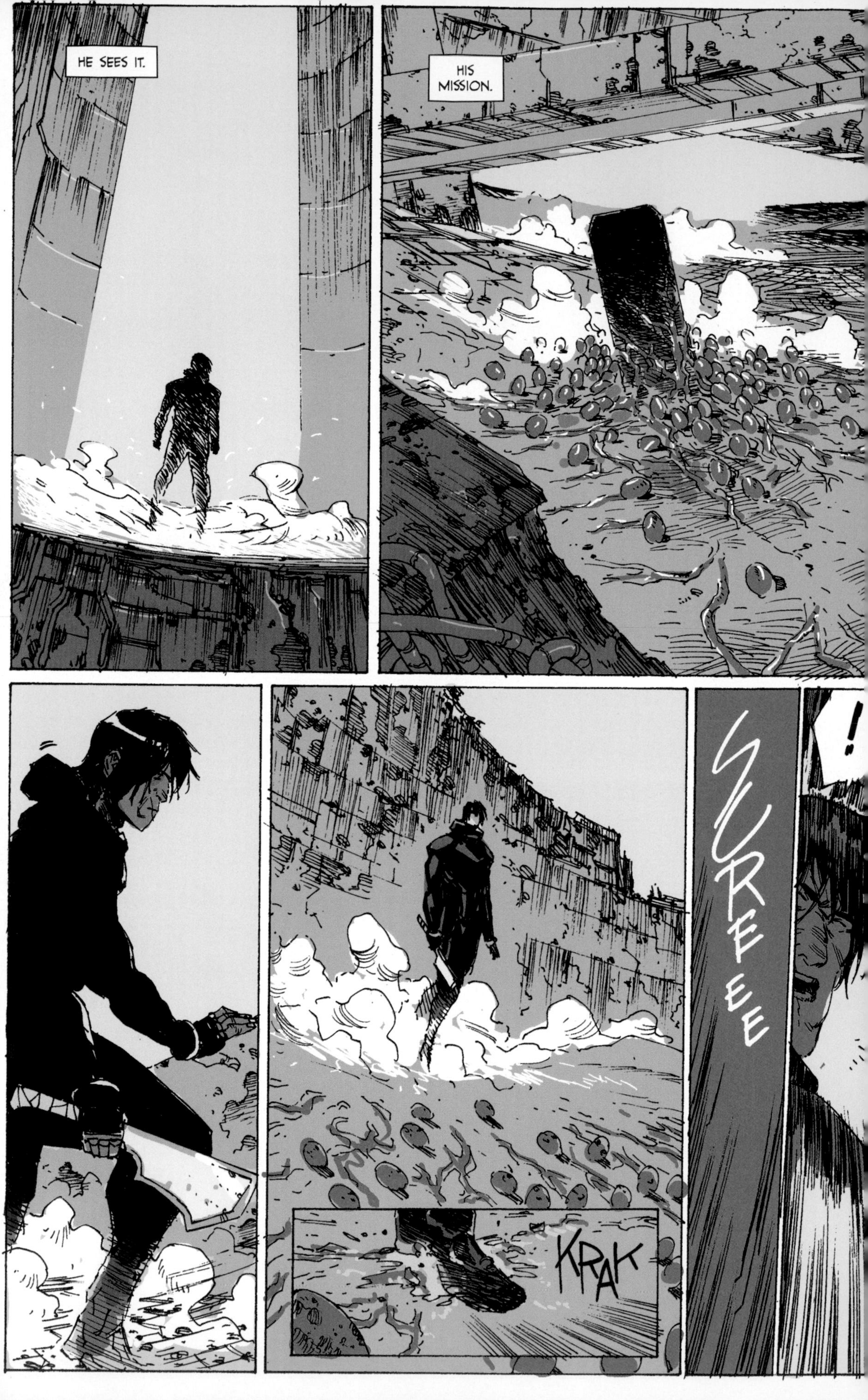
HE SEES IT.
HIS MISSION.
KRAK
SCREEE
!

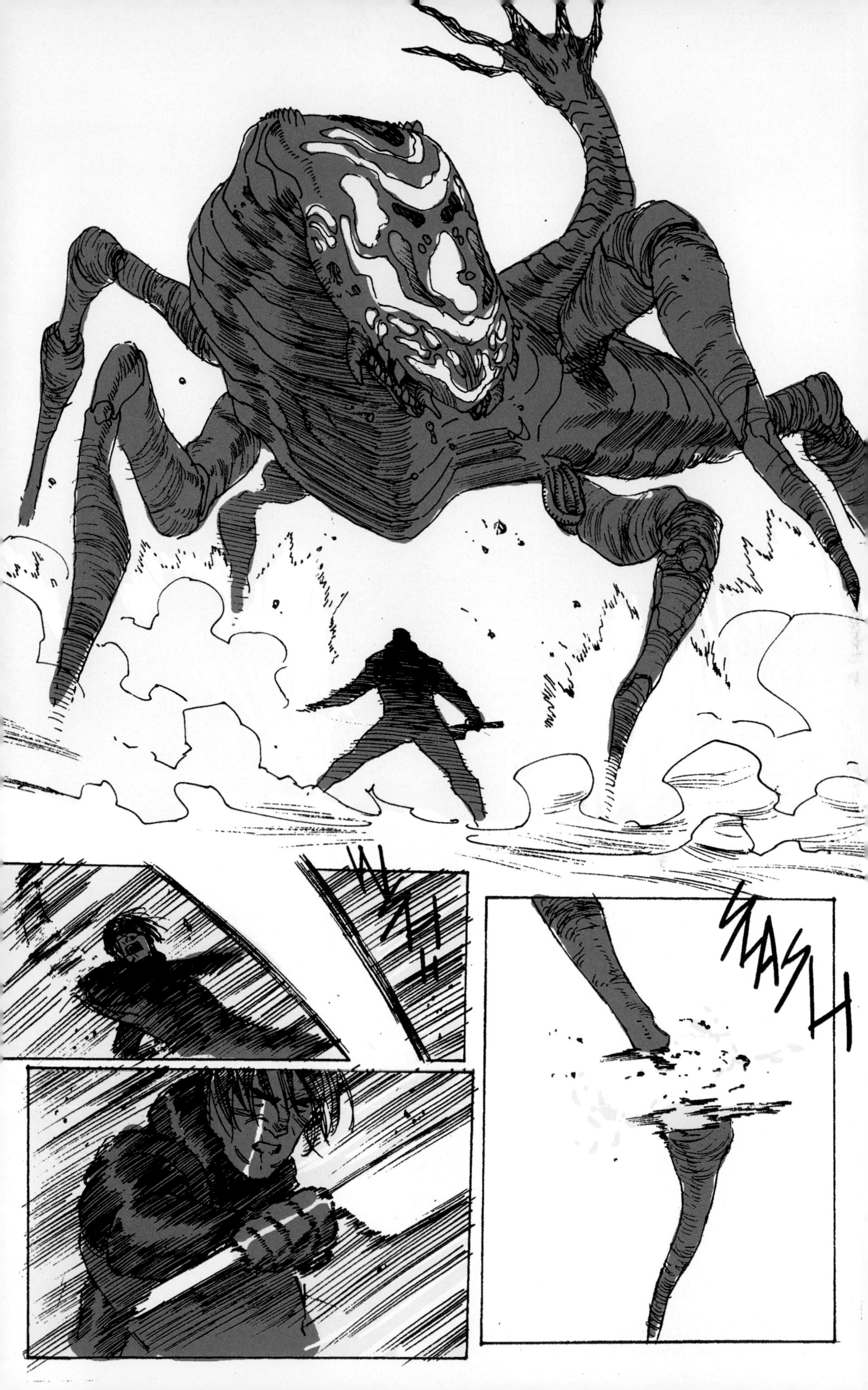
SLASH

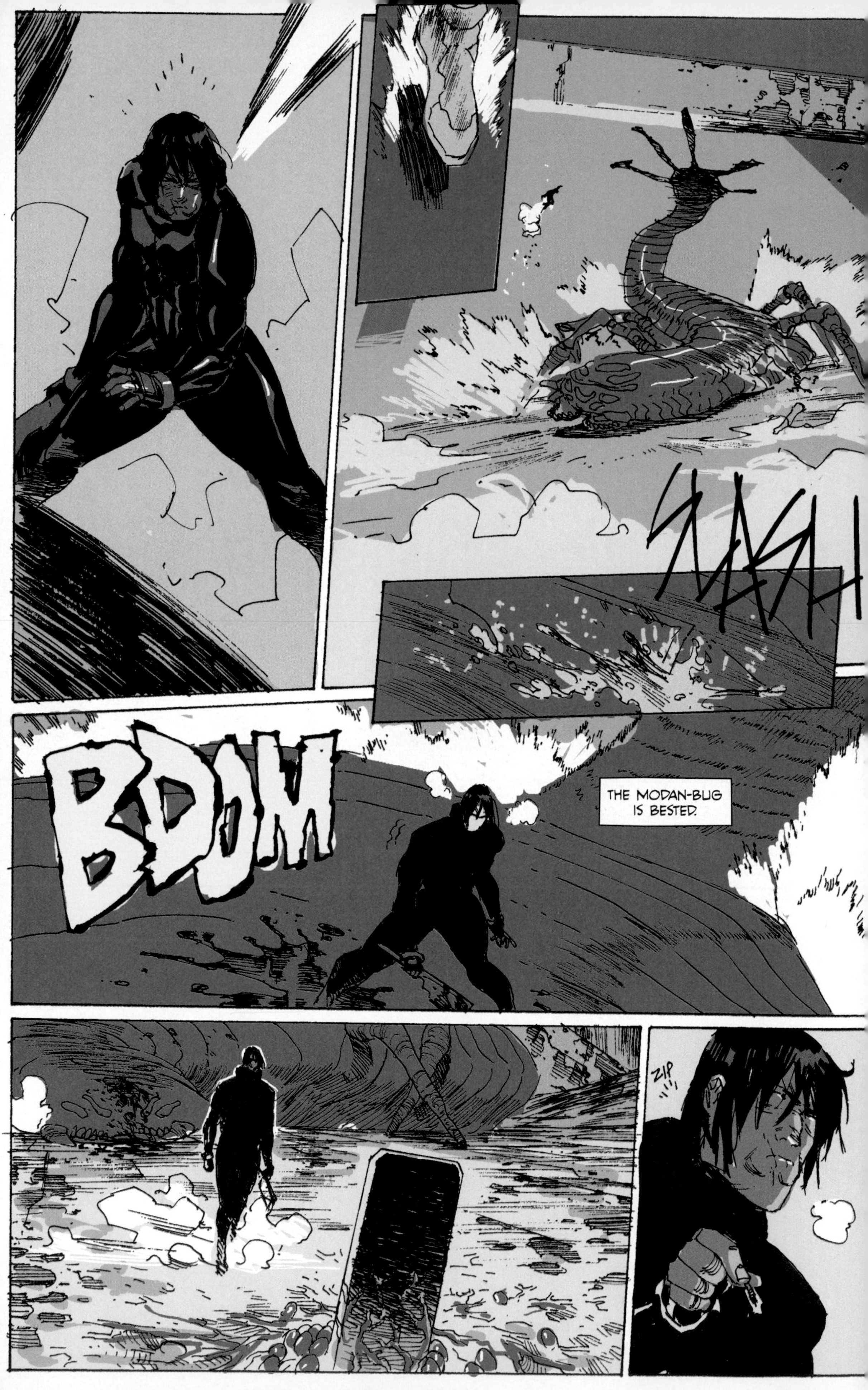
SMASH
BDOM
THE MODAN-BUG IS BESTED.
ZIP

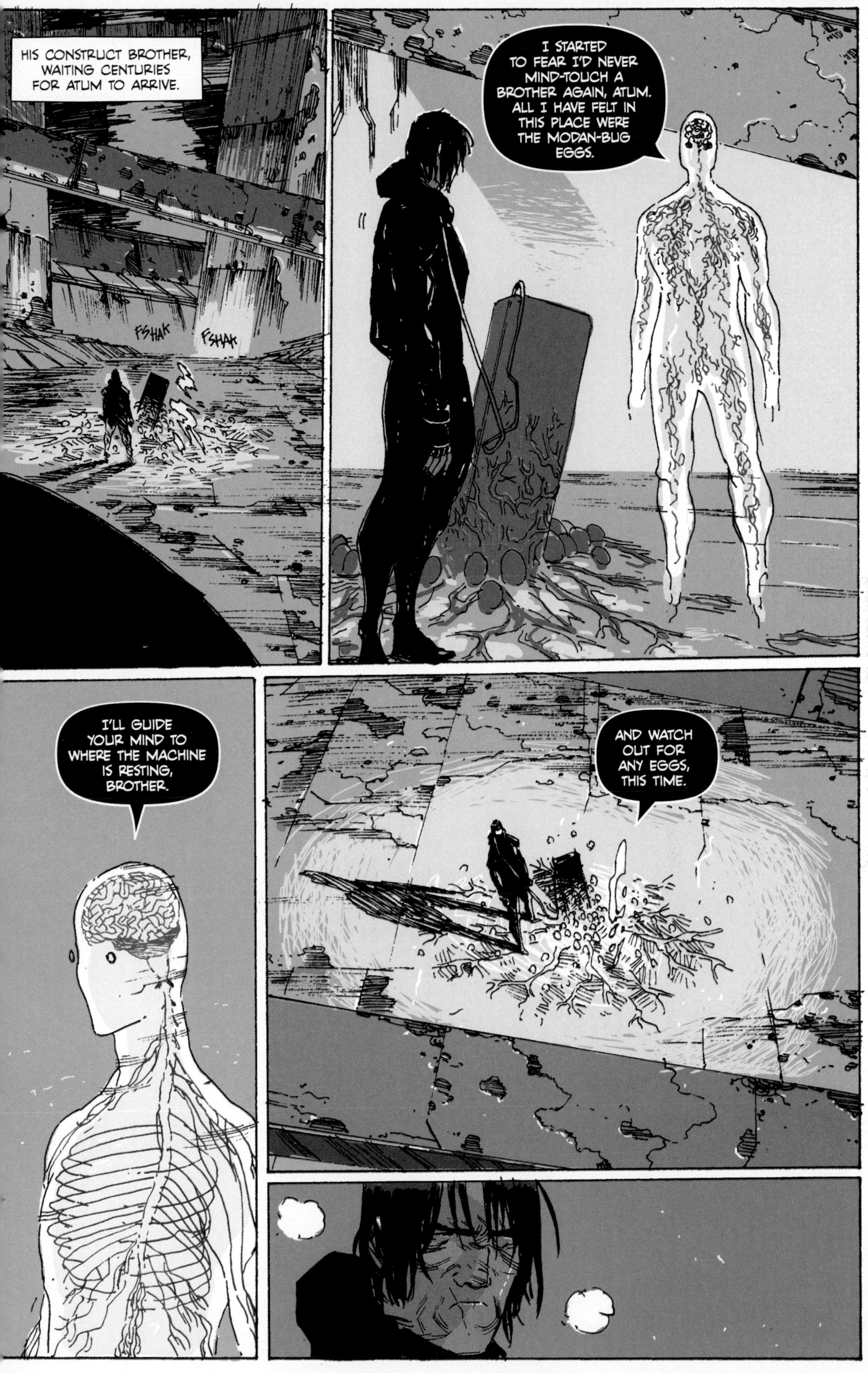
HIS CONSTRUCT BROTHER, WAITING CENTURIES FOR ATUM TO ARRIVE.
FSHAK
FSHAK
I STARTED TO FEAR I'D NEVER MIND-TOUCH A BROTHER AGAIN, ATUM. ALL I HAVE FELT IN THIS PLACE WERE THE MODAN-BUG EGGS.
I'LL GUIDE YOUR MIND TO WHERE THE MACHINE IS RESTING, BROTHER.
AND WATCH OUT FOR ANY EGGS, THIS TIME.

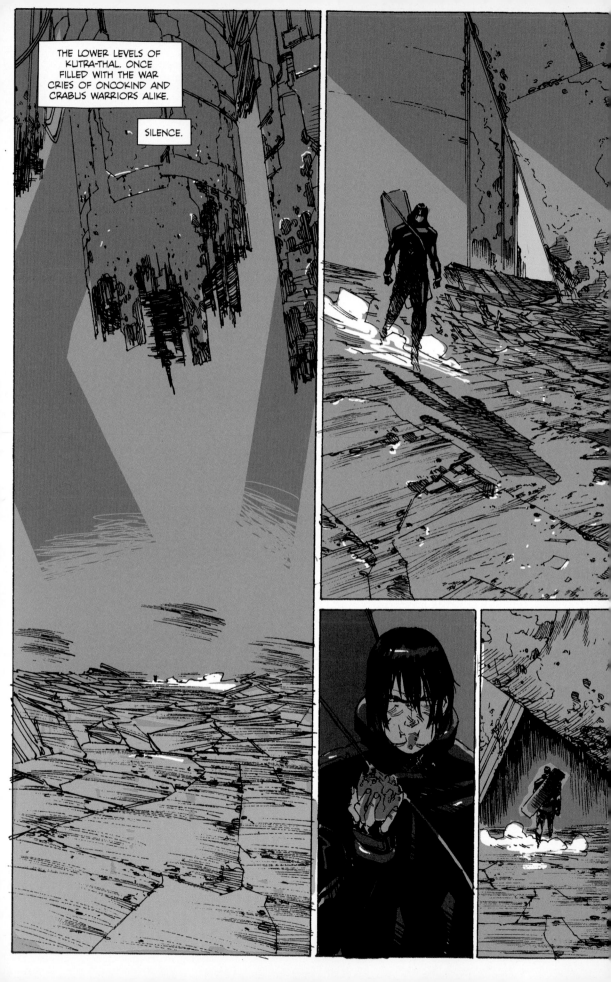

THE LOWER LEVELS OF
KUTRA-THAL. ONCE
FILLED WITH THE WAR
CRIES OF ONCOKIND AND
CRABUS WARRIORS ALIKE.

SILENCE.

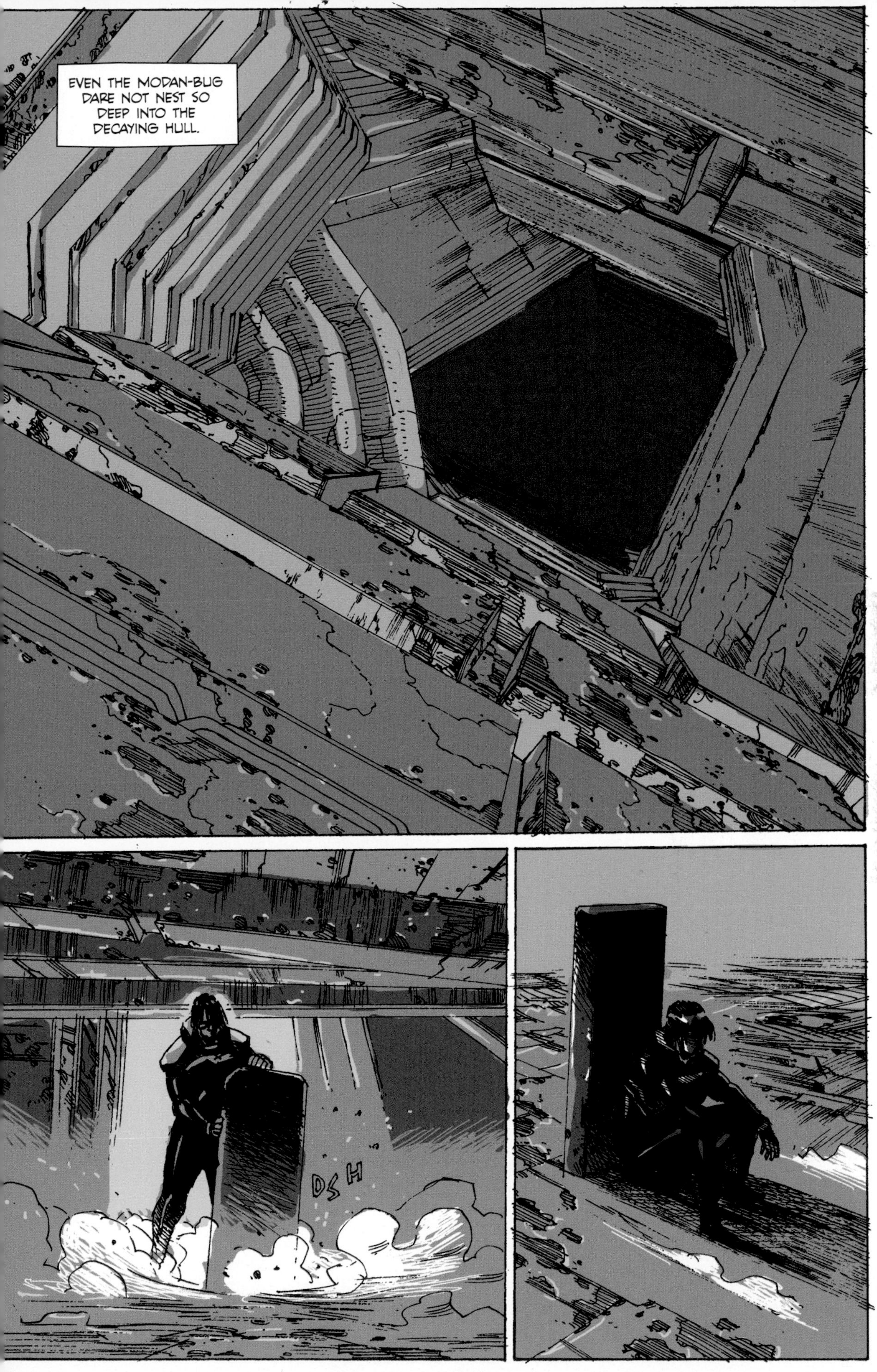
EVEN THE MODAN-BUG DARE NOT NEST SO DEEP INTO THE DECAYING HULL.
DSH

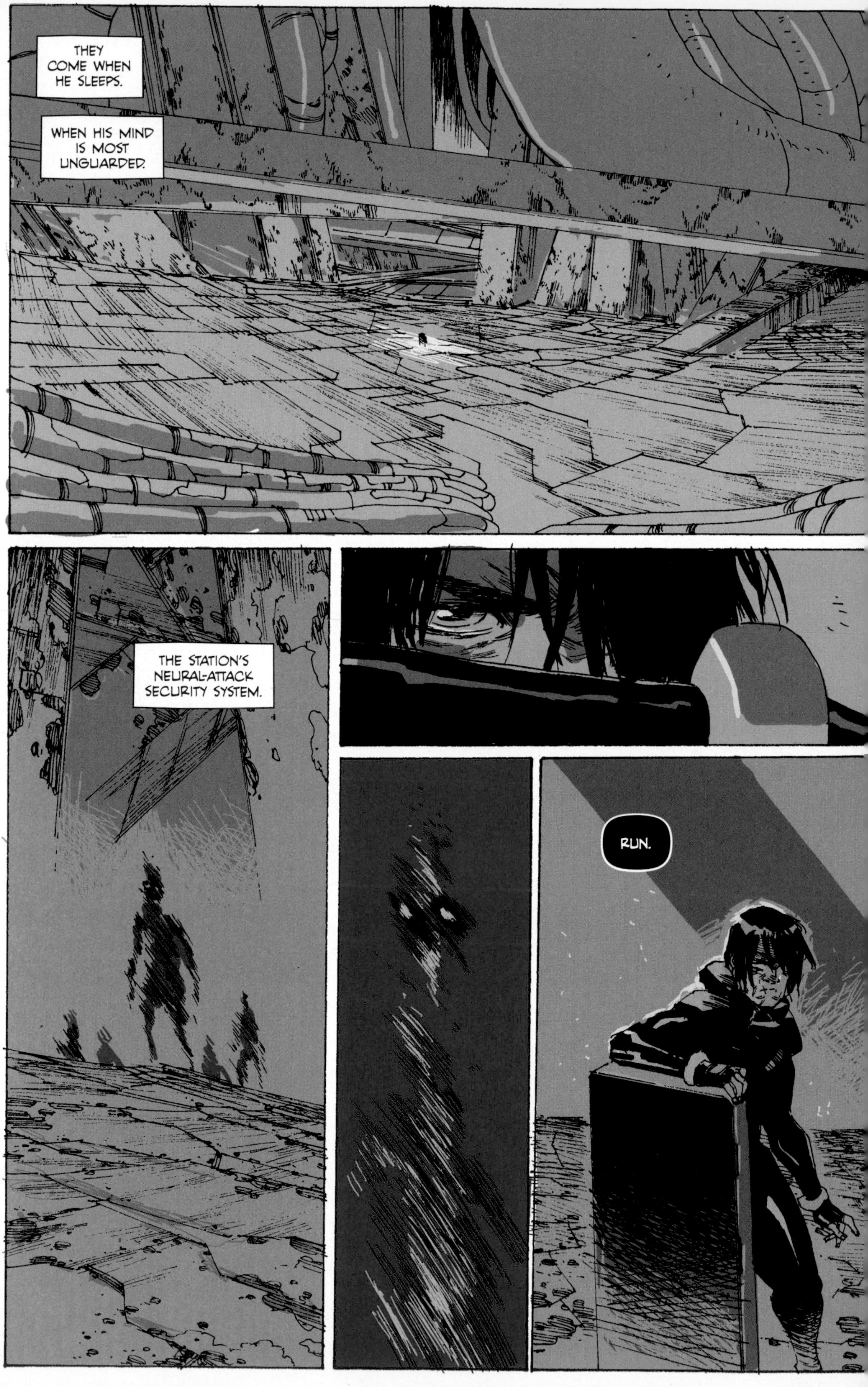
THEY COME WHEN HE SLEEPS.
WHEN HIS MIND IS MOST UNGUARDED.
THE STATION'S NEURAL-ATTACK SECURITY SYSTEM.
RUN.

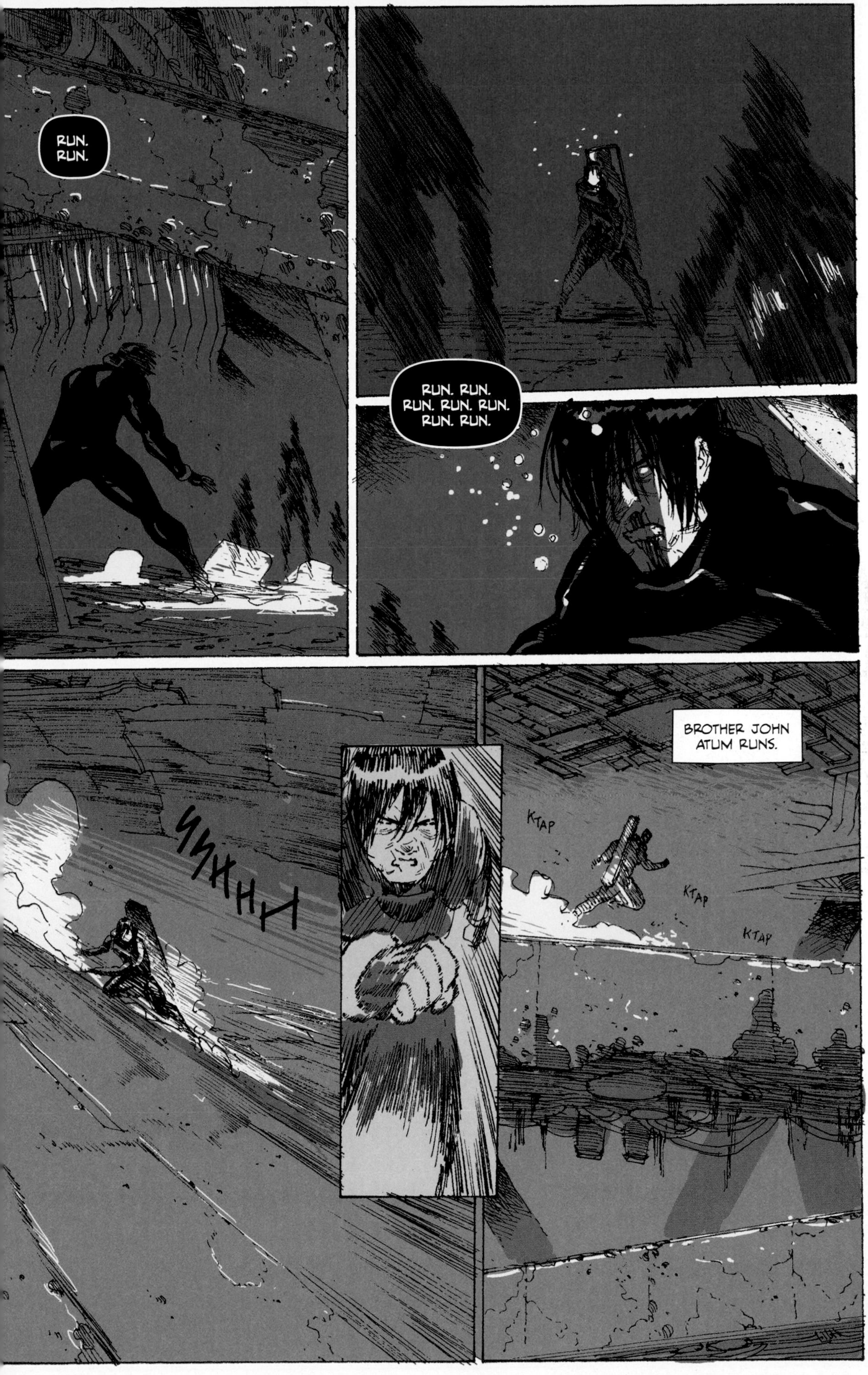
RUN.
RUN.
RUN. RUN.
RUN. RUN. RUN.
RUN. RUN.
BROTHER JOHN
ATUM RUNS.
SSHHH
KTAP
KTAP
KTAP

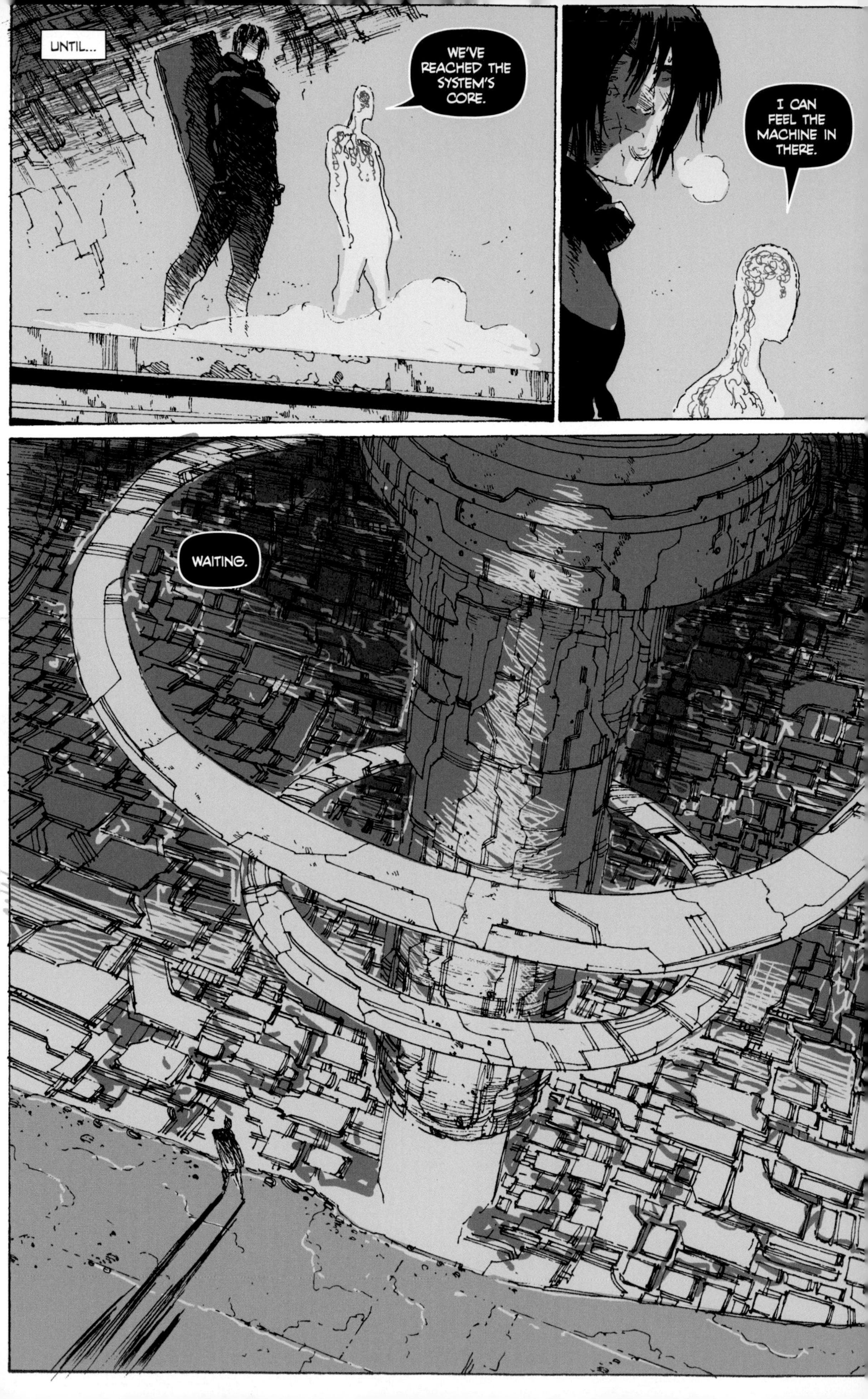
UNTIL...
WE'VE REACHED THE SYSTEM'S CORE.
I CAN FEEL THE MACHINE IN THERE.
WAITING.

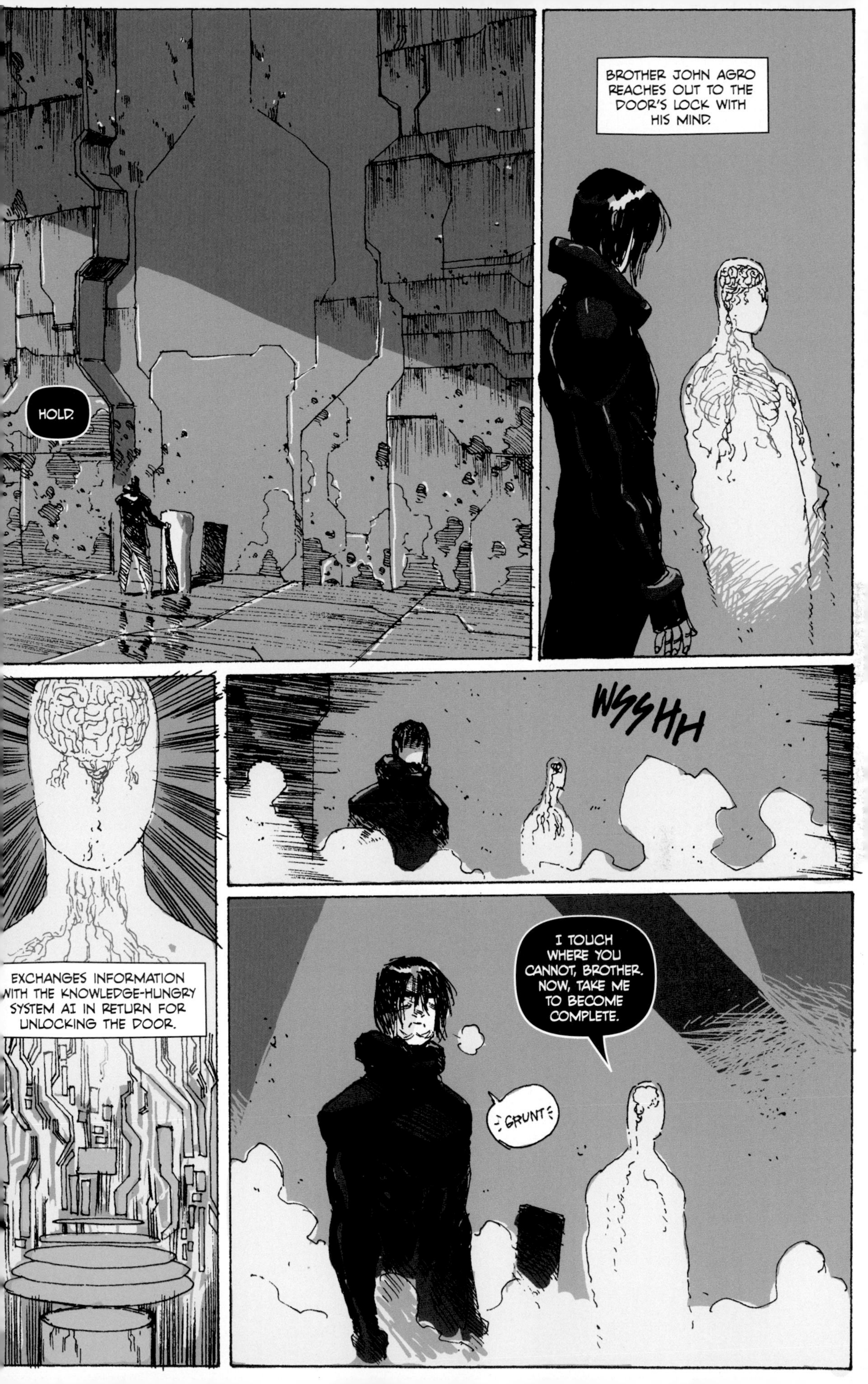
HOLD.
BROTHER JOHN AGRO REACHES OUT TO THE DOOR'S LOCK WITH HIS MIND.
EXCHANGES INFORMATION WITH THE KNOWLEDGE-HUNGRY SYSTEM AI IN RETURN FOR UNLOCKING THE DOOR.
WSSHH
I TOUCH WHERE YOU CANNOT, BROTHER. NOW, TAKE ME TO BECOME COMPLETE.
GRUNT

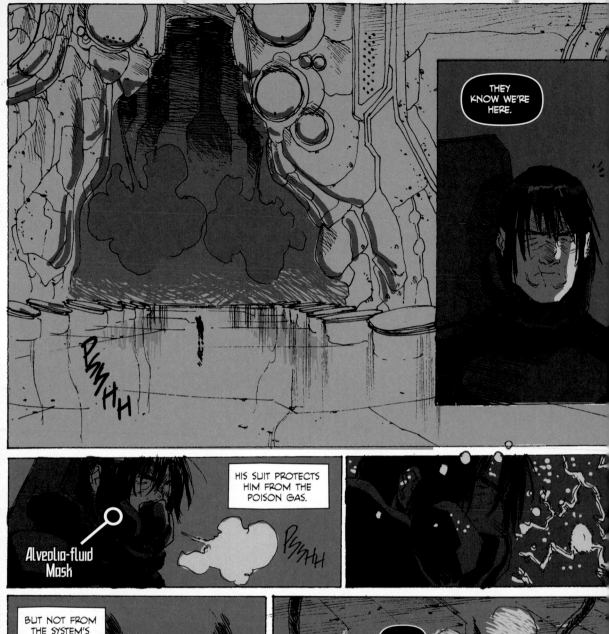

THEY KNOW WE'RE HERE.

HIS SUIT PROTECTS HIM FROM THE POISON GAS.

Alveolia-fluid Mask

BUT NOT FROM THE SYSTEM'S MIND ATTACK.

THERE.

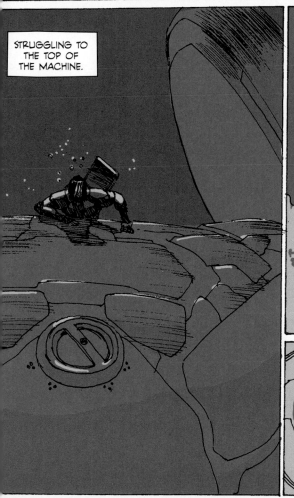

STRUGGLING TO
THE TOP OF
THE MACHINE.

CAREFUL.

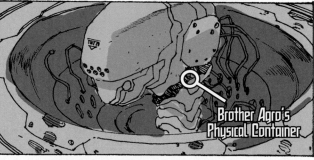

Brother Agro's
Physical Container

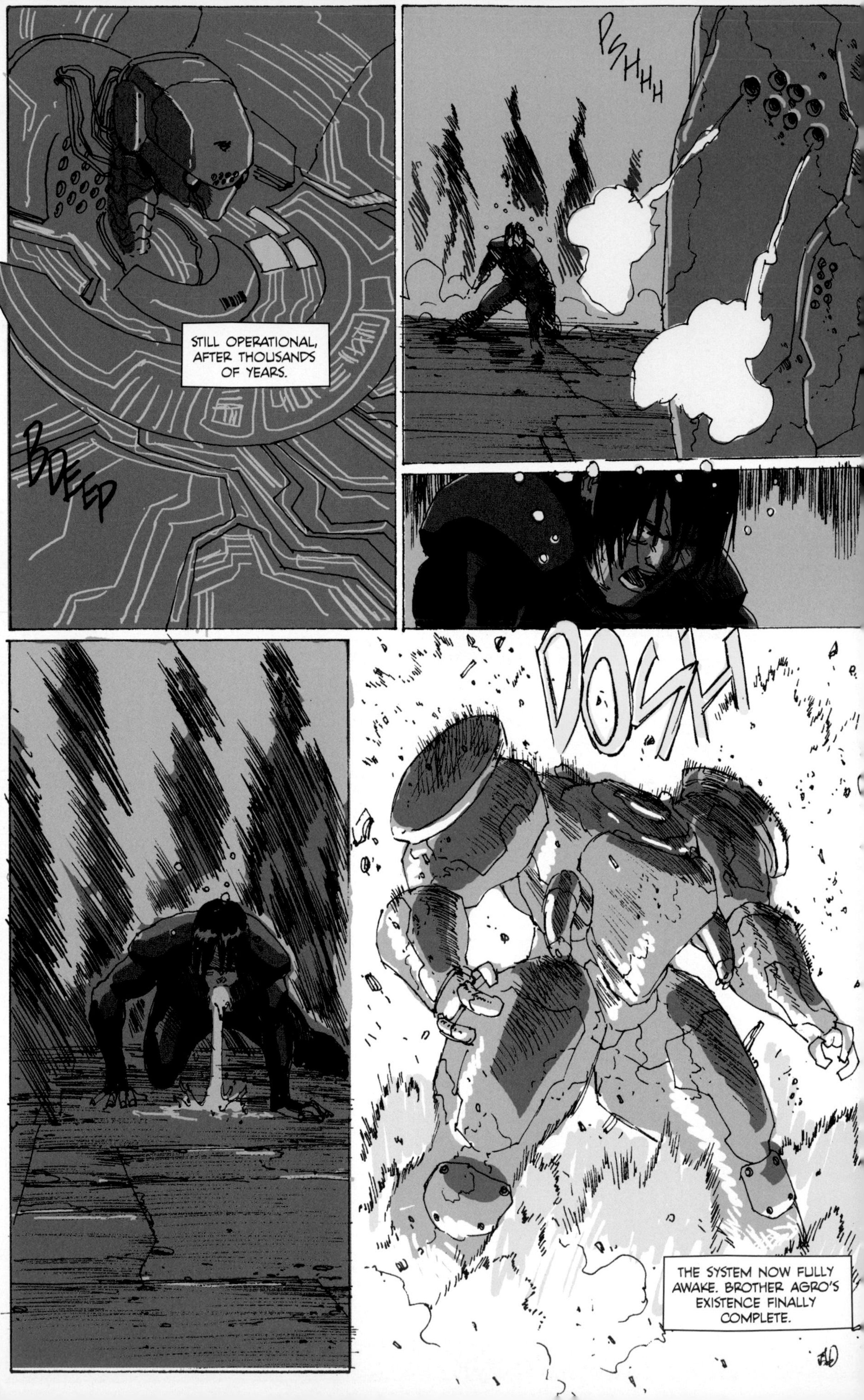
STILL OPERATIONAL, AFTER THOUSANDS OF YEARS.
BDEEP
PSHHH
DOSH
THE SYSTEM NOW FULLY AWAKE. BROTHER AGRO'S EXISTENCE FINALLY COMPLETE.

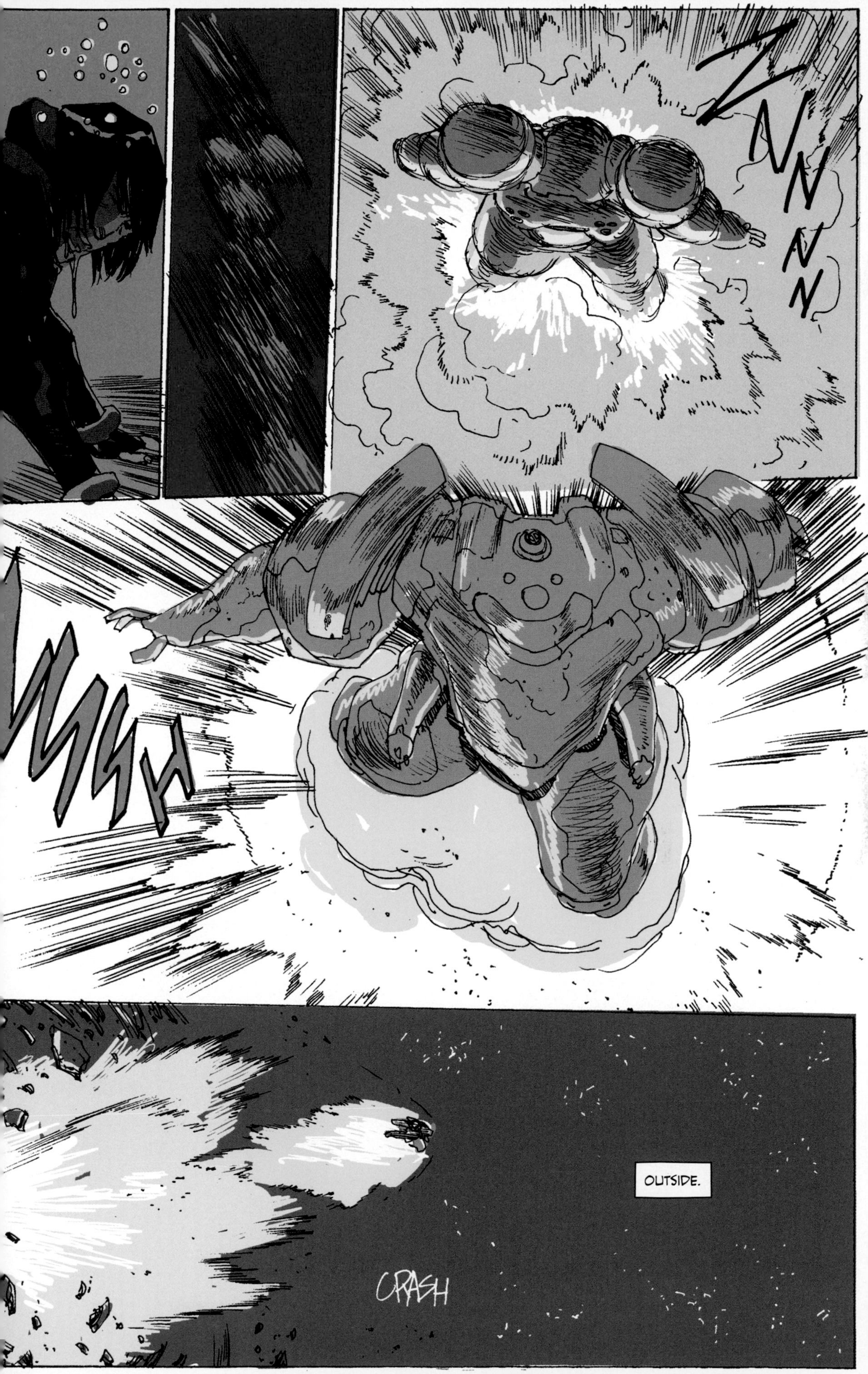

ZZNNNNN
WHSH
OUTSIDE.
CRASH

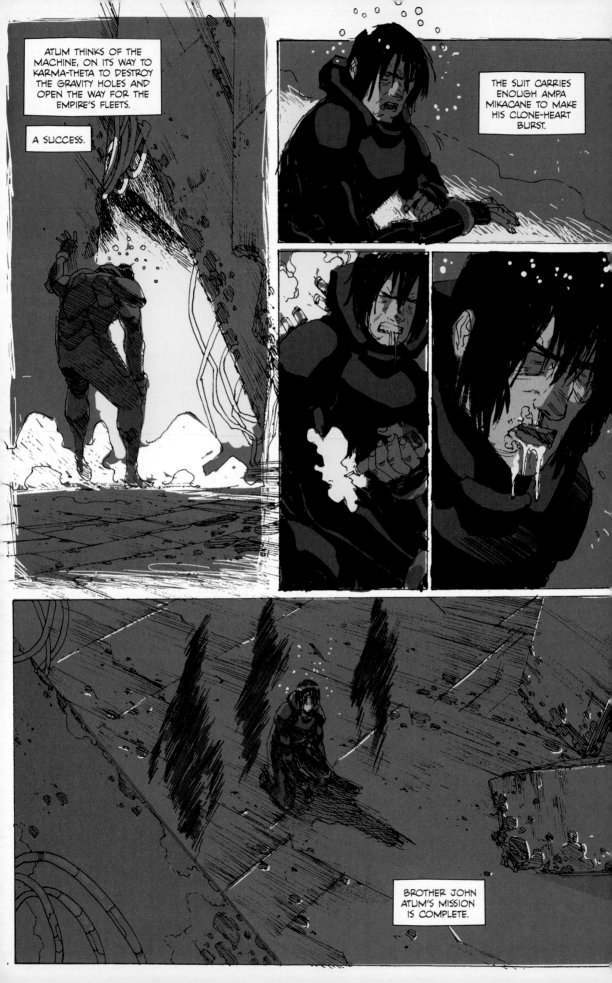

ATUM THINKS OF THE MACHINE, ON ITS WAY TO KARMA-THETA TO DESTROY THE GRAVITY HOLES AND OPEN THE WAY FOR THE EMPIRE'S FLEETS.

A SUCCESS.

THE SUIT CARRIES ENOUGH AMPA MIKACANE TO MAKE HIS CLONE-HEART BURST.

BROTHER JOHN ATUM'S MISSION IS COMPLETE.

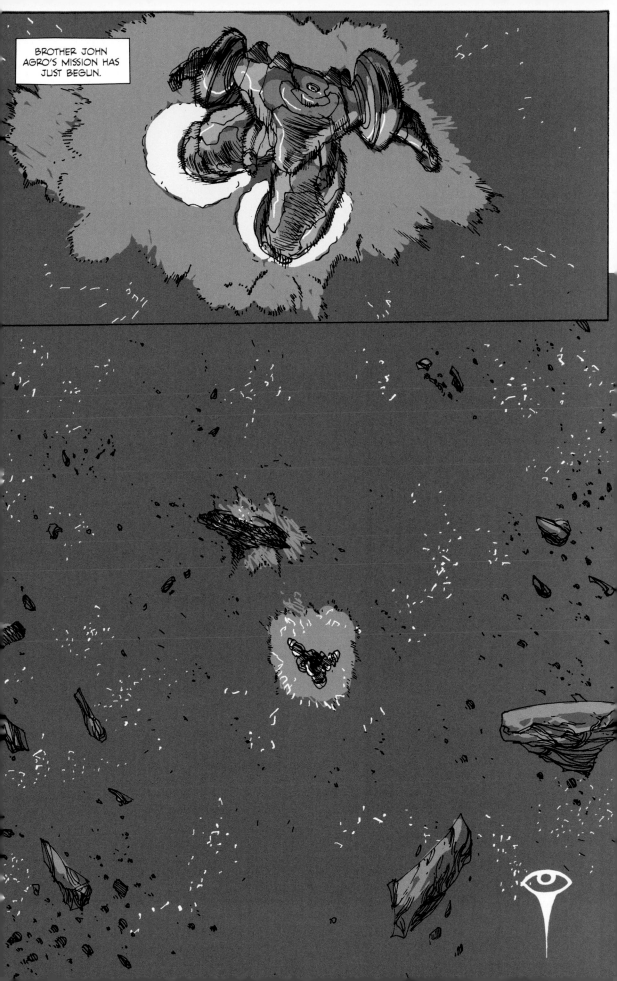

BROTHER JOHN AGRO'S MISSION HAS JUST BEGUN.

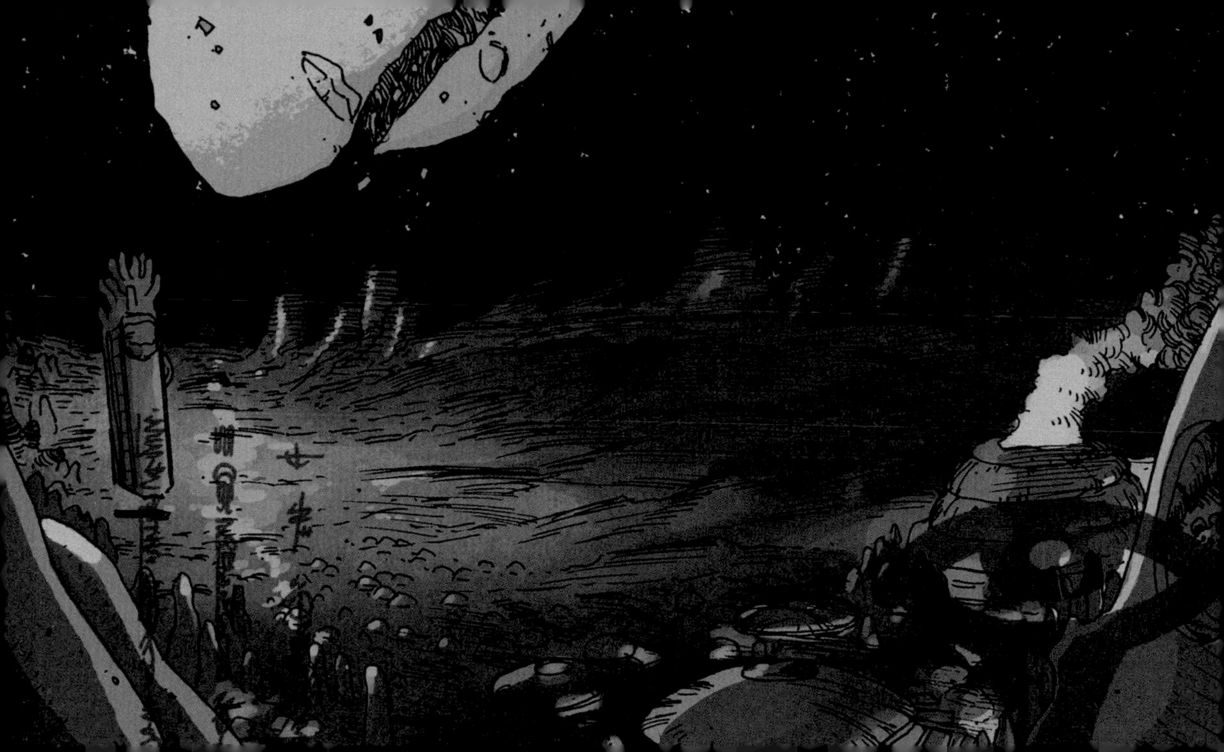

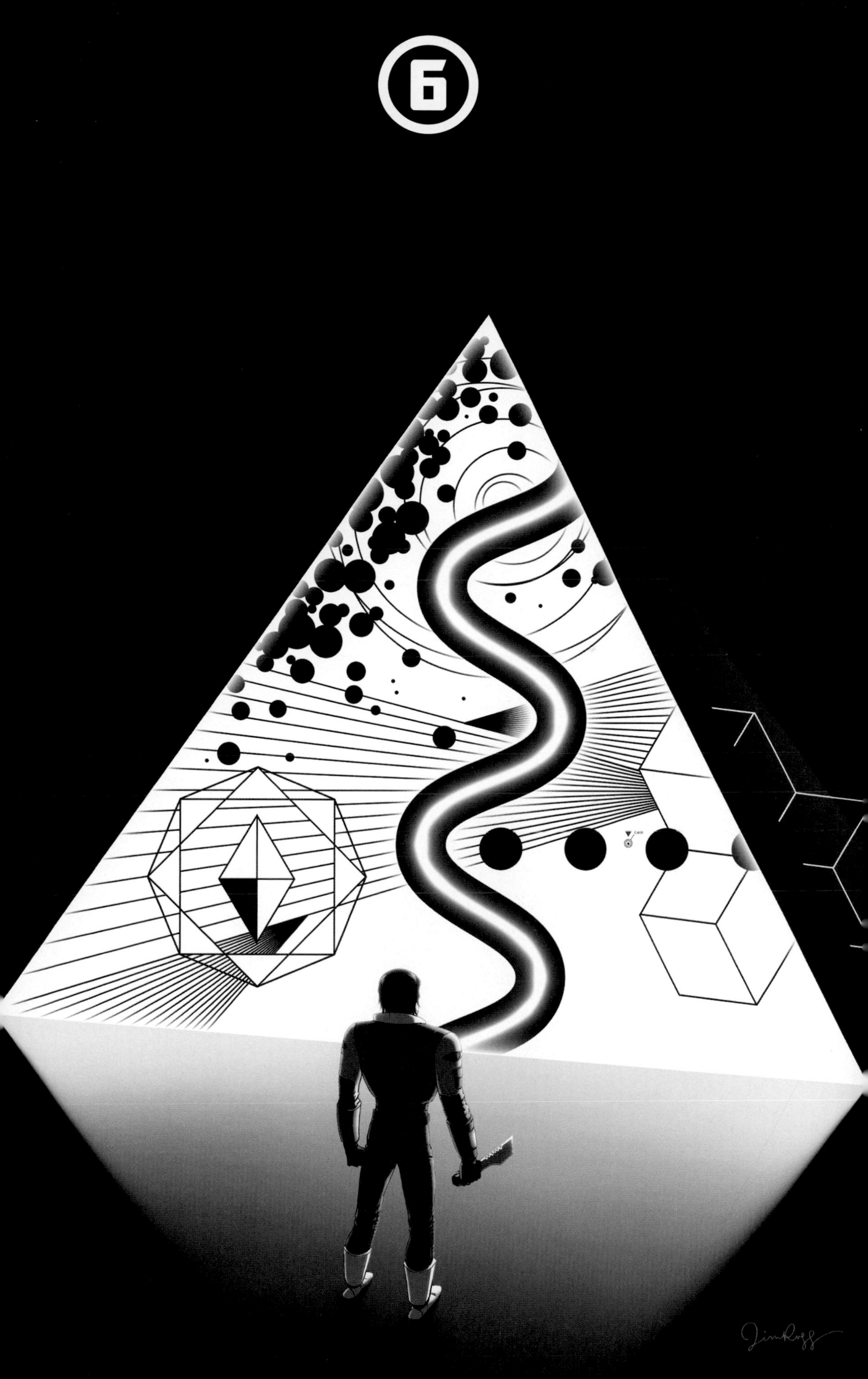
6

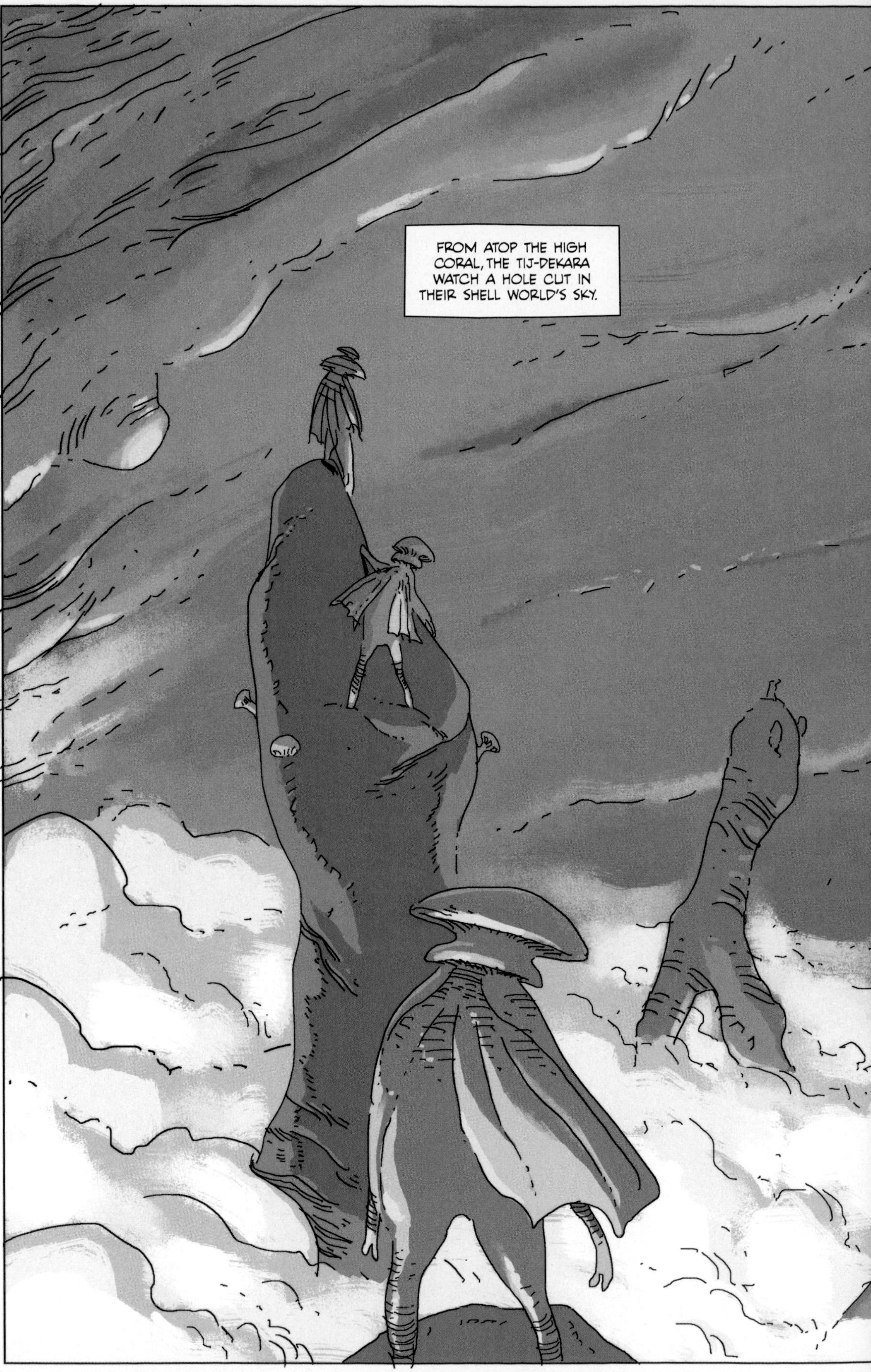
FROM ATOP THE HIGH CORAL, THE TIJ-DEKARA WATCH A HOLE CUT IN THEIR SHELL WORLD'S SKY.

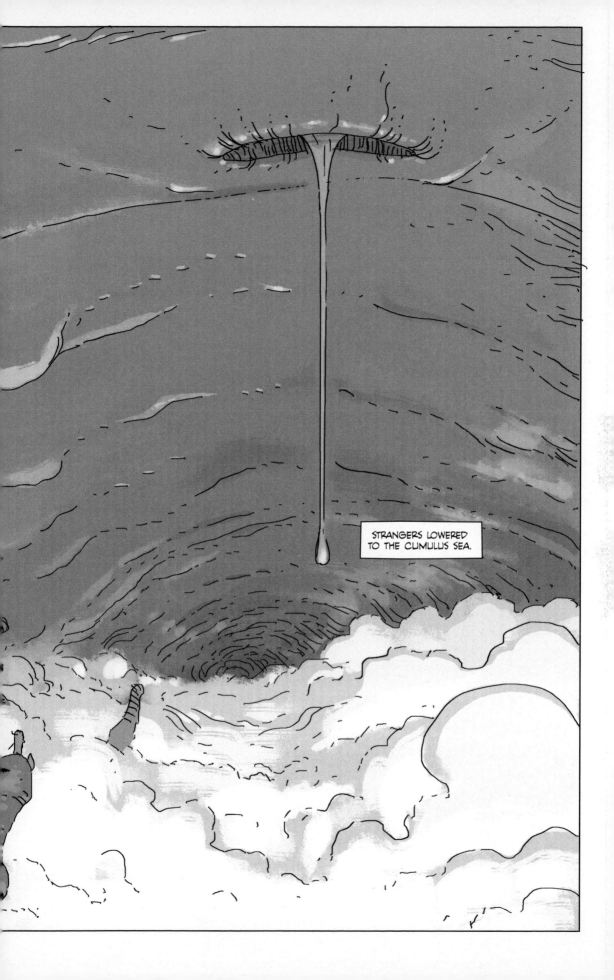

STRANGERS LOWERED
TO THE CUMULUS SEA.

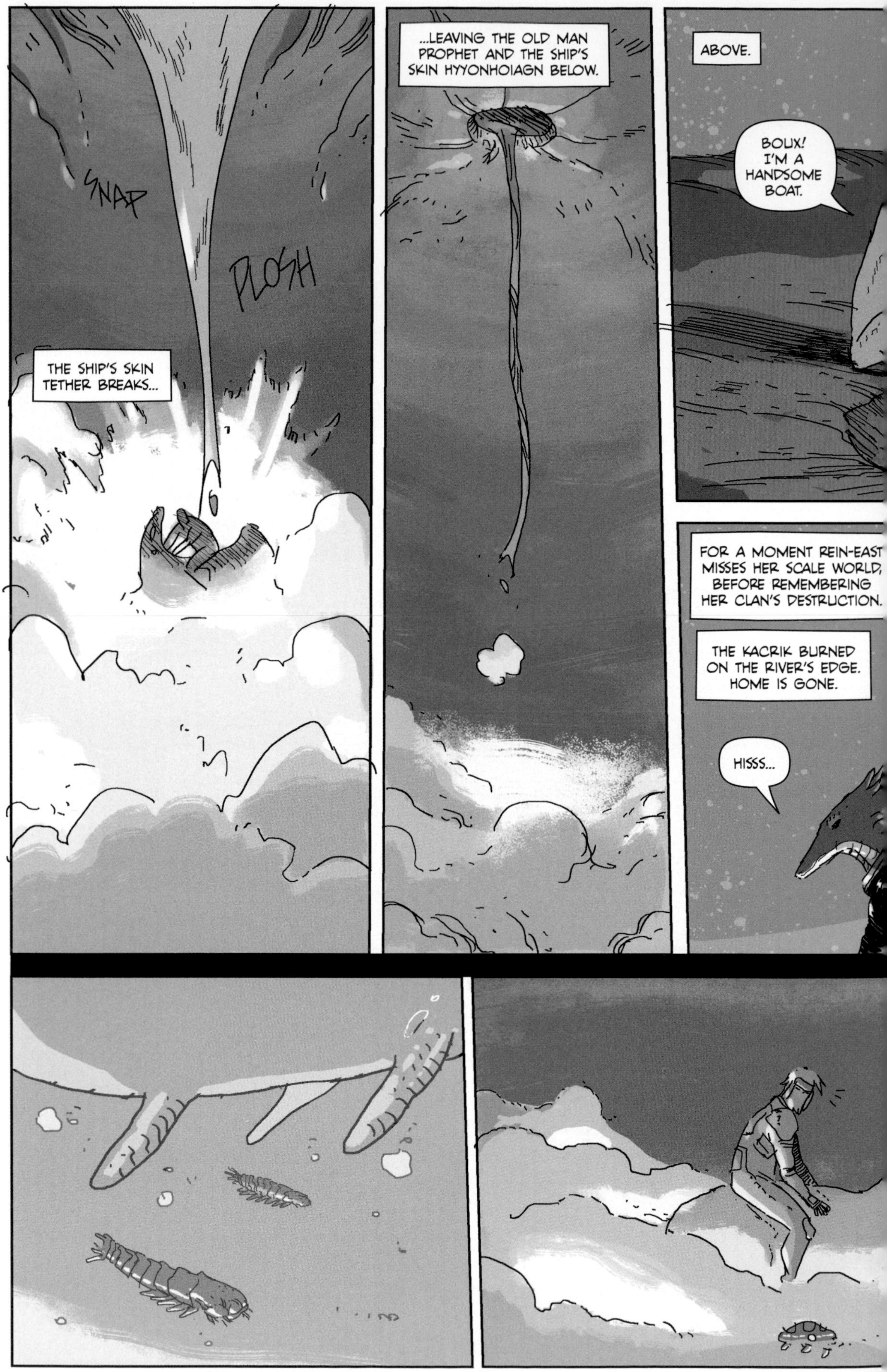
SNAP
PLOSH
THE SHIP'S SKIN TETHER BREAKS...
...LEAVING THE OLD MAN PROPHET AND THE SHIP'S SKIN HYYONHOIAGN BELOW.
ABOVE.
BOUX! I'M A HANDSOME BOAT.
FOR A MOMENT REIN-EAST MISSES HER SCALE WORLD, BEFORE REMEMBERING HER CLAN'S DESTRUCTION.
THE KACRIK BURNED ON THE RIVER'S EDGE. HOME IS GONE.
HISSS...

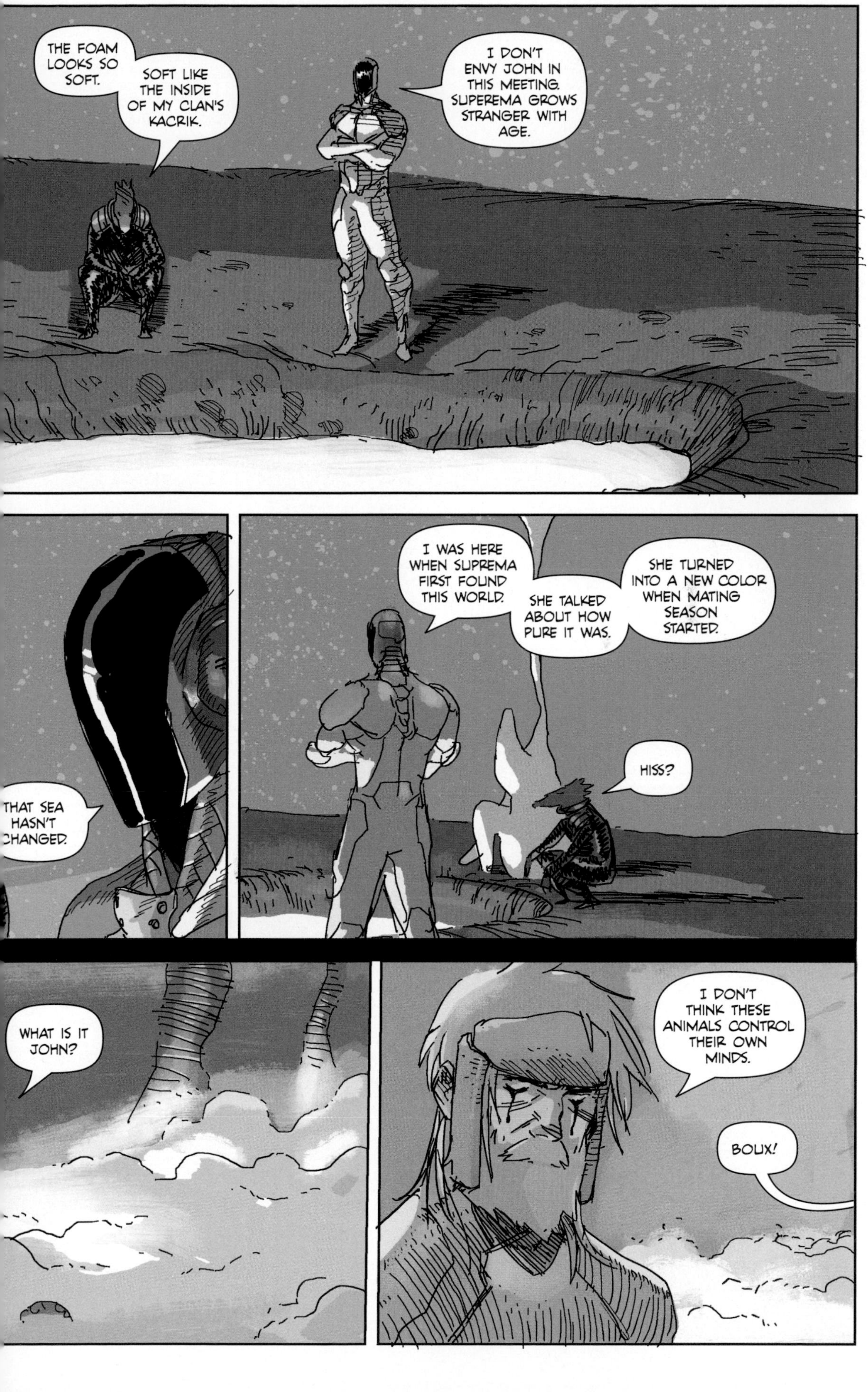
THE FOAM LOOKS SO SOFT.
SOFT LIKE THE INSIDE OF MY CLAN'S KACRIK.
I DON'T ENVY JOHN IN THIS MEETING. SUPEREMA GROWS STRANGER WITH AGE.
THAT SEA HASN'T CHANGED.
I WAS HERE WHEN SUPREMA FIRST FOUND THIS WORLD.
SHE TALKED ABOUT HOW PURE IT WAS.
SHE TURNED INTO A NEW COLOR WHEN MATING SEASON STARTED.
HISS?
WHAT IS IT JOHN?
I DON'T THINK THESE ANIMALS CONTROL THEIR OWN MINDS.
BOUX!

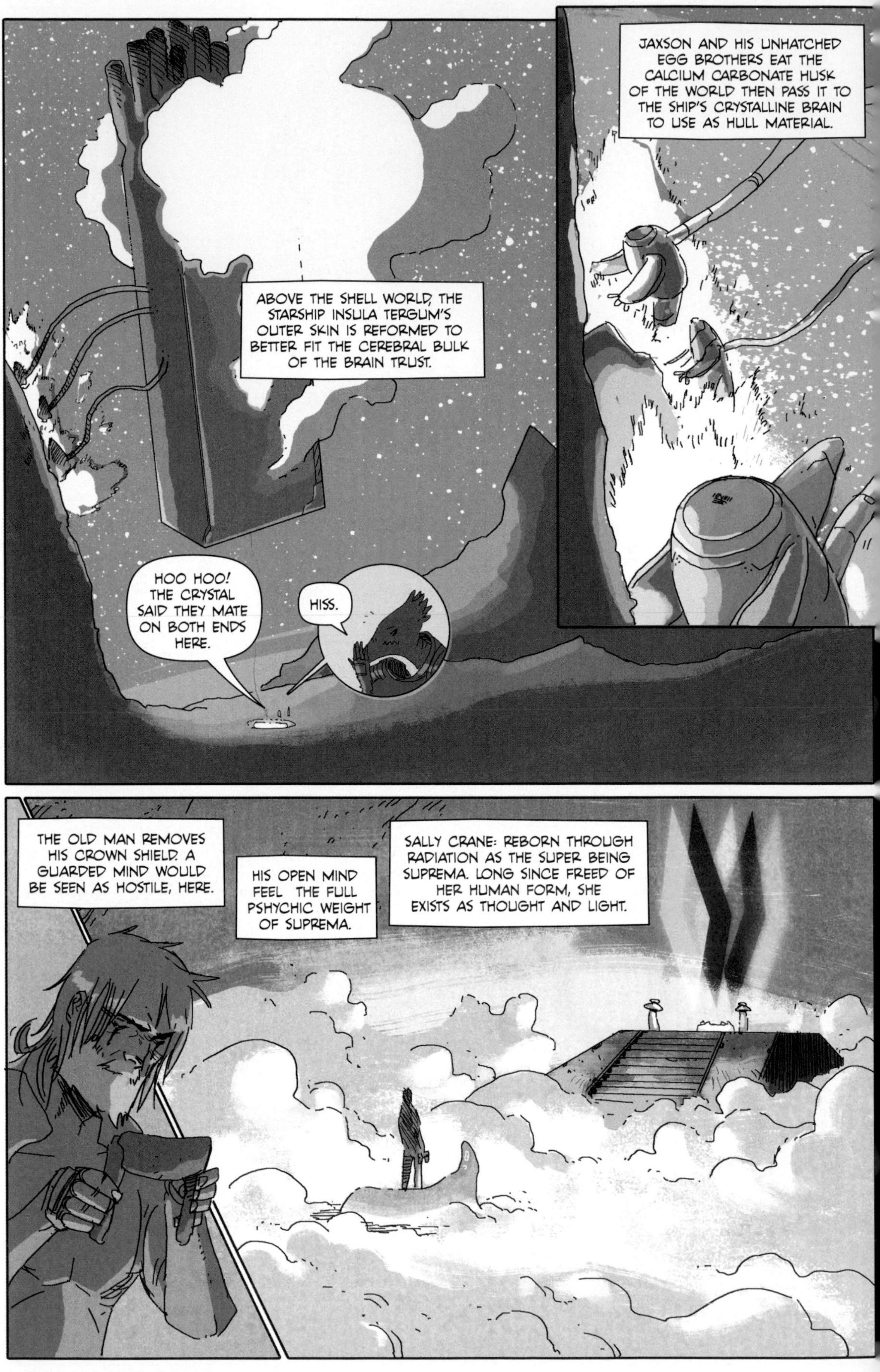
ABOVE THE SHELL WORLD, THE STARSHIP INSULA TERGUM'S OUTER SKIN IS REFORMED TO BETTER FIT THE CEREBRAL BULK OF THE BRAIN TRUST.
HOO HOO! THE CRYSTAL SAID THEY MATE ON BOTH ENDS HERE.
HISS.
JAXSON AND HIS UNHATCHED EGG BROTHERS EAT THE CALCIUM CARBONATE HUSK OF THE WORLD THEN PASS IT TO THE SHIP'S CRYSTALLINE BRAIN TO USE AS HULL MATERIAL.
THE OLD MAN REMOVES HIS CROWN SHIELD. A GUARDED MIND WOULD BE SEEN AS HOSTILE, HERE.
HIS OPEN MIND FEEL THE FULL PSHYCHIC WEIGHT OF SUPREMA.
SALLY CRANE: REBORN THROUGH RADIATION AS THE SUPER BEING SUPREMA. LONG SINCE FREED OF HER HUMAN FORM, SHE EXISTS AS THOUGHT AND LIGHT.

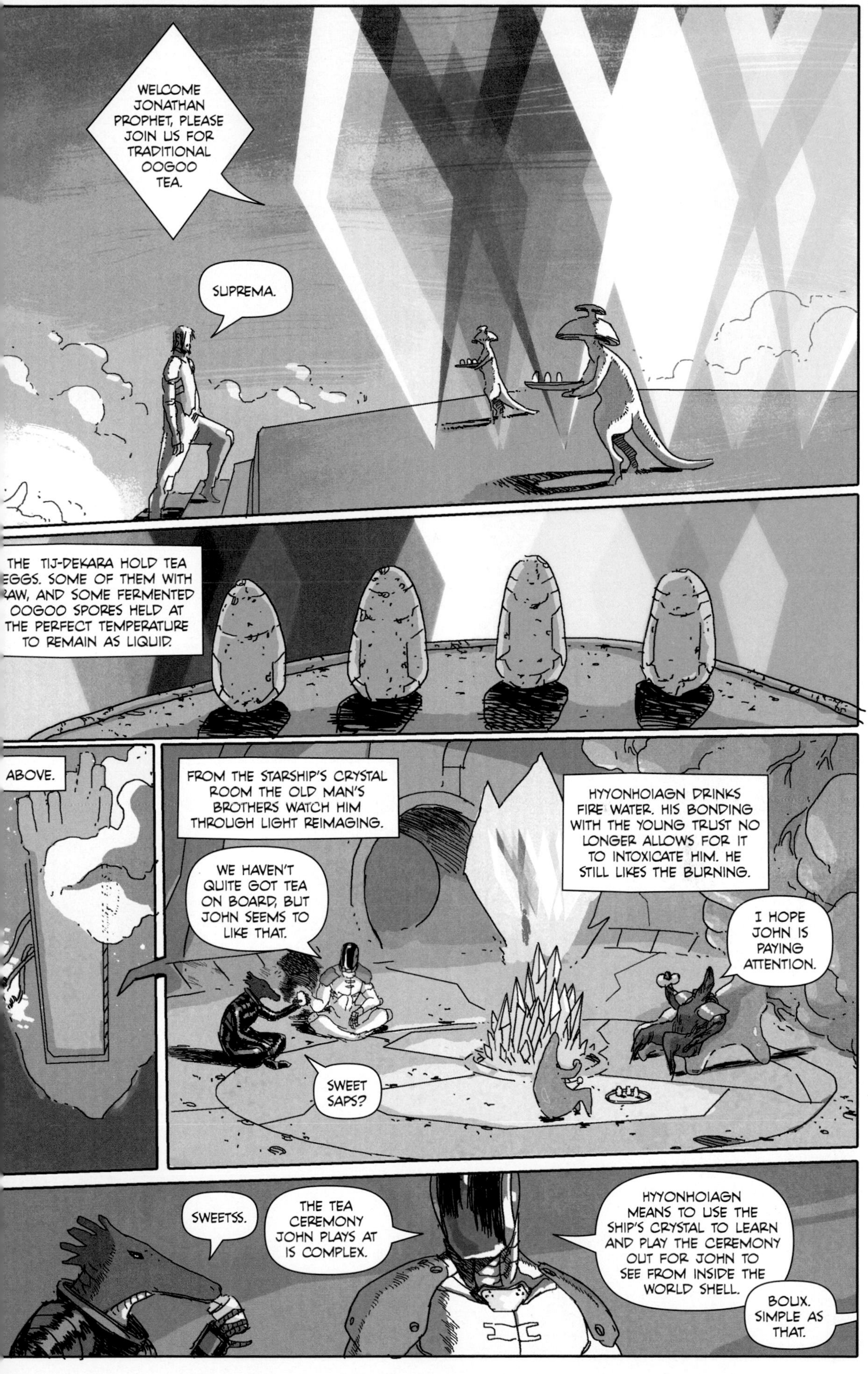
WELCOME JONATHAN PROPHET, PLEASE JOIN US FOR TRADITIONAL OOGOO TEA.
SUPREMA.
THE TIJ-DEKARA HOLD TEA EGGS. SOME OF THEM WITH RAW, AND SOME FERMENTED OOGOO SPORES HELD AT THE PERFECT TEMPERATURE TO REMAIN AS LIQUID.
ABOVE.
FROM THE STARSHIP'S CRYSTAL ROOM THE OLD MAN'S BROTHERS WATCH HIM THROUGH LIGHT REIMAGING.
HYYONHOIAGN DRINKS FIRE WATER. HIS BONDING WITH THE YOUNG TRUST NO LONGER ALLOWS FOR IT TO INTOXICATE HIM. HE STILL LIKES THE BURNING.
WE HAVEN'T QUITE GOT TEA ON BOARD, BUT JOHN SEEMS TO LIKE THAT.
I HOPE JOHN IS PAYING ATTENTION.
SWEET SAPS?
SWEETSS.
THE TEA CEREMONY JOHN PLAYS AT IS COMPLEX.
HYYONHOIAGN MEANS TO USE THE SHIP'S CRYSTAL TO LEARN AND PLAY THE CEREMONY OUT FOR JOHN TO SEE FROM INSIDE THE WORLD SHELL.
BOUX. SIMPLE AS THAT.

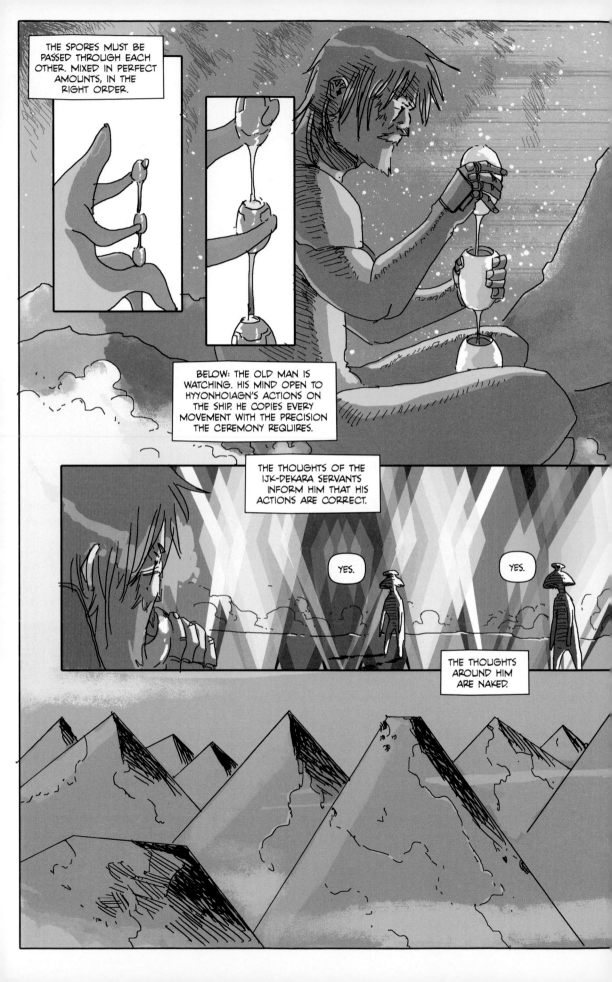

THE SPORES MUST BE PASSED THROUGH EACH OTHER. MIXED IN PERFECT AMOUNTS, IN THE RIGHT ORDER.

BELOW: THE OLD MAN IS WATCHING. HIS MIND OPEN TO HYYONHOIAGN'S ACTIONS ON THE SHIP. HE COPIES EVERY MOVEMENT WITH THE PRECISION THE CEREMONY REQUIRES.

THE THOUGHTS OF THE IJK-DEKARA SERVANTS INFORM HIM THAT HIS ACTIONS ARE CORRECT.

YES.

YES.

THE THOUGHTS AROUND HIM ARE NAKED.

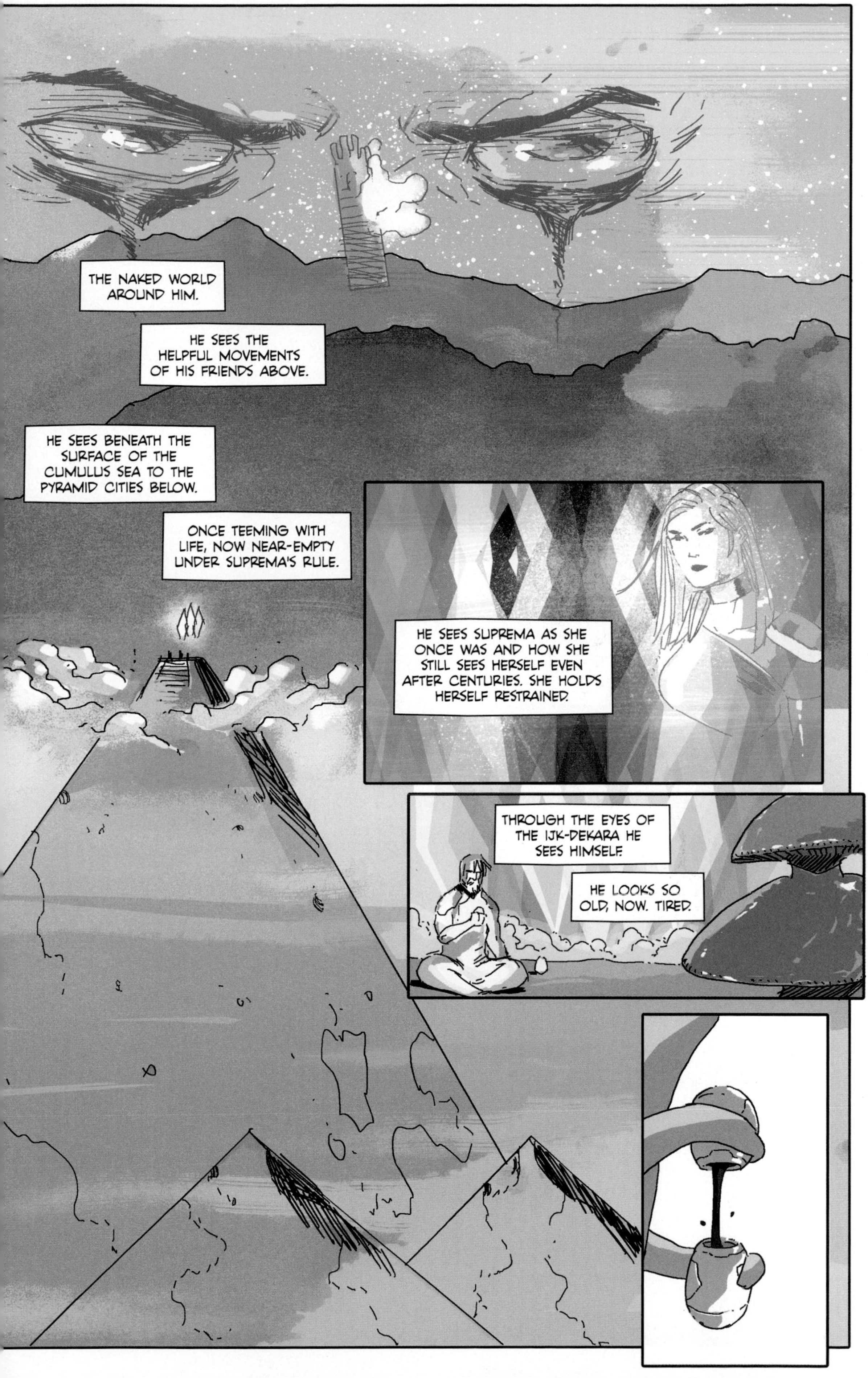

THE NAKED WORLD AROUND HIM.
HE SEES THE HELPFUL MOVEMENTS OF HIS FRIENDS ABOVE.
HE SEES BENEATH THE SURFACE OF THE CUMULUS SEA TO THE PYRAMID CITIES BELOW.
ONCE TEEMING WITH LIFE, NOW NEAR-EMPTY UNDER SUPREMA'S RULE.
HE SEES SUPREMA AS SHE ONCE WAS AND HOW SHE STILL SEES HERSELF EVEN AFTER CENTURIES. SHE HOLDS HERSELF RESTRAINED.
THROUGH THE EYES OF THE IJK-DEKARA HE SEES HIMSELF.
HE LOOKS SO OLD, NOW. TIRED.

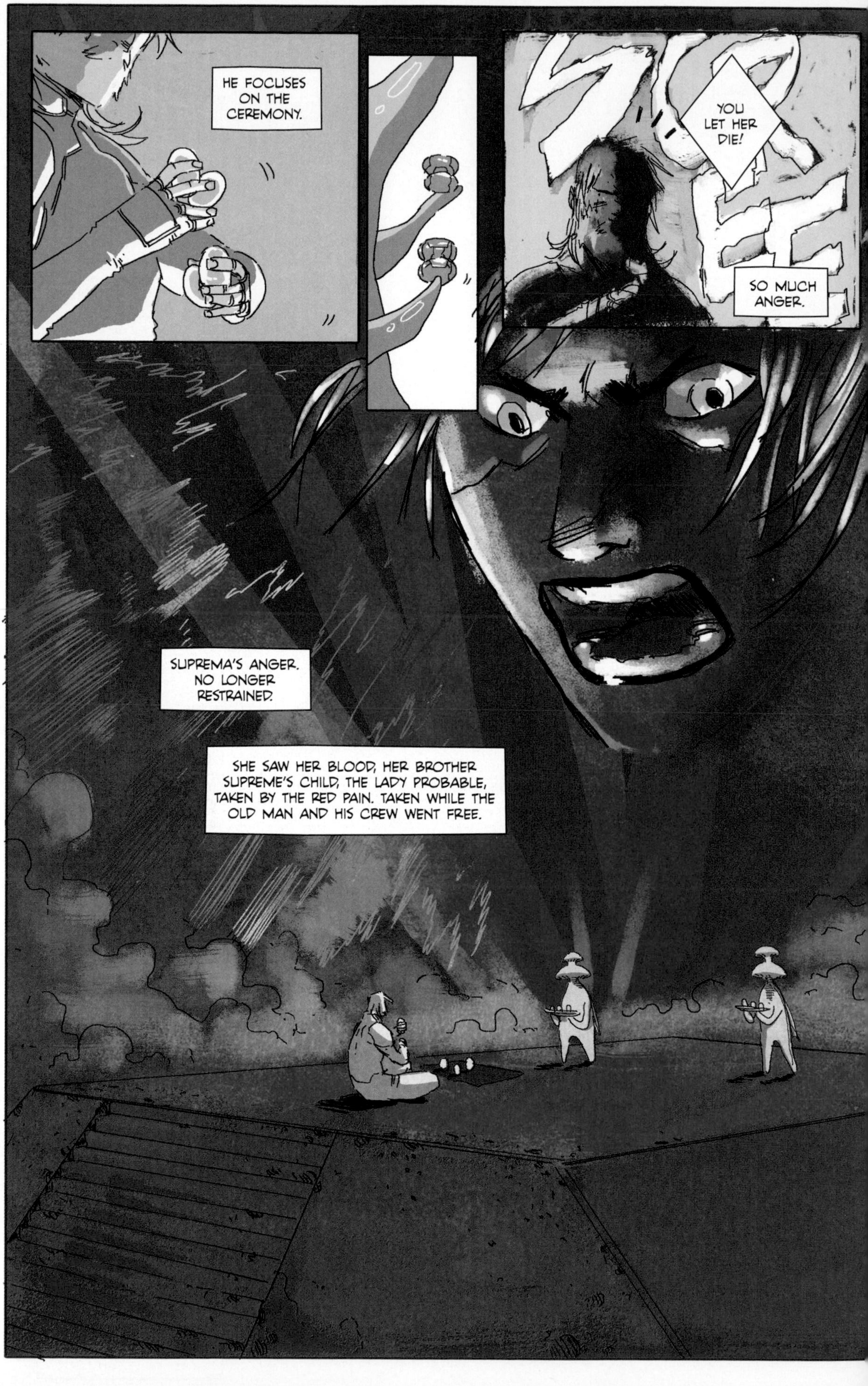
HE FOCUSES ON THE CEREMONY.
YOU LET HER DIE!
SO MUCH ANGER.
SUPREMA'S ANGER. NO LONGER RESTRAINED.
SHE SAW HER BLOOD, HER BROTHER SUPREME'S CHILD, THE LADY PROBABLE, TAKEN BY THE RED PAIN. TAKEN WHILE THE OLD MAN AND HIS CREW WENT FREE.

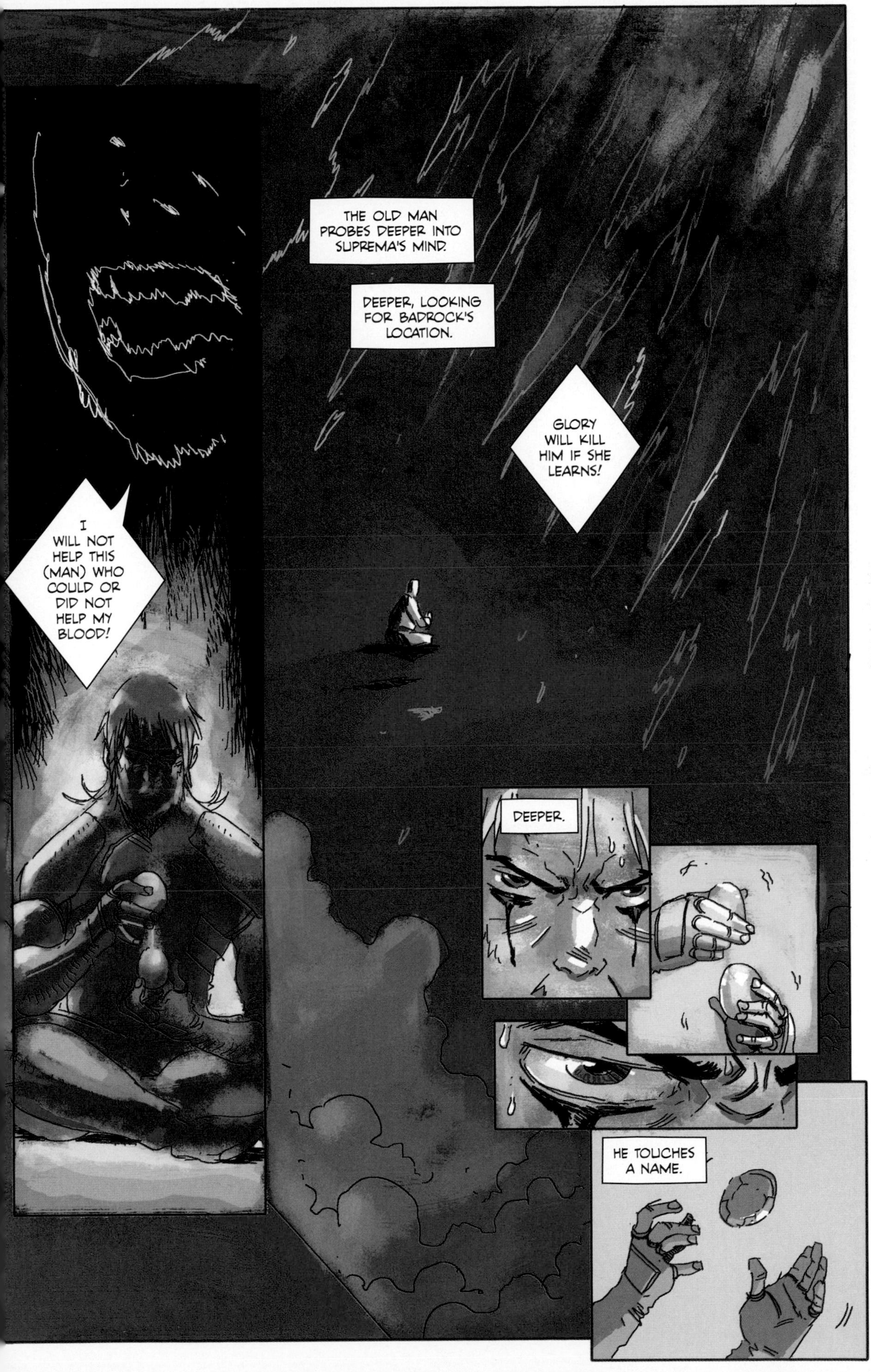
THE OLD MAN PROBES DEEPER INTO SUPREMA'S MIND.
DEEPER, LOOKING FOR BADROCK'S LOCATION.
GLORY WILL KILL HIM IF SHE LEARNS!
I WILL NOT HELP THIS (MAN) WHO COULD OR DID NOT HELP MY BLOOD!
DEEPER.
HE TOUCHES A NAME.

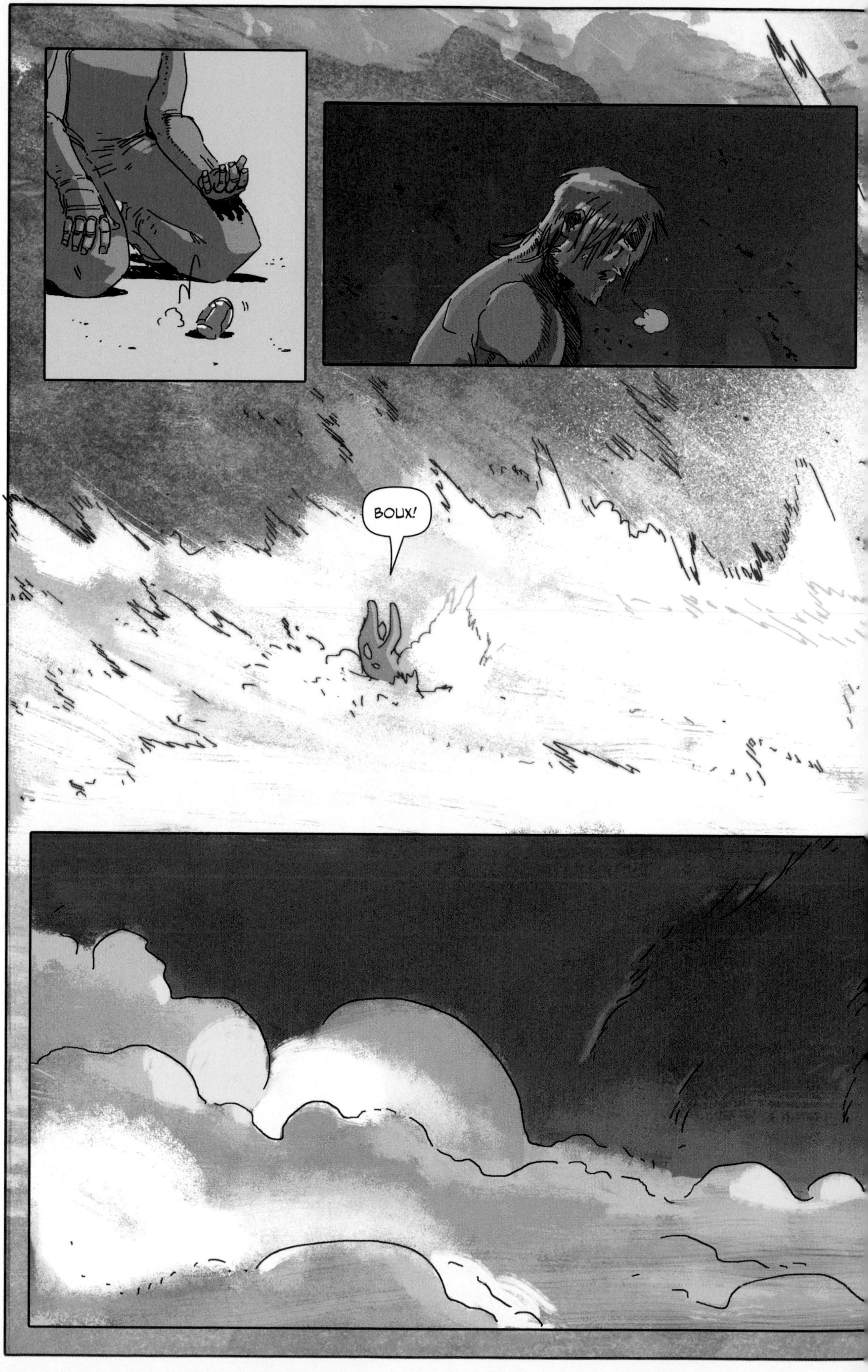
BOUX!

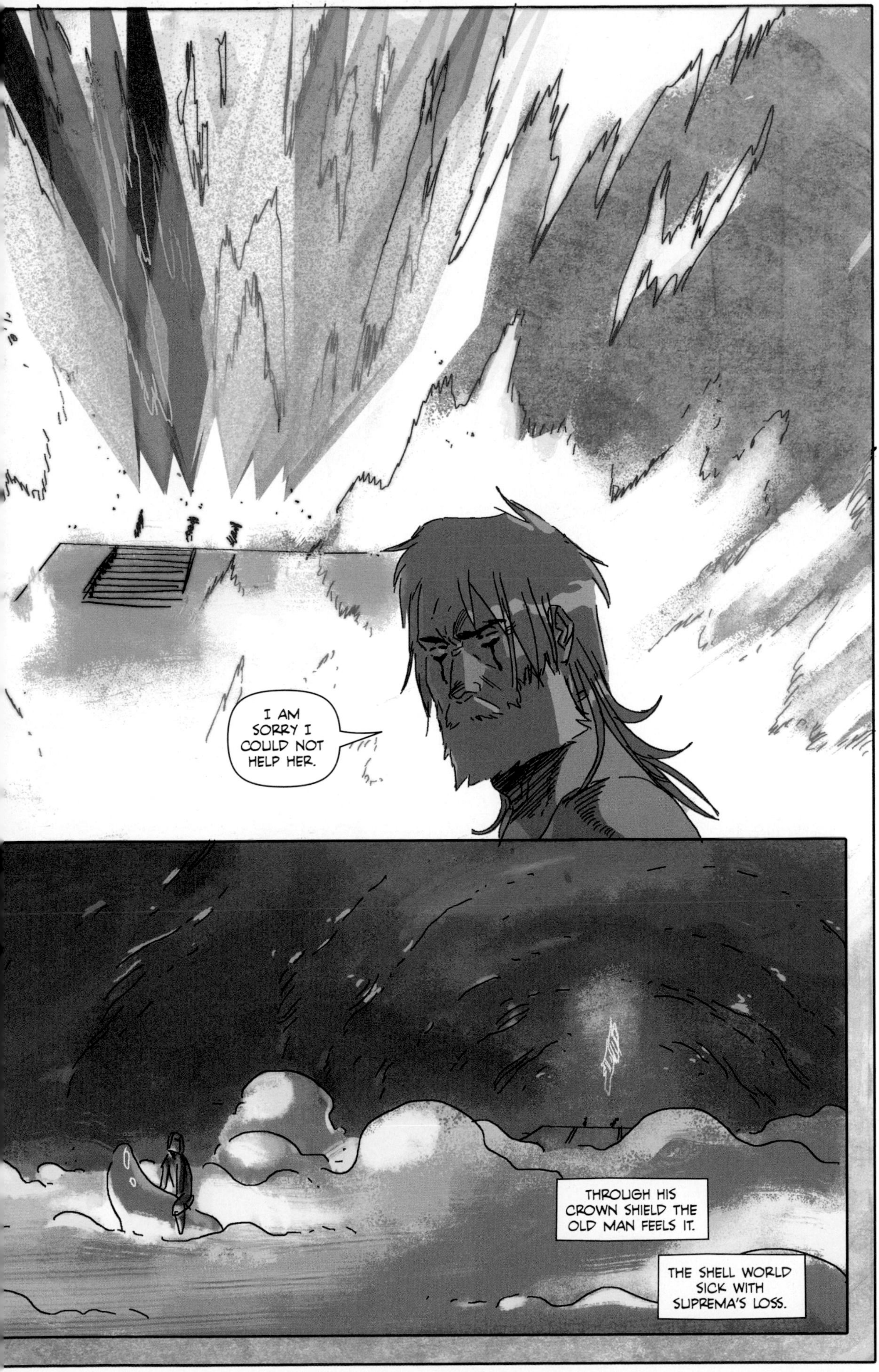
I AM SORRY I COULD NOT HELP HER.
THROUGH HIS CROWN SHIELD THE OLD MAN FEELS IT.
THE SHELL WORLD SICK WITH SUPREMA'S LOSS.

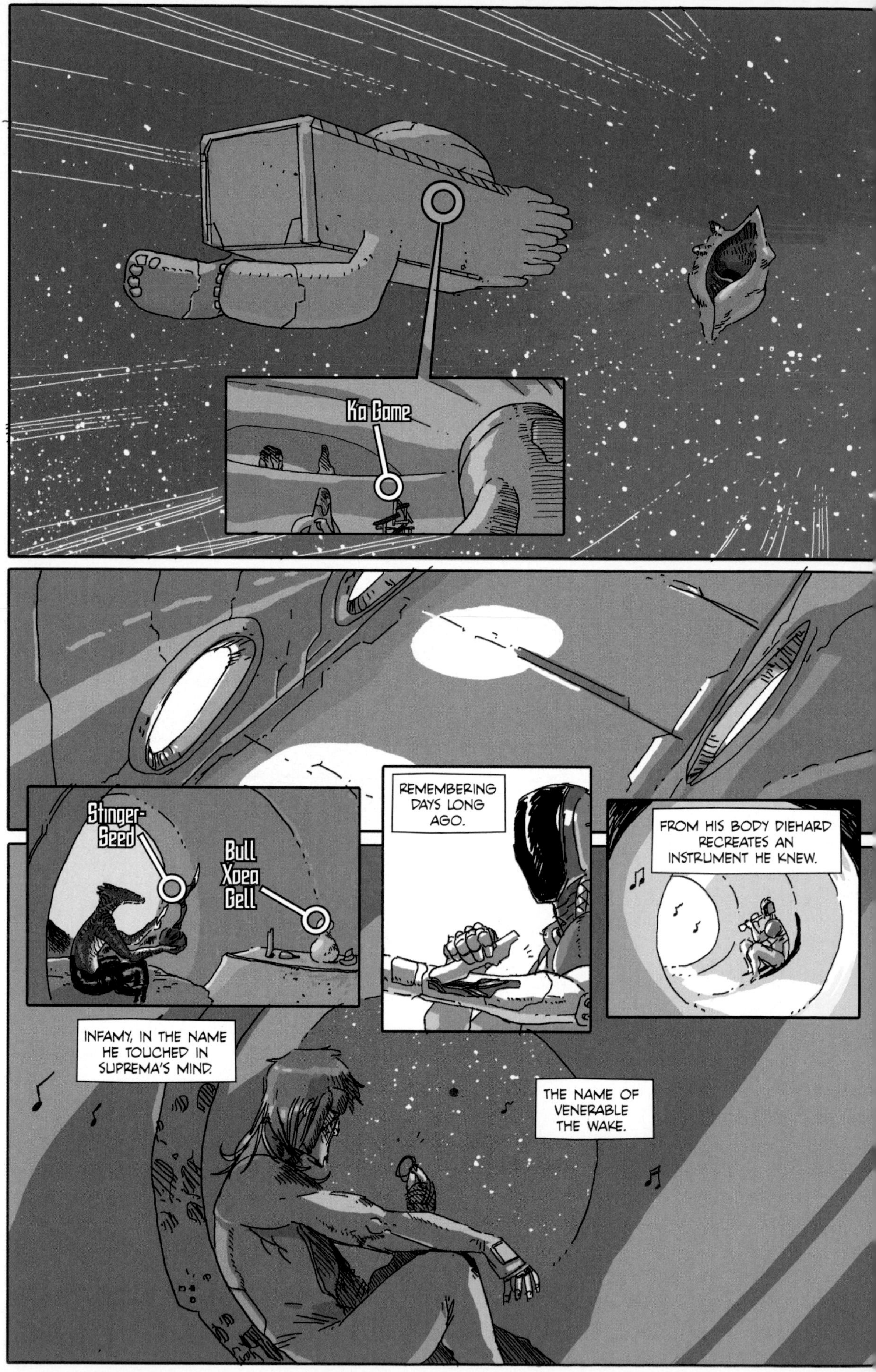
Ka Game
Stinger-Seed
Bull Xoea Gell
REMEMBERING DAYS LONG AGO.
FROM HIS BODY DIEHARD RECREATES AN INSTRUMENT HE KNEW.
INFAMY, IN THE NAME HE TOUCHED IN SUPREMA'S MIND.
THE NAME OF VENERABLE THE WAKE.

# VENERABLE THE WAKE

HEIGHT: 9'5" WEIGHT: NEGATIVE 10 LBS PLACE OF BIRTH: THE BRIDGE WORLDS

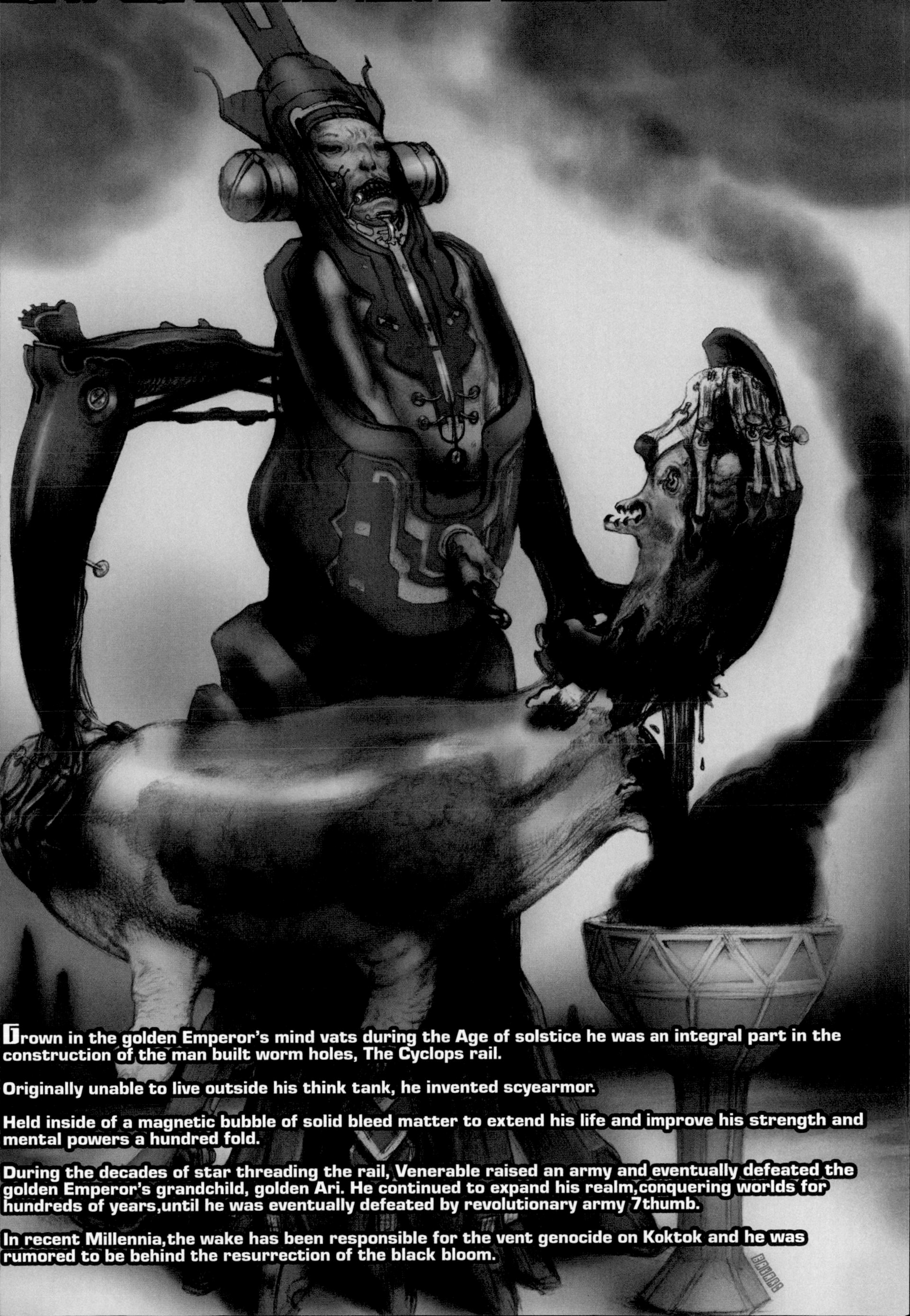

Grown in the golden Emperor's mind vats during the Age of solstice he was an integral part in the construction of the man built worm holes, The Cyclops rail.

Originally unable to live outside his think tank, he invented scyearmor.

Held inside of a magnetic bubble of solid bleed matter to extend his life and improve his strength and mental powers a hundred fold.

During the decades of star threading the rail, Venerable raised an army and eventually defeated the golden Emperor's grandchild, golden Ari. He continued to expand his realm,conquering worlds for hundreds of years,until he was eventually defeated by revolutionary army 7thumb.

In recent Millennia,the wake has been responsible for the vent genocide on Koktok and he was rumored to be behind the resurrection of the black bloom.

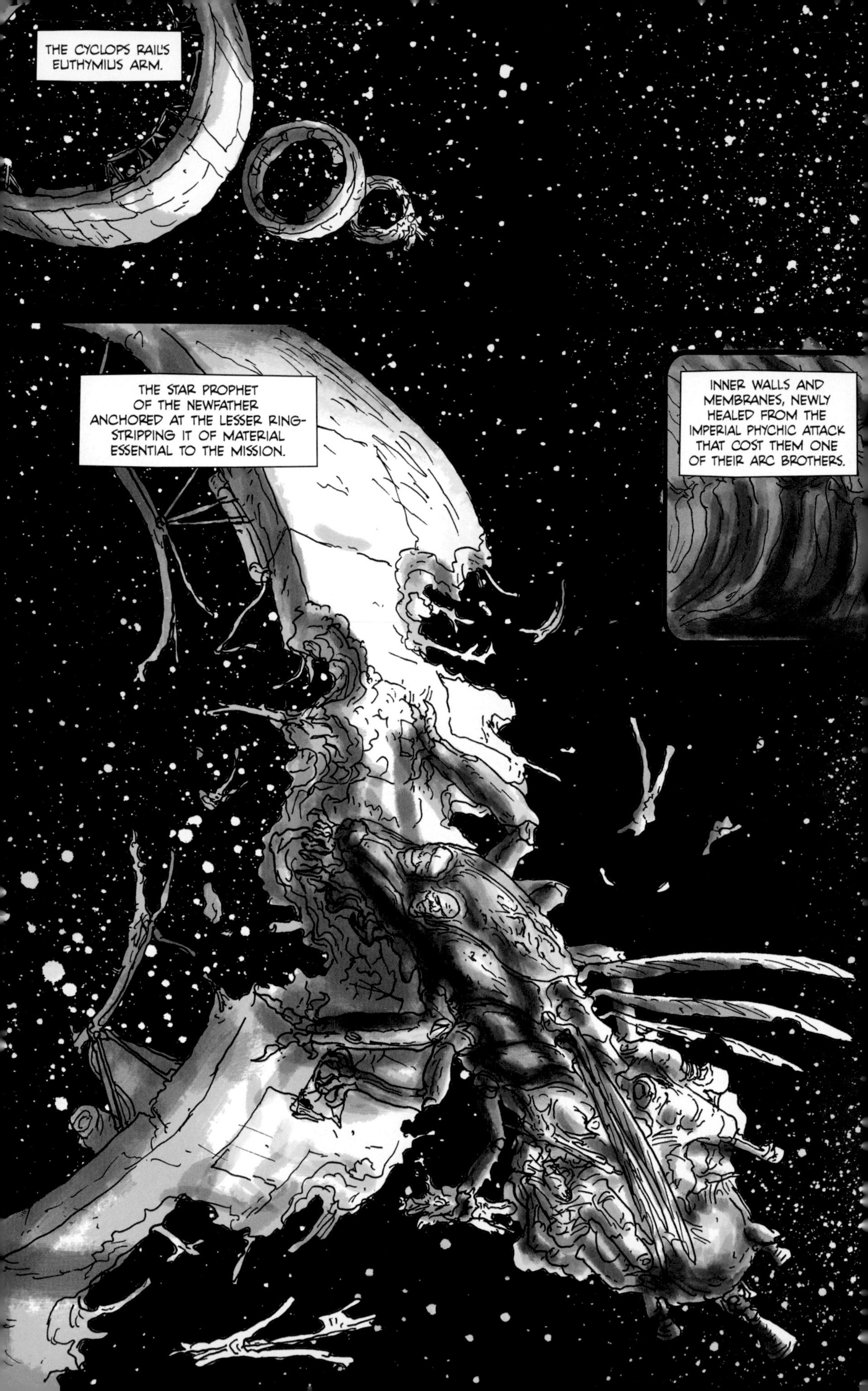
THE CYCLOPS RAIL'S EUTHYMIUS ARM.
THE STAR PROPHET OF THE NEWFATHER ANCHORED AT THE LESSER RING-STRIPPING IT OF MATERIAL ESSENTIAL TO THE MISSION.
INNER WALLS AND MEMBRANES, NEWLY HEALED FROM THE IMPERIAL PHYCHIC ATTACK THAT COST THEM ONE OF THEIR ARC BROTHERS.

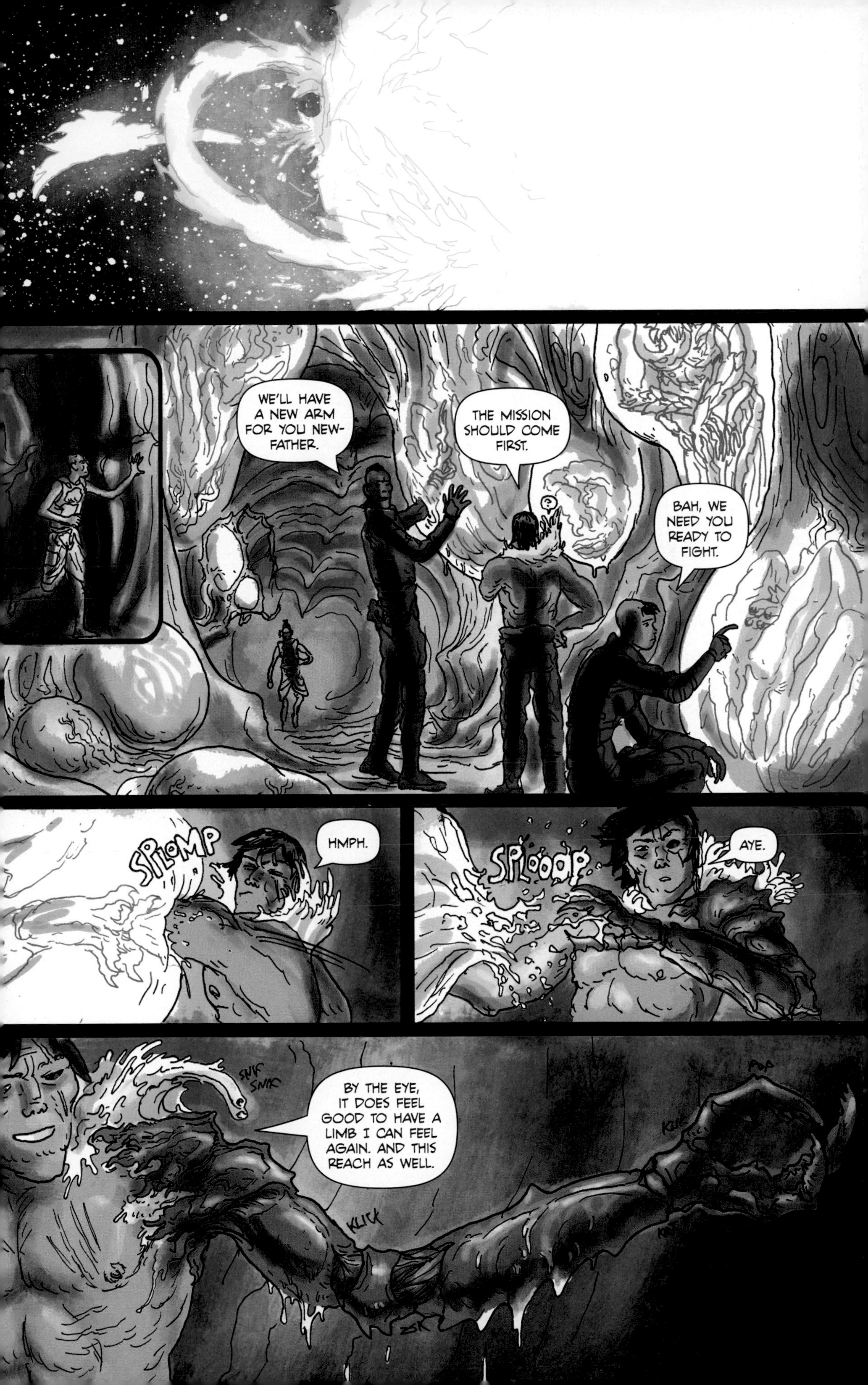
WE'LL HAVE A NEW ARM FOR YOU NEW-FATHER.
THE MISSION SHOULD COME FIRST.
?
BAH, WE NEED YOU READY TO FIGHT.
SPLOMP
HMPH.
SPLOOOP
AYE.
SNIF SNIF
BY THE EYE, IT DOES FEEL GOOD TO HAVE A LIMB I CAN FEEL AGAIN. AND THIS REACH AS WELL.
POP
KLIK
KLICK
ZSK

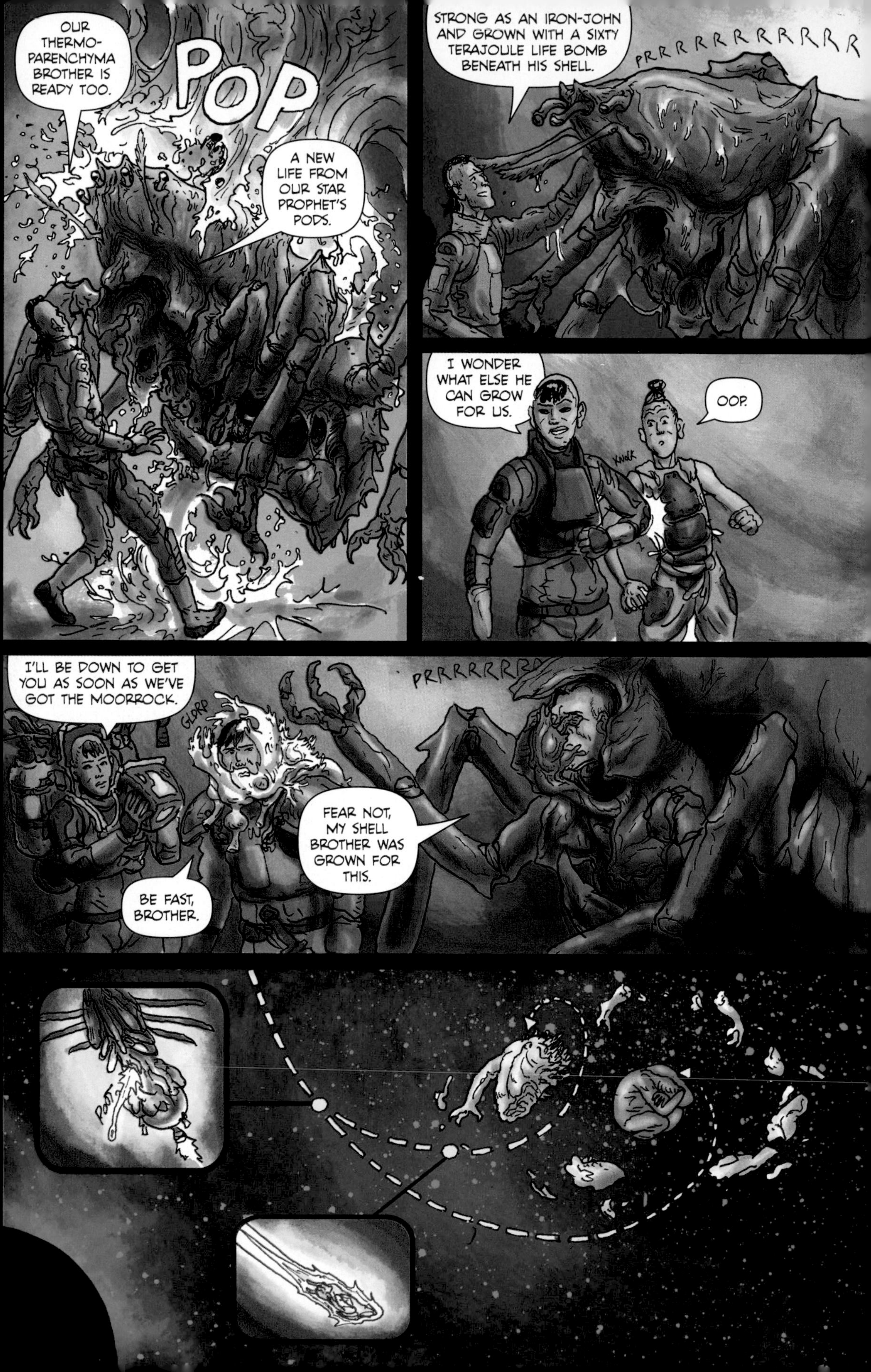
OUR THERMO-PARENCHYMA BROTHER IS READY TOO.
POP
A NEW LIFE FROM OUR STAR PROPHET'S PODS.
STRONG AS AN IRON-JOHN AND GROWN WITH A SIXTY TERAJOULE LIFE BOMB BENEATH HIS SHELL.
PRRRRRRRRRRRRR
I WONDER WHAT ELSE HE CAN GROW FOR US.
KNOCK
OOP.
I'LL BE DOWN TO GET YOU AS SOON AS WE'VE GOT THE MOORROCK.
GLORP
PRRRRRRRR
FEAR NOT, MY SHELL BROTHER WAS GROWN FOR THIS.
BE FAST, BROTHER.

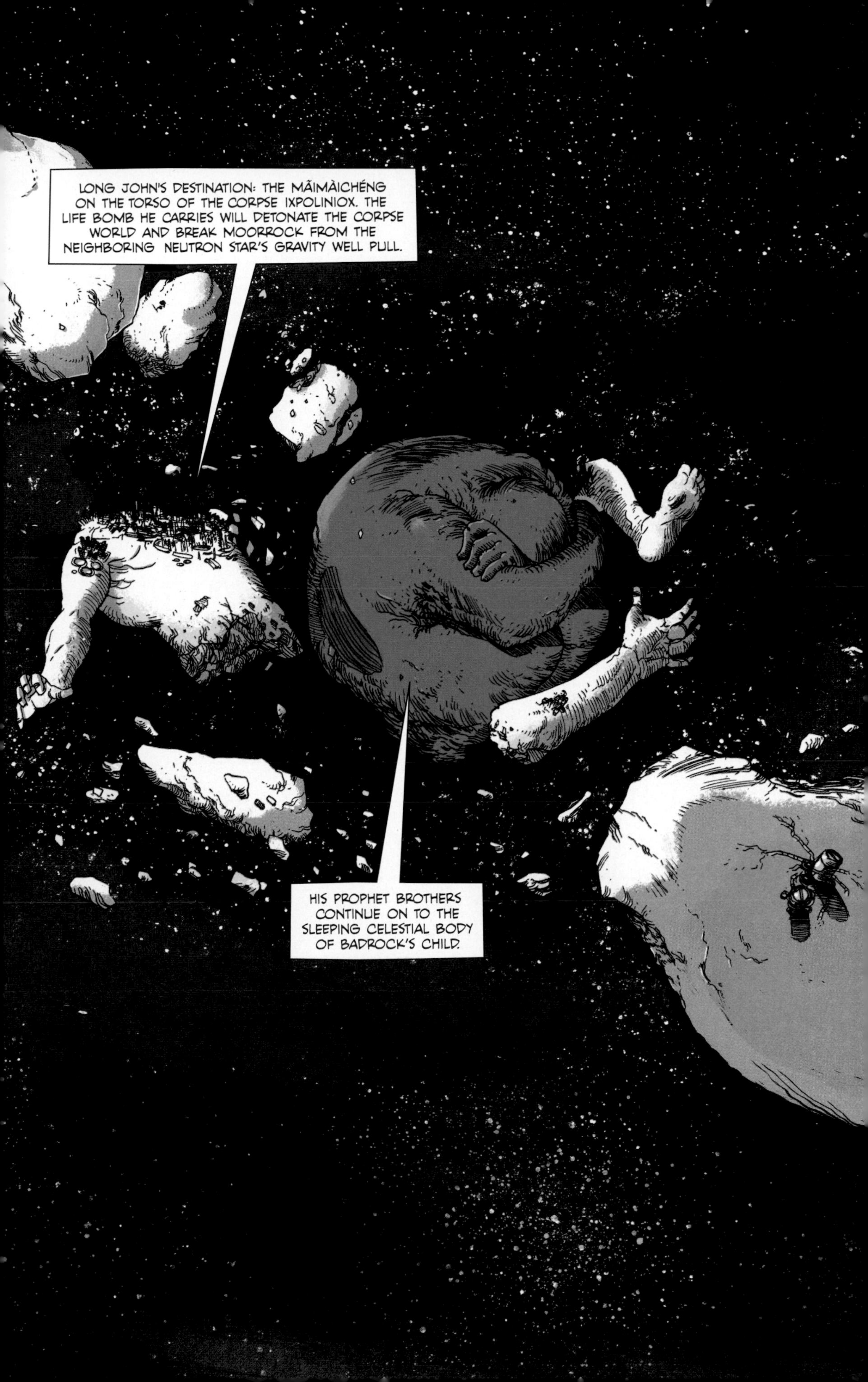
LONG JOHN'S DESTINATION: THE MĀIMÀICHÉNG ON THE TORSO OF THE CORPSE IXPOLINIOX. THE LIFE BOMB HE CARRIES WILL DETONATE THE CORPSE WORLD AND BREAK MOORROCK FROM THE NEIGHBORING NEUTRON STAR'S GRAVITY WELL PULL.
HIS PROPHET BROTHERS CONTINUE ON TO THE SLEEPING CELESTIAL BODY OF BADROCK'S CHILD.

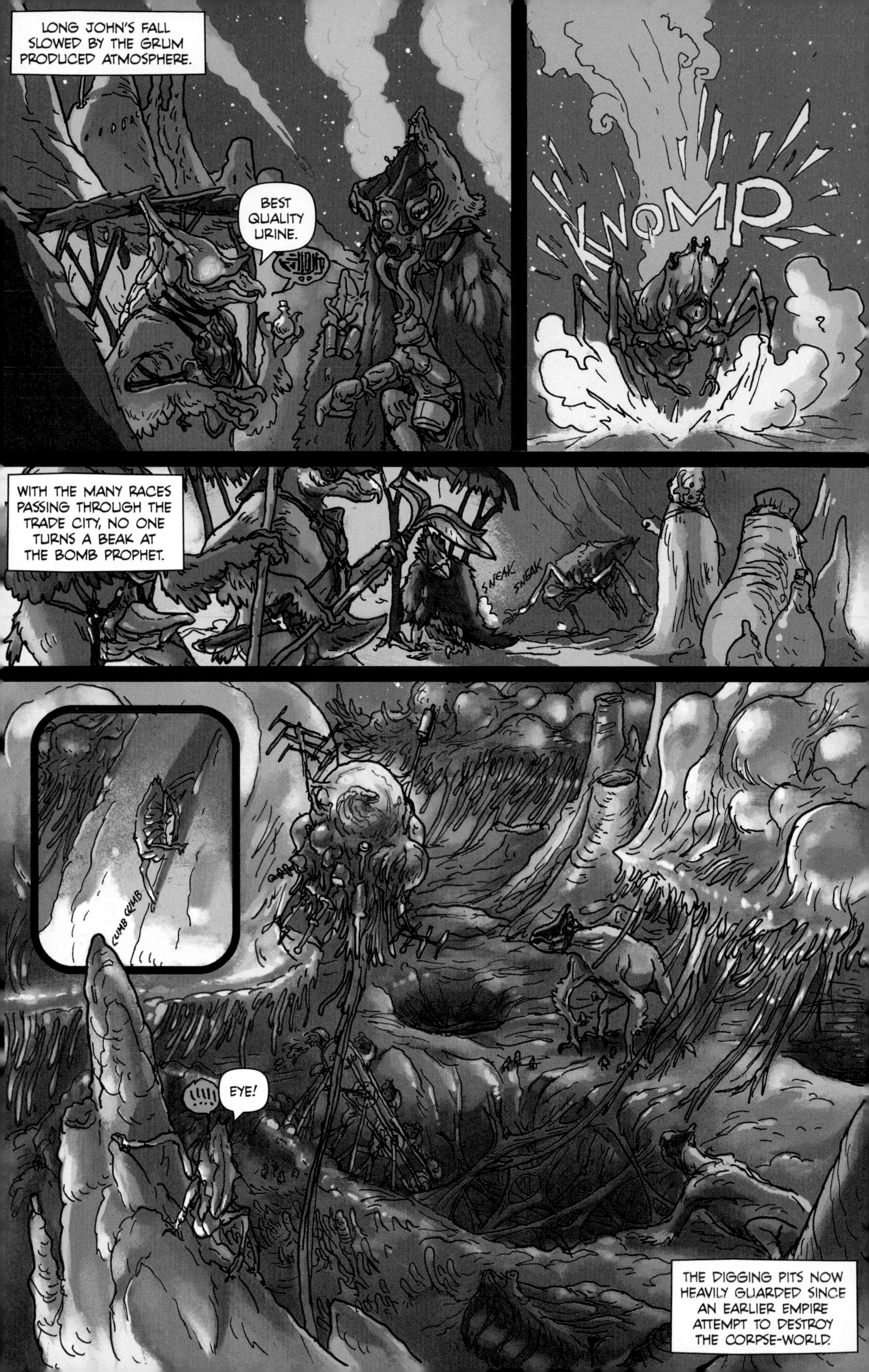
LONG JOHN'S FALL SLOWED BY THE GRUM PRODUCED ATMOSPHERE.
BEST QUALITY URINE.
KWOMP
WITH THE MANY RACES PASSING THROUGH THE TRADE CITY, NO ONE TURNS A BEAK AT THE BOMB PROPHET.
SNEAK SNEAK
CLIMB CLIMB
!!!!
EYE!
THE DIGGING PITS NOW HEAVILY GUARDED SINCE AN EARLIER EMPIRE ATTEMPT TO DESTROY THE CORPSE-WORLD.

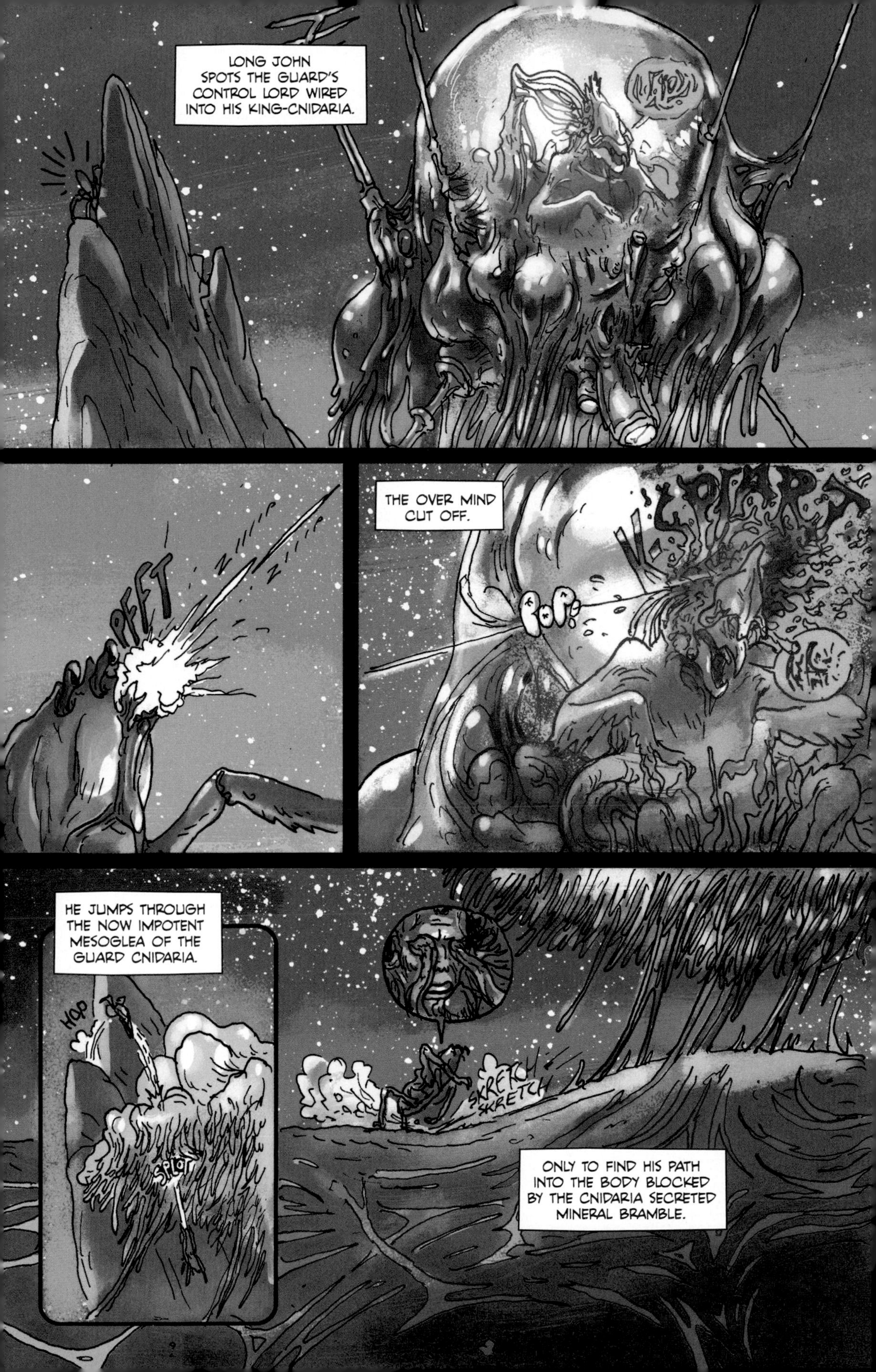
LONG JOHN SPOTS THE GUARD'S CONTROL LORD WIRED INTO HIS KING-CNIDARIA.
PFFT
THE OVER MIND CUT OFF.
POP!
HE JUMPS THROUGH THE NOW IMPOTENT MESOGLEA OF THE GUARD CNIDARIA.
HOP
SPLAT
SKRETCH SKRETCH
ONLY TO FIND HIS PATH INTO THE BODY BLOCKED BY THE CNIDARIA SECRETED MINERAL BRAMBLE.

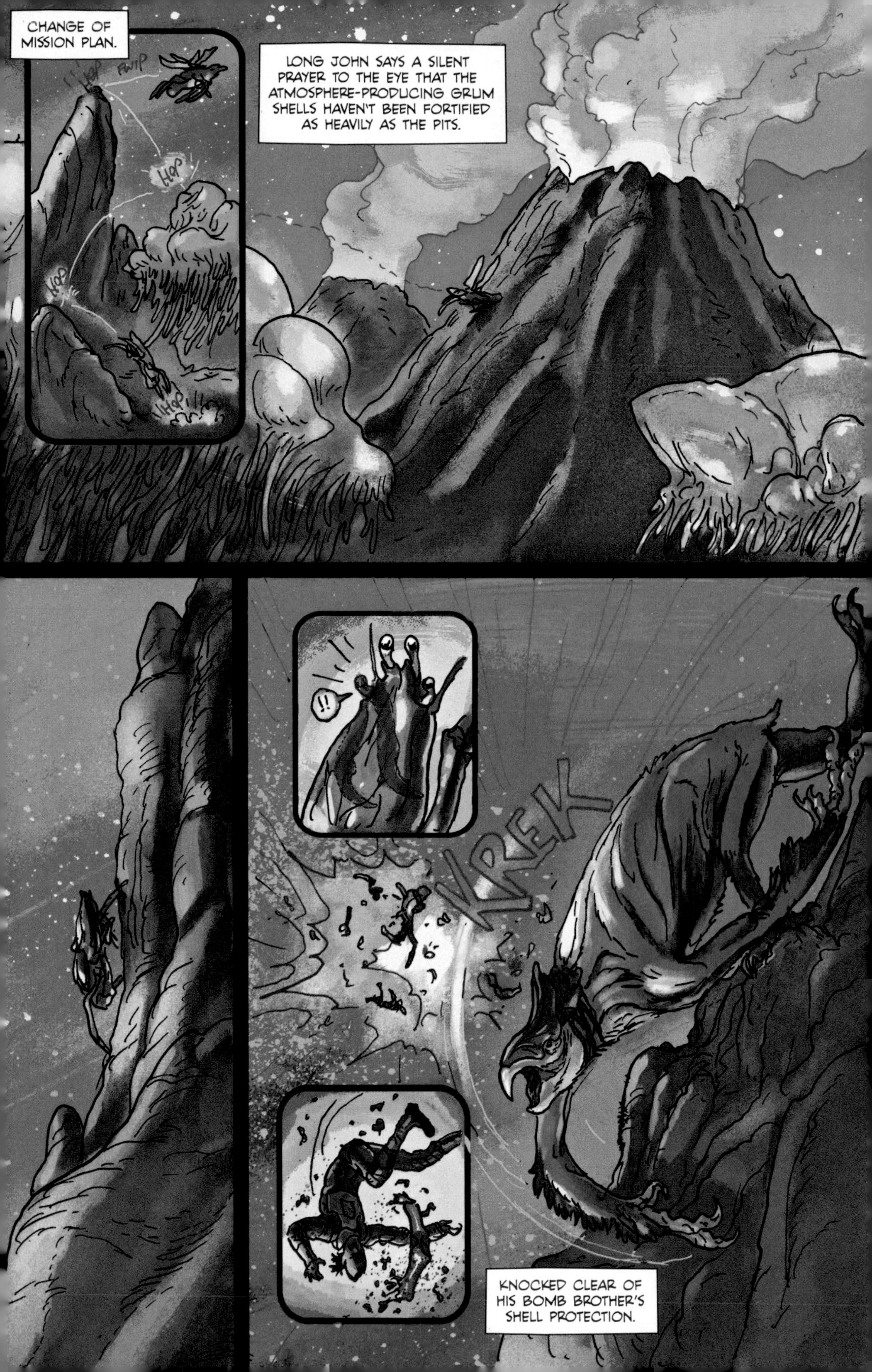
CHANGE OF MISSION PLAN.
HOP
FWIP
HOP
HOP
HOP
LONG JOHN SAYS A SILENT PRAYER TO THE EYE THAT THE ATMOSPHERE-PRODUCING GRUM SHELLS HAVEN'T BEEN FORTIFIED AS HEAVILY AS THE PITS.
!!
KREK
KNOCKED CLEAR OF HIS BOMB BROTHER'S SHELL PROTECTION.

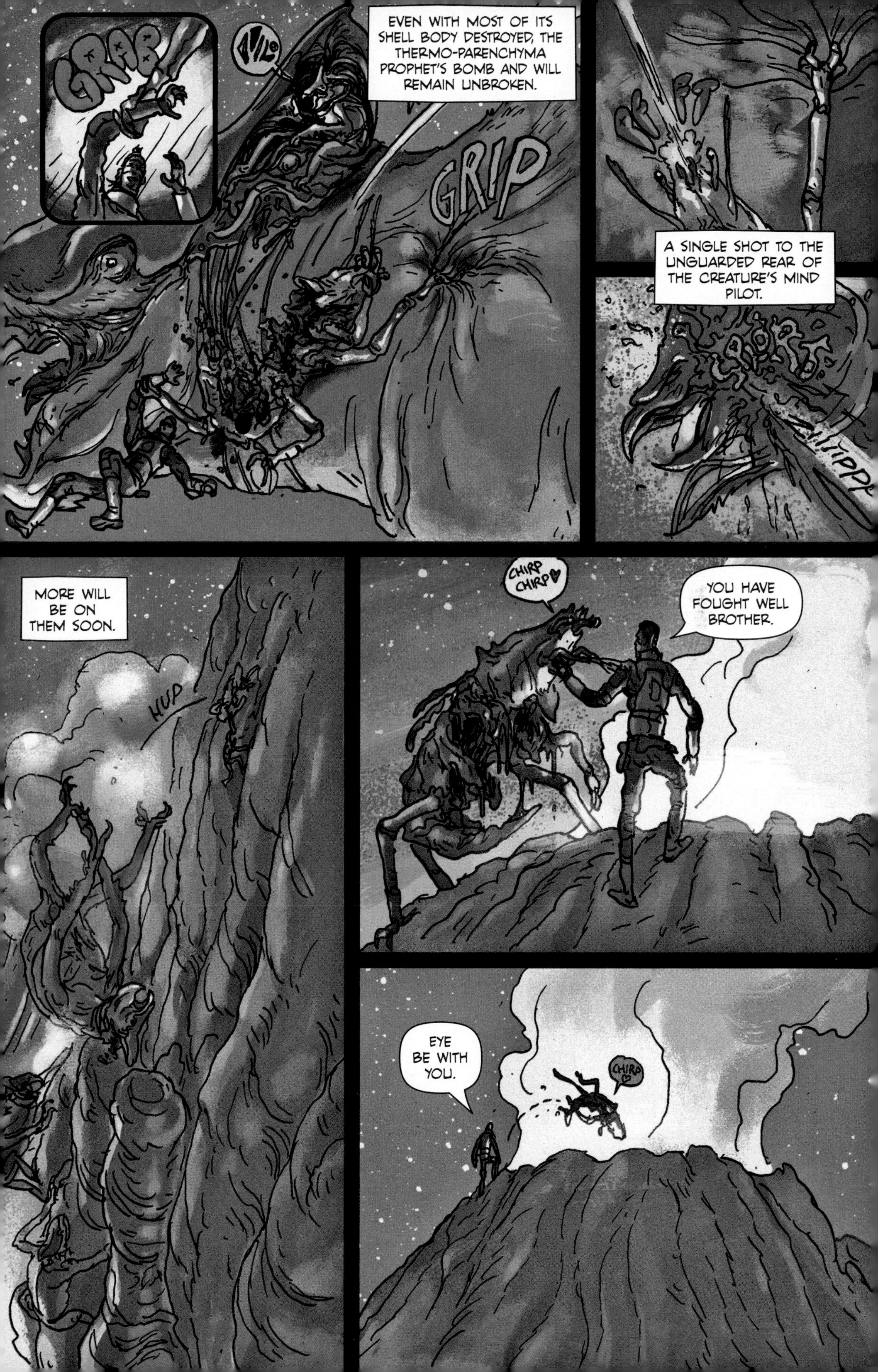
GRAB
EVEN WITH MOST OF ITS SHELL BODY DESTROYED, THE THERMO-PARENCHYMA PROPHET'S BOMB AND WILL REMAIN UNBROKEN.
GRIP
A SINGLE SHOT TO THE UNGUARDED REAR OF THE CREATURE'S MIND PILOT.
MORE WILL BE ON THEM SOON.
HUP
CHIRP CHIRP
YOU HAVE FOUGHT WELL BROTHER.
EYE BE WITH YOU.
CHIRP

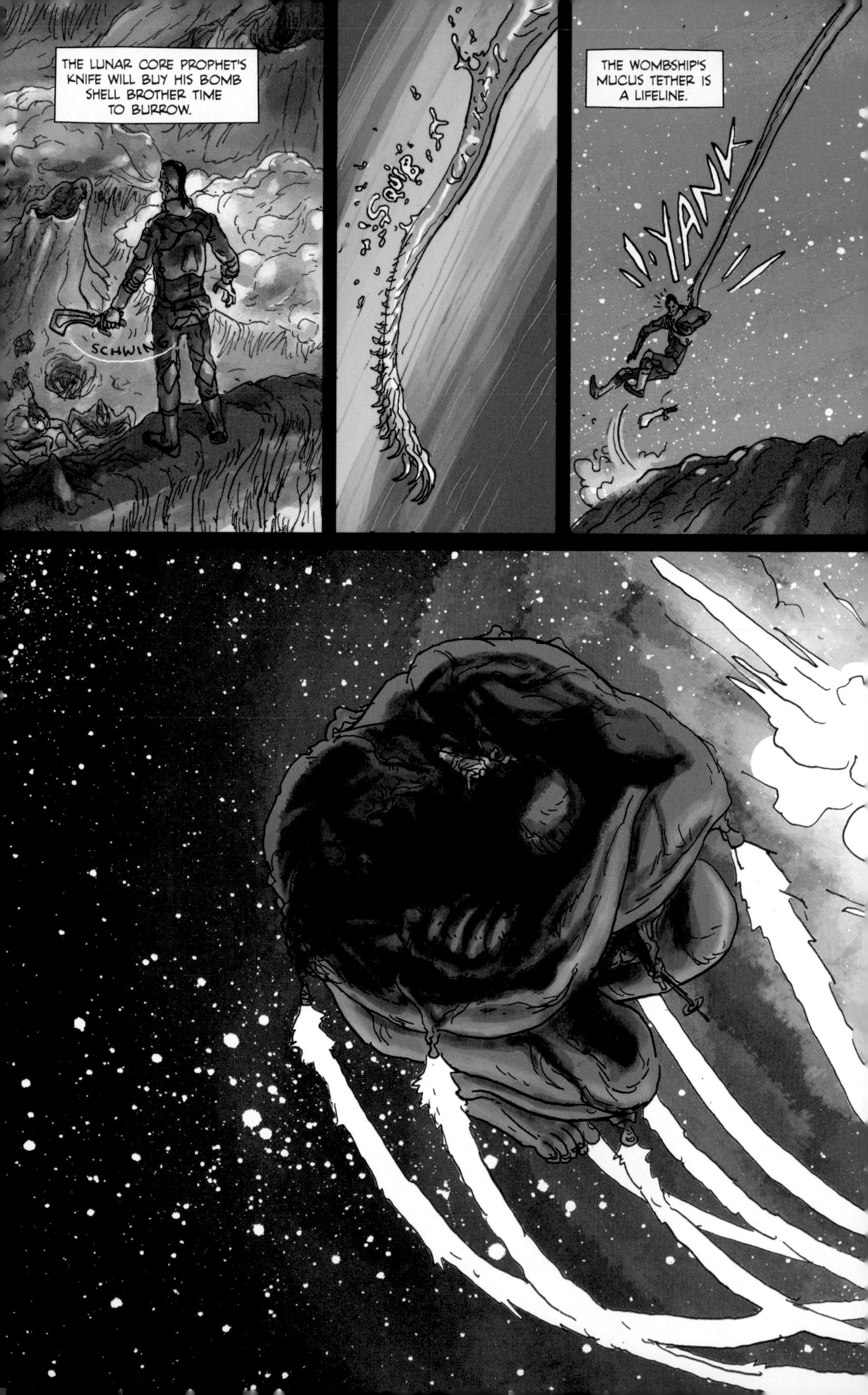
THE LUNAR CORE PROPHET'S KNIFE WILL BUY HIS BOMB SHELL BROTHER TIME TO BURROW.
SCHWING
SQUIRT
THE WOMBSHIP'S MUCUS TETHER IS A LIFELINE.
YANK

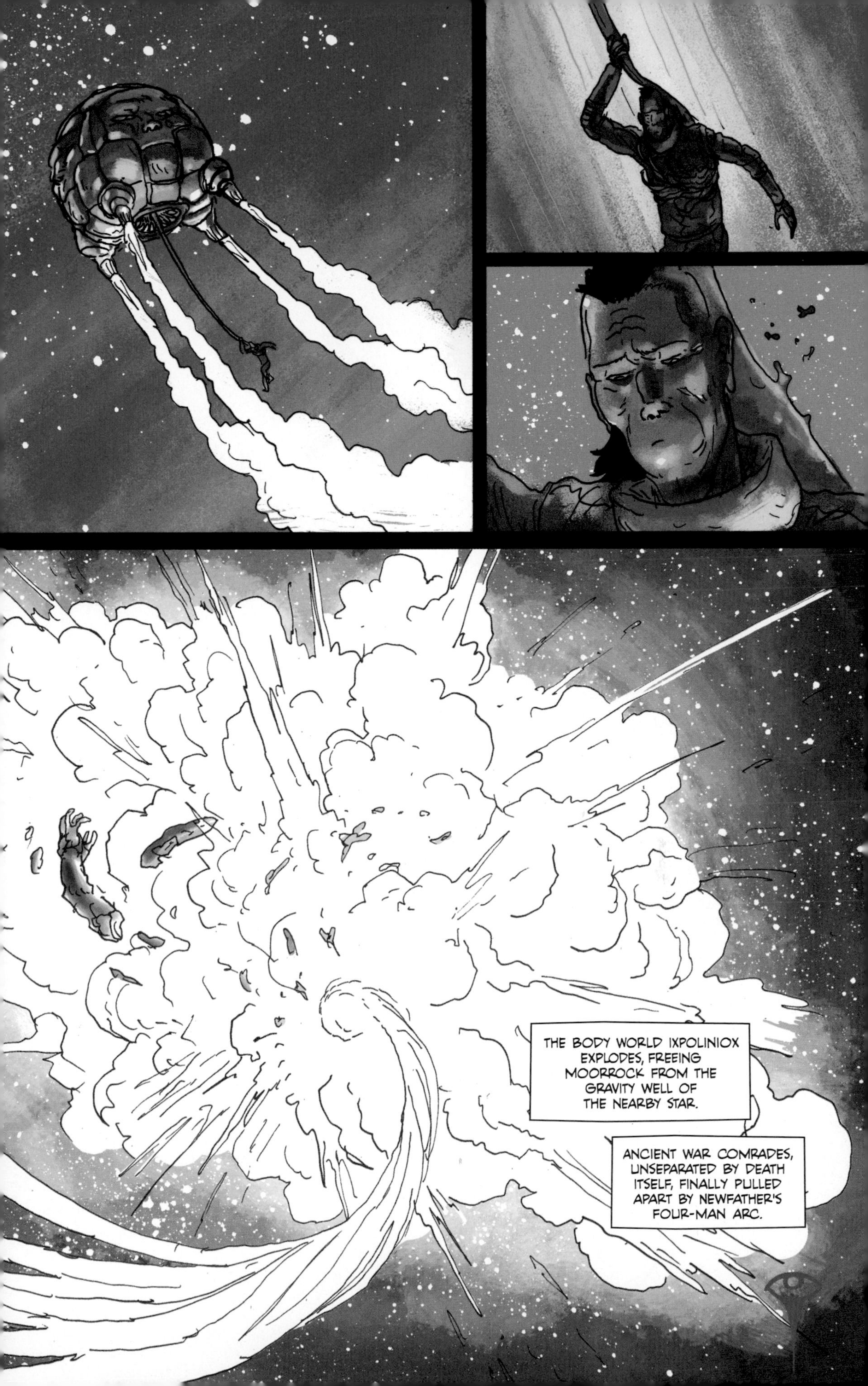
THE BODY WORLD IXPOLINIOX EXPLODES, FREEING MOORROCK FROM THE GRAVITY WELL OF THE NEARBY STAR.
ANCIENT WAR COMRADES, UNSEPARATED BY DEATH ITSELF, FINALLY PULLED APART BY NEWFATHER'S FOUR-MAN ARC.

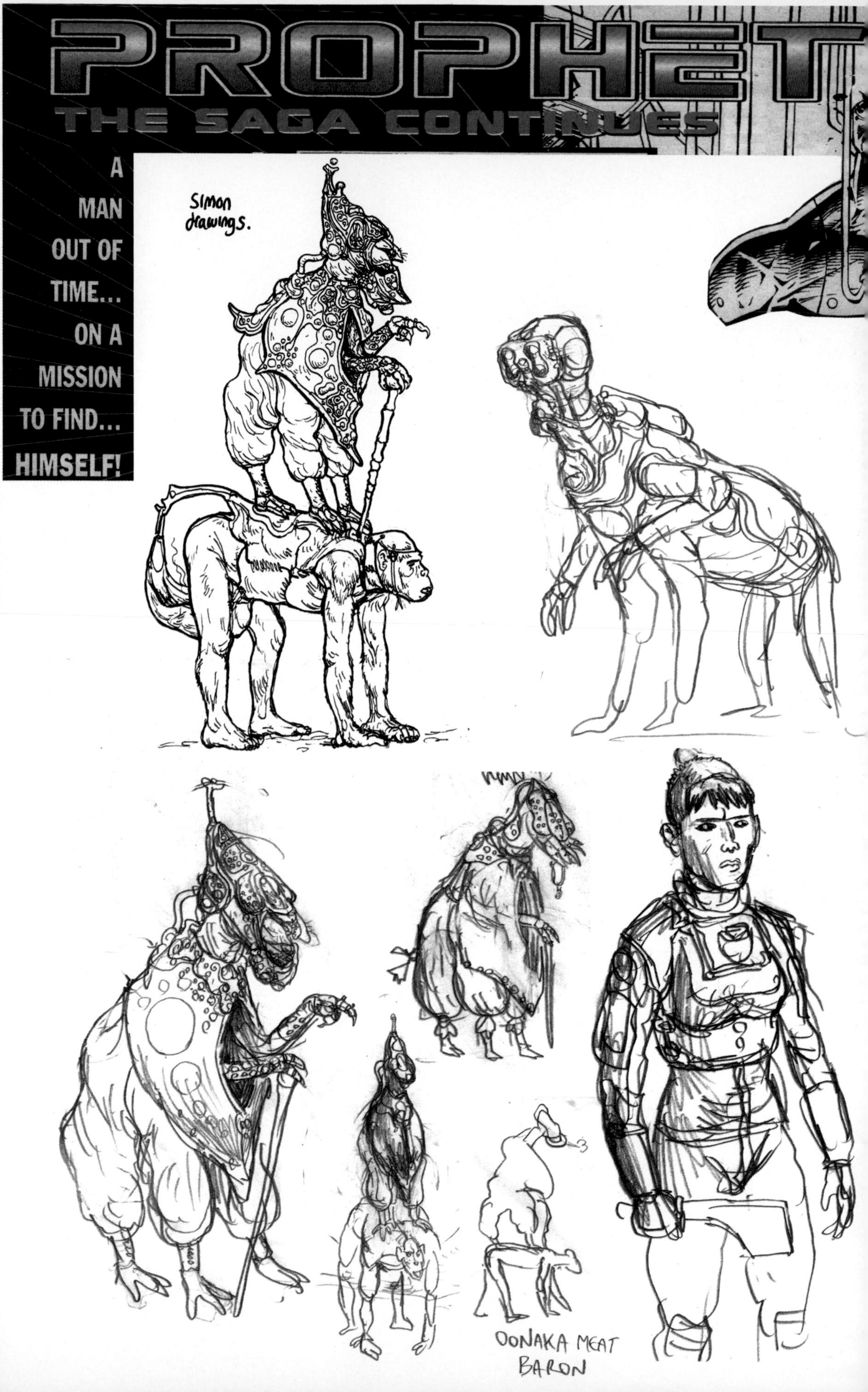
PROPHET
THE SAGA CONTINUES
A MAN OUT OF TIME... ON A MISSION TO FIND... HIMSELF!
Simon drawings.
OONAKA MEAT BARON

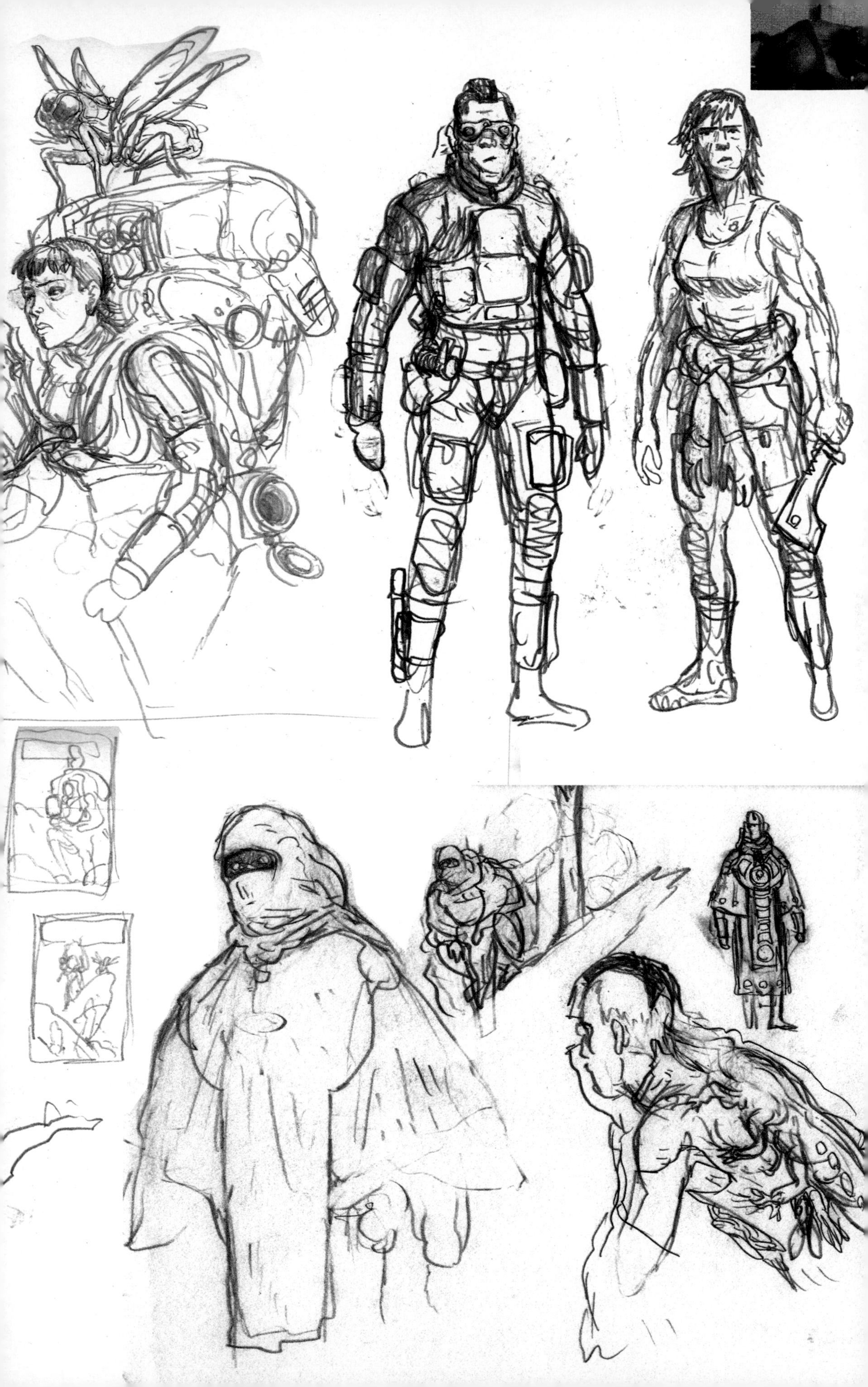

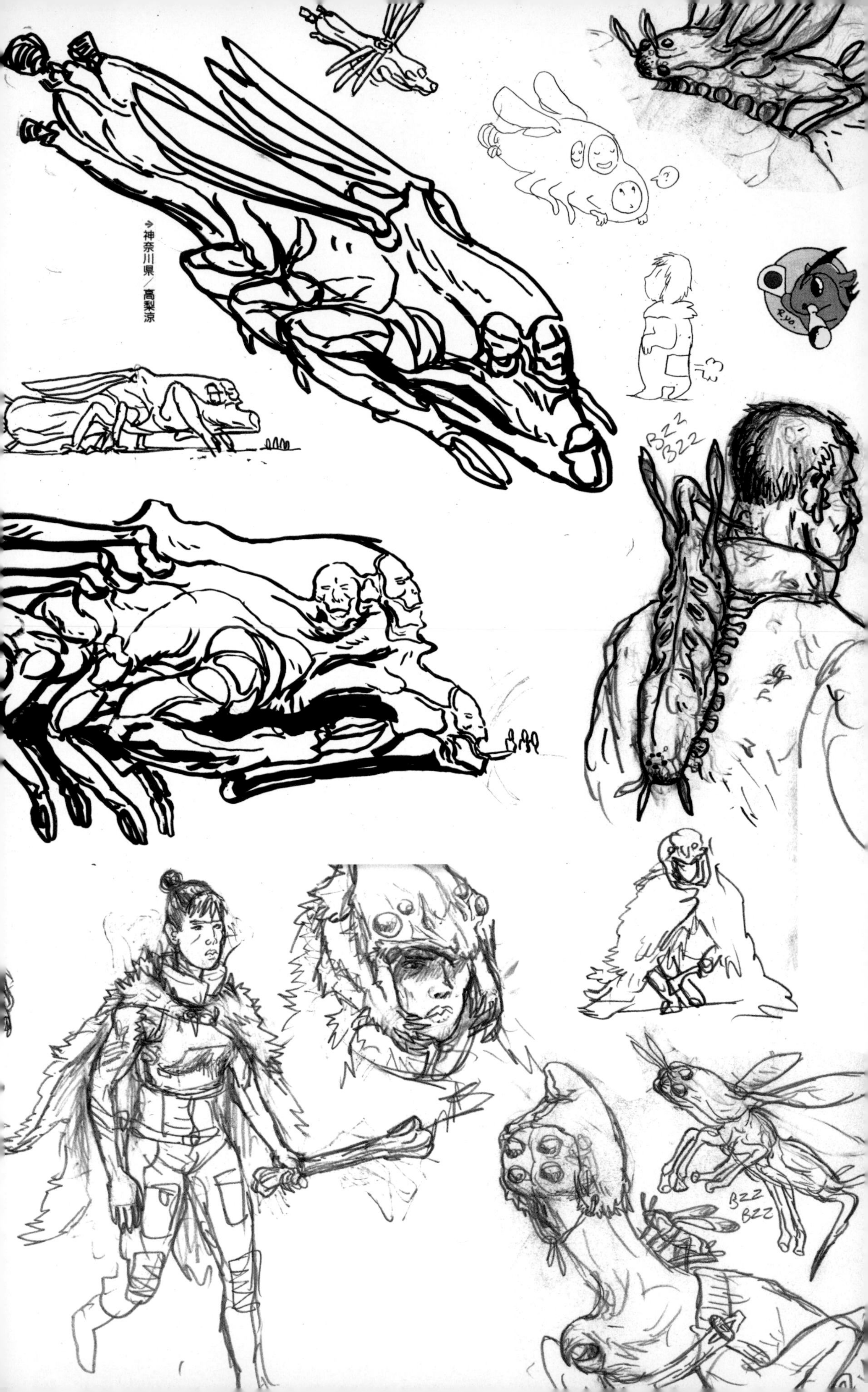

→神奈川県／高梨涼
BZZ
BZZ
RYO.
BZZ
BZZ

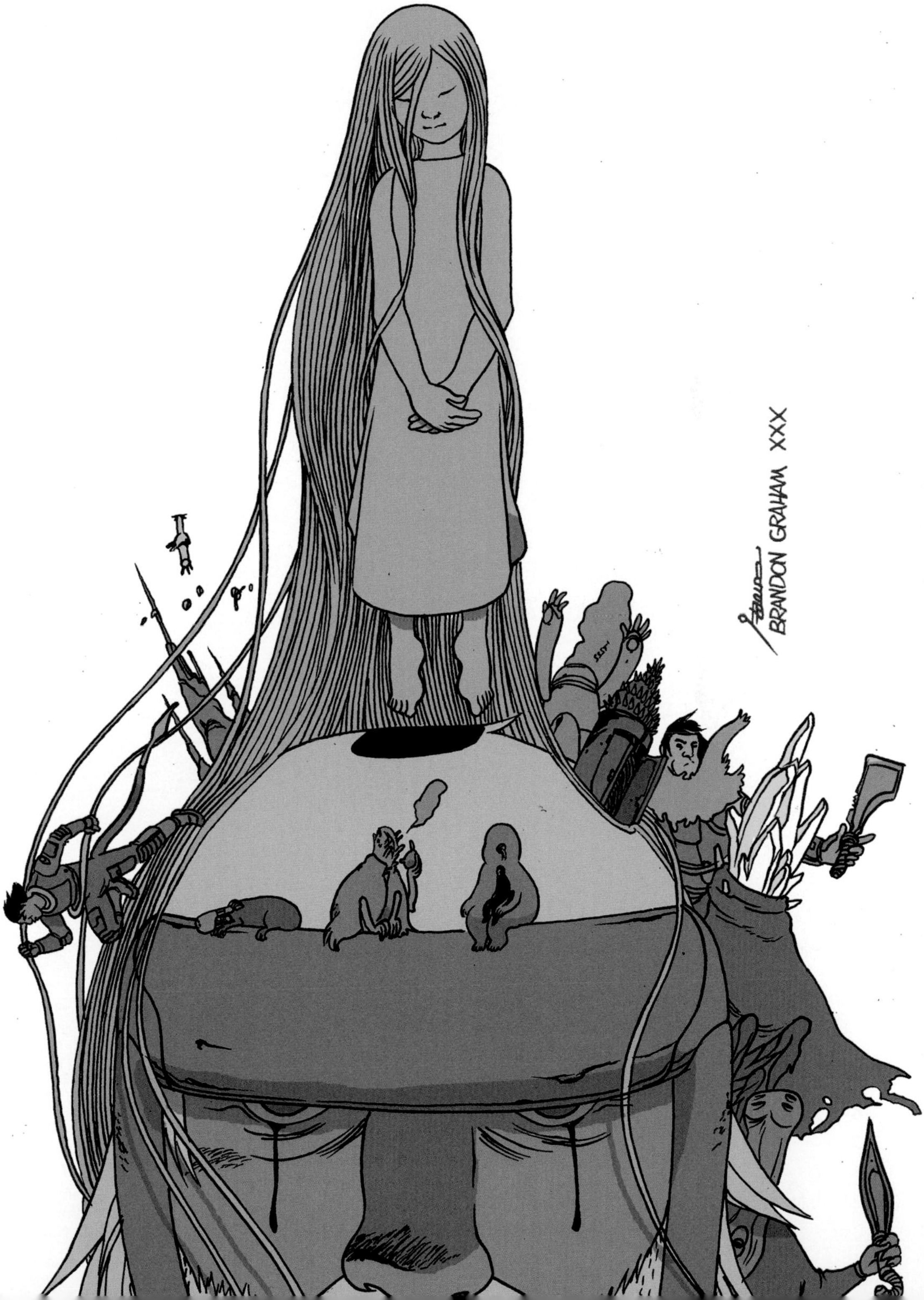
BRANDON GRAHAM XXX

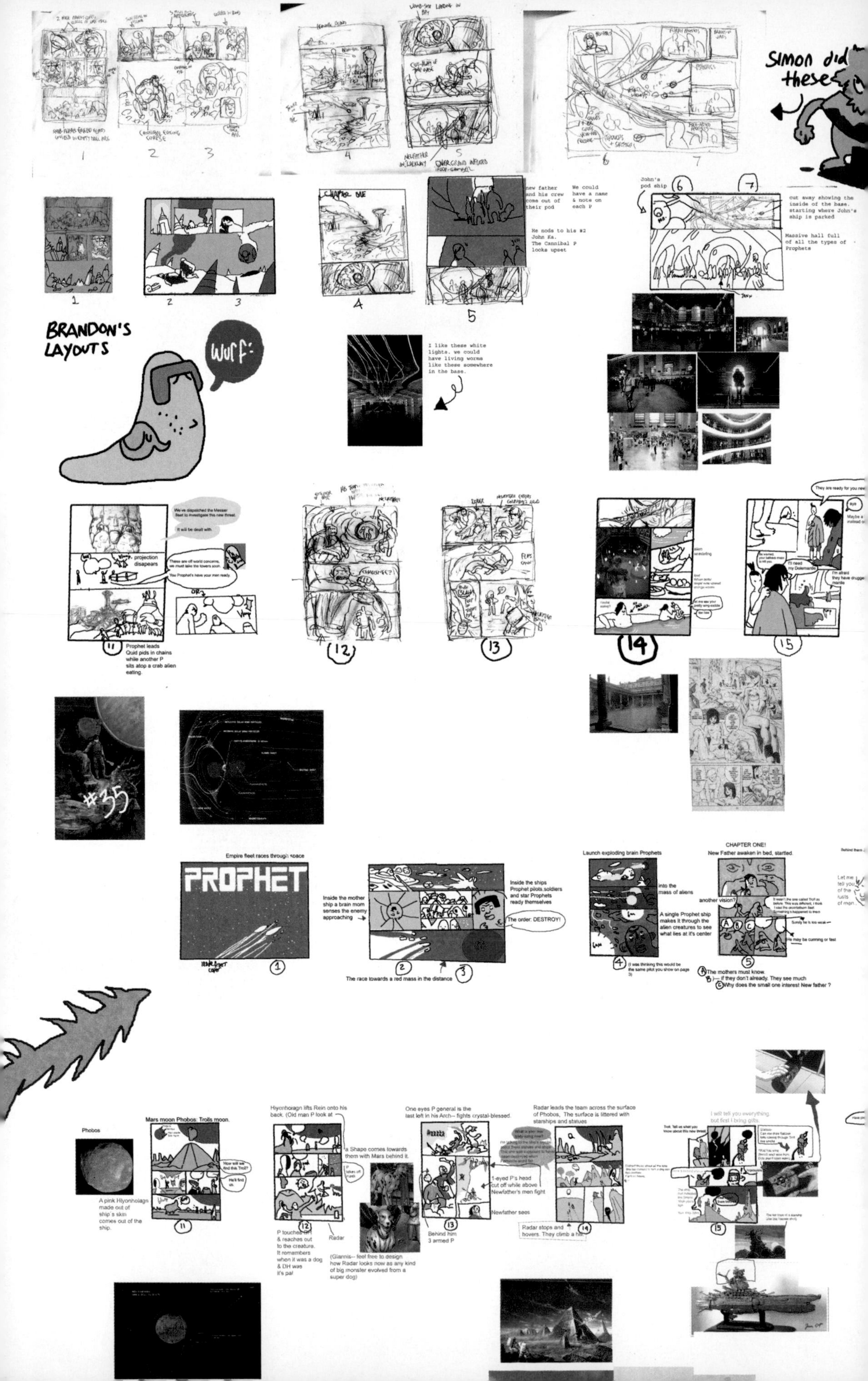

Simon did these
1 2 3 4 5 6 7
new father and his crew come out of their pod
We could have a name & note on each P
He nods to his #2 John Ka. The Cannibal P looks upset
John's pod ship
cut away showing the inside of the base. starting where John's ship is parked
Massive hall full of all the types of Prophets
BRANDON'S LAYOUTS
Wurf:
I like these white lights. we could have living worms like these somewhere in the base.
We've dispatched the Messier fleet to investigate this new threat.
It will be dealt with.
projection disapears
These are off world concerns, we must take the towers soon.
You Prophet's have your men ready.
Prophet leads Quid pids in chains while another P sits atop a crab alien eating.
11 12 13 14 15
They are ready for you now.
#35
Empire fleet races through space
PROPHET
Inside the mother ship a brain mom senses the enemy approaching
Inside the ships Prophet pilots, soldiers and star Prophets ready themselves
The order: DESTROY!
The race towards a red mass in the distance
Launch exploding brain Prophets
into the mass of aliens
A single Prophet ship makes it through the alien creatures to see what lies at it's center
(I was thinking this would be the same pilot you show on page 3)
CHAPTER ONE!
New Father awaken in bed, startled.
another vision?
Surely he is too weak
He may be cunning or fast
The mothers must know.
if they don't already. They see much
Why does the small one interest New father ?
Phobos
Mars moon Phobos: Trolls moon.
How will we find this Troll?
He'll find us.
A pink Hiyonhoiagn made out of ship's skin comes out of the ship.
Hiyonhoragn lifts Rein onto his back. (Old man P look at
a Shape comes towards them with Mars behind it.
P touches & reaches out to the creature. It remembers when it was a dog & DH was it's pal
Radar
(Giannis-- feel free to design how Radar looks now as any kind of big monster evolved from a super dog)
One eyes P general is the last left in his Arch-- fights crystal-blessed.
1-eyed P's head cut off while above Newfather's men fight
Newfather sees
Behind him 3 armed P
Radar leads the team across the surface of Phobos, The surface is littered with starships and statues
Radar stops and hovers. They climb a hill.
I will tell you everything. but first I bring gifts.

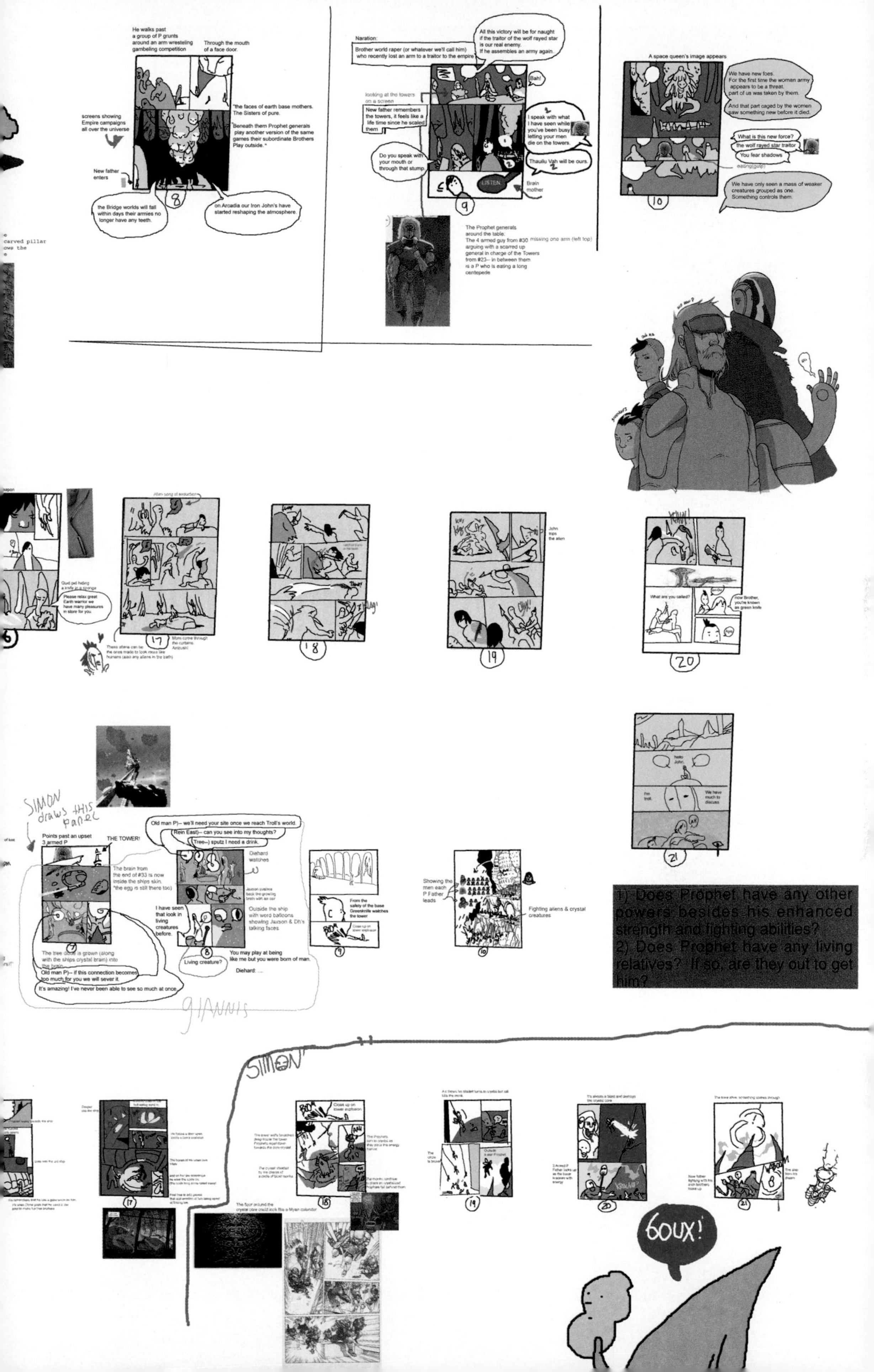

He walks past a group of P grunts around an arm wrestleing gambeling competition
Through the mouth of a face door.
screens showing Empire campaigns all over the universe
"the faces of earth base mothers. The Sisters of pure.
Beneath them Prophet generals play another version of the same games their subordinate Brothers Play outside."
New father enters
8
the Bridge worlds will fall within days their armies no longer have any teeth.
on Arcadia our Iron John's have started reshaping the atmosphere.
Naration:
Brother world raper (or whatever we'll call him) who recently lost an arm to a traitor to the empire
All this victory will be for naught if the traitor of the wolf rayed star is our real enemy. If he assembles an army again.
Bah!
looking at the towers on a screen
New father remembers the towers, it feels like a life time since he scaled them
I speak with what I have seen while you've been busy letting your men die on the towers.
Do you speak with your mouth or through that stump.
Thauilu Vah will be ours.
LISTEN.
Brain mother
9
The Prophet generals around the table: The 4 armed guy from #30 missing one arm (left top) arguing with a scarred up general in charge of the Towers from #23-- in between them is a P who is eating a long centepede
A space queen's image appears
We have new foes. For the first time the woman army appears to be a threat. part of us was taken by them.
And that part caged by the women saw something new before it died.
What is this new force?
the wolf rayed star traitor
You fear shadows
eating(gulp)
We have only seen a mass of weaker creatures grouped as one. Something controls them.
10
Quid pet hiding a knife in a sponge
Please relax great Earth warrior we have many pleasures in store for you.
Alien song of seduction
17
More come through the curtains. Ambush!
These aliens can be the ones made to look more like humans (also any aliens in the bath)
18
John trips the alien
19
What are you called?
now Brother, you're known as green knife
20
hello John.
I'm troll.
We have much to discuss
21
1) Does Prophet have any other powers besides his enhanced strength and fighting abilities?
2) Does Prophet have any living relatives? If so, are they out to get him?
SIMON draws this panel
Points past an upset 3 armed P
THE TOWER!
The brain from the end of #33 is now inside the ships skin. "the egg is still there too)
7
The tree dude is grown (along with the ships crystal brain) into the brain.
Old man P)-- we'll need your site once we reach Troll's world.
Rein East)-- can you see into my thoughts?
Tree--) sputz I need a drink.
Diehard watches
I have seen that look in living creatures before.
Outside the ship with word balloons showing Jaxson & Dti's talking faces
Living creature?
You may play at being like me but you were born of man.
Diehard: ...
8
Old man P)-- if this connection becomes too much for you we will sever it.
It's amazing! I've never been able to see so much at once.
GIANNIS
From the safety of the base Greenknife watches the tower
9
Showing the men each P Father leads
Fighting aliens & crystal creatures
10
SIMON
17
The floor around the crystal core could look like a Myan calendar
Close up on tower explosion
18
19
20
21
GOUX!

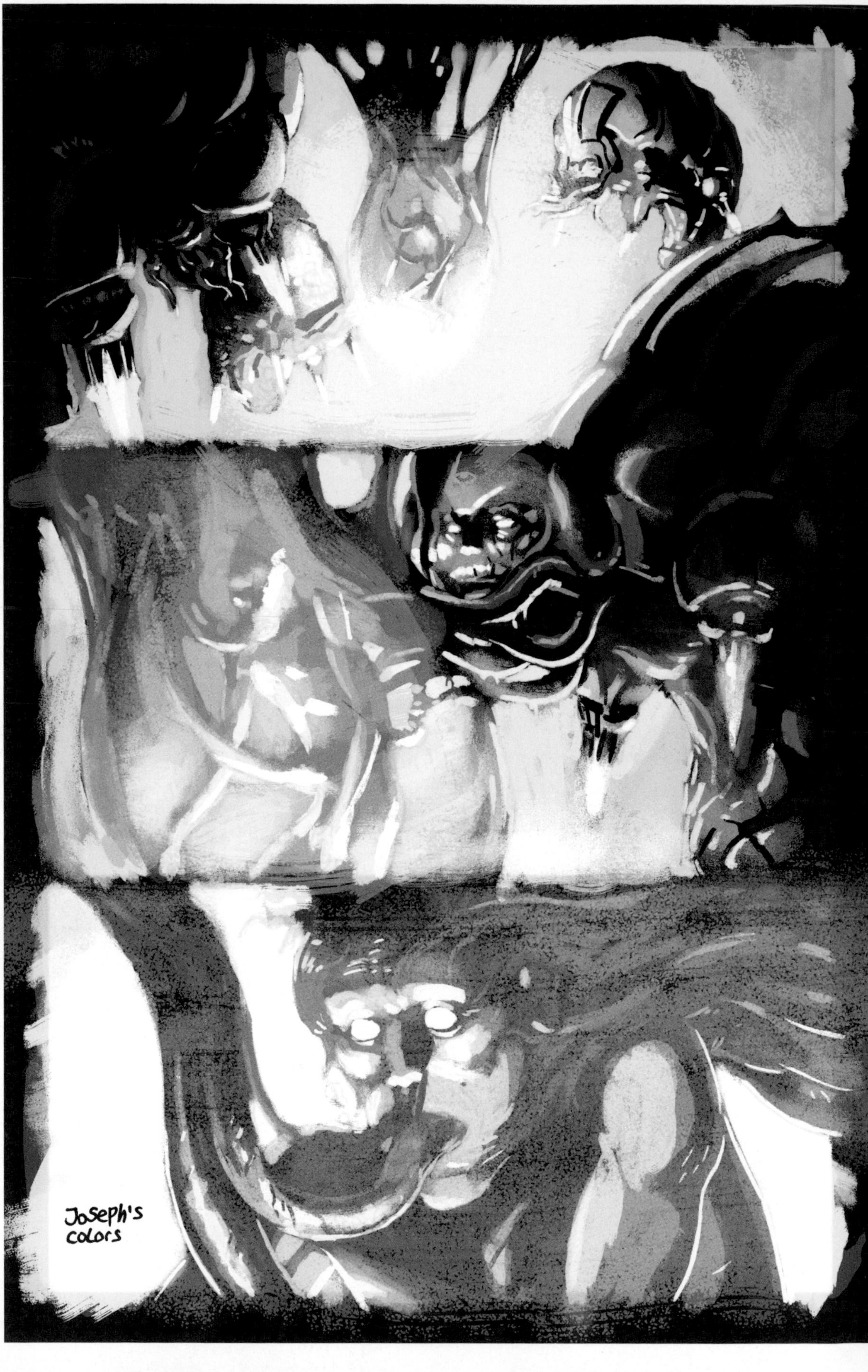
Joseph's colors

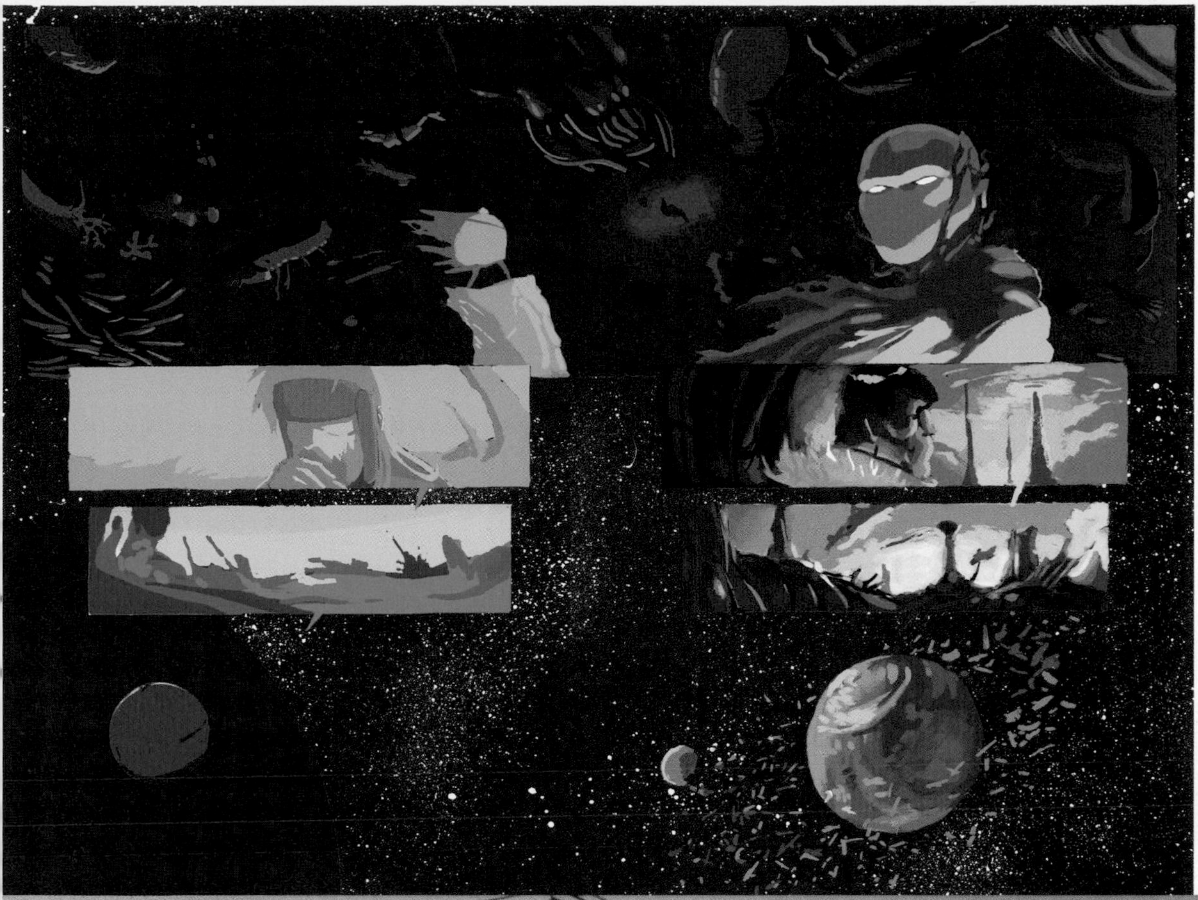

COLOR kIDS

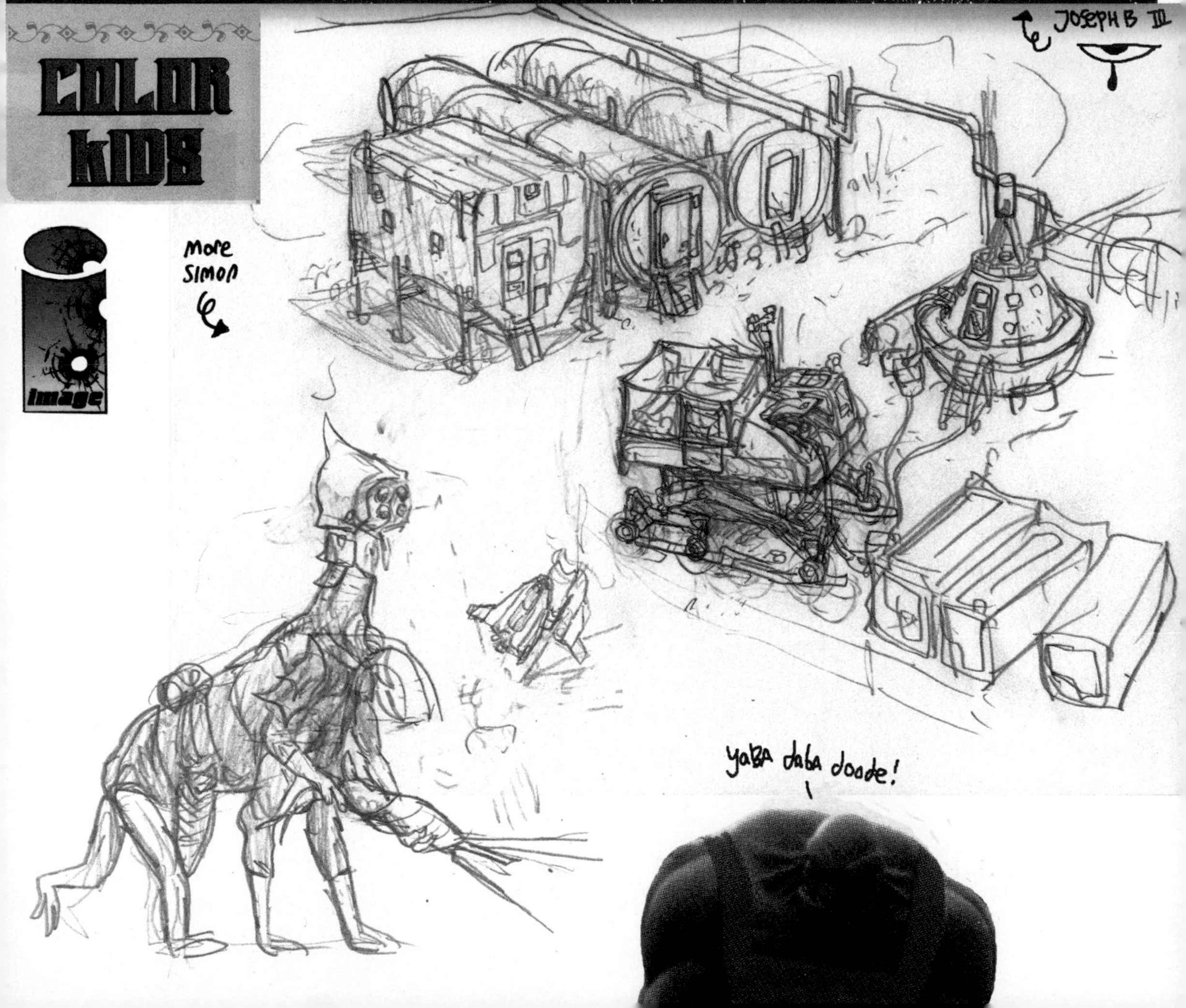
JOSEPH B III
more SIMON
yaBa daba doode!

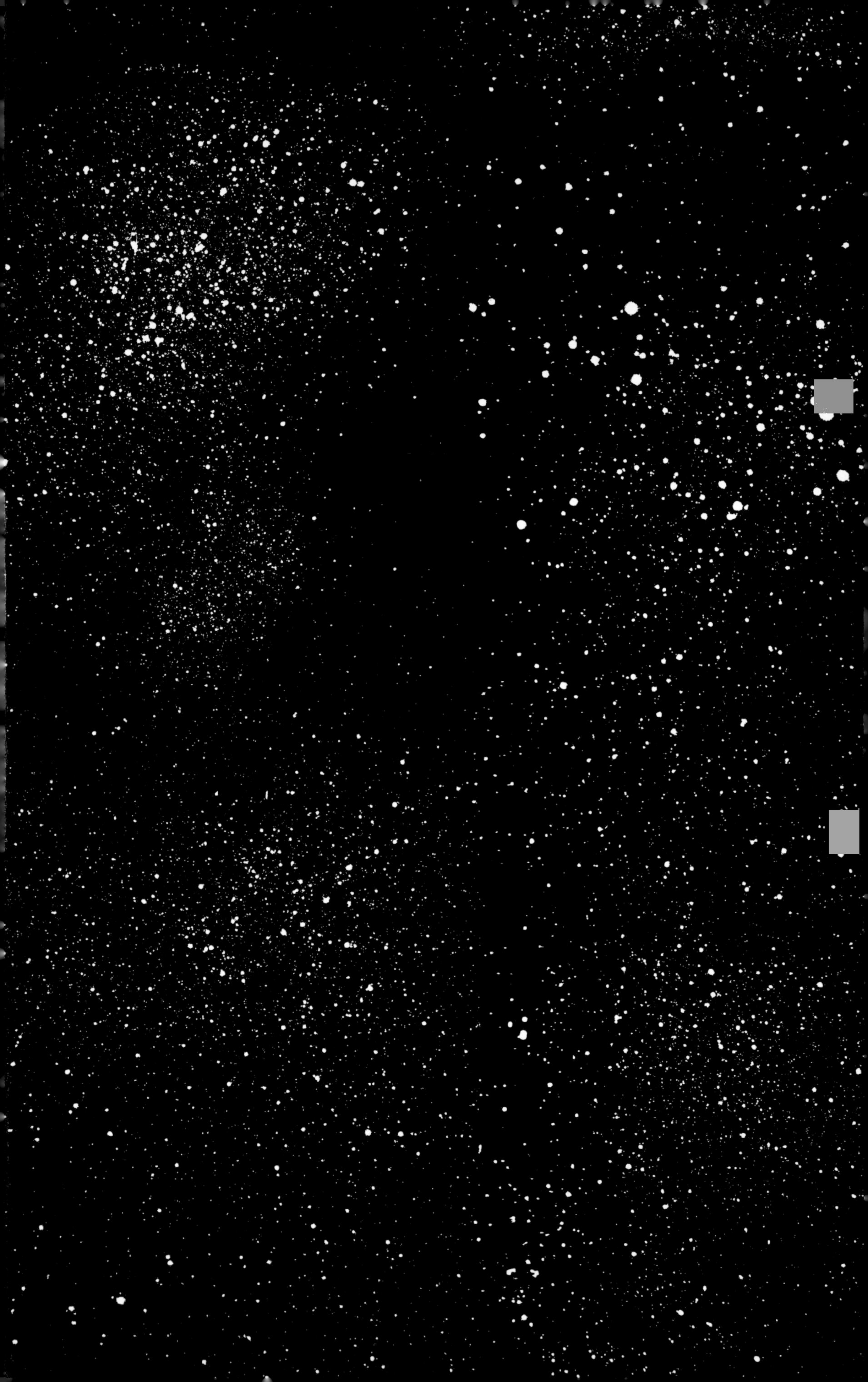